Praise for
Jenny Holiday

"Jenny Holiday has long been a go-to for funny, feel-good romance."
　　　　　　　　　　　　　　　　　—*Entertainment Weekly*

Canadian Boyfriend

"Tender, painful, joyful and, most of all, honest. This is everything a romance novel should be."
　　　　　　　　　　　　　　　—*BookPage*, starred review

"A heartwarming, healing romcom worth staying up late to finish."
　　　　　　　—Abby Jimenez, *New York Times* bestselling author

"Heartwarming, engaging…the witty banter and outrageous situations keep the tone upbeat even as characters face challenging situations."
　　　　　　　　　　　　　　　　　　—*Library Journal*

"Readers looking for emotionally intelligent romance will want to snap this up."
　　　　　　　　　　　　　　　　　　—*Publishers Weekly*

ALSO BY JENNY HOLIDAY

STANDALONES

Canadian Boyfriend

THE MATCHMAKER BAY SERIES

Mermaid Inn

Paradise Cove

Sandcastle Beach

THE BRIDESMAIDS BEHAVING BADLY SERIES

One and Only

It Takes Two

Three Little Words

Into the Woods

JENNY HOLIDAY

FOREVER

New York   Boston

Copyright © 2025 by Jenny Holiday

Cover design by Daniela Medina
Cover illustration by Leni Kauffman
Cover copyright © 2025 by Hachette Book Group, Inc.

Forever
Hachette Book Group
1290 Avenue of the Americas, New York, NY 10104
read-forever.com
@readforeverpub

First Edition: January 2025

Forever is an imprint of Grand Central Publishing. The Forever name and logo are registered trademarks of Hachette Book Group, Inc.

The publisher is not responsible for websites (or their content) that are not owned by the publisher.

The Hachette Speakers Bureau provides a wide range of authors for speaking events. To find out more, go to hachettespeakersbureau.com or email HachetteSpeakers@hbgusa.com.

Forever books may be purchased in bulk for business, educational, or promotional use. For information, please contact your local bookseller or the Hachette Book Group Special Markets Department at special.markets@hbgusa.com.

Library of Congress Cataloging-in-Publication Data
Names: Holiday, Jenny (Romance author), author.
Title: Into the woods / Jenny Holiday.
Description: New York ; Boston : Forever, 2025.
Identifiers: LCCN 2024025658 | ISBN 9781538724958 (trade paperback) | ISBN 9781538724972 (ebook)
Subjects: LCGFT: Novels.
Classification: LCC PS3608.O48432 I58 2024 | DDC 813/.6—dc23/eng/20240617
LC record available at https://lccn.loc.gov/2024025658

ISBN: 9781538724958 (trade paperback), 9781538724972 (ebook)

Printed in the United States of America

CW

10 9 8 7 6 5 4 3 2 1

For the neighbour ladies: Leacia, Andrea, Janine. Thanks for being retired from camping with me. (Probably. Unless you pour me several drinks and get me on the Ontario Parks website.) Looking forward to the crone years.

Into the Woods

1
ONCE UPON A TIME

Gretchen

Once upon a time, there was a girl named Gretchen Miller. Gretchen grew up to be a badass. She came from an OK family—nobody hit each other or screamed at each other. They liked each other well enough most of the time. But no one ever had any money. Gretchen's mom worked at a diner, and her dad worked...sometimes. He wasn't one of those stereotypical toxic men. He didn't drink too much or yell too much. He didn't cheat on Gretchen's mom, and he attended Gretchen's dance recitals—when there was money for lessons and therefore recitals requiring his presence. He just had trouble seeing himself as the kind of guy who made minimum wage doing general labor, or driving the shuttle at a car dealership, or assistant-managing a McDonald's, or, or, or. When he'd drink—not too much, but enough to get maudlin—he would say, "Is this all there is?"

Is this all there is?

Every few months he would decide he was meant for better things. Bigger things. And then he would quit his job in favor of some vision only he could see. Unfortunately, often his visions involved pyramid schemes. Gretchen's mom was a career waitress, but she didn't bring home enough to float the household on her own, so when Gretchen's dad was in one of his delusions-of-grandeur phases, things in the Miller household would get tight. Tight*er*. Gretchen and her sister, Ingrid, would get free lunch at school, which sounds great in theory but was in fact not great, as the school only served free meals to kids who qualified for them. Which meant Gretchen and Ingrid also qualified for a lot of cruelty from their peers.

But Gretchen, she didn't let any of that stop her. Gretchen was the kind of person who watched and learned. She was a hustler. She scrabbled and saved, working through high school waiting tables and teaching at her childhood dance studio. Hell, she worked through *middle* school, babysitting and shoveling driveways and doing whatever anyone would give her money to do. She saved that money. For what, she wasn't sure. For *something*.

All she knew was that she wasn't going to be like him. Like *them*. She loved her parents, but she'd seen, from a young age, that the key to happiness, to peace, was self-sufficiency. To not need to rely on a man or the Man. To be your own boss.

And I am. Me. I'm Gretchen. The badass. When I was exactly halfway through my two-year community college degree in business and marketing, I sat myself down and said, *Now. Now is the time to turn that* something *into an actual thing.*

And so Miss Miller's of Minnetonka was born. Tap, jazz, ballet, and hip-hop, ages three to eighteen. This is my seventeenth year in business. I own my own house. I have a retirement account. I don't have to wear a suit or a uniform to work. I don't have to ask my boss when I want to do something, because I am my boss.

I don't need a husband or a boyfriend to chip in on the

mortgage or the vet bills or the vacations I'm too busy to take anyway. If a boyfriend started mooching off me, it wouldn't make any difference to my bottom line. Actually, if a boyfriend started mooching off me, he'd be demoted to ex-boyfriend.

So yeah: I did it. I'm a success. All those annoying memes you see about girlbosses are me.

So what's the problem?

I'm having a fucking midlife crisis, that's the problem.

Is this all there is?

———

My best friend, Rory, stood and clinked her spoon against her glass even though it was only the two of us at dinner.

"I'd like to make a toast to—"

"Shh!" We were at Suz's, an ice-cream parlor and diner in the same strip mall as my studio. It was often full of my students and their parents, and the news that was about to earn me a toast was not public yet.

"Oh, shoot, sorry." Rory put her hand on her belly and sat back down. I didn't know why she was holding the bump. She was barely showing at seven months—she was one of those cute pregnant ladies who look like they have a miniature basketball under their shirt but are otherwise physically unchanged by the process of growing a whole other human inside them. It would have been annoying if I didn't love her so much.

Rory said, under her breath, "I get the need for secrecy, but if you think I'm not cheers-ing you, you're crazy. Here's to you and your growing empire," she whispered. "May Miss Miller's 2.0 be as awesome as the original."

I grinned. "Do you think I need a new name? Miss Miller's works for a kids' dance studio, but does the new building, with the addition of yoga and Pilates stuff, need a name that's less cutesy? More elevated?"

That's right: new building. The badass was expanding her empire. After almost twenty years renting in a strip mall, I was buying a freaking building and doubling my square footage.

The answer to the *Is this all there is?* question had been no. Miss Miller's of Minnetonka and an extremely shitty dating life that was slowly chipping away at my self-esteem were not all there was.

"Grow with Gretchen?" Rory suggested, laughing when I made a barfing noise.

"Elevated but not crunchy-granola."

I wasn't one of those woo-woo types, but I did do Pilates a couple times a week. It helped with the dancing aches and pains. Beyond that, it's good for your brain. I believed in it—and yoga—as a force for good in the world. And like the dance studio, I wanted the yoga-and-Pilates side of things to be welcoming to all. But also as with the dance studio, I wasn't in this just to do good in the world. What can I say? People who say money can't buy happiness have never been poor.

So yeah, I did deserve to be toasted, even if it had to be on the sly. I was on my way to a whole new phase of life. Midlife crisis? I don't know her.

"I say lean into it and straight-up call it Granola with Gretchen," Rory said.

"Ha ha."

"Well, whatever the name turns out to be," Rory said, "I'm proud of you."

"I'm proud of me, too, but to be honest, also slightly terrified." Even badasses get scared sometimes. "It's a lot of money."

A ginormous mortgage. A hell of a lot more than my monthly

rent payment for the existing studio. Which I wasn't even going to be able to get rid of right away, because I was keeping it open while I renovated the new space.

And I was going to have to hire teachers. I wasn't certified to teach yoga or Pilates, so unlike in the early days of the dance studio, I couldn't just teach everything myself. And beyond the cost of the reno, I had to buy scheduling software and expensive Pilates machines, and, and, and...

Granola with Gretchen—or whatever—was a whole other level.

I reminded myself that even badasses get scared, yes, but the key point about badasses is they don't let their fear stop them from doing shit.

Enough introspection. "Let's talk about something else."

"OK, how's Ethan?" Rory asked.

"Oh, Ethan's history." She was referring to my latest Tinder dude.

"Yeah?"

She wanted me to elaborate. She liked my stories from the trenches of dating. She wanted to live vicariously through me, I guess, which was funny because I wanted to live vicariously through her. It wasn't that I necessarily wanted the perfect domestic package she had—adoring husband, awesome stepkid, bun in the oven, gorgeous house on Lake Minnetonka. But I guess I had wanted it, once upon a time. So it was interesting to watch it all unfold for her, after the two of us had spent so many years as the main characters in each other's life stories.

"I do have a date tomorrow, though," I said.

"Oh! Who?"

The last man. My last date ever. Because Midlife Crisis: Averted had two pillars. Pillar One was the new studio. The

empire expansion. Pillar Two was my retirement from dating.
I wasn't going to tell Rory about Pillar Two, though. She'd try
to talk me out of it, give me the whole "hope springs eternal"
speech. Nope, I was just going to quietly let that part of my
life disappear.

After tomorrow.

"Just some guy who's visiting the Twin Cities." I shrugged.
"He seems fun." I wagged my eyebrows. "And hot."

"Oooh, look at you. Getting some."

Yes. Getting some. One more time.

———

One more time, I repeated to myself twenty-four hours later as I
pulled into the parking ramp at LaSalle and Tenth. It was a gorgeous summer night, the perfect setting for my farewell to dating. And I'd picked a doozy this time. It was probably because
I could see the end in sight. Why not go out with a bang?

Hopefully a literal bang. Ha.

Usually when I swiped right on men it was because I thought
they had potential. And I don't even mean I could see myself
settling down with them for the long term. Just that they
seemed like decent guys. They could spell, they didn't display
any overt signs of misogyny in their profiles, they were age
appropriate. Boyfriend material, if you will. I'd long since let
go of the whole marriage-and-kids thing. I wasn't sure I'd ever
wanted the kids part anyway. But I did want...a partner. I felt
like a dork admitting that, given how much I'd constructed my
sense of self around my independence and my low threshold for
bullshit. But I don't know, sometimes when I got home from a
long day at the studio, I wanted someone to be there, someone
who knew who Sansa's mom was and understood what I meant

when I flopped on the couch and said, "Sansa's mom is object-ing to the recital costumes." And then maybe that someone would hand me a drink or even, I don't know, rub my feet. Gah. It's excruciating to cop to wanting that shit, but I do.

Did—past tense.

I'd been dating as long as I'd had the studio—longer—and no one had ever stuck, not for more than a couple months. I had no shorthand and no foot rubs. Apparently I was not a girlboss when it came to love.

I was so, so tired of dating. Way-deep-inside-my-soul exhausted. I was not the kind of person who took shit from anyone, least of all men, yet when I faced my midlife crisis head-on and took a good hard look at my life, I had to admit that I'd recently started...bending a little on the dating front. Giving the benefit of the doubt where it wasn't warranted. Cen-soring what I said so as not to dent any fragile male egos. Sleep-ing with guys I wasn't sure about yet to buy time until I knew for sure I wanted to cut bait.

The stupid part was that it didn't even work. The past couple years in particular had featured so many mediocre men, fol-lowed by so much ghosting. I was utterly tired of the men of the internet.

Or forget the internet: I was tired of the men of the *world*.

I had to face the fact that happily ever after wasn't going to happen for me. And, more than that, *trying* so hard and so continuously to make it happen was turning me into someone I didn't recognize. I didn't give false compliments. I didn't laugh at jokes that weren't funny. I didn't get my undies in a bunch when a middling man ghosted me. None of this was me. I believed that. But I feared that if I continued along like I was, I might end up at a place where I didn't.

Just as bad, dating was increasingly making me sad. I was, by nature, a glass-half-full person. Sometimes people called me bubbly. Which I kind of hated, but I got it. I taught dance to kids, and my hair was usually dyed some candy color or other. I was a bubbly badass, I guess. The point was the dating grind was just that—a grind. It was grinding me down. Sanding away my natural optimism. Which sort of felt like it was sanding away *me*.

No more.

Well, one more: Scott. A dude in town for two nights for work. Not my usual type of match—not boyfriend material whatsoever.

So one last hurrah with Scott, and then it was going to be all Granola with Gretchen and embracing my forties solo. Midlife Crisis: Averted: Pillar Number Two—complete.

"Gretchen?"

There he was, standing outside the pub at which we'd agreed to meet. He actually looked like his picture. He looked *better* than his picture. The image on his profile had been blurry, but on-purpose/artistic blurry. In person, he had a lovely, symmetrical face and appealingly unkempt ash-blond hair, and he was wearing a huge smile that made his blue eyes twinkle.

"Yes, hi. Scott?"

We shook hands, and my stomach did a little flip. He had a good handshake. A big, warm hand that would probably be good at foot rubs.

I reminded myself that that was not the point here. The point was to swipe on someone I'd never see again, have a fun last date.

"I like your hair," he said, tangling his fingers in a hank of it. I was used to people complimenting my hair—it was my signature thing—but I wasn't used to people I didn't know touching it two seconds after meeting me. That was the first red flag.

The second red flag started flapping when we engaged the hostess. I'd suggested this place because it had a cool rooftop space with lawn bowling and a view of the skyscrapers of downtown. But when we were informed that there was no room on the roof, Scott said, "Oh, come on. I'm sure you can find something."

"I'm sorry, sir. You're welcome to wait. Or you can—"

Scott leaned in and aimed his twinkly-eyed grin at the woman, who looked all of twenty. "I hate to be this jerk, but do you know who I am?"

Wait, what? Did *I* know who he was?

The hostess smiled apologetically. "I do, and honestly I'm a big fan, but there simply isn't a table available on the roof at the moment."

A big *fan*?

Scott extinguished his grin. "Look. I'm sure you can—"

"You know what?" I interrupted. "Why don't we go somewhere else? There are lots of places with patios on Nicollet. I'm sure we can find a good spot."

Scott let himself be talked down, but not before asking if the hostess wanted him to sign anything. I was pretty sure she didn't give a shit, but she feigned enthusiasm and handed him a napkin.

See? This is what I mean about bending ourselves to please men. Why do we do this?

Because it's easier. We pretend to be who we aren't or like things we don't because it's easier than offending a man. Or because even though we tell ourselves that a muttered-under-his-breath

"What a bitch" or a texted "Whore" doesn't affect us, maybe enough of those little barbs do eventually accrete into a weapon that's big enough, and sharp enough, to start unraveling us.

"You want to come up to my hotel room for a drink instead?" Scott suggested when we were back outside. I'd changed my Tinder profile before my final round of swiping, making it vague and flirty. He had every reason to think I would be interested in going up to his room with him for "a drink."

And hell, maybe I still was. I didn't have to like him to sleep with him.

"Sure." As we started the three-block walk to the Hyatt, I said, "I gather you're some sort of famous person and I didn't realize."

He chuckled. "Yeah. I'm in a band."

"Oh yeah? Would I have heard of you?"

"Probably. We're in town playing the Target Center tomorrow."

Wow. Sleeping with a rock star as my last hurrah: I could get behind that. I really *would* be going out with a bang. "What's the band called?"

"Concrete Temple."

I had heard the name, but that was it. Which was surprising, as I loved music and prided myself on following lots of genres. It helped in my line of work, where I was known for my inventive recital choreography. "What kind of stuff do you play?"

"Rock. Hard rock."

That explained it. Hard rock didn't really lend itself to kids' dance recitals at studios in suburban strip malls. "Hmm," I said vaguely, not wanting to offend him. Argh!—here I was, doing it again. I started over. "Don't know you guys."

"Really?"

Here we went. "Really."

"We have a couple songs you'd know if you heard them."

"Mm."

We spent the rest of the walk talking about the band and the tour and him. Minneapolis was the second-to-last stop on a long tour. And "long" was saying a lot, because they were a "touring band," whatever that meant. He was ready to get back to his house in LA. He missed his Range Rover. He used to lift weights, but it's hard on tour; hotel gyms don't have squat racks. The other thing that's hard about touring is the food. The other guys had all this garbage food on the band's rider, whereas he always asked for a Vitamix and the fixings for green smoothies. He was getting really into Buddhism. The middle way—had I heard of that? He was going to give me the names of some books I should totally check out.

I made vague murmurs of acknowledgment as he talked, but when he informed me that sometimes the universe gives you signs that you need to be open to, I decided to wrestle hold of the conversation. Since this was my last kick at the can, I didn't have to worry if it seemed like I was interrupting. "I definitely believe in signs from the universe. I recently had one myself."

"What did it say?"

It said to take all the time and energy—and money; bikini waxes were not cheap—I'd been spending on dating and invest it in myself. Invest it in my empire. But I didn't say it like that. I told him about Granola with Gretchen.

"So yeah," I said in summation, "I close on August thirty-first, which also happens to be my fortieth birthday." It didn't "happen" to be my birthday; I'd done that on purpose, once I'd learned the seller preferred a late-summer close. I liked the symbolism of it. I would be closing on the building but also on the midlife crisis. "I'm going to have a party in the empty space. I was thinking I might make it a demo party—I'm doing a major remodel, so a bunch of stuff, including an interior wall, has to come out. What do you think? Would you be into a party where you could dance and drink but also take a sledge-hammer to the wall?"

Scott wasn't listening. I could tell by his glazed-over eyes.

I had lost my audience. I wondered why men never seemed to have enough self-awareness to realize when *they'd* lost *their* audience.

When we got up to his room, he took out his phone, and I had to listen to fifteen minutes of Concrete Temple—apparently my time to speak was over. I did recognize a couple of the songs, but only vaguely, and let's just say I was not a fan. Let's leave mumbled vocals and walls—nay, tsunamis—of guitars back in the 1990s where they belong, shall we?

When he stopped the music and looked at me expectantly, I was supposed to say nice things. Instead, I said, "I'm more of a pop person."

"You would be," he shot back.

"And you would know that how?" He hadn't asked a single question about me. I felt certain he couldn't have passed a pop quiz about the Granola with Gretchen monologue. When he didn't answer, I said, "The cool thing is there's lots of different kinds of music in the world. Something for everyone. You guys remind me of Nirvana. I'm a dance teacher, and I once tried to use 'Smells Like Teen Spirit' for a semijoking—"

He cut me off with a rough kiss.

OK, no, turns out I *did* have to like a guy to sleep with him. And I did *not* like this one. I guess if signs from the universe are real, this was mine to skip the last hurrah and retire from dating effective immediately. Pillar Number Two: activate. I pushed him off me. "I should go."

"Really?"

"Really."

"You just got here."

"I know." This was the part where I would usually make up a lie about having forgotten something I had to do in order to make my desire to leave about some external thing rather than about him, but I kept my mouth shut.

"I have to say, Gretchen," he said with a smirk, "you're passing on an opportunity here that would at least give you a good story to tell your friends. Do you know—"

"Are you about to 'Do you know who I am?' me? Because I think we've established that no, I do not know who you are."

He held his hands up in an exaggerated fashion, like he was the subject of a stickup in a silent movie. I knew that gesture. It was designed to telegraph that I was being difficult. Shrill. If there were an audience, he would have broken the fourth wall and looked at them like *Can you believe this crazy chick?*

And yep, just in case I hadn't gotten the silent message, as I was making my way out the door, he muttered, "Bitch."

So predictable, these mediocre men.

I stitched myself back together as I rode down in the elevator. Hardened myself. I *was* a bitch. I was a bitch who got shit done and didn't take crap from anyone. Back in my car, I got out my phone and deleted Tinder. And all the rest of them: Hinge, Bumble, all of it.

I gave half a thought to getting out, setting my phone against my rear tire, and backing over it.

I was almost forty, and I was retired from dating. I had a

successful business I had built from nothing and was about to take to the next level. I had family I liked and who liked me back, even if we weren't close. I had friends I loved like family.

I had a good life.

Except that niggling refrain that had been wending its way through my consciousness of late was still there.

Is this all there is?

The phone rang. Rory.

"Am I interrupting the date? I'm probably interrupting the date. But it's important."

"You're not interrupting the date."

"Aww, really?"

"It was a bust."

"Well, his loss. Next time will be better."

I didn't tell her there wouldn't be a next time. For some reason, I hadn't been telling Rory about my dating woes the way I used to. Maybe I was just sick of hearing myself talk.

"You know Imani Tran?" she asked.

"Of course." Imani Tran was a legend of modern dance. "Do *you* know Imani Tran?"

"Not personally. But I went to ballet school with someone who went on to join her company. Imani was supposed to spend the summer at this camp in northern Minnesota called Wild Arts. She's pregnant. She isn't due until December, but apparently the pregnancy has just been deemed high risk and she's been put on bed rest."

"That's terrible."

"For her, yes. For you, maybe not."

"Huh?"

"Imani felt bad pulling out so late, so she's trying to find a replacement. She asked my friend, who can't do it. My friend, knowing I'm in Minnesota, asked me."

"And you can't do it, as you're about to pop." Pregnant ladies everywhere. Maybe that was why I'd stopped confiding in Rory. I always used to be the older, wiser one, the one dispensing the advice. But now she was married and pregnant, so that just left me and my midlife crisis.

"Well, not till September twentieth, God willing. But yes, I'm not prepared to spend the summer in the woods. So I suggested you."

"That's nice of you, but I can't leave the studio." Could I? "And I have way too much going on with the new building." Didn't I?

For some reason, the idea of spending the summer in the woods was…appealing? Even though I was not an outdoorsy person. Growing up in a trailer had been, at times, a little too close to camping for adult me to have any interest in sleeping outside on purpose.

"Hear me out," Rory said. "You always do the two-week closure in the dead of summer. The camp thing is two monthlong sessions. If you did the first session only, you'd really be helping them out. You'd only need someone to cover your classes for two weeks, and that someone is me."

"Yeah, but it's not just the teaching, it's all the admin stuff. The boss stuff."

Her silence let me know what she thought of that. Rory had been my second-in-command for years, and she ran her own ballet business, too. She was more than capable.

"Fine," I said, "but what about the new place?"

"You don't even close on it until your birthday."

"Yeah, but I'm allowed two visits before that. I was going to take Justin through." Justin was my contractor.

"So take Justin through now. Then go to camp. Or I'll take Justin through." When I didn't say anything, she kept going. "This is actually perfect timing. You miss two weeks of classes, but you know I can cover those in my sleep. There's nothing you can really do for the new place at this point. I mean, you don't even have a name for it yet."

I laughed. I could feel myself softening.

"I'm not trying to bully you into doing this," she said, her tone growing serious. "I just...I don't know, I thought you could use a break. A real break."

She wasn't wrong, and it kind of...choked me up to know that she had me so thoroughly figured out.

"The gig is formally called artist in residence," she said. "It'll be you, an actor, a writer, and so on. As I understand it, you're not camp counselors per se, but more like mentors. The idea is that you do the gig, but you also get free time to pursue your own artistic aims."

"I don't have any artistic aims. Not beyond the next recital, anyway." I had entrepreneurial aims. They were taking up all the space available for aims in my brain. I didn't need to go to the forest to find my artistic soul or any bullshit like that.

But maybe they wouldn't have Wi-Fi at this camp. I thought about Pillar Two. My commitment to it currently felt a little tenuous. I'd been tempted to run over my phone so I wouldn't backslide on staying off dating apps. Being occupied teaching in the remote North Woods seemed like it would achieve the same thing, and I wouldn't have to buy a new phone at the end of it.

It could be a cleanse, if you will. A man cleanse. And when

I came out, I'd be clear thinking and ready to go on Granola with Gretchen. Hell, in the quiet of the forest, maybe the perfect name would come to me. Or maybe I'd be so cleansed and at peace that I would *like* the name Granola with Gretchen.

I had liked the symbolism of going on one last date before retiring from men, the ritualistic nature of a last hurrah, but another idea was forming.

"You know how in fairy tales, there's often a wicked witch, or a menacing old lady?" I asked. "Like in 'Hansel and Gretel.' There's that lady who lures them into the woods and... I think she eats them?" I cracked myself up. "But she always lives in a forest, it seems like."

"Yeah," Rory said. "I think there's lots of fairy tales like that. Doesn't the witch in 'Rapunzel' lock her up in a tower in the woods? Why do you ask? Are you about to manifest a Brothers Grimm–themed recital?"

I ignored her questions. "All right. I'll do it."

Once upon a time there was a girl named Gretchen. Gretchen grew up to be a badass. And then she went to the woods to become a crone.

2
INTO THE WOODS

Teddy

It was possible that the reality of the North Woods was going to be different from my idea of the North Woods.

To begin with, it was ninety-two degrees when I got out of the van at the Wild Arts retreat that was to be my home for the summer. I knew because the driver, a gray-haired woman who looked like Paul Newman's fraternal twin sister, announced as much as we drove through a giant wooden archway with a sign that read, "Nature Is the Art of God": "Ninety-two at eight forty-five at night—uff da."

She sounded like she was straight off the set of *Fargo*. But she was right about the heat. It was hotter than the subway platform at 77th Street during a July heat wave. It was hotter than a stage in the literal desert at Coachella. It was hotter than the rage boiling in my jet-black soul.

I went to the woods because I wanted to live deliberately.

Not exactly, but it was a nice idea. In my case it was more that I had come to the woods because I wanted to finish my fucking album.

No, I had come to the woods because I wanted to *start* my fucking album.

There was also the part where I had nowhere else to go.

Well, that wasn't true. My decade-plus in the band I'd just burned to the ground had made me plenty of money. I could hole up wherever I wanted to work on the revenge album. But like Thoreau, I was in search of the peace and solitude I hoped nature would provide. When the offer landed in my inbox last week, it had occurred to me that I hadn't been in actual nature for years. I hadn't even really been outside that much, except onstage at outdoor shows, on hotel balconies, or getting into and out of cars, for a year.

So it was likely that I was romanticizing the whole experience. I'd forgotten, or maybe I'd never known, that when you were in the woods, you were not alone. You were, it turned out, accompanied by approximately a million tiny mosquitoes and, in this case, one life-size mosquito wearing a T-shirt that read "I ♥ Minnesota."

I had a feeling that despite the cheery shirt, the Mosquito was almost as grumpy as I was.

Except that wasn't true. She'd been sweet as all get-out to our driver, chatting with her the whole drive from the airport to camp. And when she hopped out of the van, she closed her eyes, sighed, took a deep breath in—she didn't seem to notice or care that the air was as thick as in any mosh pit—and said, "I'm so happy to be here."

It seemed to just be me the Mosquito didn't like. Which . . . fair enough. I was no picnic at the best of times, and this was not the best of times.

She gathered her hair into a ponytail and fanned the back

of her neck. I sympathized. I had long hair, too, and it was a sweaty mess in this heat. Maybe instead of the Mosquito, I should call her Cotton Candy, because that was what color her hair was. Come to think of it, her eyes, too. Her pale-blond hair had pastel-pink tips, and her big eyes were light blue. She was an entire carnival, and that was just from the neck up.

"Hello and welcome! My late additions to Wild Arts! I'm so glad you're here!" A tall older woman with long white braids strode toward us. I slapped a mosquito as it sank a tiny, poison-tipped ice pick into my neck.

"This is the worst time of night for insects, just as darkness falls." The woman reached into a fold of the . . . garment she was wearing and produced a bottle of bug repellant and handed it to me. "You must be Teddy. We're delighted to have you with us. I'm Marion Kuhn."

I was probably supposed to know who she was, but honestly, when I'd skimmed the proposal from Wild Arts a week ago, all I'd retained was the fact that it came with a cabin on a lake for the summer in exchange for some "artist in residence" duties I fully intended to phone in. It had been the right opportunity at the right time—a life raft when I was drowning—and I'd signed on without even talking to my manager.

If he was even my manager anymore. I hadn't spoken to Brady since the last week of the tour. If Concrete Temple was no more, if it had splintered into individual shards, did those individual shards still have a management contract?

Forget management contracts. What I needed was a *record* contract. Because I intended to write a shitload of songs here in Mosquitoland.

"And you're Gretchen Miller!" Marion exclaimed, turning to the cotton candy mosquito. Oh, wait, I had the perfect name for her: the Sugarplum Fairy. It encompassed her sickly sweetness *and* her annoying buzzing. If cotton candy and a mosquito had a baby, it would be the Sugarplum Fairy, would it not?

"Thank you for stepping in," Marion enthused. "You're really saving my bacon."

"Thanks for having me," Gretchen said. "It was good timing. I'm in need of a break from real life."

Hear, hear, Sugarplum.

"I just hope I can live up to the..." Gretchen side-eyed me. "Talent pool you have in place here."

"I assume you two have met?" Marion said.

"Sort of," Gretchen said. "I introduced myself at the airport."

I had not responded in kind. That was what I meant about not being a picnic right now. In my defense, I'd thought she was a fan when she approached me at a Starbucks in the Minneapolis airport. I'd been wearing dark glasses and a hat with my hair pushed up into it, so I'd been extra undercover. Which had led me to believe she was a *super*fan. The worst kind to encounter in the wild. In general, but particularly when one's nuking of one's career had recently been on display for all to see in the pages of *Us Weekly.* So when she'd flown at me all abuzz—that was where she'd earned her initial Mosquito nickname—I'd shut that shit right down, answering her questions in one-word grunts.

It was only when we were both being greeted by Paul Newman in baggage claim that I realized my error. It was almost funny. Here I'd thought I was being fangirled, and really she'd just wanted to talk to me because we were both going to the same place to bequeath our artistic sensibilities to the masses or some shit.

I told myself to stop being such a dick. Gretchen was my colleague here.

I slapped my forearm, hitting an especially engorged mosquito so hard it left a bloody spot.

Gretchen Miller. I had eclectic taste, and I knew a lot of people across a lot of genres, but I was coming up blank on that name. Of course, this place probably drew from more of a regional talent pool.

Maybe she worked behind the scenes. If this camp was meant to teach people the music business, they'd be smart to staff it with producers and engineers and such. That kind of career was a more realistic goal for most people than, you know, that of an actual rock star.

Said the actual rock star.

But was I anymore? Could you be a rock star without a band? Could you be a rock star if you were just one self-contained shard?

Did I even *want* to be a rock star anymore?

So many existential questions. At least I knew the answer to that last one. No, I did not want to be a rock star. I never had. It just sort of happened. And really, I *wasn't* a star. That had been Scott Collier, our handsome, charismatic front man and rhythm guitarist. Runner-up on the star front had probably been our lead guitarist, Jet. I mean, when your name is Jet Lexington—Jet Lex—and you have a penchant for standing on the very edge of the stage doing your over-the-top shredding, you kind of have to be a star, right?

I'd been happy to stand in the back with my reputation as a cranky-ass and play my bass and sing backup along with Luis Costa, our drummer. I considered myself a songwriter first. The only thing I cared about was that Scott and I shared writing credit equally, à la Lennon and McCartney. I cared that we made each other better. I cared about the music.

I'd thought he did, too.

"And of course I know who you are," Gretchen Miller said, drawing me from my thoughts and reminding me that we still had an introduction in progress. "Tennyson Knight."

Her use of my formal first name startled me. No one called me that except my mother, the woman who had cursed me with it in the first place.

"It's Teddy," I said.

"OK." She shrugged.

It was a dismissive shrug.

It wasn't as if I cared if people were starstruck by me. People generally weren't—that was the not-a-star thing—and usually I *liked* it that way. I was the Mike Mills to Scott's Michael Stipe. The Michael Anthony to his David Lee Roth. Not even. I was the Duff McKagan to Scott's Axl Rose and Jet's Slash. Rock people knew me, but in the real world I could generally walk around unbothered. It was a sweet spot I appreciated. The hat and dark glasses at the airport had just been extra insurance given the upheaval—and resultant tabloid attention—of the past week.

But somehow, irrationally, this shrug, this *disregard*, from a fellow musician got my back up.

Even though I had no leg to stand on here, given what a jerk I'd been to her at the airport.

Man, I was all over the place with this woman.

"I hadn't heard much Concrete Temple before this summer," she was saying as another especially vicious mosquito landed on my cheek. "It's very..." Her nose scrunched as she searched for the word she wanted. "Emphatic."

Well, fuck you very much, Gretchen Miller.

Gretchen turned to Marion and opened a planner, which I'd noticed she'd been consulting on the drive from the airport.

Maybe Gretchen Miller was an A&R type. Maybe she had no business passing judgment on my music. Maybe she was just a suit.

Although that "I ♥ Minnesota" T-shirt was very...not suit-like. It was formfitting, and there were splotches of sweat blooming beneath her breasts.

I wiped my brow. Why was it so damn hot in *Minnesota*? I'd never been to Minnesota other than to play shows in Minneapolis or Saint Paul. We'd played Minneapolis only a few days ago before heading to Chicago for the last show of the tour, which of course had turned out to be the last show period.

"I hope it's OK that I gave out your fax number," Gretchen said, showing Marion her binder. She turned to me and explained, "I have a real estate deal pending," as if I'd asked. "I don't know why bankers and lawyers and Realtors cling to the Stone Age technology that is the fax machine, but apparently they have to send some documents that way."

Gretchen was definitely a suit, even if she didn't look the part.

"And this is the day I have that meeting booked," she said, tilting her calendar toward Marion. "I want to make sure that's still OK."

"All good. I'll keep an eye on the fax, and you'll be in charge of your own schedule here. I'm just grateful that you could fill in on such short notice." Marion turned to me. "And you, too. The campers are going to be thrilled to meet an actual working musician."

I made a vague hum of acknowledgment. I wasn't sure that was an accurate description of me anymore, but I didn't want to get into it. I just wanted to get into some air-conditioning, take a cool shower, and crack open the bottle of Maker's Mark I had in my bag. Also, what the hell was this camp if the other staffers weren't working musicians?

"Hello." A tall, skinny man wearing a mud-splattered black T-shirt approached. "You must be our final two colleagues." He strode over to Sugarplum and stuck out his hand. "Danny the Potter."

"Gretchen the Dancer."

Well, shit. I guess this *wasn't* band camp.

"I love your hair, Gretchen the Dancer," Danny the Potter said as they shook hands. "There's a painter here who has blue hair. They should have sent a memo." He ran a hand through his shaggy blond mane.

"Are there any other musicians here?" I asked. Not that I cared. I wasn't planning on making friends, and when it came to music, I wouldn't be collaborating on my next project or maybe on any other project again ever. What had seventeen years of collaboration gotten me? A broken-up band. A broken-up friendship.

"Just you," Marion said. "Which was why we were so glad you could step in when we lost George." She turned to Gretchen. "And you when we lost Imani. It was touch and go for a while there, but I'm so relieved everything is going to be OK with them and the baby."

I had no idea who Imani or "the baby" was, but George was George Tran, a classical pianist my sister knew from her New York artsy circles. George knew the owner of this camp, who I gathered was some sort of socialite artist-wannabe. I was triangulating that information with this Marion person, who was wearing one of those sculptural dress-tunic hybrid garments favored by wealthy women of a certain age. When George had to bow out of his plan to be here this summer, he'd leveraged

his networks to suggest a replacement. And my sister, not looking forward to my spending the summer moping in her guest
room, had voluntold me. Really, though, Auden hadn't had to
twist my arm. I had heartily agreed that my newly unemployed
ass could do with a change in scenery. I needed a fucking break.

So here I was. A summer off the grid. Peace. Nature and
shit—I slapped a mosquito. Hopefully in a large enough dose
for me to write enough decent songs—no, enough *great* songs—
for an album. Over my dead body was Scott fucking Collier
going to be the only ex-member of Concrete Temple coming
out with a solo album.

So I needed to write some songs. That was my priority. Then
I would come out of the woods and sort out all the legal and
contractual shit. Decide what my next move was going to be.
Professionally but maybe also literally if Karlie, my ex, didn't
get out of my fucking apartment.

"The blue hair belongs to Maiv Khang, our visual artist—she's
a painter," Marion said. "Then we have Danny Frangopoulos—
you just met him. And you, Gretchen." Marion was counting off
on her fingers as she listed the summer's artists in residence. "At
least we have you for the first session." She made a frowny face.

"Yes, sorry," Gretchen said, "I can't leave my dance studio
for that long."

"I know, I know. We'll figure out something for the second
session—I already have some leads. But for now, we're so happy
to have you. We also have a novelist and an actor—there are six
of you total. You'll meet everyone at sunrise circle tomorrow."

Sunrise circle. I did not like the sound of that—the circle
part or the sunrise part.

"The counselors will be joining us after lunch. We'll go over
schedules and procedures then."

"And the kids come Monday, right?" Gretchen asked.

Hold on. Kids?

"The kids come Monday," Marion confirmed.

I had thought this was going to be band camp for grown-ups. Aging dudes who never got over Pearl Jam and fancied themselves rebels even though they'd just made partner at their accounting firms.

"As you know," Marion said, although I, of course, did not know, "you artists won't have extensive duties as it relates to the campers. But we are going to have some training on policies and procedures tomorrow, as well as a session on CPR and first aid."

Fuck. This was what I got for not reading the fine print. Or any print.

I slapped yet another mosquito, eyeing the Sugarplum Fairy. Why wasn't she getting bitten? She looked sweet enough to rot a man's teeth. In addition to the candy-tipped hair, she had heart-shaped lips, pale skin, and a pretty fucking cute nose—when she wasn't wrinkling it in disdain. She looked like a Disney princess fused with Katy Perry circa 2010. She looked like she could make small woodland creatures do her bidding as she sang girl-power anthems while dressed as a lollipop or some shit.

Slap.

"Teddy, you're getting eaten alive!" Marion said. "Let's get you to your cabins—they're screened." She turned to our airport chauffeur. "Lena, can you take them?"

They're screened. That did not sound promising. I mean, it sounded better than *They're not screened*, but I was the guy who always turned the hotel thermostat down to sixty-five. Back in the band's early days, when we'd all bunked together in one shitty motel room, the guys and I had always done battle over the room temp.

I examined the buildings nearby. They were large and made of logs. The one behind Marion sported a sign that read "Office," and it had some lights on inside. It also had windows that were cranked as wide as it looked like they would go.

All right. Yes, it was hot as hell, but I wasn't such a diva that I couldn't survive a summer without air-conditioning. I hadn't had it my entire childhood. Hell, half the time we hadn't even had power or running water, depending on what was happening with the rent strikes. I would have to settle for a long, cold shower.

Marion said good night, Danny proclaimed that he was off to visit the kiln—I realized now that what I'd thought was mud on his shirt was clay—and I followed Lena and Sugarplum to a golf cart. "It's a fifteen-minute walk to your cabins, but with your luggage, we'll drive. Well, I'll take you as far as I can, and then you'll have to hoof it the last bit. The paths between the cabins are muddy since we had some rain this afternoon. You might want to keep that in mind when you walk up for sunrise circle tomorrow." I followed her gaze to our feet. "You're fine." She pointed at the ancient Docs that housed my over-heated feet. "But you"—she pointed at Gretchen's feet—"might want to rethink your footwear choices. Mud aside, there are Lyme-bearing ticks in these woods." Gretchen was wearing denim shorts and silver, flat, strappy sandals. Her toenails were painted fire-engine red. I experienced a pang of longing as I eyed her perfect cherry toes—but only because I was jealous of how much cooler her feet seemed relative to my sweaty dogs.

"Got it," Gretchen said. "Thanks for the heads-up."

Gretchen sat up front with Lena. From their conversation,

I gleaned that Lena was the camp's longtime caretaker. "Used to be owned by the Girl Scouts," she said. "Then it was a corporate retreat for a couple years. Then the yoga people." I gathered from her tone that she hadn't thought much of "the yoga people."

"And it's going OK now as Wild Arts?" Gretchen asked. "This is the third year of Wild Arts, right?"

"Yup, it's going great. And I gotta say that though I'm not really an art kind of gal—I went to a play once in the Cities when I was young, and I didn't care for it—it's good to have Marion here. This place was falling apart when she bought it. I'd been doing the best I could, but as I told the yoga people, you can't meditate your way to new shingles."

The last stretch of the drive was through the woods, and we emerged into a clearing that contained a small parking lot. Lena cut the engine and pointed to a dirt path that extended into the trees. "You guys are in cabins five and six. They're both music cabins, so I'll let you sort out who gets which." I was closer to her, so she handed me two keys, each attached to a red-and-white plastic ball.

"Oh, bobber keychains—cute!" Gretchen said.

I had no idea what a bobber was, but I handed Gretchen the key for cabin five, reasoning that if there were six artists in residence, cabin six was likely to be the end of the line and therefore to have a neighbor only on one side. I had been imagining living in Waldenesque solitude, not in a God damn neighborhood.

Waldenesque solitude with air-conditioning, but still.

"You got flashlights?" Lena asked. Dusk had become dark, and it was *dark*.

"Nope," I said.

Gretchen dug around in her giant shoulder bag and produced a flashlight she flipped on and proceeded to blind me with.

I swallowed a curse and shielded my eyes as I slid my phone out of my pocket and turned on the flashlight.

I intended to take off—we both had our keys and our lights—but Gretchen struggled with her suitcase as she tried to keep her tote bag on her shoulder and hold her flashlight aloft at the same time. Sighing, I slung my guitar across my back, grabbed her suitcase and my duffel, and took off. I could afford to be generous because my shower, if not the AC of my dreams, was so close I could practically feel it.

Also because maybe I was a teeny bit sorry I'd been such a dick at the airport. Or, if I was the kind of person who cared what people I didn't know thought of me, I would have been sorry.

I didn't know Gretchen, so I didn't care.

Which probably meant I should stop thinking about it.

I did not respond to Gretchen's protests that she could carry her own bag, just trudged down the path.

I'd been wrong about cabin placement. Tidy cabins lined both sides of the path, which ran parallel to the shore, the even numbers on the water side and the odds on the forest side. I took in cabins one and three as we approached and extrapolated that Gretchen in five would be "across the street" from me on the beach in six. I would indeed be at the end of the line, though. Three of the cabins we passed were dark, but there were signs of life—a swimsuit draped over a porch railing, windows cranked all the way open. Cabin two had its lights on, and I could see the outline of a person moving around behind a thin curtain. Yep, this was definitely a *Mr. Rogers' Neighborhood*–type situation. Fuck me.

As we approached the end of the line, it occurred to me that a gentleman would offer to give Gretchen the cabin with the lake view, but I'd already carried her suitcase, which I deposited with a grunt on the porch of cabin five. It featured a single rocking chair.

Instead of using the steps, Gretchen leaped from the path onto the porch, landing more softly than I'd expected. She was light on her feet. I looked down at said feet, shining my flashlight on them. Her red-lacquered toes were streaked with mud. There was something about the juxtaposition of such perfectly done toes covered in mud that—

"Well," she said loudly, "good night."

I blinked, which had the effect of detaching my gaze from her feet. I didn't return her farewell, just raised my hand in nonverbal acknowledgment and headed across the road.

My cabin faced the lake, so I walked around to find my own porch. It was bigger than Gretchen's and featured a double glider. I couldn't see the lake in the dark, but I could hear the lapping of the waves.

I had definitely taken the nicer cabin. I did not feel bad about that.

Not bad enough to do anything about it, anyway.

I let myself in with my bobber key thing and was hit by a wall of stale, humid air. The place had been closed up tight, so after confirming that there was no thermostat or window unit hiding anywhere, I moved around and opened the windows, shedding my clothes as I went. I took in the dark outline of a double bed on one side of what was essentially one big room and a table and kitchenette on the other. There was a mini-fridge, a hot plate, a microwave, and a small sink. Through the kitchen was the bathroom, where I found a toilet and a sink and...a toilet and a sink. No shower. No bathtub, no means of washing my sticky, sweaty self.

"Fuck," I muttered into the hot, still night.

I made my way back to the kitchen and shone my phone light around as if I were expecting to stumble on a shower I had somehow missed on my first pass. The shower in the Greenpoint apartment of my childhood had been in the kitchen. But no such luck. My light snagged on a three-ring binder on the counter, cover emblazoned with the words *Welcome to Wild Arts*. Flipping past a text-dense letter up front—What can I say? I really do not like to read the fine print—I found a map of the property. Mr. Rogers' Neighborhood was indeed where the artists in residence were housed. The central area we'd come from had a camp office and a dining hall—those had been the log buildings I'd seen. Behind them was some artsy infrastructure: a visual arts studio, a kiln, indoor and outdoor performance and practice spaces, and a dance studio—hopefully Gretchen would be spending most of her time there. Beyond that was what I would consider normal summer camp stuff, though I'd never been to one: an archery range, a canoe shed, an area of the lake labeled "Swimming." Beyond all that and along the lake were cabins I assumed housed the campers. Near them was a building labeled with a shower icon. I looked for something similar in Mr. Rogers' Neighborhood, but there was nothing.

"God damn it!"

I could feel the anger rising, this new but increasingly familiar visitor of mine. It was the same ire that had had me being such a jerk to Gretchen. That had made me lose my cool with

Scott a week ago in that hotel room. The same anger he was now blaming for the breakup of the band, when he knew full well our demise was on him.

The unfairness of it all made me rage.

I swept my arm across the counter, and the binder hit the floor. The clatter it made—it was eerily silent here—was a wake-up call. It was one thing to get mad because your life's work was crumbling before your eyes, another because you were too much of a fucking child to wait a day to take a shower.

More importantly, I wasn't this guy. I wasn't the rock star who trashed hotel rooms, the entitled manbaby who got pissy when the world didn't offer itself up exactly to his specifications.

So I needed to stop fucking being him.

I took a breath and told myself to listen to the silence. To appreciate it. The silence was why I was here, right? I was going to write a shitload of songs in this silence.

It wasn't actually silent, though, when you paid attention; there was a rhythmic background humming of some sort. Crickets? Cicadas? I didn't know nature stuff, but it was a pleasing sound.

I headed for the bed, but as I walked, I moved the phone light around the rest of the cabin. There was an old but comfortable-looking love seat near a small bookshelf and...holy *shit*.

A keyboard.

I detoured over to it like a moth drawn to the light that is ultimately going to be its demise. The keyboard and a lamp next to it were plugged into the wall. So hey, no shower, but at least there was electricity—come to think of it, why the hell had I been using my flashlight in here when we'd seen a light on in one of the other cabins? Idiot.

I switched on the light to reveal a full-size Yamaha. This

must be what Lena meant when she'd said five and six were "music cabins." Gretchen must have a keyboard, too.

What was Gretchen going to do with a keyboard? She was—

I interrupted this train of thought—what the hell did I care if Gretchen had an extraneous keyboard?—and stepped closer.

Concrete Temple had been all guitars—lots and lots of guitars, which was probably what Gretchen meant when she'd called our sound "emphatic." We were the grandchildren of Phil Spector. I had a baby grand piano in my apartment in New York, but I hadn't been home much over the past year. And honestly, I never tried to write anything on it. It was for show, for grandstanding at parties, where I was known for being able to play pretty much anything anyone requested.

I hadn't written on a piano in any meaningful way since my teen years. We'd had a shitty, perpetually out-of-tune upright in Greenpoint. Mom had inherited it from a guy in the building who'd overdosed. I had found a needle and a spoon in the bench seat.

A memory rose, seemingly from nowhere, a snake rising to the sounds of its charmer: Mom and Auden and I, singing in the dark while I played that piano, candles all around us. "The Times They Are a-Changin'." "For What It's Worth." "Both Sides, Now." Mom had been obsessed with the folk songs of her parents' era. I'd absorbed it all, replicating what I heard on the scratchy records she was always playing. There had never been money for formal lessons—I only learned to read music as an adult—but I taught myself to play both piano and guitar from that stack of Pete Seeger, Bob Dylan, and Joni Mitchell records. My grandparents' records, I supposed, though I'd never met them. Peter, Paul and Mary had been a favorite of

Mom's because our little family of three could do the trio's harmonies. "Leaving on a Jet Plane." "500 Miles."

"Lemon Tree." We'd even had a potted lemon tree in the apartment in homage to Mom's folk heroes.

That fucking lemon tree. I'd have thought it was long forgotten, but nope. Apparently it had been lying dormant under the soil that was my psyche all these years, sour as ever.

The night I was remembering had been dark. The electricity had been cut by the landlord, which in retrospect was not an unreasonable thing for a landlord to do when faced with a building full of hippies and artists who didn't much care for paying rent. We had often gone without things most people would consider necessities—power, running water. Food.

But we'd sit in the dark and sing by the candlelight. We'd had no power, but we'd had the piano.

I wasn't romanticizing those days. I wouldn't go back for anything. Lemons could grow on trees in pots, even in semi-converted warehouses in Brooklyn, but a kid couldn't live on lemons.

A kid couldn't live on love, either, though Mom had sure preached that gospel. It had taken Auden and me years to deprogram ourselves. To understand that Mom's version of love had been more about rallies and songs and whatever her agenda du jour had been than about actually caring for her kids.

"*'Don't put your faith in love, my boy,' my father said to me. 'I fear you'll find that love is like the lovely lemon tree.'*"

It was funny how, like the memory of the tree, the song was still there, hiding out in the folds of my brain. I hadn't thought of it or heard it for literal decades, but it had risen to the surface of my mind like the rubber balls Auden and I used to play with in the McCarren Park pool. We'd sit on them, hold them under water, and laugh when we lost our balance and they shot to the surface.

We'd go to the pool when the water was turned off at home. We'd swim, shower and shampoo in the locker rooms, and emerge clean and cool into the early evening. That had been a good feeling. A respite.

I looked over my shoulder, out the window into the blackness. I didn't have a shower, but I had a whole damn lake outside my front door.

Turning back to the keyboard, I hit the power button, my throat tightening as a green light came on. The first note of "Lemon Tree" was a G. My finger hovered over the key for a few seconds as I swallowed a hard lump of emotion. The anger from before, from the past week—from the past *year*— had alchemized into something heavier and slower. Something more like sadness. It was thick and metallic in my throat.

I pressed the key. It was weighted, so it was both soft and heavy under the pressure of my finger, both familiar and strange to my guitar-calloused hands. I let the note ring out into the night and waited until the reverberations had fully faded before walking out the door and into the lake.

3
CELEBRITIES: THEY'RE JUST LIKE US!

Gretchen

I have seen Teddy Knight naked. I have seen Teddy Knight naked. I have seen Teddy Knight naked.

The refrain looped through my mind as I stepped onto Teddy's porch and knocked on his door. He didn't seem like the kind of guy who was good at setting alarms, and I didn't want him to miss sunrise circle.

Well, no, LOL, that was a lie. I wanted to yank him abruptly from a peaceful slumber because I was so sick of smug, entitled, self-impressed men that I wasn't behaving rationally.

Or maybe I was rational for the first time in my life.

It did occur to me—after I knocked—that since I was at Wild Arts to take a break from men, the best way to do that was probably to…take a break from men. As in, not let the first one I saw get me riled up enough that I started plotting ways to annoy him.

What were the odds? To think that Teddy Knight had likely been nearby in the Hyatt when I'd taken the unheard-of step of rejecting his bandmate. Honestly, if I believed in fate or any of that woo-woo bullshit, I would say that landing at Wild Arts with a member of Concrete Temple meant something. But I didn't, so the most my atheist self would allow was that the randomness of the universe could be pretty funny sometimes. And not ha-ha funny, but fuck-me funny.

I knocked again, louder, my fist thudding on the door bringing to mind the thud in my gut when I'd googled Teddy Knight early yesterday morning after reading Marion's email to both of us with instructions on what to do at the airport. Tennyson "Teddy" Knight, bassist for Concrete Temple. Or maybe I should say ex-bassist, as Google had informed me that the band had broken up after the last stop on its tour the previous week.

I'd told myself to give Teddy the benefit of the doubt. He was going to be my colleague at Wild Arts, and it wasn't fair to lump him in with Scott. For all I knew they'd broken up due to personality differences. And I *had* given him the benefit of the doubt—for all of ten seconds, until I clicked on a TMZ post reporting that the band had broken up because Teddy had thrown a tantrum and trashed a hotel room.

And the way he acted when I tried to introduce myself at the airport: sheesh. I'd just been going to say, *Hey, I think we're both late additions to the Wild Arts faculty*. I'd been able to google him, but there are hundreds, maybe thousands, of Gretchen Millers in Minnesota. There's also the part where I'm not famous. But OK, message received. At least, unlike with my Tinder dudes, I hadn't wasted any time dating him or any vulnerability sleeping with him. No, that was the job of his Instagram-influencer girlfriend, Karlie Carroll, God bless her.

I sent myself back to last night. After getting settled into my cabin, I'd walked across the road to check out the lake. I'd been standing there, staring at the dark water, thinking about whether I would be the kind of crone who cursed men or if I'd take it up a notch and be the kind of crone who cursed men and *also* lured stupid young women to the forest and ruined their lives, when Teddy appeared. He was carrying his lit-up phone, he was stomping across the beach—he passed maybe ten feet in front of me—and he was stark, raving naked. He was holding the phone at waist level, and I could see all the goods. I mean, I could also see a hint of some abs and some tattoos—when it came to rock star torsos, Teddy Knight's was very on the nose—but can you blame me for focusing on the goods? They weren't anything extraordinary, just your basic penis and balls at rest in a thatch of dark hair, but it was weird to be seeing a dude's junk in a nonsexual context.

But maybe also a little gross? He didn't know I was there; he had the reasonable assumption of privacy. I forced my gaze up—even assholes deserved privacy—and took in more tattoos and inexplicably attractive shoulders.

I needed to cut it out with the stealth ogling. I was turning out to be as bad as the men of Tinder when it came to basic human decency. I transferred my attention to the public, above-the-neck region of Teddy Knight and had to stifle a sigh. He had thick, lustrous, mahogany hair pulled back into a hefty bun my ballet girls would have killed for, a sharp, angular jaw, and a few days' worth of beard scruff. I tried to tell myself that anyone would look good in shadows like this. It was a lie. Even in the harsh overhead light of baggage claim back at the airport, Teddy Knight had been gorgeous. It didn't seem fair that someone with such a pretty face should also look like a Greek god. Or maybe a Greek god's tattooed, black-sheep, wayward brother—though come to think of it, they probably had Greek gods who fit that bill.

No wonder he was such a jerk. If someone that beautiful was also a nice person, it would probably violate some rule of the universe. Tinder Lesson #1 was that the hot guys were the worst.

But the not-hot guys were also the worst, so I wasn't sure how much stock to put in Lesson #1.

But it didn't matter because I was on my way to being a post-Tinder crone.

Teddy's stomping became more pronounced when he hit the dock. *Bam, bam, bam, bam.* After he passed me, I got a view of his butt.

He barely broke stride as he approached the end of the dock, just paused momentarily to set down his phone before walking off the edge. He slipped into the still water without a splash.

It had been interesting to appreciate him from afar. To admire his admittedly smoking self with my mind, with no attachment to the *idea* of him, no eye toward a possible future, no worries about if I'd groomed sufficiently or had enough funny anecdotes on deck to make for good conversation. Setting aside the fact that I don't sleep with known jerks—no, I just sleep with guys who *later* turn out to be jerks—I wasn't here for that.

Under no circumstances was I going to have sex with Teddy Knight. It was never going to happen. So I'd been able to watch him with an air of detachment. That, in turn, made me realize how much I normally didn't, or couldn't, do that. I evaluated every man I met through the pathetic lens of *Could he love me? Could I love him?*

Gah. Gross.

Here, with me actioning Pillar Two on the whole Midlife Crisis: Averted project, everything was different.

Teddy Knight was never going to love me, and I was never going to love Teddy Knight. I found that oddly freeing.

So I would like it stated for the record that my *I have seen Teddy Knight naked* earworm was *not* about the fact that he was famous. It was merely that Teddy Knight was a human male I had seen naked and was *not* going to sleep with. It was another one of those the-universe-has-a-sense-of-humor moments: Here I was, day one of my naked-human-male moratorium, and what was the first noteworthy thing I saw? A naked human male. A naked human male formerly of the same band as Scott fucking Collier. All you could do was laugh.

I *was* laughing, in fact, when Teddy yanked open his door and growled, "*What?*"

Right. Because I was standing on his porch, where I'd pounded on his door purely to provoke him. Which was something I was going to knock off. I had a feeling that neither Teddy nor I was our best self around the other.

He was still naked. Mostly. He was holding a strategically placed pillow over his junk. Which I had already seen.

I still felt guilty about that.

"What do you want?"

I want to annoy you because I can tell you don't get enough of that in your regular life? "I came to get you for sunrise circle." Realizing I was talking to the pillow, I transferred my attention to his face. He was all sleep-mussed, his hair half in last night's bun, half around his shoulders.

He squinted against the bright light. "Seems like the sun's already up."

"Sunrise circle turns out not to be literal. Which you would know if you'd read the welcome package."

Listen to me. What did I care if Teddy Knight read the welcome package? "You know what? I'll just see you there." I didn't need Teddy making me late for day one anyway. I was a punctual person. I ran a tight ship, at the studio and in regular life.

I was about to step off Teddy's porch when I heard a "Hey."

I turned back. "What?"

"Do you have a keyboard in your cabin?"

"Yes." I'd had some fun last night plunking out songs I remembered from my brief tour through piano lessons as a kid—I'd had to quit when we had to sell the piano—but the keyboard was wasted on me. This camp was, as Rory had reported, partially meant to be a retreat for the artists. The rest of them were staying for ten weeks. There were the two four-week camp sessions, but also a two-week interstitial period in which the artists were meant to do arty things without the distraction of campers. I was only staying for the first camp session. I had to get back to my real life.

That was fine, though, as I wasn't an artist in the sense the others were. What would I even do over that interstitial period?

Too bad they didn't want anyone to teach people how to write a business plan. I would kill at that.

"Do you want to switch cabins?" Teddy asked.

"Do you not have a keyboard? Sure, I'll switch with you." Teddy Knight might be a smug, entitled ass—with a very nice actual ass, my mental tape from last night reminded me—but I could hardly deny the musician among us the cabin with the keyboard.

"No, I have one."

"Then why do you want to switch?"

"If you take this cabin, you'll have the lake view."

"Oh." That was…nice? It was, right? I tried to imagine what ulterior motive he might have but came up with nothing. So I switched to trying to think what ulterior motive the shitty men of Tinder might have in this situation, but then I realized they—and Teddy—were not worth the mental energy. "I'm good, thanks. I'm only staying the one session. Anyway, I'm all unpacked and organized."

He rolled his eyes as if to communicate that being unpacked and organized was somehow a character flaw. The dude probably had a manager and an army of handlers and personal assistants who told him when it was time to take a shit. The rest of us had to run our own lives, our own small businesses. So yeah: tight ship, no apologies.

We stared at each other for a few seconds. His intense, unstinting attention made me squirmy on the inside, but my years of dance training had taught me to keep my body perfectly still when the situation called for it.

I reminded myself that I didn't owe him anything. I wasn't trying to make him like me. So I just said, flatly, "See you." I had sunrise circle to get to. I stag-leaped off his porch. Time for some kumbaya nature shit.

———

There was no one outside at the flagpole where sunrise circle was supposed to be held, so I headed for the dining hall, where I could see a door propped open. The hum of chitchat grew louder as I approached, but the moment I emerged into the large room filled with long, Hogwarts-style tables with benches, everyone fell silent.

Four sets of eyes swung toward me. One set I recognized: Danny. I knew the other three, too, as I'd done extensive googling of the other artists in residence. Well, all of them except Teddy, as I hadn't realized he was coming until I received Marion's email yesterday morning. It all made sense, though, now that I knew that the musician Teddy was filling in for was married to Imani Tran, the dancer I was filling in for.

"Hi." I waved to the group. "I'm Gretchen Miller."

A tall Asian woman I knew from my research to be the painter Maiv Khang grinned. I'd cruised an online version of a recent exhibition of hers at the Walker Art Center. Her paintings were amazing. Just seeing them on the screen had me in awe of her talent. "Hi, Gretchen. I think we're all being so weird because we were talking about Teddy Knight, and we thought you were him." She rolled her eyes self-deprecatingly. "You know, caught gossiping about the celebrity."

Apparently even acclaimed artists were awestruck by rock stars.

"But is he really a 'celebrity'?" Danny asked. "Would you recognize him on the street? I feel like the other guy is the famous face of Concrete Temple. What's his name?"

"Scott Collier," I supplied, ordering myself to keep my sneer internal.

"And that's probably at least partly because he's married to that model, Cinda Lewis," Danny said.

Scott Collier was *married*?

Of course he was.

There was a sniff from a man I recognized as Jack Branksome, a novelist who was famous for two things. One, his debut novel, which the *New York Times* had called a tour de force. Two, his refusal to let Hollywood actress and power producer

Blair Kellermoon use his tour de force in her book club. The latter had earned him a reputation as a snobbish elitist.

"Well, Teddy sure acts like a celebrity if you believe what you read," said Maiv, who was wearing a Minnesota Twins T-shirt. I was a baseball fan myself, so this endeared her to me. "He's kind of a grump, I gather."

"Can confirm," I said.

They started asking me questions about him since I was the only one there who had seen him. And I had *seen* him. Heh. Was Concrete Temple really broken up for good? Had Teddy said anything about the hotel room incident? What was he like?

I did my best to answer as I poured myself a coffee from the breakfast buffet. I didn't know if Concrete Temple was broken up for good, but they must be broken up for at least the summer, right, if he was here? He had not said anything about the hotel room incident. "As for what he's like, hmm. He is very..."

Rude. Humorless.

Gorgeous. In possession of hair that would make teenage ballerinas weep.

What could I say that was truthful but wouldn't sound like I was running him down? Or objectifying him? Not that I cared, really, but it was probably a good idea to behave with decorum in front of my colleagues. "Teddy Knight is very..."

"Here!" Maiv whispered.

I turned, knowing what I'd find because I had that same squirmy feeling I'd gotten earlier when Teddy had been staring at me.

"Don't let me interrupt," Teddy drawled as he approached. He was wearing a ratty gray T-shirt, a pair of cutoffs, and the combat boots that had passed muster with Lena last night. His hair was in a fresh bun.

"Good morning! It looks like we're all here!"

Saved by Marion.

She strode in and clapped her hands, drawing everyone's attention. If I were prone to intimidation, I would say Marion was a bit intimidating. To begin with, she was ultrarich. She'd have to be, to be funding Wild Arts. She was also smart and stylish and had that air about her that people do when they feel confident about their place in the world. Of course, it's probably easier to feel confident about your place in the world when you're ultrarich. Some of us had to work to acquire that attitude, had to constantly nurture it.

"Has everyone had enough to eat?" She gestured at the buffet. "The kitchen isn't up to full speed until tomorrow. The binders in your room list the hours of meal service. You're welcome to eat here or to get your food to go—though I note that campers must eat here. For now, let's grab what we want and decamp to the flagpole."

Outside, there were rows of rough-hewn wooden benches around the flagpole. Marion explained there was a morning ceremony to kick off each day. "It'll be led by the counselors. Your attendance is optional, but I'd love it if you could make it a few times each session. As you know, your role here is to mentor. Beyond your initial one-on-one meetings with campers, your office hours, and your help with and attendance at the closing performances, I leave it up to you as to what that mentorship will look like. The counselors will run activities—of both the arty and non-arty variety—and rehearsals as we get closer to the end of the session, but you are more than welcome to join in at any time.

"But I'm getting ahead of myself. Now that we're all here, let's do introductions. Tell us who you are and a bit about your artistic goals for your tenure here."

Danny I'd already met. He talked about the distraction of regular life and his desire to get a bunch of pieces made this summer, including some with natural, experimental glazes he was working on. I didn't know anything about pottery, but he seemed interesting.

Maiv said she wanted to "play with the tension between urban and natural." "We treat it as a binary," she said, "but as I learned when I did a recent show on the encroachment of nature in abandoned urban spaces, nature takes over pretty fast. I want to explore what that means. I've been doing this in the city, but I thought it would be interesting to come here and approach it from this angle. What is nature like when people suddenly occupy it?" That sounded cool and ratified my initial impression of Maiv as a person worth getting to know.

Next was Jack Branksome. As far as I could tell, as he talked about his novel in progress, which "plays with themes of celibacy as metaphor for the post-postmodern," his reputation as an elitist snob might be at least a teeny bit justified. He said he worked best in silence and had trouble concentrating at his condo in Minneapolis, so he hoped the quiet here would enable him to get a draft done. Good luck to you, Jack Branksome. May Blair Kellermoon have mercy on your soul.

Then there was Caleb Lyons, a theater actor from Minneapolis who was working on a one-man show. "I've somehow got myself typecast as a serious tragic hero—I've done Hamlet and Romeo, and I'm aging into Lear and Vanya. Which is fine. No, it's *great*. I adore my job, and I consider myself lucky to have it. But I got into theater originally because I loved musicals—I was that musical theater kid. So I started thinking about writing a one-man show that would combine my love of classical theater with music. Most of what you see in that space is parody—the complete works of Shakespeare in sixty minutes, that kind of thing. Which is also great—there's room for all of that. But I've been working on a piece that is basically a memoir told through the roles I've played, but with music. It's hard to explain. As for why I came here specifically, honestly, I got ahead of myself and applied for and got a spot at the Brooklyn Fringe Festival in October, so now I'm in panic mode." He performed a grin that became an exaggerated, self-deprecating grimace.

Ha. I liked this guy. I liked what he said, and I liked his refreshing candor.

"But it's all good," he went on. "It's almost done—I'm just fiddling with it at this point. And I have some connections to an off-Broadway theater that may pick it up if they like what they see at the festival. So I just have to, you know…finish fiddling."

It was my turn. "My name is Gretchen Miller. I'm a pinch hitter. You probably know that Imani Tran was supposed to be here. You might not know the name unless you know modern dance, but she's a big deal. I am not a big deal. I'm a dance teacher. I think I might be the living embodiment of the saying about 'Those who can, do; those who can't, teach.'"

There was a polite murmur of disagreement. "It's OK. I'm not saying that to run myself down. I'm a great teacher, if I do say so myself. And businesswoman, too." I really was. I was proud of the way I, someone from a modest background and with no entrepreneurial experience to speak of, had built my studio from nothing into a place that celebrated dance in a way that—I hoped—turned its back on some of the garbage that often came along with dance culture. "I have my own studio, and I'm getting ready to expand it.

"Because I wasn't planning on coming, and because, to be

honest, my focus on dance has always been nested inside my identity as an entrepreneur, I can't say I have a coherent artistic goal for my time here. And I'm only here for the first session. I'll probably turn my attention to some choreographing for the upcoming season at my studio, but to be totally frank, I'm here more to achieve some personal goals."

Wait. I should not have said that last part, given that I was not prepared to follow it up with a monologue about dating apps and my impending and voluntary crone-ification. So I went in with some humor for the save. "Yes, very important personal goals, which I should not have mentioned, because now I'm probably supposed to tell you what they are, but I am not going to do that." I grinned, and so did some of my audience. "Let's just leave it that I am in need of a reset, so I'm appreciating the change of scenery."

"Thanks, Gretchen," Marion said. "We're so glad to have you here. We support artistic goals and personal goals alike. A reset, whatever form it takes, sounds like a worthy aim. And last but not least, Teddy?"

Teddy was still looking at me, as if he hadn't registered that I'd stopped speaking. Marion had to call on him again, and he finally shook himself loose. "I'm wanting to write enough songs for an album."

That was all he said, which cracked me up. These people were dying for more from Mr. Rock and Roll. I knew Teddy better than they did—I'd seen him naked, after all; did I mention that?—so I knew they were going to be disappointed.

"I hope that some of you will become real friends," Marion said when it became clear that Teddy's three-second speech was all she was going to get out of him. "Or at least camp friends."

Maiv asked what camp friends were, and Marion explained

that teenagers tended to form fast, intense friendships at camp. "I suppose they're aided by the fact that there's no technology here. Probably also by their hormones. There's something about the setting, too, away from the distractions and pressures of their everyday lives. They latch on to each other, and they latch hard. And if they come back the next summer, they pick up right where they left off."

The rest of the morning was spent going over stuff we'd need to know. The counselors were the ones responsible for the campers on a day-to-day basis, but Marion briefed us on the rules anyway, which covered everything from life jackets to shower schedules.

"What about showers for us?" asked Teddy, who had so far remained silent to the point of sullenness except for when he'd been made to speak about his goals.

"There's a single-stall shower room behind the artists' cabins," Marion said, and Teddy perked up. "Sorry, I should have told you about it last night. It's not on the map, just to minimize the opportunity for pranks—camp pranks are also a thing."

"I'm intimidated by the idea of high school kids, to be honest," Maiv said. "I did not enjoy my high school years."

"Artsy kids are different," I said. "They're not going to fit your image of the typical high school kid. I'm not sure any kid is, actually." I grinned. "Well, they are kind of obsessed with each other—and themselves—so in that sense they are. I can totally see how this concept of 'camp friends' is a thing."

"Even if they're not the terrifying teen-movie kids we're imagining, how do we *relate* to them?" Danny asked.

"With this age, and in this setting, I think the key is not to try to relate to them as kids," I said. "Sure, they're not fully mature people. Their brains are still wiring themselves, which is good to remember. But for our purposes, especially since we're not doing any of the direct supervisory stuff, try thinking of them as peers who are not quite as far down the road as you are." I shrugged. It wasn't really that hard. "Listen to them. Try to help them."

After lunch, we met the counselors, most of whom were college students. They were earnest and smiley and very, very hyped. The world had not yet worn them down. The meet and greet was followed by a session in CPR and first aid. I was already certified in both, given my job, but it was good to have a refresher.

We were dismissed around three and told we were on our own until dinner. "Anyone want to go swimming?" I asked. I loved swimming. There was something about floating in water that buoyed me. Literally, but also mentally. Also, it was still hella hot.

Maiv and Caleb were up for it—yay. They were the two I had in my sights as camp friend material. Danny said he was going to the kiln to check on some pieces. Teddy initially said nothing, but when Jack said, "It's cocktail hour," he grunted in a way that sounded vaguely enthusiastic, and soon the musician and the writer had a plan to drink together. Fine; they deserved each other.

We walked back to the cabins together, as Maiv, Caleb, and I needed to change into our swimsuits.

"What's the deal with Marion?" Teddy asked once we were underway.

"Her family manufactures cheese spread," I said. I was a huge fan of the Kuhn family product line. "She runs the family foundation."

"They sell enough cheese spread to support a foundation?" he asked.

"Oh yeah, it's like a cheese spread empire," I said.

"What the hell *is* cheese spread, anyway?"

No one answered, so I said, "You know, cheese that you spread?"

"Like cream cheese?"

"No. It comes in a tub and it's usually cheddar and sometimes it has stuff in it like chives or bacon bits."

"Is it orange?"

I tried not to chuckle. I wasn't sure why, but the question, and/or its deadpan delivery, hit my funny bone. "It is orange."

"So what you're saying is this place is run by a processed cheese heiress."

"You say that like it's a bad thing, but have you ever had cheese spread?"

"I had something called pub cheese when I was at school at Oxford, but I can't say that I enjoyed it." That had come from Jack, and I was a bit startled by it. It had felt for a moment as if it'd been just Teddy and me talking, as we'd bantered back and forth, but of course that hadn't been the case.

Teddy and Jack went into Jack's cabin—he apparently had some kind of rarefied sake in there, and they were planning to take it to Teddy's lakeside porch to drink it. I dashed into my cabin and changed into my bathing suit. I didn't want to keep my new friends waiting, so I went quickly, and when I emerged, I crossed paths with the sake boys making their way over to Teddy's.

"You sure you guys don't want to come with us?" I regretted it the moment it was out. I didn't *want* them to come with us— I was going to work on locking down my camp friends—and I generally tried to avoid partaking in the standard Minnesota Nice politeness-for-its-own-sake bullshit. Or at least the new me did.

Teddy looked at me blankly. He had a way of doing that. Like it took his brain a few seconds to shake loose whatever else it was thinking about and participate in the conversation at hand.

Belatedly realizing I was standing there in my bathing suit, I wrapped my towel around my shoulders. Not that there was anything wrong with my suit. It was a two-piece, but a modest one with lots of coverage on both top and bottom. But their attention, particularly Teddy's ultraintense brand of scrutiny, made me . . . what? What was this strange feeling? Was it *shyness*?

No. Crones did not do shy. So I dropped the towel. I was wearing a swimsuit at a summer camp. That was a perfectly reasonable thing to do. If they wanted to secretly judge me, or secretly ogle me, that was their business. Teddy was still look-ing spacey, so I didn't give him a chance to respond to the invitation I regretted issuing. "See you."

Teddy started to speak and got as far as "Actually we could bring our—" when he realized Jack was talking, too, and stopped.

Jack said, "No thanks. I think I'm going to stick close to home. Gonna try to get some writing done after a drink."

"Yeah," Teddy said. "Me, too."

"Suit yourself."

The others had not emerged from their cabins yet, so I did a cabriole-sauté series to propel myself over to Maiv's cabin to wait for her.

4
LITTLE WOMEN, BUT WITH DANCING

Teddy

Jack Branksome was going to be an acquired taste. But honestly, if I was going to acquire a taste for anyone here, it was probably going to be for him. He was smart, and he didn't feel the need to fill every silence with words. We did talk a bit as we sipped our sake, but it wasn't oppressive. I hadn't read his book, but I wasn't much of a reader these days—I'd read a lot as a kid, but somehow I'd lost the habit. He, however, seemed familiar with Concrete Temple.

"You guys broke up, huh?"

"It would appear so."

"It would appear so?"

Yeah, that had been an idiotic thing to say. It was just that *breakup* sounded mutual. A civilized parting of ways after both parties realized the relationship had run its course. That was what Karlie and I had done.

That was *not* what Scott and I had done. Nope, he'd just sat me down in the fucking Hilton Garden Inn in Chicago after the last show of the tour and told me he was done. Our record contract had been fulfilled, and he had no interest in re-upping with our label or any other. In fact, he had studio time and session musicians already booked for a solo album, which meant he'd been sitting on this news for a long time.

Well, he'd been sitting on it for a long time, and then he'd gone and told Jet and Luis before me.

Nothing against Jet and Luis. They were great musicians. But Concrete Temple was Scott and me. The other guys hadn't been with us from the beginning. They didn't write. Sure, Jet was a star, but he was still, to be blunt, replaceable. Luis was replaceable.

Scott was not replaceable. There was no Concrete Temple without Scott.

There was no Concrete Temple without me, either, thank you very much.

I guess the problem was, I wasn't sure if there was a me without Concrete Temple.

I maybe could have dealt with all that junk from Scott—the news he was leaving, being the last to know, the studio already booked for a solo album—if he hadn't gone on to spew all this shit about how Concrete Temple hadn't been fulfilling him artistically for fucking *years*.

You sure managed to cash those unfulfilling checks, I'd snarked back. And then when he called me a hack, I'd smashed the TV.

It was still so mortifying. No, it was more than that. It was *terrifying*. Because I was not that guy.

And yet, apparently, I was.

I cleared my throat, forced myself back to the here and now, where I was sitting on a porch next to a novelist, looking out at a lake in the middle of a forest where I was meant to get my shit together. "Yeah. We broke up."

"Too bad."

"Mm."

"What do you think of the others here?"

"They seem fine." What did he want me to say? I didn't care about paintings or pots, but I could understand that other people did.

"Everyone seems very...perky."

"Mm." I raised my glass in agreement, thinking of how every time Gretchen departed my company, she literally leaped away. Which, come to think of it, maybe wasn't perkiness so much as it was sensibleness. I was no longer feeling the Hulk-smash energy that had animated me the day of the hotel room incident, but I would freely admit that I was not sparkling company right now.

Anyway, I wouldn't really call Gretchen perky. She *looked* perky, with her pink-tipped hair and her retro, pinup-style bikini. But *she* wasn't perky. She was...well, the word that came to mind was actually *sour*. Maybe that was my fault: realistically, she'd only turned sour after I'd been a dick to her. But the fact was, I could feel the coolness emanating from her.

I'd thought of her, last night, as the Sugarplum Fairy. The fairy part tracked: she was always leaping through the air. Maybe I should start calling her the *Sour*plum Fairy. I laughed to myself over what a perfect descriptor that was for her.

"What's funny?"

"Nothing." I needed to turn my attention to something besides refining nicknames for Gretchen. I needed to remember why I was here: the album.

After a couple drinks, Jack took his leave, and I intended to start writing. I brought my guitar out to the porch. I went so far as to take it out of the case.

Then I sat on my ass and did nothing. For a long time.

So long that I was still sitting there on my ass doing nothing an hour and a half later when Gretchen pulled up in a God damn paddleboat.

"I don't know what I was thinking," she said when she realized I was sitting there, "but apparently I'm arriving by boat."

"I can see that." There was no way *not* to see her, with her bright hair and her bright...self. The sun was peeking out from behind a bank of clouds in a way that made her skin glow.

And there was a lot of skin. She was wearing that same swimsuit from before.

She was wearing that same swimsuit from before. Listen to me. What did I think? She would have executed a costume change while at the beach?

Her swimsuit was white. The top looked like a sports bra, except the straps that went over her shoulders were wide ruffles, and the hem also had a ruffle. The bottom was high-waisted—it covered her belly button—and there were smaller ruffles around the leg holes.

That was...a lot of ruffles for someone so sour.

"I think this is one of those 'It seemed like a good idea at the time' scenarios." She made quotation marks with her fingers even as her legs kept pedaling.

I shook myself out of my thoughts. She was trying to pull up alongside the dock that extended from the little beach in front of my cabin, but she was having trouble.

"It turns out that while one person can do a paddleboat built for two, precision maneuvers are tricky," she said.

I sighed and put down my guitar—it was apparently only a prop anyway—and rose to mount a rescue mission. "Where's everyone else?" I asked as I crossed the beach.

"Still swimming. I'm starving all of a sudden, so I decided to come back and change and head up to the dining hall. Marion said we can take the paddleboats back and forth between the swimming area and this beach. There's supposed to be a post here to tie it to?" She looked like Fred Flintstone with her legs pumping. "I should have just walked, but this looked like fun." She snorted. "Famous last words."

"Throw me that rope." She did, and I hauled her in and secured the boat.

She was on the seat on the far side of the boat, so there was some to-ing and fro-ing as she disembarked. I offered her a hand and was surprised when she took it.

When she alit on the dock, she didn't immediately let go. She was completely waterlogged. Her hair hung in blond-pink hanks around her face, and there was makeup smeared under her eyes.

She shivered. "The lake is colder than it looks. But you probably already..." She swallowed the rest of her sentence.

"I probably what?" Her smile disappeared, which was unsettling for reasons I could not articulate. "OK, well," I said, attempting to extricate my hand from hers.

She did not let go. "Were you named after the poet Tennyson?"

I was discombobulated by the abrupt change of subject. "My mom was a fan."

" 'It's better to have loved and lost than never to have loved at all,' " she recited. "That's Tennyson, right?"

"It is," I said warily. Where was she going with this? Most people had vaguely heard of Alfred, Lord Tennyson, and most people knew his most famous line, but in my experience, they didn't know it was *his*, or that it was from a poem at all. That line was more likely to appear in Etsy shops that also sold shabby-chic wooden signs that said *Live, Laugh, Love*.

Maybe if I couldn't get any fucking songs written, I could launch an Etsy shop that sold signs that said *Die, Cry, Hate*. Auden could help me make them look good.

"Well," Gretchen said, abruptly letting my hand drop, "that's complete bullshit."

"I…" Had no idea what to say to that. Struck dumb by Sourplum. Ha. That rhymed. Watch your back, Alfred, Lord Tennyson.

I was still trying to think what to say when Gretchen turned and walked off. No leaping, just walking. Which seemed wrong, somehow. I guess I'd gotten used to the leaping.

But her thesis was *not* wrong. It *wasn't* better to have loved and lost than never to have loved at all. I learned that early from dear old Mom.

——————

At the end of week one, I was beginning to think I'd made a mistake coming here. Not only had I done zero songwriting, I was up to my eyeballs in children.

There were eighty kids at this camp, and they all had a declared area of focus. Like college majors, except at camp. I felt a little bad for them. My childhood had been shitty in many ways, but I wouldn't trade the wide-open, unprogrammed summers of my youth for anything. Auden and I had had the city at our feet, and we'd gleefully abandoned both the strictures of school and the unpredictability of Mom in favor of roaming free.

Fifteen kids were doing music, and I was supposed to meet with each of them at least once. Which on paper seemed reasonable enough, but it also meant I was seeing three kids a day that first week, Marion having suggested we try to do our one-on-ones early in the month so the kids could benefit from our wisdom or some shit as they planned their end-of-camp performances. I was keen to get this obligation over with, as after this week, all I would have to do was show up at a few sunrise circles and hold twice-weekly "office hours" in the music studio, where kids could come see me for…I wasn't even sure. Help tuning their guitars? Straight talk about the music industry that would crush their fragile little dreams?

By Friday afternoon, I was exhausted by the week's tsunami of teens. They were so oily and awkward. But I'd almost made it; I'd survived fourteen kids of wildly varying abilities. And honestly, I'd done it by putting into action Gretchen's advice about treating them like adults who were less far along in their careers than I was.

Kid number fifteen was—I consulted my schedule—Anna, going into tenth grade at St. Paul Academy. I think they told us the kids' schools because it was supposed to mean something to us. I, of course, was clueless. Anna could be a Juilliard graduate for all I cared.

"Hi," she said shyly, as she appeared in the studio.

All right. One more kid, and it was the weekend. I tried not to look as unenthused as I was. It wasn't her fault she was stuck with me. "Tell me about you and music, Anna."

"Um, I love music."

Great. Don't we all. I raised my eyebrows.

"I play piano, guitar, and banjo," she added.

"Banjo!" I exclaimed. I couldn't help it. So far this week, I'd seen guitar and piano and drums, which I could work with, and a saxophonist who would be better off with YouTube than with me—woodwinds were not my forte. Then two kids who only sang, which was fine for them, but I didn't know what they expected from me. I'd only sung backup for Concrete Temple, though I supposed that was going to have to change if I intended to put out a solo record.

I gestured Anna in—she was still hovering near the doorway—and pointed at the empty stool next to me. The camp provided a piano and a drum kit, but the kids were supposed to bring their own instruments if they played anything else, and sure enough, Anna was laboring under the weight of a guitar case and a banjo case.

"Let's hear something on banjo."

She got her instrument out and said, "You want to hear a cover or an original?"

Well, hell. "Both. Why don't you start with a cover?"

She proceeded to blow me away with a cover of the Eagles' "Take It Easy." I'd have thought that if a kid this age was going to cover music with actual banjos in it, rather than just banjo-ify a current pop song, she'd have gone with the Chicks or Mumford & Sons or something, not a dude-rock band from before her time—and mine. She changed the opening lyric about having "seven women on my mind" to be about having seven boys on her mind. At first the gender swap delighted me. She was making the song her own, and this girl could *play*. But then the song took a turn, became kind of creepy. When you thought about the lyrics—being owned, having a truck slow down as you're minding your own business, the simple change of pronouns made it unsettling. Which I was pretty sure was her point. Damn. I hadn't felt this awake since I arrived here.

I got that buzzing feeling in my limbs, as if someone had replaced my blood with gin and tonic. I used to get the feeling from being in the studio with Scott. Though come to think of it, I hadn't gotten that feeling during the last record.

When Anna was done, I said, "Now let's hear an original."

She took a deep breath. She was nervous. But she relaxed as she started playing. Her song was short, and she stumbled over a couple chord changes—she didn't have this one down like her Eagles song—but it had a hell of a lot of potential.

"No lyrics yet," I said when she was done.

"No. I don't have them yet, but I know what it's going to be about."

"And what's that?"

She paused.

"You don't have to tell me." I did desperately want to know, which was an odd feeling. I hadn't felt this strongly about something in a while. Well, no, I had to issue a mental correction as I thought back to that shattered TV at the Hilton Garden Inn: I hadn't felt this strongly in a *positive* way about something in a while. But I respected people's songwriting processes. It could be an oddly private experience. It could make you feel exposed. Vulnerable.

Which was why I'd only ever done it with Scott. Because I trusted him. Or I used to trust him.

"No, it's OK," she said. "I just think you might think it's dumb. Immature."

"Try me."

"It's about a boy at school I hate."

I laughed. Gretchen popped to mind, for some reason. If camp was school, I was pretty sure I was the boy Gretchen hated. Probably deservedly so.

As Anna's face shuttered, I rushed to say, "I'm not laughing at you. That was a laugh of delight. If anything, I'd have expected you to say it was about a boy you *liked*. Which would have been cool. Most songs are love songs for a reason. But a boy you *hate*—that's a great twist."

She smiled tentatively, and I asked, "How'd you learn to play banjo?"

"I grew up in a tiny town in West Virginia where there was nothing to do, and my grandpa taught me."

Well, damn. Anna was officially my favorite camper. Not that there was much competition.

"My mom and I moved to the Twin Cities when she and my dad got divorced. She met a guy online, and we moved to be with him. He has *money*." The way she emphasized "money" made me think the guy must not have a lot else going for him.

I had to swallow a laugh. Once again, I wasn't laughing *at* her, I was just fucking charmed by this kid and her talent. "Maybe you should write a song about that." The best songs were authentic. And what was more authentic to a teen girl's experience—I imagined—than hating her mom's boyfriend who had upended her life?

"I've thought about it," she said, "but I decided he's too much of a dick to bother with." She inhaled quickly. "I mean jerk. He's too much of a jerk to bother with."

I grinned. "I get it. OK, Anna, you want to meet up next week at this same time? I can't pretend to know banjo." I'd noodled around with one here and there over the years, but banjo was not in Concrete Temple's wheelhouse. "But I can try to help you with songwriting—if you'd like. Or we can just jam."

"That would be great," she said.

And hell, maybe *she* could teach *me* banjo. "You know any

Pete Seeger?" I asked as she packed up her instrument. Maybe my Appalachian musical wunderkind would know some of the folkies of my youth.

"Never heard of him."

———

Thanks to Anna, I closed out the week with a spring in my step. Metaphorically. I was still wearing my Docs, as I'd neglected to bring any other shoes, and though the temperatures had come down from their previous Dante's *Inferno* heights, the afternoons were still hot. My attitude adjustment didn't mean I wasn't glad the week was over, though. Well, I guess nothing was "over" since we lived here, but the kids did normal summer camp things on weekends. And there were no sunrise circles on weekends; the kids were allowed to sleep in.

I knocked on Jack's door to see if he was in the mood for a drink. We'd fallen into the habit of having one before dinner. "You want to go to your place, look out at the lake?" he asked. His cabin was on the forest side of Mr. Rogers' Neighborhood.

"Nah. Let's just stay here," I said, though I had no idea why. It was likely that soon the Sourplum Fairy, who always went swimming with Maiv before dinner, would come flitting home to change into her ridiculous swimsuit that made her look like a ruffly marshmallow, and did I want to see that?

No.

Mostly no.

It was complicated.

I liked the swimsuit, OK, as absurd as it was. I was capable of appreciating a pretty woman even if I didn't appreciate the woman herself.

Soon we were set up on Jack's porch with more of his sake, which wasn't my favorite, but it had been a long week and a drink was a drink. Like clockwork, Gretchen appeared a few minutes later. She was only walking, not leaping or pirouetting or whatever the fuck, but she had a lightness and grace about her, which I guess shouldn't be that remarkable given her line of work. I'd noticed, though, because I was an asshole, that the lower body that was the engine of all her light-footedness was hella strong. She had a sizable ass and big, muscular thighs. The combination of that physique and the ruffly swimsuit was...really something.

Maybe I would tag along for swimming today. Gretchen always asked Jack and me if we wanted to join—though she never seemed to actually want us to say yes. I used to love swimming, back in my McCarren Park days, and I'd been known to hit hotel pools for laps with some regularity. It had been a long time, though. When had tours stopped being fun and started feeling like such a grind? Had the switchover been gradual or abrupt, and how had I not noticed?

"Hey!" Gretchen called when she spotted us. "Just the gentleman I was hoping to see. Can I join you for a sec?"

We didn't give her an answer, but she didn't require one. She barged in and leaned against the railing of Jack's small porch. "It's about my dance girls and their end-of-camp show." I belatedly wondered if I should give her my chair. Jack had one of the small porches with a single chair, and I'd dragged the chair over from Danny's place next door. "They want to do *Little Women*."

"Uh, OK," I said, as Jack said, "*Little Women*, like Marmee and Jo and Meg donate their Christmas breakfast to the poor and stuff?"

"Yep. *Little Women*, but with dancing."

"*Little Women*, but with dancing," Jack repeated, a hint of mockery in his tone. More than a hint.

"So," I interjected. "*Little Women*, but with dancing. What about it?"

"I was hoping you could help us adapt it?"

"And here I would have thought Louisa May Alcott didn't need any help," I said.

I was trying to be funny, but she scrunched up her Disney princess nose, seemingly giving serious consideration to what I'd said. "You would?"

"Well, it's a classic for a reason, isn't it?"

"And here *I'd* have thought *you'd* have thought you were above Louisa May Alcott."

"What?" What were we even talking about?

"Your self-esteem is very...robust," she said. "You also don't seem like the kind of person who's into books about, like, sisterly bonds."

"I have a sister. We have a bond." A bond forged in the fire of parental neglect, not the unconditional love of a wise and loving mother à la *Little Women*, but whatever.

"Hang on, it's going to take me a sec to process the idea of you as a sibling. As a child. As having a past that didn't involve being birthed into the world as an adult man with a scowl and calloused guitar hands." I looked down at my hands. I hadn't thought my calluses were that noticeable. "Nope," she went on. "That is not computing; I'm getting an error page. I'll have to work on that later. In the meantime, I have *Little Women*, but I have nine girls and no boys. And I'm actually talking to Jack here." She swiveled to face him.

Of course she'd been talking to Jack. She wanted help with a writing problem. Why had I thought *I* was "just the gentleman" she wanted to see? I stood, which caused her to swing her attention back to me questioningly.

"Why don't you sit?" I asked.

"That's OK. I'm not going to stay long." She turned back to Jack. "I want everyone to have roughly the same amount of stage time. So do I make more little women? Or do I rethink completely?"

"I think if you're redoing *Little Women* to make it a musical, you can do whatever else you want to it," Jack said. Again, he was being kind of a dick, but in a way that was hard to put my finger on.

"I never said musical," Gretchen said. "Although…" Her eyes narrowed and she swung back to face me. I was still standing, not having sat back down after she rebuffed my offer of a chair.

"Why do you want everyone to have the same amount of stage time?" I asked, though I had no idea why I cared. As was well established, she wasn't here for me.

"Why *wouldn't* I want everyone to have the same amount of stage time?"

"Because some of the kids are more talented dancers than others?" I posited. "Or smarter? Or just generally better? Because the world is, or should be, a meritocracy?"

She blinked. Yeah, that had been an odd thing to say. But I couldn't square Gretchen's plan with reality. Though I wasn't sure why I felt the need to. I sat down.

"Sure," she said. "But this isn't the world. This is summer camp for teenagers. There's plenty of time for meritocracy when they grow up. The world can crush their dreams later."

"I thought you said to treat them like adults."

She looked momentarily confused. But she *had* said that, that first day when she was talking about how to deal with teenagers, and it had been good advice. It had gotten me through the week.

She shrugged. "I guess I contain multitudes." She turned to Jack, either not getting or not caring that he wasn't interested in her show. "Also, what do I do about Laurie?" She paused. "Laurie is a boy character in *Little Women*."

"I am aware," Jack said, and there was nothing subtle about the snobbery in his tone that time.

"OK, sheesh."

"Maybe you should talk to Caleb," Jack said. He was dismissing her.

"I will find you a Laurie," I said suddenly, because apparently I'd taken leave of my senses.

"You will?"

"Yep." I had the perfect kid for the job. A self-impressed little shit who fancied himself a guitar god. He was the kid version of the accountant I'd imagined going to adult band camp. "He's a music kid, but I don't see why he can't do double duty in the dance show."

She eyed me skeptically, as if waiting for there to be a catch. I stared back until she shrugged and said, "OK, thanks."

I waited for her to ask if we wanted to go swimming. A Friday-night swim was sounding good. But she took her leave and disappeared into her cabin. When she came out a few minutes later wearing the ruffled monstrosity, I thought surely she would invite us. She had every other day this week.

But she didn't. She just waved and disappeared down the path.

5
RESET

Teddy

I didn't see Gretchen again until after dinner the next day. She hadn't been in the dining hall for dinner, which was unusual. But then, it was Saturday. Jack had driven to the nearest town for "an injection of life," which was amusing because he was always talking about how he hated noise and needed silence to write. Maiv hadn't been at dinner, either, so probably she and Gretchen were off doing something. The two of them seemed to have really hit it off.

I was sitting on my porch enjoying an after-dinner drink when I heard them. You couldn't *not* hear them—they were laughing maniacally as they approached in a paddleboat.

"Land ho!" Gretchen called as they aimed for the dock. I wasn't sure what their problem was, as there were two of them, so the boat wasn't unbalanced, as it had been last time Gretchen had returned home via nautical means. But they were coming in at a bad angle all the same.

I got up and jogged out to meet them. "Slow down," I called, which only sent them into further fits of laughter. Eventually I got them to throw me the rope, and I tied up the boat and helped them disembark. I headed back to my porch but kept an eye on them as they lingered on the dock. I wanted to make sure they didn't fall in the water, as I suspected they'd had quite a bit of fun this evening. They were talking about *Little Women*. It sounded like Gretchen had gotten Maiv to agree to help with the sets. Damn. The counselors were in charge of the end-of-camp performances, so I hadn't concerned myself with what the music kids were doing. What could they really do besides play some music, recital style? But it was sounding like we might all be shown up by *Little Women*, but with dancing.

Not that I cared.

I cared about writing my songs.

Which did not explain why I hadn't even bothered to bring my guitar out here with me this evening.

Eventually the women hugged and parted ways. Gretchen approached—she had to pass my cabin in order to get to hers. She tripped as she stepped from the sand of the beach to the dirt of the path, and I instinctively stood and moved toward her.

"I'm OK!" she shouted. "I'm OK! I'm OK!"

"Say it like you mean it," I said.

"Sorry." She winced. "I'm having some trouble with volume control." She stage-whispered, "I am a little bit drunk."

"So I gathered."

"What's that?" she asked, pointing to my glass.

"Bourbon."

"Can I have some?"

"Is that a good idea?"

"Meaning what? It's not seemly for a woman to drink too much? Bourbon's not a girly drink? It's acceptable for you to drink but not me? It's—"

"OK, OK." I was already on my feet. "Sit. I'll be right back."

I came back with her drink and a bag of almonds I'd gotten from the camp store. "You want something to eat?"

"Oh, yes. I surely do." She took a sip of her drink and promptly started coughing. I refrained from saying anything as I sat. I only had the glider, so I was stuck sitting next to her. She'd sat on her towel, but she didn't have it wrapped around her, so my denim-clad thigh was an inch from her naked one. There wasn't an ounce of fat on her thigh; you could see the outlines of the muscles beneath the skin.

She blew out a long, theatrical breath, interrupting my thigh-gazing. "What a week. I'm exhausted."

I could see why. I was tired, and from what I could tell, in addition to her discipline being inherently more physically demanding than mine, Gretchen had spent the week running around being an unpaid camp counselor. I would say she was putting the rest of us to shame, but since I had none, it didn't bother me.

She did look tired, though. Even in the golden-hour light this place was so good at, she had dark circles under her eyes. "Have you been...dancing a lot this week?"

What a stupid question. Of course she'd been dancing a lot. She was a dancer. I'd been thinking back to her intro speech about how she didn't have an artistic goal for her time here. I'd found it refreshingly honest. Also, I was dying to know what the "personal goals" she'd referenced were. The "reset" she'd said she needed.

"Not really," she said. "I haven't been dancing as much as I would in a normal week of teaching at my studio."

Hell, I was going to just ask her. She might even tell me, if she was a loose-lipped drunk. "Why so tired, then? Those secret personal goals of yours wearing you out?"

She looked at me for a really long time. So long I was sure she wasn't going to answer. OK, so not a chatty drunk.

"My personal goals are not really the kind that I have to work on. Just...being here...achieves them."

Well, damn, color me intrigued. The Sourplum Fairy had put a spell on me. But how could I get her to say more without looking like an idiot?

She took another sip, eyeing me over the rim of her glass. "I might as well just tell you."

Jackpot.

"It's not like it's anything shocking. I just have had a really long, really bad run on dating apps. I keep saying I'm quitting them, deleting them from my phone, but then, I don't know, hope springs eternal, I guess." She gave a self-deprecating shake of her head. "But I can't keep getting my heart broken. I...can't."

Wow. I was astonished that she'd spoken so openly. I guess that was the booze talking.

I was also annoyed. I was not the president of the Gretchen Miller fan club, but I was irritated by this alleged parade of heartbreakers.

"Anyway, I made some big life changes before I came here." She was back to her usual assured tone. "On the professional side of things, I'm expanding my business. And on the personal side, I've sworn off men. Deleted the apps—for good this time. That's the being-here bit." She shrugged. "I don't know. I thought a dramatic change of scenery might help."

"Not to mention the patchy cell service."

"Exactly." She sighed and slouched against the back of the rocker, which made me realize that normally her posture was ramrod straight. Must be a dancer thing. "Teddy Knight, what is the secret?"

"The secret to what?"

"The secret to love. Mind you, I'm only asking theoretically, since I'm done trying to chase relationships. But I'm curious. You're in a long-term relationship, aren't you?"

I was flattered that she knew that, given it must mean she'd googled me. But of course Google had not reported accurately on my relationship status since Karlie had not informed her followers of our breakup. And since *I* had *no* followers—I was not on social media—and also was not the kind of person who had a publicist inform *People* of changes in my relationship status, news hadn't gotten out. Maybe I should be that kind of person— maybe that would finally get Karlie out of my damn apartment.

"I was in a long-term relationship," I said in answer to Gretchen's question, "but we broke up last Christmas." I wasn't sure why I was telling her this when basically no one other than the band and my sister knew, except I guess that Gretchen had shown me her heartbreak and I wanted to respond in kind. Not that I was heartbroken. In fact, I'd barely thought about Karlie since the breakup, which was probably telling. It had only been in the week before coming here, as we'd been bickering over the apartment, that she'd been front of mind. I knew the feeling was mutual. We'd had our time, but that time was over.

"I'm sorry. It must be hard keeping a relationship going when you're on the road so much."

"Yes and no. We were on-again, off-again for years, and..." I tried to think how to sum up our relationship and its ultimate demise. "Sometimes our interpretations of when we were on and when we were off did not line up."

She looked shocked.

Shit. I had to say more, because for some damn reason I didn't want Sourplum thinking poorly of me. I was afraid she was having visions of me living it up with groupies on the road, when really, what I did on the road was do sound check, play shows, eat, sleep, swim laps, watch TV, and noodle around with Scott on song ideas. I mean, yes, back in the days when things were officially "off again," I'd had some fun, but I had never lived the stereotypical rock-and-roll lifestyle. It didn't take a genius to figure out that my childhood of chaos and deprivation had turned me into someone who didn't want to mess with the status quo—at least when that status quo meant paying the bills by making music. Smashing that TV was the most "rock star" thing I'd ever done—which was probably why I could not stop thinking about it.

"A couple years ago, we decided to get serious, and we moved in together," I said. "Or maybe I should say *I* decided to get serious. I flew home before the holidays to surprise her, and let's just say *I* was the one surprised—unpleasantly so— by what I walked in on." In my apartment. In my bed. "That's what I meant about our interpretations of when we were on and when we were off not always lining up. Call me crazy, but I think living with someone makes you in a permanent state of on."

"Yikes. You must have been devastated."

"Not really." I hadn't been gutted or heartbroken or any of that. My reaction really had been one of unpleasant surprise. I'd been more upset about the fact that I had to, on principle, throw away my nice sheets.

"Maybe you should have had a don't-ask-don't-tell agreement for when you were on the road," Gretchen said.

I thought that was an odd thing to say, but I also thought it was easier to just agree. "Maybe we should have."

"Did any of the other band members have arrangements like that with their significant others?"

That also seemed like an odd thing to say—an odd question. "Not that I know of," I said noncommittally. I'd always been vague when questioned about rumors of Scott's extracurricular activities. But why now? Scott and I were done. And anyway, he and Cinda had been separated for a year now, speaking of being done with Scott.

But I didn't want to talk about Scott. I wanted to talk about me. Which was weird, but I went with it. "When I walked in on them, I was more relieved than sad. It felt like it had been over for a long time. Like she was already an ex. A distant one I could think back on fondly. Or maybe not fondly, maybe just neutrally, you know?" Huh. I had never really thought of it that way, much less articulated it to anyone.

"Did you love her? Before, I mean?"

I didn't know how to answer that. "I thought I did. I *said* I did." When prompted, I'd said it back. I tried to think if I'd ever said it first. I came up blank. "But if I really had, wouldn't I be more upset? Honestly, I'm much more worked up over the apartment than I am the breakup."

"What do you mean?"

"She's still in the apartment. I don't have a place to live now that the tour's over. That's why I'm here." Well, that was part of it, but really, I was here for the revenge album that I was apparently incapable of writing.

"Why don't you have a place to live? Were you living with her?"

"No, she was living with me. I mean, we'd lived together

for two years—when I wasn't on tour, anyway—but it was my place to begin with. It's my name on the lease, and I pay the rent."

"But she cheated on you!"

"Yeah, I just..."

"She cheated on you *six months* ago! In *your* apartment!"

I rolled my eyes at myself. "I know. I know. When we first broke up, I was going to be on the road for months, so I was happy to have her stay for a while. It's hard to find an apartment in New York, and she has a lot of stuff." I did hear how that sounded. It was just that Karlie wasn't going to be able to afford a place that was up to her standards. I didn't wish her ill, and what use was an empty apartment to me? "Anyway, she was supposed to be out by now, and she's... not."

I was coming off as such a doormat. This was not how I wanted Gretchen to see me, though I understood that having a way I did or did not want Gretchen to see me was not a good look. I tried to summarize my last "discussion" with Karlie in a way that would put an end to this topic. "We agreed she'd be out by September," I said decisively. "So here I am."

That seemed to satisfy her, at least in the sense that she dropped the subject, but she was staring off into space, and she looked sad.

"A penny for your thoughts," I said, though I had no idea why. The conversation had come to a close, and she was the one who'd intruded on my solitude to begin with.

"My thoughts are worth way more than a penny," she said, and based on just her words, you'd have thought she was kidding—it was a jokey thing to say—but she still had that wistful vibe about her, and she was still staring at the darkening sky.

Fuck me if I didn't respond by reaching into my pocket and pulling out a crumpled ten-dollar bill—I had stopped at the camp store for the bag of almonds Gretchen was eating as we talked, and I still had cash on me. I moved over a bit and set it on the glider between us.

That cracked her melancholy. Her laughter rang out over the lake. "I was thinking about that don't-ask-don't-tell thing we talked about earlier. Or on-again, off-again. Maybe that's actually the way to go. Like, by design. Call it what it is from the outset of a relationship."

"Nah, I'm just damaged goods. Karlie and I were not a match, not elementally."

"No, seriously. I'm trying to think how I would react if a Tinder dude outright *said* he was only interested in getting in my pants." My eyes zoomed back over to her thigh. Her pants-less thigh. "I'm not sure I'd go for it, but I think I would respect it. I'd certainly respect him more than all the terrible guys I ended up with."

I cleared my throat. "Aren't most people on those apps only looking to hook up, though? Isn't that pretty much the point?" I wasn't on any apps, but that was the impression I got.

"Maybe for a lot of people, but not for everyone. I have it right in my profile that I'm looking for a long-term relationship." She glanced sideways at me. "I want love. I know you probably think that's naive and foolish, but I don't care." I tried to object, to tell her I had no opinion on what she did or did not want out of life, but she waved me off and tossed back the rest of her drink. "I should say I *did* want love. I *did* have that junk about long-term relationships in my profiles. I'm over it now." She stood abruptly. "I should go."

I didn't want her to leave.

Which was weird as hell, but Drunk Sourplum was pretty good company. "Tell me about these Tinder guys."

She screwed up her face like what I was asking was the most bizarre thing ever. When I raised my eyebrows, she made a silly face and said, "Well, how much time do you have?" I shrugged. I didn't have anywhere to be. All I had were some songs that were not going to write themselves and also, apparently, were not going to be written by me.

"OK, but I'm taking this, then." As she sat back down, she picked up the ten-dollar bill, and I chuckled. But I sobered pretty fucking quickly when she shoved it into her bikini top— like, slid it into her cleavage and then just...out of sight. That was—

Shit. I realized she'd started talking—about the thing I'd told her to talk about—and I'd missed the start.

"...anyway, most of them are your garden-variety bait-and-switch."

"Meaning?"

"You'd message back and forth a bit and think, *We're on the same page*. I mean, they'd read my profile, right?" I wanted to say that maybe they *hadn't* read her profile. Maybe they'd seen her pink-and-blond hair and her blue eyes—and her killer thighs if her profile contained any full-body pictures—and swiped without reading a word. But I held my tongue.

"Eventually the messaging is promising enough that you go on a date. Then, I don't know, either you sleep with them and they ghost you, or you *don't* sleep with them and they ghost you. Or God forbid you decide it's not a match and deign to say so in the politest possible terms, intending to save everyone time, and they send you a tsunami of harassment, usually involving an itemized list of everything that's wrong with you and/or an essay riddled with grammatical errors about how they didn't want you anyway."

"Really? Jesus."

"Yeah. I think the problem with dating apps is everyone is paralyzed by choice. Like, why settle for me when there are so many other people out there? Or in there." She leaned over and pointed at my phone, resting on the armrest of the glider on my side. Her breast brushed against my arm, but she didn't notice.

I thought about the ten-dollar bill.

"It's been years since I've had a real relationship." She threw a handful of almonds in her mouth, then appeared to have a memory that amused her, because she started laughing—then coughing and spraying out fragments.

I sat up, alarmed—did I remember any of that CPR?—but she waved me off. "I was remembering this one guy. Talon."

"His name was *Talon*?"

"You should talk, *Tennyson*."

Yeah, yeah. I rolled my eyes.

"Anyway, Talon was a bank teller, but I only found that out later, because he said he worked 'in finance.' Now, I have exactly zero problem dating a bank teller. I do, however, have a problem dating liars. But anyway, when this came out, I somehow talked myself into giving him another chance. So we're on date number three. And, incidentally, we're at a sushi restaurant, which I always avoid because I have a shellfish allergy, and even if you don't order anything with shellfish, I find there's often cross contamination. Anyway, having had enough bad reactions, I steer clear of the sushi category entirely—alas. He knew all this. But he really wanted to try this new place, and he gave me the puppy-dog eyes, so I agreed. No, actually, I faked enthusiasm." She did the nose scrunch, but this time it looked like she'd smelled something bad. "I faked enthusiasm over miso soup and seaweed salad, which was all I felt I could safely have. Why did I do that?"

I had no idea. "You don't seem like the kind of person who fakes anything."

"Right?" She seemed cheered by my assessment. "I'm not. Or at least I didn't used to be. Which is exactly why I'm here. Having the reset. Anyway, after dinner Talon 'invites me back to his place.'" She paused and gave me an exaggerated wink. "Do you know what that means?"

I chuckled. "I know what that means." Drunk Sourplum was cute.

"Well, for all I know, famous people have a different code."

"If they do, they haven't told me about it."

"I wasn't really feeling it, but at some point you have to fish or cut bait or you lose them. So we're at his place, and things got…" She rotated her wrist in a way I took to indicate that things got heated between them. "Do you know what that means?" She rotated again.

"I know what that means."

"So fine, we're kissing. But then he starts pushing my head into his lap."

"Wait. What?"

"Yeah, not that unusual." She was on a roll with her story now, and I had to make a concerted effort to keep up, to not remain mentally snagged on the idea of a dude named Talon pushing Gretchen's head into his lap. "And honestly, usually you're going to get there eventually. Unless you want to give up on the prospect. Which is what I generally told myself, anyway. I'm a pragmatist."

Well, shit. "That's just—"

She cut me off. "But *this* guy." She snorted. "He said, 'Polish my talon, babe.'" She burst out laughing. I chuckled along with her, but inside I was unsettled.

"So I had to call it. Couldn't do it. I got up, wished him well, and left. I could hardly keep a straight face, and that was my mistake. When I got home, I had seventeen text messages telling me I was a frigid bitch, a talentless whore who deserved to be—"

"I get it." I couldn't hear any more.

"I wanted to be like, *Which is it? Am I frigid or a whore? I think you have to pick a lane there, dude.* But you have to give Talon credit for his vocabulary skills. Most of them are..." She trailed off, and she was back to looking at me strangely.

"Most of them are what?" I prompted.

"Most of them are more succinct. They might just call you a bitch, for example, without the adjectives. There's something about all this Andrew Tate 'men's rights' bullshit that I honestly think is poisoning an entire generation of men. Though to be fair, some of the Andrew Tate crew aren't throwing the word *bitch* around necessarily, but they're looking for a 'high-value female.' Apparently that isn't me. I also had one guy tell me I wasn't 'obedient.'"

What. The actual. Fuck. I was dumbfounded.

She was silent a long time, and just as I was coming around to the idea that I had to let the evening wind down, she said, "So *then* what happened is my best friend fell in love. Like, real, cinematic, happily-ever-after shit."

"That must be hard for you."

"Yes and no. I'm over the moon for her. She's expecting a baby. She's younger than I am, and I used to give her dating advice. She used to have this crappy boyfriend, before Prince

Charming—who's a retired NHL player, by the way—and I was always on her case about settling and all that. But really, what was I doing but exactly the same thing? It maybe looked different because I was always on to the next guy. So it seemed like I was picky, or had high standards, or whatever. But really, I was making myself small to please men, same as she was. Only I couldn't even hold on to one for more than a couple weeks at a time, even with all that shrinking."

"I think you're being too hard on yourself," I said softly. But I did admire the fearless way she confronted her perceived shortcomings.

"I'm not, though," she insisted. "I'm being *good* to myself. By making myself face the truth. I don't want half relationships. I don't want to sleep with people who don't care about me as a person. I'm tired of twisting myself into something I'm not to please other people—to please *men*." Her voice had risen, and she seemed to realize it. "So I'm not going to do that anymore," she finished quietly. Almost primly. "I know you think that's dumb, but I don't care."

"I don't think it's dumb." I didn't like the way she kept prefacing what she was saying with declarations about how she knew I was going to think it was dumb, or pathetic, or naive—what did it say about me that those were the vibes I was giving off? Her little speech had been oddly moving, actually. Gretchen and I were different sorts of people, and we'd gotten off on the wrong foot, but authenticity was something I dug. And Sourplum, she was very much herself.

And her thing about coming to the woods for a reset—it was a nice idea. It was basically what I was trying to do, too, though I hadn't given it a name.

"It sounds like you know literature," I said, thinking about how she'd known that stupid "Better to have loved..." line came from Tennyson. "You know Thoreau? *Walden?*"

"Never read it, but yeah, I'm familiar."

" 'I went to the woods because I wanted to live deliberately,' " I quoted.

She pointed at me. "Exactly, Teddy Knight, exactly."

"You want another drink?"

I was disappointed when she said no. "I've already had too much." She heaved herself to her feet. "You know I only told you all this because I'm drunk, right?"

"Right."

"Which means you can't hold it against me tomorrow."

"I won't."

She shook her head and sounded genuinely dismayed when she said, "I can't *believe* I told all my pathetic shit to the local rock-and-roll asshole."

"I promise your pathetic shit is safe with me." I made an X over my heart.

She looked momentarily confused, then seemed to give up on whatever thought was dogging her, shrugged, and executed one of her signature leaps off the porch.

I was glad the leap was back.

————

I was jolted awake in the middle of the night by my phone.

It was a FaceTime from my sister, and I fumbled to answer.

"Oh my God, you were *asleep?*"

"Yeah," I mumbled, checking the time. Eleven twenty.

"I'll call you tomorrow," Auden said.

"No, no, it's OK." Calls from Auden were the one thing in my life that were a constant, and I wanted to talk to her more than I wanted to sleep. I reached for the bedside lamp, and when my fingers found the switch, I was confronted with the sight of myself blinking and befuddled. I'd been having a dream. Something about Scott. We'd been at his parents' apartment, but as adults, not as teens. We'd been...doing something with a marching band? The more I tried to send my mind back to it, the more the fantastical tendrils loosened their hold on me.

"Look at you! Dead asleep, and it's barely past midnight!"

My sister and I were night owls. It was normal for one of us to call the other in the wee hours—after my shows, after her late-night bursts of work.

"It's not even midnight here," I said. "Minnesota's on central time."

The exaggerated funny-shocked face she made turned my yawn-in-progress into a grin. Like me, Auden had "made it." She'd transcended our tumultuous childhood and made a life for herself. She was an actuary. I sometimes thought she'd chosen that line of work because it was lucrative and stable—the opposite of our scrabbling, chaotic childhoods—but she seemed to really like it. She was a kick-ass musician, but she had also always been freakishly good at math. But even though she'd changed pretty much everything about her circumstances—job, borough, personal style, you name it—that face she was making was the same. It was her all-purpose Teddy face, and I loved it. Depending on the circumstance, it could express shock, outrage, amusement. It was the same one she'd made when Mom had decided to demolish an interior wall once in the middle of the night. But also the one she made when Scott and I first got signed. The key, with this face, was that whatever else it was doing, it was always expressing solidarity. Auden and

I, we were siblings, yes, but we were more than that. We were fellow soldiers.

She exaggerated "the face" and said, "Who are you and what have you done with my brother?"

It was actually a good question, but she was joking, so I answered in kind. "I dunno. I guess the deep dark North Woods has a lulling effect?"

"Or, call me crazy, you're completely exhausted by the implosion of your career?"

I made my own face at her, deciding to stay on the joking train, but she wasn't wrong. Concrete Temple had been a touring band. Yes, we'd made records, good ones, but our success and longevity had been largely down to the fact that we'd spent most of the year, every year, on the road. We had a die-hard fan club, and people would come to see us year after year, some of them road-tripping to hit more than one city. It had been awesome, but it had also been exhausting.

It was possible that I was only now realizing how much.

"Well, either way," Auden said, "I like this for you. Rest. Real rest. Are you writing?"

"Yes."

"Liar."

"How do you do that through a phone screen?" I loved it, though. This was what I meant about Auden. No one else was ever going to get me like she did, because no one else had lived our life. I'd thought Scott got me, because even though he came from a wealthy Upper East Side family, he'd been around since we were teenagers. But I guess that wasn't long enough. I guess you had to go further back for someone to really get you.

"I wouldn't beat yourself up about not writing," Auden said.

"Honestly, I don't think you should rush whatever's going to come next."

"I don't think I asked you," I said with a wink.

"Since when has that stopped me?"

"That's true."

"I just mean that your next album shouldn't be reflexive, you know? Reactive."

"Well, I don't think you have to worry about that. I've been here a week and I haven't written a note."

"I'm serious. It's OK to stop and take a breath. Don't just react to the circumstances you currently find yourself in. Stop and think about what you actually *want* to do next."

As usual, she was right. I *had* been thinking of the next record as a "revenge album." Revenge was pretty damn reactive.

"So what are you doing while you're not writing?" she asked.

"There's been a lot of camp counselor–type bullshit this first week, getting the kids set up with their plans for the month."

"Kids!" she shrieked.

"Yeah, turns out I didn't read the fine print."

She snorted. "And are you canoeing and doing camp-y stuff? Oh, are you swimming? Tell me you're swimming!"

I knew Auden was thinking back to our childhood pool days. Hell, even our adult pool days, as Auden was a regular visitor to the pool at my building. Our shared affection for the water, developed out of necessity as kids, had endured.

Which was why I was disappointed in myself when I had to tell her, "I went once, the first night I got here, but I haven't been since."

"What's the matter with you? I googled that lake you're on, and it looks like a postcard. That is some prime North Woods shit."

"I know."

"Do you know I've never swum in a lake? Only pools. Well, I guess I went in the ocean once when I had to go on that company retreat in the Hamptons. But I only went in up to my knees." She shuddered. "Seaweed, ugh. Why can't we ever do retreats at the Four Seasons?"

It was wild, sometimes, to think how far we'd both come. That Auden was in a position to casually talk about the Hamptons versus the Four Seasons, and that I had just come off a world tour. Yes, my band had fractured, but still. Auden and I had made it. I didn't think I'd ever stop marveling at that fact.

"Well," she said, "you'd better get some swimming in, or else I'll come there myself and push you in the water."

"I would love that." I didn't know what Marion's policies on visitors were, but it didn't matter because Auden's threat was an empty one. She was a city girl. A New Yorker, more specifically. I could never even get her to come see one of my shows in another city she ought to find suitably large—Chicago, say, or Boston. The idea of her in northern Minnesota was almost laughable. But how great would it be to sit on the glider with her and look out at the lake?

I thought back to my earlier episode of glider sitting, my thigh an inch from Gretchen's, the electric current between our legs shocking me yet drawing me closer, a dance of proximity and distance, like a binary star system.

"So you're having a good time?" Auden was leaning toward her phone like she was trying to see through it, straight into my soul. She did that.

"I guess I am." In my own way.

"Good. I was starting to feel guilty for making you do this."

"'S'okay. You don't want me underfoot all summer."

"Well, actually, I do want you underfoot. I've missed you this past year."

The last tour really had been a grind, even by our standards, and when I thought back to the breaks I'd had that had allowed me to fly back to New York, I realized I'd spent most of them with Karlie. Karlie who I now could barely remember being with.

"I just didn't think it would be good for you," Auden said. "You needed to do something this summer besides sleeping in my guest room and moping around."

"I need to do something bigger."

"No, I think you need to do something smaller."

I thought of how big the sky was here. How tall the trees were. How dark it was. But then I thought of that single G note I'd played when I first turned on the keyboard in my cabin. The first note of "Lemon Tree," and how it had reverberated through my chest. "Or maybe both at once."

"Maybe."

"You sure I can't lure you out here for a visit?"

"You cannot."

6
FOOTSIE

Gretchen

I was in Target when I saw him, and good Lord, was there any escaping this guy? He was in the remote North Woods; he was in a multinational chain store a forty-five-minute drive from the remote North Woods.

He was also, unfortunately, in my brain. I would like to say the reason I'd had trouble falling asleep last night was that I was thinking about my artist-in-residence duties. About *Little Women*, but with dancing.

But no, I couldn't sleep because I'd fallen down a Karlie Carroll rabbit hole. Yes, I'd creeped Teddy's ex-girlfriend's social media. She was everything you'd think a rock star's girlfriend would be: skinny, generically pretty with big eyes and long balayaged blond hair styled in perfect beachy waves. She did sponsored posts on protein powder and retinol. But as much as I wanted her to be only that—macros and skin care—she was also into refinishing vintage furniture. Her pieces looked amazing.

If you scrolled far enough back, Teddy made the odd appearance in her posts. There were the usual "Happy birthday to this goofball" pictures with him in the background photobombing her and "Celebrating two years with the most amazing person in the world" posts with her on his arm on the red carpet at the Grammys. But there was also the odd domestic post. A picture of two sets of legs tangled together on a sofa, one barefoot and the other in a pair of Doc Martens I recognized. Or a flute of champagne and a glass of beer on a table on a balcony with an amazing city view.

I was embarrassed by how much I had told him last night. I'd had a lovely evening eating with Maiv on the beach. And drinking with Maiv on the beach—she had a literal box of wine in her cabin, and we'd filled water bottles from its spigot and, after our swim, toasted the end of week one at Wild Arts. And then toasted some more.

I hadn't been *drunk*-drunk. But I had been happy enough, and vehement enough—I got overly invested in everything when I was tipsy—that I'd opened my mouth and vomited all my thoughts and feelings on Teddy Knight. Teddy Knight! Who didn't even like me!

I'd been so relieved when he wasn't in the van today. This morning Lena announced she was "going into town"—which apparently meant not into the tiny town fifteen minutes from camp that had a bar, a variety store, and a boat mechanic, but to a bigger place farther away that had a wider range of shopping—and had invited any of the adults to come. Danny and I had taken her up on the offer.

It wasn't as if I'd said anything supermortifying last night, just that in the sober light of day, I felt I'd exposed myself too much. Or to the wrong person. Mistaken the level of emotional intimacy that was appropriate. So while I didn't have anything to apologize for, or even any cause, really, to be more than slightly chagrined, I'd been happy to keep out of Teddy's way. To let time soothe my self-consciousness. Monday would come, with its work and its routines, and things would feel more normal.

But no. There he was. Standing at an endcap in the men's shoes section at Target examining a pair of orange Crocs knockoffs.

I gave some thought to ducking down an aisle, hiding among the shower curtains and toothbrush holders, and pretending I hadn't seen him. But was I the kind of woman who hid from uncomfortable situations? I thought about the last time I'd seen Talon—speaking of last night's oversharing—which had not been on our final, disastrous date, but in a situation much like this, where I'd seen him at a restaurant and then immediately departed said restaurant before he saw me. So maybe the answer was yes, I *was* the kind of woman who hid from uncomfortable situations. At least lately, if not historically.

But not anymore. I was here for the reset, right? I'd come to the woods because I wanted to live deliberately—to quote Teddy quoting Thoreau—right?

So I sidled up to him. "I'm not sure those are really your style."

He seemed profoundly unsurprised to find me standing next to him at Target. "The problem is this is the only pair of remotely sandal-like shoes in my size, and I can't do the rest of the summer in these." He lifted a Docs-clad foot. The last time I had seen that foot had been on my phone screen, and it had been playing footsie with Karlie Carroll. "It's too fucking hot for these. But yeah"—he shook the not-Crocs—"these are atrocious."

"So you're standing here contemplating the trade-off between self-respect and comfort."

He barked a laugh. "I guess I am." He set down the shoes and examined me. "What would you do?"

"This summer? I'd choose self-respect." I made a face, and he intensified his study of me. "But also, they're just shoes, not a moral statement on your self-worth, so probably you should choose comfort."

"Hmm." He put the shoes down.

"I for one would love to see you in orange fake Crocs at camp," I added, feeling bad about projecting my issues onto his footwear choices, "and I'm sure the kids would, too."

"Ha ha. It was probably dumb to think I could find decent shoes here. I only came in search of better bug spray"—he held up an industrial-looking aerosol can—"and I got distracted on my way to meet Jack."

Ah, the cool kids drove on their own instead of taking the Lena bus. "What do you mean 'better'?"

"The stuff Marion gave me doesn't work. I'm getting eaten alive. Aren't you?"

"Not really. When they start to get munchy, it's a reminder to reapply, and then I'm mostly fine. Not so with you?"

"Nope. Doesn't seem to matter how much I put on, or how often." He held out his arm, and it was indeed covered with welts.

"Aww. I guess you're so sweet they can't resist you." The notion was so amusingly outrageous that I cackled.

He looked around. "What are you doing here? You in the market for new shoes, too? Those shoes aren't going to be good for hiking and shit."

Those shoes. I wasn't sure how he even knew what shoes I was wearing, as my feet were hidden from his view by a stool/mirror thing between us. But he was right. I stepped out from behind the fixture and examined my sandaled feet. My pedicure was starting to chip. "I packed hiking boots. I just haven't gotten them out yet."

When he didn't say anything, just looked sternly down at my feet—Karlie Carroll probably never let her pedicures chip—I added, "I'm here to buy a couple essentials." I held up a travel alarm clock. "I've decided to take the radical step of putting my phone away for the rest of camp, but I need a way to wake up for sunrise circle, so I'm going old-school." Next I held up a bathing suit, a utilitarian red one-piece. "And I got this."

"Don't you...already have a bathing suit?"

"I need a second one. I've been swimming so much that my suit doesn't dry by the time I'm ready to wear it again, and there's nothing worse than trying to shimmy into a damp bathing suit." When he still didn't say anything, I kept going, for what reason I do not know. I didn't think of myself as a person who rambled. "So now I'll have this ugly Target suit for my morning swims and my existing suit for my evening swims."

"You've been swimming in the mornings?"

"Not at the beach proper. Just a quick dip off the dock in our neighborhood."

"Right in front of my cabin."

"Yes." What, did he think he owned the lake outside his cabin?

He blinked. "I gotta go find Jack." He checked the time—he was wearing an old-fashioned wristwatch, which was, for some stupid reason, charming. Apparently I was into analog time-pieces now. Maybe that was a crone thing. Made sense: Weren't curses always coming due at midnight or princesses going into comas for a hundred days or whatever? A crone needed a way to keep track of this stuff.

"I'm overdue to meet him in the books section," Teddy said.

"Jack's in the books section? Why? So he can turn up his nose at everything there? So he can peel the Blair's Book Club stickers off books he doesn't approve of?"

"Probably." He smirked. "See you."

"Teddy," I called after him, and he turned, eyebrows raised. I already regretted what I was about to say, but somehow that didn't stop me from saying it. "I said a lot of stuff last night, and some of it was kind of embarrassing. I was hoping we could keep it between us." He'd promised as much last night, but I wanted to make sure.

He came back toward me. "So you had some shitty dates. Who am I gonna tell?"

"Jack?"

"Nah." The way he said it, as if Jack wasn't worth telling secrets to, gave me a little thrill. "Anyway, right back at you." He pointed at me with the orange not-Crocs.

"What do you mean?"

"I told you some embarrassing stuff, too."

"Well, I can say, 'Right back at you,' too. Who am *I* gonna tell?"

"The tabloids? 'Disgraced Musician Walks in on Influencer Girlfriend Cheating.' They'd *pay* you for that scoop."

"Oh, well, in that case..." I lifted my phone to my ear and pretended I was talking on it but cut off the joke when I saw something flash in his eyes. Just for a second, but it looked an awful lot like hurt. "Just kidding." I slid the phone into my purse. "You know I'd never do that."

"Do I?"

He had a point. He didn't know me, not really, despite my

drunken confessions. "You do," I said firmly. "You might not like me, but you can trust me."

"Who says I don't like you?" The question came out with a hint of cockiness, of challenge. He was back to his old self.

"Don't worry," I said. "The feeling's mutual."

"Well." He softened. "You can trust me, too."

The weird thing was, I knew that I could.

———

Little Women, but with dancing wasn't going superwell, and the kids could sense it. It wasn't a disaster, but it wasn't really coming together.

"All right," I said at the end of our Monday-afternoon session, "everyone gather round for a minute, sit."

I was probably overdoing this. This wasn't in my job description. I was supposed to help with their end-of-camp performance, but I wasn't expected to be knee deep in it like this. Caleb, for example, was letting the counselors run the drama sessions and popping in every couple of days to give notes. I could have done the same with the dance counselors, Grace and Brianna.

But Grace and Brianna seemed happy to have me around, and honestly, what else was I going to do all day? Unlike the other artists, I didn't have a creative masterpiece making demands on my time.

"I think we need to regroup," I said. "Maybe we're overthinking the narrative part of this. This is the dance group, right? We don't need to put on a play—that's for the drama group. So why don't we think of our mission as choreographing some dances that are inspired by *Little Women* rather than literally doing *Little Women*? We're so focused on the start of the book, the idea of introducing the girls and their trip to visit the poor. I'm not saying there's anything wrong with that, but what if we set that aside for now and think about the book as a whole?" I paused. My brain was racing ahead of me, ideas zinging around faster than I could put words to them. "Or…what about scenes that encapsulate the themes of the book as a whole?" I made a mental note to ask the girls what they thought those themes were, but I had to keep going so as not to lose the idea that was coalescing.

"Consider the party scene," I said, suddenly picturing them in it. "It already has dancing. We could do something with Meg and Jo sharing the pair of gloves, and Jo having to skirt the edges of the room because the back of her dress is burnt." I'd loved that scene as a kid. I'd identified with the girls trying to hide their poverty among their peers. I'd downloaded the book and reread it on my phone over the last couple of days, and it still stood out. "But it's not just about a dance, right? It's a way to show the economic differences between the March sisters and everyone else. It's about how being poor shapes a person, and about the eternal human desire to fit in."

"*Yes*," Brianna said vehemently. "We've been focusing on plot. On what happens to the characters. But the story is *also* about other, bigger stuff. And that big stuff is what makes the book resonate with people a hundred and fifty years after it was written." She turned to me. "That's what you're talking about—there's for sure an economic theme here."

"It's funny how they're helping the poor, but *they're* also kind of poor," said one of the campers, Addison, a fifteen-year-old I'd clocked as the smartest in the group, if not the best dancer from a technical point of view. "I guess they're just less poor?

Or they're something in between, because they're poor but they're going to fancy parties?"

"Great observation," I said. "Maybe there's a way we can represent all this."

"But isn't the book also about sisterhood?" asked another girl. "I hear what you're saying about poverty and exclusion, but what I like about the book is how the sisters love each other, but sometimes they hate each other. That's timeless."

The other girls laughed, and one said, "Amen. I hate my sister, but I kind of miss her, too."

"Yes!" I exclaimed. "This is all great. We should plan to sit and talk more in depth about what we think the themes of the book are. But do people agree that one of our dances could be the party scene? Beyond all this high-level, thematic stuff, it would be fun, don't you think?" My other motivation for wanting to do the party was that it would be easier for everyone to have a good part. "We could do some actual ballroom stuff, some period dances"—I'd have to figure out what that would look like—"but then maybe we nest inside that some modern dance that communicates how out of place Meg and Jo feel."

The girls loved this idea, and I did, too. I was getting a buzzy feeling in my body. Excitement, for me, had always taken on a physical form like this. It made me want to dance. Which I suppose was why I loved dance to begin with. It was a physical manifestation of what was going on inside me. It discharged emotions.

"Yeah, but what about Laurie?" one of the girls asked. "He's central to that scene."

"I have a lead on a Laurie for us," I said. I hoped I did, anyway. "He won't be a dancer, but maybe we can make that work for us."

"Yes!" Brianna piped up. "He can be the eye of the hurricane, the still center around which the scene revolves."

Everyone seemed excited by that idea, and when we broke
for the day, I kept Brianna and Grace back. "Am I stepping on
your toes too much here?"

They assured me I was not. Grace said, "It's cool to have
a real choreographer. Last year we had a ballet dancer, and
she was great, but mostly she just helped the kids—and us—
with technique. So the show was more a straightforward dance
recital. A bunch of pieces that didn't relate to each other. Which
was fine. But I like this better."

"I think you're right on with the idea that we do something that's less than a play but still has some thematic coher-
ence," Brianna said. "I have to choreograph a big piece next
year"—Brianna was doing a BA in dance at the University of
Minnesota—"so this is good practice for me."

I was happy to have them on board but felt compelled to say,
"You know I'm *not* a choreographer, right?"

Brianna shrugged. "Well, I don't know what it is you're
doing here if not choreographing."

Hmm.

On my way back to my cabin to get changed for my pre-
dinner swim, I passed by one of the music rooms. I could hear
Teddy singing. I edged closer and peeped around the open
door—it wasn't as oppressively humid as that first day, but it
was still hot enough that most of us kept our studio doors open.
Teddy was playing guitar and a girl was playing banjo and they
were both singing "Leaving on a Jet Plane."

I sneaked closer. They sounded *great*. Teddy was singing
harmony to her melody, and though I didn't know that much
about music performancewise, I could tell he was letting her

take the lead instrumentally, too. Maybe not literally—he wasn't playing a bassline or anything—but he was a fraction of a beat behind her, as if he wanted her to make her own way but was there to support her if needed.

I was transfixed. After they finished, Teddy complimented her, and they talked about a chord change that had been giving her trouble.

"Peter, Paul and Mary did 'Puff, the Magic Dragon,' too, right?" she asked after the debrief. "I feel like I remember that from the music classes I took when I was little."

"They did. They did a bunch of songs you'd probably know if you heard them. They did a great cover of Dylan's 'The Times They Are a-Changin'.'"

"They don't let us have phones here, otherwise I'd listen to a bunch of their stuff."

I had intended to follow that no-phones rule, too. I'd bought that alarm clock yesterday for that very reason, but the pull of the Karlie Carroll rabbit hole had been too strong. What a waste. I needed to recommit to ditching the phone. I was done with my reread of *Little Women*. I was doing a virtual walk-through of the new building with Justin next week, but until then, I had no more excuses.

"You should listen to some of their stuff when you go home," Teddy said. "It's banjo friendly, and I think your voice would lend itself well to their songs—to the extent that you're looking for songs to cover."

"I have to say, I'm surprised you're a fan of this kind of music."

"You mean because my own music is harder?"

"Yeah—not that you're not allowed to like different kinds of music," she said.

"My mom was into the folky protest music of the sixties.

Pete Seeger and Woody Guthrie and early Dylan. But especially Peter, Paul and Mary. I learned to play music—piano, initially—on their songs."

"What's your favorite song of theirs?"

There was a pause that seemed a little fraught, like it signified more than just Teddy trying to settle on his favorite song. He finally said, "I guess it's this one called 'Lemon Tree.' My mom and sister and I used to sing it all the time."

"Can you play it for me?"

There was another pause before he said, "How about this one instead? It's called 'Where Have All the Flowers Gone?' It was actually written by Seeger—a lot of Peter, Paul and Mary's hits were written by him."

I shamelessly settled in to listen. The song seemed to be about the futility of war. It was beautiful. I didn't dislike Concrete Temple, but I tended to mentally discard any music I couldn't use for my kids at the studio, and Concrete Temple was too hard for Miss Miller's of Minnetonka.

This song wasn't recital material, either. It was—at least as performed by Teddy—plain, almost stark, but it was all the more beautiful for it. He had the perfect voice for it—a perfectly imperfect rasp. His voice reminded me of his calloused hands.

The song was circular—each verse built on the next, and the simple but powerful chorus was repeated frequently. Eventually Teddy's student picked it up and started singing high harmonies on the choruses, then on the verses, too. As she grew more confident with the song structure, they both started messing around vocally, with volume and with more elaborate harmonies.

When they finished with a decisive chord, stopping the song abruptly, it was if I snapped out of a trance. Damn. That had been *fantastic*.

I could hear them wrapping up, so it was time for me to flee. I had to go to my cabin and get out the phone I wasn't supposed to be using and look up "Lemon Tree."

———

Later, on my way to swimming, I stopped by Jack's porch, where he and Teddy were parked with their end-of-day drink.

"Hey, Knight, you promised me a Laurie, and I've come to collect."

I'd listened to "Lemon Tree" three times back-to-back in my cabin, trying to figure out what Teddy thought about it. Why he called it his favorite but didn't want to play it. The conclusion had been pretty obvious. It was a blatant antilove song, warning that no matter how pretty or fragrant a lemon tree was, its fruit was always sour.

Clearly Teddy wasn't over Karlie yet. Which made me feel weird. Which was why I'd addressed him by his last name. We'd accidentally spilled some secrets to each other, and I wanted to put some distance between us.

But as his last name rolled off my lips, it sounded more like an endearment than a formality. Everyone else called him Teddy, but here I was calling him Knight, like I thought I had special status or something.

"Right," Teddy said. "I'll talk to him tomorrow." He looked at me as if waiting for me to say something else, but I couldn't imagine what. I transferred my attention to Jack, who was looking at me the same way he always did: with indifference that felt like it could tip over into disdain given the slightest nudge.

I didn't wait for that to happen, just danced off. I had a lake to get to.

———

The next morning I slid into my crappy Target bathing suit. It must have been too late in the summer for there to be a lot of selection left; I'd had to settle for what I could get. It was a basic red one-piece that was not my color at all. With my pink-tipped hair, I probably looked like Pamela Anderson's less endowed, arty cousin had come to visit the *Baywatch* set. But the suit was gloriously dry as I fumbled it on in the early-dawn light—I liked to not turn on any lights in my cabin and let the dawn function as a reverse dimmer switch, turning on the day while I was in the lake. And no one else was ever going to see this suit, so aesthetics didn't matter.

"Hey."

I shrieked as my heart kicked into high gear.

I had crept around Teddy's cabin, as I did every morning. But unlike every morning, today he was sitting on his porch holding a guitar. It was momentarily discombobulating: that was his *evening* spot.

"Sorry. I was trying to *not* scare you. Didn't want to startle you once you were in the water."

So much for no one seeing my ugly suit. Well, what did I care? I was here on my man cleanse, right? My crone-ification project. Although crones probably swam either naked or in Victorian-style bathing costumes.

"A morning swim sounded good, so I thought I'd invite myself to join you." He paused. "Unless I'd be in your way."

"It's a big lake," I said with what I hoped was an air of nonchalance, but I was feeling very non-nonchalant all of a sudden. Very chalant, one might say. Because unlike Evening

Teddy Knight with Guitar on Porch, Morning Teddy Knight was wearing swim trunks. And nothing else.

I reminded myself that I had already seen Teddy Knight naked and walked by him and stepped off the dock. I swam underwater for quite a way, and when I surfaced, he was in the water, too, but close to the shore. He was only up to his knees. I wanted to go closer so I could see his tattoos, but I refrained.

"Wow," he called. "This is *some* seaweed. Do you call it that in a lake? Lakeweed?"

"Not much of a swimmer, I take it?" I called back.

"A swimmer, yes, but not in lakes."

"Swim out farther. You'll get to a point where it's deeper and the weeds aren't so high."

He started out toward me, his arms working in the diffuse dawn light. He had a strong stroke.

"They cut the weeds in the official swimming area, out by the kids' cabins, so it's not as icky getting in over there," I said as he began treading water a few feet from me. "If you're getting in here, it's better to jump off the dock than to wade in from the shore.

"Just a tip," I added. Though I wasn't sure why I was giving him tips. I didn't *want* him to make a habit of crashing my morning swims, did I?

No. What I wanted was to get a look at his tattoos, but now that he was close enough, he was submerged up to his neck.

He rotated in a slow circle, treading. "I gotta say, this is worth the icky entrance."

It was. A person could get complacent about lakes, living in Minnesota, the land of ten thousand of them, but this one, especially at this time of day, was objectively gorgeous. The sun was just coming up over the treed shoreline. "Look," I said, pointing. "You can still see the moon. I love when you can see the sun and the moon at the same time."

"I don't think I ever have before."

"Really?" That surprised me.

He'd been turned toward the moon, and when he looked back at me, assessing, he added, "I grew up dirt poor in New York, so there were no trips to the Hamptons or views from penthouse terraces where you could see the whole sky."

That surprised me even more. Though I didn't know why. I knew as well as anyone that people could transcend their humble upbringings. I didn't want to make a big deal of it, though, so I kept my response light. "They should probably call it something other than 'dirt poor' when you're in a city. Pavement poor?"

"I wonder if the phrase comes from the notion that you have dirt roads or dirt floors rather than pavement, so pavement is the fancy option in that sense? But yeah, no dirt roads in New York."

"Hmm. I grew up dirt poor—well, cyclically dirt poor—in the suburbs. We lived in a trailer that I was embarrassed by, so I never had friends over. It wasn't a well-to-do suburb, and most people lived in modest houses, but they were, you know, *houses*. So I guess I grew up trailer-trash poor."

If he was surprised by that admission, he didn't show it. "I suppose if you grow up poor in Minnesota, you still get to see the moon and the sun in the sky at the same time."

"Yeah. Open spaces abound. Lakes, too. Lakes are more democratic here, I guess because there are so many of them. Even our trailer park had a 'lake' that was really a glorified pond in the middle of it. But this one is spectacular."

"Yeah." He sighed—a good sigh, like he was sinking into his

body, making an overdue surrender. "What does it mean to be cyclically poor?"

I probably shouldn't have said that. But hell, he'd started this whole confessions-while-treading-water thing. And the dim, slanted orange light of the sunrise gave the scene an air of un-reality, like a stage set. Like if I told him secrets, it would only be an actress playing the role of Gretchen doing the telling.

"My dad would have these phases when he worked, and things would be relatively OK. We were still poor, but we could..." I assessed him. I'd never really told anyone the details of my child-hood. Even Rory only knew the CliffsNotes version. So I had no idea why I was suddenly telling Teddy. And I was not an actress playing me; I was me. "We could still eat, you know?"

"Yeah," he said gruffly, and somehow that one word tele-graphed that he *did* know.

So I kept going. "He would have these periods where he would have 'normal' jobs. Low-wage ones working retail, or being on a landscaping crew, or whatever. Things would still be tight—my mom was a waitress—but money was coming in. But my dad..." I tried to think how to explain Len Miller. "He always had this idea of himself as bigger than he was. Like he'd found himself living the wrong life. So he'd do stuff like quit to write a novel—and then not write the novel. Or he'd get roped into pyramid schemes and we'd have a shed full of unsellable herbal supplements but no money for lunch at school."

Teddy made a noise of understanding. A noise of understand-ing that was totally neutral: it contained no judgment, or pity.

He said, "I used to pretend I wasn't a breakfast person to get around the fact that there was never any breakfast in my house."

"But you were a breakfast person," I said, because I recog-nized this strategy.

"Yep. Always used to wake up starving. But for a while I made 'not a breakfast person' into an identity. I started drinking coffee at thirteen because it was cheap and suppressed my appetite. It got me through to lunchtime. I got free lunch at school—when I was going."

"You weren't keen on school?"

"It was more that my mom wasn't keen on it. She was...arty. She thought of herself as arty, anyway. We lived in a run-down building that had been colonized by artists—I was never clear on if everyone was there legally. And I guess my mom *was* arty in that she had a lot of natural talent, both musically and in terms of visual art. But she never did anything with it—nothing practical, anyway. She was always taking my sister and me out of school in service of her various whims—one week we'd be busking in Central Park, the next she'd have my sister on modeling casting calls. I *wasn't* really keen on school—I was never that smart—but at least it was predictable." He paused. "At least it came with lunch."

"Do you find..." I thought about how to phrase this. I'd never imagined asking anyone this question. "Do you have any hang-ups about food as an adult that you think probably date back to childhood? Like, I do this thing where I hate to share food, even though I'm completely financially comfortable nowadays. It's OK if I can plan for it, like I'm having a party and I'm feeding my guests. But if you want to share fries at a restaurant? I hate that. It gives me a genuinely bad feeling. I can't shake the notion that I might not get as much as I want if I let someone else start eating my food before I'm done with it." I huffed a self-deprecating laugh, slightly appalled that I had shared so much so easily. "I'm superfun on dates."

"So maybe your dating problems were partly your fault."

"Maybe they were."

His expression turned stricken. "I was kidding. Not wanting to share your fries is not a character flaw." He paused. "You know what a rider is?"

"Yeah. Like *I demand M&M's in my dressing room, but the green ones only?*"

He chuckled. "Exactly. Concrete Temple had a lot of lean years as a band. We won a Best New Artist Grammy ten years ago, but we'd been together for seven by that point. We did a lot of tours where my practice being hungry came in handy. But it felt different from childhood. It was part of a trying-to-make-it sort of hustle."

"It was part of a life you chose," I said. "It was in service to something, rather than this thing that was happening *to* you that felt like it was never going to end."

"Exactly. And eventually things started taking off, and we started booking bigger venues. We upgraded to a tour bus, and later we started flying around. The funny thing is that as you're making more money and you can afford to buy what you need, the venues start to come with all this free stuff. You can literally order whatever you want, like they're your God damn butlers. The bigger we got, the more outlandish the guys got with their riders. By the time we were in arenas, their demands were, to my mind, insane."

"Like what? Sushi served off the body of a model?" I thought back to that date with Scott. He'd told me he was "getting really into Buddhism" and accused the others of having crappy taste. He'd made it sound like he was subsisting on organic pomegranates and tempeh made by monks.

Teddy chuckled again. I was pleased with my ability to make him laugh. "Not quite, but all the stereotypical stuff you'd imagine. Tons of junk food, but also steaks, top-shelf liquor. Our lead guitarist always wanted a whole cheesecake with cherry topping. But then they'd *also* ask for all this healthy stuff they were never actually going to eat. Our lead singer would ask for fixings to make smoothies—he had this whole list of kale and mangoes and shit—and a Vitamix blender to make them in. Had to be a Vitamix. No other brand would do. But then he almost never made the smoothies."

What a shocker, given what I knew of Scott Collier. "I imagine the idea of a rider is a little wild if you grew up like we did."

Like we did. I'd phrased that as if there were a kind of solidarity between us, between this rock star and me. But the weird thing was, *something* was stretching out between us, here in this quiet, cool water, and it felt an awful lot like solidarity.

"Exactly," he said. "There was so much waste. Of the healthy stuff, but also of other stuff. They wouldn't be in the mood, or they'd say they weren't hungry. Regardless, it would have been impossible for anyone to eat everything they ordered. It used to drive me completely batshit."

He was talking fast, his arms paddling faster. I could sense his irritation rising. "What did you order?"

"You're going to laugh at me, but usually a Caesar salad with chicken and a small amount of sushi—on a plate, not a model."

"Not very rock star–like," I said, and look at me, *teasing* Teddy Knight.

"I wanted to make sure I'd eat everything I ordered, and honestly, I never wanted to eat that much before a show. I'd eat the sushi, which was a good infusion of protein and carbs. Then I'd eat the salad afterwards. I did go through a phase where I asked for a chocolate croissant, but I had to nip that in the bud when I realized I'd gained ten pounds in six months and the only thing that had changed was those croissants. You don't get a lot of exercise on tour. I used to swim laps when we were in hotels with pools, but that was pretty much it."

"I always thought performing was very physically taxing."

"Maybe if you're Taylor Swift. Or, speaking of Minnesota, Prince—that dude was amazing live. But when you're the grumpy bassist in a band like Concrete Temple, not so much. I mean, it was a lot of standing, but there was also a lot of time on buses and planes."

The thought of Teddy Knight watching his weight was mind-blowing. But so was the idea of him having had a hungry childhood.

Not to mention the fact that we were treading water in a lake talking about all of it.

It started to feel like too much. An unsettling, heavy feeling rose through me, and my legs were having to work harder to keep me afloat.

"You OK, there, Miller?"

My discombobulation was showing. "Yeah, yeah."

"I don't know why I'm telling you all this. I guess because you haven't called the tabloids yet."

I hadn't, but I had continued to creep his ex-girlfriend, lately because I wanted a look at her apartment that was really his. She'd had an overnight oats phase, and Teddy had a really nice kitchen. But now that I knew more about him, I felt kind of...icky for ogling his kitchen? I didn't even know. I just felt weird. I guess it was going to take a while to adjust to the fact that Teddy Knight was actually, maybe, at least somewhat, a decent person. Celebrities! They *are* just like us!

"Haven't called the tabloids," I said. "In fact, I'm going to put my phone away."

For real this time. I would call Rory, Justin, my Realtor, and my lawyer and tell them to call the camp office if anything came up, and then I would power that sucker down.

"That's why you bought an alarm clock at Target, right?"

"Yep, but I've faltered a bit and have yet to fully cut the cord."

"Have you backslid on your reset? Are you back on the dating apps?"

"No." *I'm just on your ex-girlfriend's apps.* "But what's the point of being here if I'm on my phone all the time? You know how sometimes you look up and you realize you've been on it for two hours and you didn't even feel the time passing?" He was looking at me blankly. "You don't, do you?"

"I mostly use my phone to talk to my sister," he said. "Some of the other guys in the band were attached to theirs like it was an umbilical cord. I don't mean this to sound all judgmental. I certainly have my vices. But I don't think cell phones were good for them. They're probably not good for *anyone*. I have this theory that you should only use cell phones as proxies for things that existed *before* cell phones—so, like, use it as an actual phone, use it as a map, read a book on it. But don't use it for things that can *only* be done with a cell phone, you know? By which I mean, don't do social media. It messes with your brain. Changes your personality, and not in a good way."

"How'd you get so enlightened?"

He smirked. "I guess it just comes naturally."

I rolled my eyes. Time to get out of here. I was less unsettled than a moment ago, but here, again, I'd just told Teddy all this really personal stuff. And I didn't even have alcohol as an excuse this time. "Well, it's been nice chatting, but I gotta go. I'll see you later. You still owe me a Laurie."

7
GIRLS, GIRLS, GIRLS

Teddy

My idea for Laurie was this kid called Tristan Barnes. He was sixteen, and he was a little shit.

On Tuesday afternoon, I dropped in on the music kids during a group meeting. They and the counselors were settling on the order of operations for their recital or whatever. I hung back until it was over and intercepted him. "Hey, Tristan, want to do me a favor?"

I didn't wait for his answer, just started walking, trusting he would follow. Which he did. "Sure, yeah."

I was shamelessly exploiting the fact that some of the kids, Tristan among them, were visibly in awe of me. It was funny how there was an inverse relationship between how starstruck the kids were and how much I liked them. I wondered if that said something about the kids or about me.

"Where're we going?" Tristan asked.

"I need you to help the dancers with something."

He stopped in his tracks. "What?"

"They need a guy for their show."

"To play guitar?"

"Not sure," I said vaguely, and I kept up a brisk pace until we reached the dance studio. The doors were propped open on account of the heat, so we could hear the music before we could see them. It was Beyoncé's "Run the World (Girls)."

We peeked in. Girls in leotards were dancing. Most of them were paired up, doing an old-fashioned-looking dance, a waltz maybe, but two of them were doing a modern solo thing—except they were doing it side by side, so was that a duet?—in the middle. It was striking, these two girls doing contemporary moves in the middle of these stylized waltzes, all set to Beyoncé. I mean, I didn't get it, but it was cool looking.

Gretchen shouted some encouragement, and I swung my attention to her at the edge of the dance floor. She was wearing a leotard, too, and it stopped me in my tracks. Which was dumb because I'd seen her in a swimsuit. I'd seen her in two different swimsuits.

The leotard was light blue, and she was wearing a pair of ratty shorts over it. It was, theoretically, nothing special. But damn, there was something about it. Or maybe it was the way she was moving in it. She was following along with the girls in the center, doing the moves they did but in a smaller, more restrained way. From my vantage point, she was in profile, and she was nodding and whispering to herself. When the girls leaped, she made a leaping motion with her arms but stayed on the ground. When they turned, she stayed where she was but made a looping motion with one hand. She looked a bit like a classical conductor.

If classical conductors perspired. She was *sweating*. Her hair was pulled back into a ponytail, but it was wet along the hairline. Her face was shiny, and there were blooms of sweat under her arms and down the gentle valley made by her breasts.

There was something oddly compelling about all that sweat. And about the intensity of her concentration.

One of the girls stumbled over a move, a sort of leap-twist hybrid, and Gretchen went over to her and said, "You have to lift with the leading hand. Like this." I was, frankly, astounded at the version of it she performed. I could not believe how she could just be standing there one moment and the next be propelling herself up and around so high and so thoroughly. And she did it casually, like it was no big deal.

She caught sight of us as she spun, and I worried for a moment that we would distract her, make her trip on her landing, but no. She merely completed her spin, landed much more lightly on her feet than should have been possible given the height she'd achieved, and came toward us smiling. "Is this our Laurie?"

Tristan said, "Huh?" at the same time I said, "Yep."

"Thanks so much for helping us out." She held her hand out to Tristan. "I'm Gretchen."

Tristan shook her hand but didn't say anything—fair enough, maybe he was struck dumb. I understood. "This is Tristan," I said.

"Aka Laurie," Gretchen said.

"I thought you needed a boy," Tristan said.

"We do."

"What's with the Lori thing, then?"

"Oh, it's Laurie." She spelled the name. "It's short for the character's last name, Laurence."

He made a face of displeasure, which was my cue to leave. I was halfway out when she called me back. "Actually, Teddy, hang on. We have a question, if you don't mind."

I probably should have minded. I had shit to do. Or shit to not do, if I was going to take my sister's advice.

The point was, I'd signed up to deliver a Laurie, and I had delivered a Laurie. But my body turned, and my mouth said, "Sure."

"We're not sure about the music for this piece. We want to set it to a song that has the word *girl* or *woman* in it. We came up with a list, and we're thinking that we want a song that's emblematic of the female gaze." My face must have conveyed my confusion, because she said, "Brianna can explain. I didn't know what it was, either."

One of the counselors stepped forward. "There's this thing called the male gaze. It's a theory, I guess, like a philosophical thing. It's about how a lot of depictions of women in art or movies or music are through the male gaze. They represent women as seen through men's eyes—so mostly that means women are depicted as objects of sexual or romantic desire and not fully realized characters in their own right."

Huh? My first instinct was to get the hell out of there—this was above my pay grade—but I didn't want to be rude.

Wait. I didn't want to be rude? Had I met me? What was happening here?

"You know," Gretchen said. "Like 'California Girls.' Everyone loves that song, but it's about girls as seen by boys, right? Versus, say, this Beyoncé song?"

I ran through the lyrics to both songs in my head, and I could kind of see what they meant, but those were only two songs. "I guess I'd have to think about that."

"Yeah, sure," Gretchen said. "We were just chatting about it, and I thought I'd get a musician's take on things."

Gretchen led Tristan over to the girls, and everyone—except Tristan—was talking a mile a minute. They formed a circle around him, and I chuckled to myself. I didn't know whether to pity him or envy him.

———

After Anna and I finished our session that afternoon, I asked her about the dance girls' "male gaze" theory. She was my go-to person here to bounce ideas off. I realized that what Gretchen had said on day one was true—thinking of Anna as a peer was working. Not only in terms of Anna's development, but also in terms of mine. I was learning to play banjo. From a teenager. It was wild. She had ended up writing a song about the rich but shitty stepfather who'd upended her life, and it was amazing—catchy and vicious. Now she was working on one she said was inspired by Peter, Paul and Mary. She didn't have lyrics yet—she was a melody-first writer—but it was sounding great so far. I was helping a bit, or trying to—it could be tricky to know how interventionist to be. I was aware of the fact that we were in a student-teacher role. This wasn't cowriting, like I would do with Scott.

"I think they're onto something," she said, after enduring my rambling recounting of what the dancers had said about the so-called male gaze. "All the famous 'girl' songs from, say, the 1960s to the 1980s are songs about girls by men. The Beach Boys' 'California Girls,' like you said. Billy Joel's 'Uptown Girl.'"

"Foreigner's 'Waiting for a Girl Like You.'"

"Don't know that one, but yeah, probably."

"Mötley Crüe's 'Girls, Girls, Girls.'"

"Gross. Exactly."

"'The Girl Is Mine'!" I was on a roll now.

"I don't know that one, either."

"A Paul McCartney and Michael Jackson duet. Surely you know who they are."

"I do, but the idea of them doing a duet is not computing."

"Well, it's basically about them fighting over a girl—they take turns calling dibs."

"Gross," she said again, and I had to think about what it must be like to be a young woman as talented as Anna and to be surrounded by this all the time.

"So that one's gross," I said, "but are they all gross?" The idea was alarming. "What about Van Morrison's 'Brown Eyed Girl'? There's nothing wrong with that, right?" I suddenly felt invested in finding a not-gross song from the old days, though I had no idea why.

"I don't think it's that there's anything wrong with that, or with most of these songs, per se." I could see that she was thinking though this stuff as she talked. "In some sense, a love song is always going to objectify the other person."

"And a lot of songs are love songs," I said, thinking about my own catalogue. But also about how delightful I found it that Anna seemed to be developing a "hate song" niche.

"Yeah. It's just that when men write about women, that's pretty much all it is. It's like there's a spectrum from romantic to creepy, but everything to do with women is somewhere on that spectrum, you know?"

I did know. When she said it like that, I got it. The male gaze. Damn.

"Men aren't writing about women, I don't know, starting companies," she added. "Helming empires."

"Like Beyoncé is."

"Like Beyoncé is," she confirmed. "I think it's only more

recently that you get women writing and producing their own stuff in a meaningful way, so you get, like, the more defiant 'girl' songs. 'Hollaback Girl.' 'Girl on Fire.'"

I thought about Anna's "Take It Easy" cover.

"I have an idea," I said. "Hear me out. I know you're only... what? Seventeen?"

"I'm flattered, but fifteen—sixteen next month, though."

That gave me pause. The closest thing I had to a peer at this camp was too young to drive.

Hell, the closest thing I'd had to a peer in a long time.

I told myself to get over it. She was a prodigy, OK?

"You could do a whole album of cover songs like you did with 'Take It Easy.' You're making me see that if you change the pronouns in a lot of songs and sing them today—like, in the modern era—it changes everything. Can you imagine a whole album of those songs?"

She laughed but sobered when I didn't. "Oh, you're serious."

"I don't want you to get a big head, but you're very talented."

"But I'm fifteen."

"Sixteen next month!" She laughed. "Anyway, wasn't Taylor Swift around that age when she started?"

"How am I supposed to make an album?" she asked incredulously.

I wanted to say that I would help her. But the truth was, I had the same question. How was *I* supposed to make an album?

"Anyway," Anna said, "If I ever get to make an album, I wouldn't want it to be all covers. I hear what you're saying, and clearly you got what I was going for with that 'Take It Easy' cover, but a whole album of that would be repetitive, don't you think? I think one song makes the point as well as ten would. I don't want to be a one-trick pony."

"Yeah, you're right."

"But..."

"Yeah?"

"I do hope I get to make an album someday," she said quietly, almost sheepishly, as if it were presumptuous to voice such an ambition. I thought about Tristan, wondered how he was getting on with the dance girls.

"You will." I had no doubt.

"But I need a record deal for that. And, what? A manager? Agent? I don't even know."

"Manager first, probably. They manage your overall career and are more engaged on the creative side of things. Agents do the actual booking of tours and negotiating record deals."

"How do you find a manager? Do you have one?"

We hadn't spoken about the Hilton Garden Inn debacle, but I had to assume she knew about it. "You know what? I don't know. I might be between managers."

Back at my cabin, I decided to call him to find out.

I was half-surprised when he picked up. "Hey, Brady," I said. "Are you still my manager?"

"And a good evening to you, too, Teddy."

"Yeah, yeah. Are you still my manager?"

"Do you want me to be?"

"I want to make an album." That was true. I didn't have any songs to put on said album, but I did want to make one. Eventually. To my surprise, the project no longer seemed so urgent. Probably because, also to my surprise, the notion of revenge was no longer gnawing at me. It had receded, like a wave on the lake outside my door. It had left a scar, mind you, but dealing with scars was better than being actively eaten alive. "And...I want to produce an album."

"For who?"

"An up-and-comer."

"A nobody."

"I guess technically, but when she is somebody, which is absolutely going to happen, do we want to be the ones who helped or the ones who said no?"

He chuckled, and I thought for sure that was it, he was going to fire me, but he said, "I always liked you."

"You *did*?"

"Yeah."

"Even though I smashed a TV at the Hilton Garden Inn in Chicago?"

"Not your finest moment, but yeah." He added, snarkily, "You want me to line up some anger management classes?"

He was needling me, but I took the question seriously. I was still unsettled by my own behavior that day. "I think being here is kind of its own anger management course."

"Where is 'here'?"

"I'm at this arts summer camp thing." I explained the setup.

"You should have had me look at the contract."

I should have. Then maybe I'd've realized what I was getting myself into. But I was glad I hadn't, because then I wouldn't have come. And I was, despite the mosquitoes and the heat, settling into a certain groove, even if I wasn't writing anything. "Does this mean you're still my manager?"

"Yeah, sure, if you want me to be."

"What about Scott?"

"What about him?"

"Are you managing him, too?" Because I wasn't sure if I could do that. It would feel too much like Scott was my stepbrother or something, like Brady had custody of us on alternating weekends.

"Scott's decided to go in a different direction," Brady said.

"Wow, you got the same line I did." He chuckled. "Why didn't you call me?"

"I don't know. Maybe because you destroyed a TV at the Hilton Garden Inn in Chicago?"

Fair enough. "You should know that when I do make a record, I think it's possible it will be quite different from Concrete Temple."

"OK," he said mildly. "You got any songs?"

"Nope," I said, almost cheerfully. "But I'm going to write some." Eventually.

"Well, you want to send me a tape of this up-and-comer of yours, and any songs you manage to write for yourself, and we'll talk when you're done communing with nature?"

"Yes." That was exactly what I wanted to do.

This felt, in a real, profound way, like the right next move. It wasn't reactive, to use my sister's term. It was just about making some great music. It wouldn't look the same as making great music in a band, in a songwriting partnership with Scott. But I was feeling, for the first time, like maybe that was OK.

———

Some of the artists had taken to having campfires on our little beach. Not every night, but maybe twice a week. I hadn't joined them. I guess I was still sticking to my image of myself as a cranky-ass loner. The only person I actively hung out with at Wild Arts was Jack, and that was because we didn't talk very much. We just sat and drank. But when I heard them out there on Friday night, the crackling of the fire and the sounds of their laughter carrying into my cabin, I grabbed my guitar and walked out to join them. I had no idea what had come over me, just that my head was...full. Of songs, mostly. Not the ones I was supposed to be writing, but others: "girl" songs and Anna's songs. But also Tristan's simplistic guitar god wannabe songs, which, when I was being generous in my thinking, were probably perfectly appropriate for a teenage boy to be into. I couldn't expect everyone to be a prodigy like Anna. And I was thinking about my drummers, and what songs I could give each of them that would provide the right amount of challenge.

Honestly, if this was what teachers felt like all the time, it was exhausting. I needed to discharge some of this frenetic energy.

"Yeah, but who am I going to choreograph?" Gretchen was saying as I approached the fire. "You can't just anoint yourself a choreographer. I need dancers."

"Don't you have a whole school of them?" Danny asked.

I hovered outside the circle, eavesdropping.

"Sure, but you know that's not what I mean. I used to do some choreographing at local high schools, for their musicals. I'd come in and teach the Von Trapp Family Singers or the Munchkins in Oz to do their dances. I stopped when the studio really started to take off, but maybe I should get back into that."

"But is that any different from what you do at the studio?" Maiv asked gently.

"No. It's less, in a way. At least at the studio, I pick the music, and the theme." Gretchen, who apparently had supersonic hearing, or eyes in the back of her head or something, turned toward me. "That you, Knight?"

Busted. I stepped into the light, sheepish, conscious of disturbing their cozy circle, of derailing the conversation. If I wanted to be in the circle, I should have been less standoffish earlier. I should have said yes to a swimming invitation when they were still being issued. I should have gone to a sunrise circle.

To my shock, though, Gretchen slid over on the log she was sitting on to make room for me. The circle absorbed me without comment, and the conversation continued.

"What if we did something together?" Caleb asked Gretchen.

"What do you mean?" Gretchen asked.

"A theatrical piece, but one where the movement *is* the theater, or at least part of it. Where the movement is integral to the story."

"But who writes the story?" Gretchen asked.

"We do."

"Well, *that's* terrifying."

"That's probably a sign that you should do it," Maiv said, and Danny murmured his agreement.

Gretchen sighed, and Maiv turned to me. "What do you think, Teddy? Don't you find that when you're terrified of something artistically, it usually means you should do that thing? Run toward the fear?"

I immediately thought of that G note. Of "Lemon Tree." "Jeez, I don't know, I just thought we could sing some campfire songs. This shit is too deep for me. But you guys carry on."

"No, no, let's sing!" Gretchen said. "What's a good campfire song? 'Kumbaya'?"

I started strumming it even as I said, "No way." Everyone laughed. I was startled by how easy it had been to summon collegial laughter from the group.

"I heard you playing some Dylan the other day," Caleb said.

"Yeah, I guess I've been revisiting the music of my youth." I switched to strumming "The Times They Are a-Changin'."

"Your youth?" Caleb exclaimed. "Dude, how old *are* you?"

"Revisiting the music of my mother's youth. She was really into 1960s folk music, and, I don't know, it's been front of mind lately."

"That's weird," Caleb said. "Weird in a good way." I must have made a face that contradicted his assessment, because he added, "Or not."

Everyone was looking at me. This was my cue to explain. I wasn't sure I knew how to, even to myself. But I'd just been wishing I'd taken opportunities when they were presented. "I grew up in this unofficial artists' colony in a falling-down warehouse in Brooklyn."

"Sounds cool," Danny said.

Gretchen stiffened beside me. Yeah, she already knew about the ways in which my childhood had been very much not cool. "In some ways, I guess. It definitely made me into who I am as a musician." I left out that I didn't actually *know* who I was as a musician. Not anymore, anyway. "But in other ways, it sucked. It wasn't the starving artist, Bohemian paradise you're probably imagining." The starving part, yes, but I wasn't going to say that. I didn't mind Gretchen knowing that part, but I didn't see the need to trot out my childhood junk for everyone. I summarized: "It was actually pretty miserable. But my mom..." I thought about how to make sense of it—to myself, even as I was trying to explain it to them. "We never had money for rent. Or utilities or any of that. But instead of getting a job, she threw herself into organizing the tenants. She made the fact that most of them were artists into this big moral statement. We shouldn't have to pay rent because we made art. So she'd get these rent strikes going, get companies to donate generators for when the power was cut off. She was a pretty good amateur musician, and my sister and I were both musically inclined, so she taught us all these 1960s protest songs. And she'd organize the neighbors for these…well, rallies, I guess, and everyone would sing those songs."

"It was her theme music," Gretchen said. "The way she defined herself."

That was exactly right. How had I ever thought of Gretchen as annoying? I swiveled to look at her. The fire was making her face glow like some kind of Renaissance painting of the Virgin Mary—if the Virgin Mary had pink-tipped hair.

"Let's hear one of her theme songs," Danny said.

"Unless it brings back bad memories," Maiv said.

"No," I said, though it was a lie. These songs did bring back bad memories, some more than others. *One* more than others. "They're great songs. Perfect for singing around a campfire." I was still amazed that they'd let me into their conclave with such ease. I wasn't used to ease.

We ran through a bunch of them. I'd start a song, and they'd pick it up. Many of these songs had simple verses that swapped in one thing for another—the hammer in "If I Had a Hammer" became a bell in the second verse—so they were easy to get the hang of. Then Maiv asked if I knew any Beatles. Soon I was taking requests from everyone. Maiv was a Beatlemaniac, Danny was into Pearl Jam, and Caleb favored show tunes.

"Is there anything you *don't* know?" Gretchen laughingly asked after I'd played the Go-Go's "Vacation" at her request, except I'd slowed it way down and made it into a ballad.

"I'm embarrassingly ignorant about country and bluegrass. I know some of the classics, but nothing new." Though Anna had turned me on to a couple artists I planned to learn more about.

"I was kidding, but I love how you answered that earnestly," Gretchen said.

Before I knew it, the fire was down to embers and it was almost midnight. "That was awesome, thanks, Teddy," Maiv said as she stood and fished her flashlight out of her pocket. Everyone concurred, and I had to agree. I felt recharged. I'd come to the fire thinking I needed to *dis*charge all my jumpy energy, but instead it felt like I'd redirected it. Amazing that sitting around aimlessly singing could do that.

But that was the power of music, wasn't it? That was what I loved about it. That was probably what my mother had loved about it, too. Music could change you.

When was the last time I'd sat around singing for no reason? I used to love writing with Scott, but those sessions had always been about creating something new. Making something out of nothing. Tonight reminded me of all the singing with my family when I was a kid. There had been, back in that dark apartment, a kind of purity to sitting together and singing for the joy of it. I'd forgotten about that, that there had been some good in and among all the shit.

"You coming on the big hike tomorrow?" Caleb asked as he smothered the embers with sand. "If you are, you should bring your guitar."

I was about to ask *What big hike?* when Maiv said, "It's only a day trip, though, so when would we sing? We're not going to be building a fire. It's just in and out."

The fact that I had no idea what they were talking about probably didn't reflect well on me. I was embarrassed when Gretchen, who clearly realized I was confused, had to say, "Day trip to a nearby state park tomorrow. Hiking in to a waterfall, lunch, swimming—there's apparently a pristine swimming hole there—hiking back out. Optional for the kids, but a lot of them are going. And obviously optional for us, too."

As we ambled back to our cabins, I heard myself say, "A waterfall might be fun." When I could feel Gretchen raising a skeptical eyebrow—it was too dark to actually see it, but somehow I knew it was there—I said, "What?"

"I didn't say anything."

"You thought it."

"You, Teddy Knight, have no idea what I think."

8
FOREST FRUIT ROLL-UPS

Gretchen

"This is all your fault."

I didn't know exactly how, but the fact that we were lost in the freaking North Woods was Teddy's fault. It had something to do with whatever had come over him this past week. His personality transplant. He was so easy to talk to now. He was so *distracting*.

"My fault!" he protested. "You're the one with the compass."

"Yes!" I doubled down. "Your fault!"

After surprising me by showing up at the bus that morning, Teddy had continued delivering shocks: Posing for pictures by the waterfall when asked. Swimming with good cheer—even going so far as to join some kids in a competition to see who could make the biggest splash cannonballing into the swimming hole.

And the last one, which I'd felt as a *literal* shock, a visceral, galvanizing bee sting: falling into step with me on the return trip and asking, earnestly and with seemingly genuine interest, about the conversation he'd walked in on last night—about my burgeoning choreographic ambitions. Which, in the light of day, with Teddy freaking Knight and his split personality, I was more than a little sheepish about.

"You're the one who kept asking questions!" I added. "You're the reason we fell behind!" I shook my useless compass at the sky. Sure, I had a compass, but since I didn't know which way was "out," it wasn't any use. "Definitely your fault!"

"That...might be true."

See? Case in point about how *weird* he was being. All agreeable and interested in other people and just generally...decent. It was disarming. I didn't know what to do with this new Teddy. At the best of times, but this was not the best of times. This was lost in the God damn woods times.

We'd tried shouting. We'd tried retracing our steps to see if we'd missed an obvious turnoff.

"Oh wait!" Teddy said. "Duh! We can call someone. I don't have my phone—get out yours."

"I don't have my phone, either!"

"Why not?"

"Because I gave it up, remember? You're the one who was all holier-than-thou about it! You're the one who said phones mess with your brain!"

"Since when do you listen to me?"

A terrifying thought dawned, and I answered his question with one of my own. "Are there bears in these woods?" I could hear the panic in my voice, but I couldn't control it.

"How should I know? You're the Minnesotan."

"Oh my God!"

"We're going to be OK. Come. Sit. Take a breath."

That...was probably a good idea. We were both sweating from running around trying to get unlost, and my breath was coming in shallow huffs, like it had the other day when I'd spent an hour working on hook jumps with the girls. Then the breathlessness had been in service of something: after we were done, the girls could do hook jumps. Kind of. Most of them. Here I was just panicking, and I had enough sense left to know that panicking wouldn't help.

Teddy settled himself on a flat rock and patted the space next to him. I sucked in a slow, shaky breath and sat.

He shrugged off the pack he was carrying. "You've got water, right?"

"Yes!" I was disproportionately pleased with this morsel of good news. I extracted my water bottle. "This is still about half-full."

He nodded at my day pack. "Anything else in there?"

I upended the bag. "Wet swimsuit, sunscreen, and—oh! Granola bars. So we won't starve."

"And hey, if it comes to it, we both know how to starve, right?" He bumped his shoulder against mine, and I experienced another wave of that odd solidarity, though come to think of it, it was starting to feel less odd.

More importantly, the solidarity was subsuming the panic. I took another deep breath; this one sounded smoother.

"All I have is water," he said, "but Marion gave me one of the first aid kits to carry." He broke the seal on the bag and started pulling out items. "Bandages, gauze, tape, scissors."

"So we can wrap presents," I said, trying to keep my fear at bay with a joke, and I was pleased when he smiled.

"We have one of those tinfoil survival blankets."

"Hopefully it won't come to that."

He made a hum of agreement. "What's this?" He held up a multicolored cylinder, tilting it so he could read the side. "EpiPen." He did the same with a bunch of other items.

"Painkillers, antihistamines, antibiotic cream." He kept rummaging. "Damn. I was hoping for flares or something."

My semisoothed state didn't last. "It's a first aid kit, not a survival kit! What good is first aid if we're not going to survive?" My voice was going shrill, like Minnie Mouse had taken control of it.

"Gretchen, Gretchen. It's going to be OK." He held my hand. Like, actually picked up one of my hands and held it in one of his. The resultant shock tipped me out of my panic. "They're going to notice we're missing, they're going to find us, and this is going to make a great story someday. Probably not even that far off. Monday's sunrise circle."

"Are you going to come to Monday's sunrise circle and tell it?"

"I wouldn't miss it."

"You've missed all of them so far."

"I was waiting until I had a really good story to tell."

I looked down at our joined hands. He wore a bunch of silver rock star rings, and there were the calluses that I'd been finding so…interesting. I kind of felt like rubbing my thumb against one of them would be soothing in the way textures sometime are. It would be hella weird, though.

Well, fuck it. We were lost in the woods, and I was trying to keep my terror at bay. So yeah, like a complete freak, I stroked one of Teddy Knight's calluses.

There was a thin line of black around the edges of two of his fingernails. "Is that the remnants of nail polish?"

He joined me in looking down at his hand. "Yeah."

"Huh."

"Are you going to say something about how nail polish is for girls?"

He sounded like he'd heard that a lot. "Oh my God, no. I would never do that. It's…" *Uncannily attractive.* "I'm just surprised." It occurred to me that I was using the words *surprised* and *shocked* a lot today as they related to Teddy Knight. He was being so *nice*. I didn't know if I could trust it.

"My sister used to paint my nails sometimes when we were kids," he said. "She went through this nail art phase, and I'd let her practice on me." He shrugged. "When you play guitar, you look at your hands a lot." He pulled his hand out of mine, which, I'm not going to lie, was disappointing, and held it up to examine his nails. "I liked seeing an interesting color rather than my own boring nails. And honestly—this is going to sound gross; I've never said this out loud, and if you tell anyone I will have to murder you." I got a little thrill at the idea of being about to hear something that Teddy Knight had never told anyone else. "The water at our building was often shut off. So we were…well, we were dirty sometimes. I'd have this dirt under my nails that was, like, a permanent feature. The polish covered it. I preferred being the weird arty kid people slung homophobic insults at to being the dirty kid."

I didn't say anything. Being cool over this revelation seemed like the right move, so I didn't react with outrage or concern or anything, though I felt all that stuff swirling around inside me.

"But I did actually like it aesthetically," he went on. "So I kept it up. Not all the time but occasionally when we had a day off on this last tour, I'd go get my nails done."

"In a salon?"

"Not salons. No-frills nail bars where you don't need an appointment—you know, like in a strip mall? I'd just look up the closest one to wherever we were."

"I'm trying to imagine a nail tech in, like, Cincinnati, looking up at her next client and it's Teddy Knight from Concrete Temple."

"Oh, no, they usually had no idea who I was. Scott was the face of the band. And anyway, nail techs in Cincinnati weren't generally our demographic—nothing against nail techs in Cincinnati."

"Who do you think was your demographic?"

"Good question. One thing I noticed is that our fans grew with us. Aged with us. You didn't really see teenagers or people in their early twenties at shows."

"So Concrete Temple wasn't a growth proposition?"

He barked a laugh. "I guess not. I would have said I didn't care. If you're lucky enough to have an audience, who cares if they're the same age as you? In our case dudes—and I feel like they were mostly dudes—in their thirties and forties. Maybe some a bit older."

"You would have said that, but you don't anymore?"

"Well, at the risk of ruining my image as a curmudgeon, this week has been eye-opening. I have this one kid. She's...well, she's fantastic. She's basically a songwriting prodigy, and I'm not throwing that word around lightly. I'm learning so much from her."

This must be the girl I'd heard him singing with. "Nice."

"It's like this for you all the time at your studio, isn't it?"

"No. Definitely no. But I know that energizing feeling that you sometimes get when you're teaching."

"But no dance prodigies at your studio?"

"It's not really that kind of place. A lot of my kids, and I say this with love, are not natural dancers. Which is fine. More than fine—it's kind of the point. I pride myself on running an inclusive studio that doesn't deal in a lot of the garbage that many dance studios do. I have this sign that displays my—you're going to think this is dorky—philosophy of dance. It's distilled into three rules I call Miss Miller's Morals."

"That doesn't sound dorky. What are they?"

Well, look at me: lost in the woods, telling Teddy Knight about Miss Miller's Morals. I started ticking them off on my fingers. "Number one: 'Everybody is welcome at Miss Miller's.' Two: 'Everybody can dance.' Three: 'Dancing is supposed to be fun.' Then there's a joking number four that just reads, 'The end.'"

"That's great."

"It *is* great. You probably don't know much about how dance culture messes with kids'—girls' mostly—mental well-being. And physical."

"I can imagine. Am I sensing a 'but,' though? You have this great, inclusive, evolved studio, but...?"

I sighed. I hadn't even articulated this to myself, so I didn't know how to explain it to him. But we potentially had hours of time to fill before our rescue, and Teddy had proven himself a not-bad listener on several occasions now. "I think I have to start from the beginning for this to make sense."

"I'm afraid we might have a lot of time to fill," he said, echoing my thoughts. But the prospect wasn't so scary anymore.

"OK, so, I've already told you about my shitty childhood." He nodded. "When I was in high school, I decided I wanted to be my own boss. I looked at my parents, and I thought about what they did. My mom waited tables for forty years. Forty years! Not that there's not honor in that job, but you know. She took a lot of shit, worked long shifts, often at night, and income was up and down because it depended on tips. And I told you about my dad." I sighed. "Sometimes I think I'm too hard on him. I can see some of myself in him. He was really creative."

"Was?"

"He died a few years ago."

"I'm sorry."

"Thanks. We weren't close as adults. I mean, I loved him. He loved me. I was sad when he died. But—and I'm aware this sounds bad—in some ways, his death was a relief, because then I only had to worry about my mom. Between my sister and me, we were able to get her into a little condo." I paused. "Is your mom alive?" He had talked about her, but only in the past tense.

"As far as I know."

I waited for more, but he didn't say anything. So we weren't going there. Fair enough. "I could see my dad bristling against 'the Man.' Like, he didn't want to have to wake up early to be at work by a specific time. He didn't want to work to enrich others—some of his jobs were really physical, hard on his body. I get it. I think I even got it at the time, at least to some degree, but I didn't have a lot of patience for it. This is the way of the world, I used to think. If you wanted to opt out of capitalism, you shouldn't have had kids who needed things like food and clothes, or hell, maybe even a musical instrument or the occasional vacation, you know?"

He snorted. "Oh, I know. Believe me, I know."

More solidarity with Teddy Knight. Which was still weird, but maybe a little less so. "But I think in some elemental way, my dad and I were alike. He was creative. He just never had the opportunity to nurture it. He hadn't grown up with money, or access to higher education, so he never had a shot at a white-collar job, which, while it might have been soul destroying, would at least have been more lucrative."

"So you took your dad—your parents—as a cautionary tale."

"Exactly. I got to the end of high school, and I thought, 'I want to do something where I'm my own boss.'"

"That was some serious foresight."

"And/or naivete." Maybe it had been both. I did look back on my teenage self with empathy, and with gratitude. In some ways, it was for her that I was embarking on my man cleanse. My become-a-crone quest was the completion of a project she'd started so many years ago. She had always looked to the future with clear eyes and a sense of what was important to her, and I owed it to her to keep doing that.

I returned to my story. "I did a two-year community college degree and learned basic accounting and marketing. I started thinking about what I wanted to do specifically. I narrowed it down to the two things I loved the most: dance and cats."

He barked a laugh. "Cats!"

"Yeah, I'm a cat lady."

"Hmm."

"What?"

"I just realized that I know you, but I don't really *know* you. Camp feels like a pause in the normal space-time continuum."

"I know what you mean. It's that camp friends thing Marion was talking about. Like, in the normal world I would never be lost in the woods with Teddy Knight. I'd be lost in the woods with a nonfamous person."

"Ha. No. It's more that people have contexts, you know? Or at least some people do."

"You don't have a context?"

"Well, I did."

I didn't know if he was talking about the band or the ex. Probably both.

"Anyway," he said, "go on. Cats versus dance?"

"Yeah, I narrowed it down to opening a dance studio or a pet grooming place. But I'm not really a dog person, so I went with dance." I paused. "It sounds so cold and calculating when

I say it like that. I love dance. I love it inherently, but I also love it because it has allowed me the life I have. I work hard, but I'm the boss."

"Sounds ideal."

"I guess."

"I'm sensing a 'but' again."

"I myself managed to avoid most of the toxic dance culture garbage, probably because as a kid I only had lessons on and off, as we had money or didn't. So it wasn't until high school, when I was on the dance team, that I had any consistent instruction. I saw a lot of girls on my team damage themselves with eating disorders, body dysmorphia, all that junk."

"Can I just say again that you seem to have been remarkably self-aware from a young age?"

"I'm not sure if it's that. It's hard to develop an eating disorder when you don't consistently have enough to eat to begin with. Or if I *was* unusually self-aware, maybe it's only because I was forced to be by circumstances."

"Yeah."

"You, too?"

"No. Well, maybe, but I was thinking of my sister. You remind me of her in a way."

"What way?"

"We'll do me later."

We'll do me later. I got a thrill at that notion. "Well, that's pretty much it for me. I decided to open a dance studio, but I was determined that it be inclusive, that it not perpetuate all the harm that can be endemic to dance. Hence Miss Miller's Morals. I have a one-strike-you're-out policy on body-shaming, bullying, all that. I run a tight ship."

"But? We keep almost getting to the 'but.'"

I sighed. "I think it's what you said about camp being a pause in the normal state of things. At the studio, I choreograph all the recitals—we have two a year. I'm known for my chore-ography, in fact. This is part of the Miss Miller's Morals thing. I'm not into little girls shaking their asses in skimpy costumes. So oftentimes I theme recitals based around older music. Or they're funny on purpose—once I did an entire 'Weird Al' Yankovic recital. But—and here's the 'but' finally—being at Wild Arts has made me see how what I'm doing *isn't* really cho-reography. It's choreography lite. Or maybe that's not fair. But the girls here, and the dance counselors, are *really* into dance. They're talented technically, but they're also creative about how they *think* about dance and what it can do. It's exhilarating to work with people like that. To think about not only setting steps to music, but about telling a story, or communicating a message. It's like solving a puzzle. It's, well…it's awesome."

"So what's the problem?"

"I feel bad even thinking all that stuff I said, because it feels like it goes against Miss Miller's Morals, like it goes against my whole life's purpose. On the one hand, I'm saying everyone can dance, it doesn't matter how good you are, dancing is about fun. I've built my whole professional life, and my livelihood, around that idea. But on the other hand, here I am with these elite, talented dancers, and it feels like…I don't know, like it's waking up this dormant impulse inside me."

"Does it have to be one or the other, though?"

"What do you mean?"

"Well, your studio sounds pretty great. Can it be great, but also not be enough for you at this stage of your life, creatively? It's doing an important service, it sounds like, meeting a com-munity need. And it's paying your bills. But…" He trailed off

and scrunched up his forehead. "It's OK to want to do something different, or more."

"Why do you have that funny look on your face?"

"We'll do me later."

That was the second time he'd said that. I hoped we didn't
get rescued too soon to "do him." Look at me—suddenly *not*
wanting to be rescued.

"Anyway," I said, "it's a moot point. I literally just bought a
new building."

"Yeah? This is what you meant when you said you were
expanding your business?"

"Yep. I've been renting in a strip mall all these years, but I've
bought my own building, and I'm going to double the studio
space and start offering yoga and Pilates. I'm about to be up
to my eyeballs in renos and bills. So I can't suddenly decide to
'become a choreographer.'" I made air quotes with my fingers.

"What about Caleb's offer to do something with him? You
could do that on the side, even if you're busy."

"I don't know how to write."

"Yeah, but you know how to dance. Isn't the point of what he's
suggesting that the story is told, at least partially, through dance?"

"Yeah. It's just…"

"Terrifying," he said with quiet surety.

Yet again, I was startled. "You sound like you're speaking
from experience."

"Maybe I am."

"Is it time to do you now?"

———

We didn't "do" Teddy for a while. He deflected, suggesting we
try yelling for help again. "Maybe it took them a while to realize

we were missing," he said. "Maybe they've doubled back for us."
After a round of shouting proved unfruitful, we used the scissors in the first aid kit to hack off sections of gauze, and Teddy
began an exercise wherein he would walk away from our spot
in a straight line and tie strips of gauze to trees to make a trail
leading to us. We would call back and forth to each other as he
walked, and he'd only go as far as he felt he could without losing
touch with me. I imagined the finished product from above as
a sort of mummy-sunshine hybrid, gauzy "sunbeams" radiating
out from where we were at the center. It probably was going to
make no difference unless they sent helicopters. And if they had
to send helicopters, we were more screwed than I had imagined,
even in my moments of panic. I told myself that Teddy was
right: they would come back and find us. We couldn't be that
far off the path we'd walked as a group. Still, our little art installation gave us a purpose, and having a purpose was calming.

Eventually, though, dusk was upon us. The temperature
began dropping, and I could feel the fingers of panic starting
to slide up my spine.

No. I wasn't going there again. "I think we should prepare
for the possibility that we might have to spend the night here,"
I said when Teddy came back from his latest tree-decorating
excursion. "And I don't think you should go off on your own
anymore."

He blew out a resigned breath. "Agreed."

"When it gets dark, it's going to get *dark*."

"The question is, How cold is it going to get?" he asked.

"Not cold enough to harm us, I don't think. But probably
cold enough to be unpleasant."

"It's been so hot at camp so far. There were nights I would
have killed to be 'too cold.'"

"Should we try to make a fire?" I asked.

"With what?"

"I don't know. Rubbing sticks together? Does that only work on TV?"

"I have no idea," he said, "but I guess it's something to do."

As the ambient light around us dimmed, we went around and collected leaves and twigs and made what looked like a decent approximation of a firebed—neither of us had experience with outdoorsy pursuits.

"I have concluded this does only work on TV," I said after a good ten minutes of rubbing two sticks together.

He stopped, too, and shook out his hand. "I think maybe you need a flint for this to work?" He paused. "Is that a real thing? I don't even know what a flint actually is."

"Remind me never to go on *Survivor* with you."

"Oh yeah, we'd be dead immediately."

We laughed and gave up. He came to sit next to me where I was leaning against a tree. We sat in what I would have called companionable silence, except it was more like companionable anxiety.

"Let's eat the granola bars before it gets fully dark," I finally said. We'd been holding off, but I didn't want to die because a bear had sniffed out my Kashi. Teddy tried to make me eat both of them, but I forced one on him. We tapped them together as if we were cheers-ing, and after we ate, we returned to our companionable anxiety.

Eventually, and out of the blue, he said, "That thing you said about contexts. I think I'm freaking out right now because I don't have a context. Well, not *right now*–right now. *Right now*–right now, I'm freaking out because I'm lost in the woods."

"Maybe you're lost in the metaphorical woods." I paused. "In addition to the literal woods."

He blew out a breath that made his lips vibrate, which I was starting to recognize as something he did when confronted with a perhaps-uncomfortable truth. "Basically. The band that's been my life for the last seventeen years is dead."

"And you got dumped."

"Yeah, but I'm over that." He waved a hand dismissively. "That's just a logistical problem at this point, not an emotional one. I need her out of my apartment, but she's already out of my heart."

I thought about the lyrics to that "Lemon Tree" song. I thought about how happy he and Karlie looked when he'd appeared on her Instagram. "Are you sure?"

He shot me a quizzical look. Fair. When a person repeatedly questioned if another person was over an ex, it was generally because Person A was getting jealous and territorial.

And jealous and territorial were states of being associated with dating. Which I did not do anymore.

"Pretty sure," he said mildly.

I needed to stop poking at the girlfriend thing. "It's like you got divorced."

"What? No. I mean, yes, we were together for a few years, but it's not like that at all." Cue another quizzical look. A more serious one: he was staring at me like he was trying to see my thoughts.

"No, sorry, I meant the band. I meant Scott Collier."

He looked away. "Right."

Things had become awkward. He drew a breath like he was going to start talking, but he didn't. The easy fellowship of before, when we'd been talking about me, felt miles away. I wondered if I should tell him about my disastrous date with Scott. On the one hand, it wasn't any of his business. And did Scott even deserve the airtime? What was he but another example of a bad date with a mediocre man—the kind of date that was firmly in my past?

On the other hand, it was starting to feel weird that Teddy was grappling with stuff to do with Scott while I was keeping quiet about my own recent encounter with him.

There was also the issue of Scott's wife, Cinda Lewis. I'd crept her Instagram, too, but there wasn't much to see. All her posts were professional—fashion shows and the like.

Anyway, now was not the time for any of it. It could wait until we were unlost. "So I remind you of your sister, huh?" I asked, sending myself back to the part of our previous conversation where Teddy had first deflected attention from himself. Talking about his sister was probably less fraught than talking about himself.

"Yeah. She's that same mix of creative and practical." I could hear the affection in his voice.

"Is she a musician, too? You said you grew up singing together?"

"She sings and plays piano and paints and does photography. And she's always picking up these oddball arts and crafts, like one minute she'll be doing origami and the next she's learning traditional rug hooking."

"Wow."

"But it's all in the hobby realm. By day she's an actuary."

"Wow again."

"Yeah. Don't get me wrong, she likes her job. She was always really good at math. But I think she probably made a conscious choice to follow a career path that would bring money and stability to her life."

"I get that."

"I thought you would."

"But is she undergoing a dark night of the soul that's making her question her life's path?"

He chuckled. "No, that's you." He paused. "And me."

"Do go on." We had circled back to the topic, but this time the awkwardness was gone.

"It's not some big thing. Just that I'm supposed to be writing songs for a new album, and I'm...not."

"What do you mean 'supposed to be'?"

"That was my whole goal for my time here. The point in coming. I was going to write songs for a solo album."

"You're allowed to change your goals. Marion didn't take notes on anything anyone said. You didn't sign your name in blood. You're allowed to change your mind—*you* just told *me* that."

There was a pause before he asked, "Did you change your mind about your goals for your time here?"

"I'm befuddled on that topic. As you know—we just talked about that."

"That's not what you said your goal for your time here was."

Oh. "You mean my man cleanse. My become-a-crone project."

"Your *what* project?"

I ignored his question. I didn't want to get into it. "No, I'm not changing my mind about that goal. My man cleanse is...still underway." *Say it like you mean it, lady.* Jeez. I cleared my throat and said, with false cheer, "We're supposed to be doing you. So you're not writing the songs you thought you would, or should?"

He sighed but did not speak. I'd made things too heavy with my questioning. I had a sudden inspiration for how to lighten the mood and reached into my pocket, where I had some cash. "Ten dollars for your thoughts."

He cracked up as I handed him a wrinkled bill. "Is that the same ten dollars?"

"Yep. We were supposedly stopping for fast food on the way home." I moaned. "What would you give for a Big Mac right now?"

He took the money with a wry smile. The awkwardness had dissipated, and he looked right at me and said, "I think I'm not writing because I don't want to write the same kind of stuff anymore."

"So don't write the same kind of stuff."

"But that's what I know how to write, and..."

"And what?" I asked gently, feeling as if we were on the precipice of something.

"I don't know if I can write without Scott."

"Ah. I don't have a pat comeback for that."

"Yeah, I've never done it."

I had a feeling he *did* know how to write without Scott, or at least that he could discover a way to, and I hated the idea of that jerk making Teddy feel less than, but what did I know about any of it? "Literally never?"

"Well, usually one or the other of us would start a song, but we'd always finish it together."

Well, maybe I did have a pat comeback. "You know what? You don't need that asshole."

"Whoa!" he said—but laughingly.

"I said what I said." Of course, he didn't know *why* I'd said it—which probably explained the bewildered look I somehow knew he was giving me. It was now officially too dark to see, but I'd gotten to the point where I could sense his bewilderment. Maybe because I was so often the cause of it.

"I guess not only do you not call the tabloids, you don't read them," he said. "I'm the one who threw a fit when he tried to dump me. So, logically, I think I do need him."

"Screw logic. This is sounding more and more like a divorce, and you know how it works: when your friend gets divorced, you're automatically on their side. So it's Team Teddy here."

"It is, huh?" He was trying to be wry, but he sounded chuffed. "You know what? I think 'screw logic' is the right approach in general. For writing songs, I mean. I think I'm way too up in my own head. I need to, like…rely on muscle memory or something. I know how to write songs—you were right about that. It's just…"

"It's terrifying, right? Like you said. I guess we both need to figure out whether being terrified is sufficient reason not to do something."

"Yeah, I guess we do."

———

I woke up with a start sometime later with my head on Teddy's shoulder and his arm around me. I'd fallen asleep. "Oh, shit," I mumbled. "Sorry."

"No problem."

I made an involuntary squeak of dismay when I pulled away. It was cold and he was…cozy.

"Yeah," he said, as if he could read my thoughts—read my squeak. "How is it so fucking freezing here? It's not this cold in our cabins at night."

"I don't know, maybe something sciencey to do with the

trees? Or just the simple fact of shelter. Anyway, it's probably not as cold as we think it is. We're not going to die of exposure." I paused. "I'm saying that to myself as much as to you."

"I didn't want to wake you, but now that you're up, I think we should get out that blanket."

"Yes." I completed the unwelcome task of disentangling myself from him and hopped around to try to get my blood flowing while he dug in the first aid kit.

"OK, come back," he said.

My eyes had adjusted to the dark. He was settling himself back against the tree trunk with the blanket wrapped around his back and shoulders like a cape. He was holding up one side of it, making a space for me next to him. I went willingly but winced audibly as I tried to arrange myself into anything remotely resembling a comfortable position.

"Sorry, I have a crick in my hip. It's an old injury that acts up when I'm cold. And when I sit too long." The solution was to extend my leg, so I did that as well as I could while keeping my upper body cozied up to the heat sources that were the blanket and Teddy.

"Maybe we should put it over us actually like a blanket," he suggested.

"Let's try."

Several minutes of awkward logistical wrangling followed. We'd get one end of the blanket tucked under one of us, but then the other end wouldn't quite reach over and around the other person, and it would end up flapping in the breeze.

"Argh!" I said.

"All right. Pause." He held up both hands like I was robbing him. "Pause." He got up and pulled me to my feet. "Here's what we're gonna do. Step one: we're going to kind of...hug."

He moved toward me and put his arms out as if to embrace me but stopped short of actually doing it. "Except horizontally, on the ground, OK?"

"Horizontal hugging. Is that what they call it these days? Sheesh, no wonder I quit dating."

"Shut up."

"You say that to all the girls, don't you?" I lowered my voice in a parody of masculinity. "Come on, baby, let's hug horizon-tally."

He ignored me, pulling me against his chest with one hand and using the other to measure the amount of space we took up relative to the blanket. "This is going to work. And we should try to sleep, right? It will be easier if we're lying down."

"Yeah, OK," I said, and he lay on the ground and pulled me down with him.

"Do we actually have to hug, though?" I asked. "Can't we lie side by side?" Because not only was I not going to sleep if we were hugging, I was not going to relax even one iota. "I feel like we take up less room this way than we did sitting."

"Let's try." He tucked one edge of the blanket under himself and handed me the other. I tried to do the same, but I had to tug it into place.

"No, no, it's coming out on my end," he said.

"It's not wide enough," I said. "It's not going to work."

"It's going to work, but I'm sorry to say, we have to resort to hugging. Here, come here."

Somehow, I wasn't even really sure how it happened, we ended up lying face-to-face, or face-to-neck—my face to his neck—near the edge of the blanket. There wasn't time for it to be awkward, though, because he shouted, "OK, roll!"

"What do you mean, roll?"

"Roll!" He hoisted me onto his body. Before I could adjust to the fact that I was literally lying on top of Teddy Knight, he'd rolled me down the other side. "Oh, I see what you're going for—like a burrito." I tried to bring the bottom of the blanket up with my feet.

"No!" he said. "We're going for flauta, not burrito."

"What's the difference?"

"We're just rolling, we're not fussed about filling coming out of the bottom, so there's no tuck-in."

"Well, I for one am fussed about stuff coming *in* the bottom, so maybe there *should* be a tuck-in!"

"What's going to come in the bottom?"

"Bugs! I don't know…wolves? Frigid air?" My face was jammed into his neck—which smelled weirdly good—so I couldn't see his face, but I suspected he was rolling his eyes. "You know what I mean!"

"Yes, but the blanket isn't long enough. We can either have our feet in it *or* our shoulders covered. We have shoes on, so we should prioritize the shoulders. Yours are bare."

They were. He was wearing a T-shirt, but I was wearing a tank top. "OK, OK. I surrender. Flautas. Or maybe a Fruit Roll-Up is a better analogy."

"Let's start again." He pulled away from me and futzed with our setup. "OK, roll!"

I rolled.

But I also started laughing.

"Be serious!" he admonished, but there was amusement in his tone, too. "We can get this. Try again."

By the time he was yelling, "Fruit Roll-Up, take three!" I was snorting with laughter, though I tried my best to roll at the same time.

He was laughing, too, and he had a great laugh: low and rumbly and, I don't know…hard-won sounding. It called to mind a rusty engine taking a minute to start but then roaring to life. My face was once again nestled into the crook of his neck, so I could *feel* his laughter. It was like the purring of my cats—but more. Bigger. Like the purring of a lion, maybe: cozy but dangerous.

Soon enough I had to abandon my high-minded similes because we were in hysterics. We weren't even trying to tuck ourselves in anymore, we were just lying there smooshed up against each other, convulsing with laughter.

"Oh my God, my stomach!" I gasped. I was laughing so hard my stomach hurt. When was the last time *that* had happened?

It took a while for it to wear off. We'd stop, but then one of us would start again, and off we'd go. Eventually, though, we wound down, and I was left with my nose in his neck. "Sorry I got your neck wet. I was laughing so hard I cried."

"'S'okay," he rasped. After a pause, he said, "Are you *smelling* me?"

"I…" Had been. It was impossible not to notice, jammed in there like I was, his aftershave or whatever it was. It was medicinal, like eucalyptus maybe, or rosemary, but with an overlay of something citrusy. "Sorry," I finally said. "You smell good." I could feel my face flush. At least that was one perk of being lost in the woods at night—no one could see you blush.

"Uh, thanks?"

I tried to adopt a businesslike tone as I said, "I think this is going to work better if we spoon."

"Oh, for God's sake!"

"Do you want to spend the whole night with me lying here smelling your neck?"

"All right, all right."

I wrangled myself over and settled back against him. He half sat up and tugged the edge of the blanket over me. "Lift your knee," he prompted, tucking me in. When he settled back, we did some scooching and adjusting and, finally, we were settled.

"I guess I shouldn't have assumed I'd get to be the little spoon," I said into the darkness.

He shushed me and threw an arm over me. It was...nice.

"We're stuck here now," I said.

"Yes. You can't move. This was too hard-won."

"What if I have to go to the bathroom?"

"You should have thought of that before."

I made a little noise of dismay, and he said, quickly, "Of course if you have to go to the bathroom, you have to go to the bathroom."

"I don't. That was just a generic expression of unease."

"Are you thinking about bears again?"

"*Now* I am."

"Sorry. Can you try to sleep?"

"Maybe." Surprisingly, I thought I could. I felt like I was having an adrenaline crash. "Don't leave me, though." For some reason, I needed to not be alone for my hypothetical bear mauling. Everyone dies alone, they say, but not me. I was going to die with a rock star named after a poet.

"Never," he said gruffly, his tone more in keeping with a solemn vow than comforting my scaredy-cat self.

"I just mean if you have to pee or something. Can you wake me up if I'm asleep and you need to get up?"

"Yes." His top arm tightened around me, and it was...still nice. It was *really* nice. I wouldn't say I was warm, but I was no longer freezing. I felt...not safe exactly, but...sorted.

I yawned.

The next thing I knew, I was waking up, unsure how long I'd been asleep. I was cold and uncomfortable—so much for sorted and not cold.

"Hey," he whispered.

"How long was I out?" I whispered back.

"I don't know, maybe an hour?"

"Did you sleep?"

"Nah."

"How come?" I answered my own question with a self-deprecating snort. "I guess because not everyone can lose consciousness on the ground in the middle of a probably-teeming-with-bears forest they're lost in."

"It's more that I thought I should, I don't know, keep watch? Is that dumb?"

It was actually sweet. Chivalrous. If you went for that kind of thing, which I no longer did. I'd developed an immunity.

"Also, there was a mosquito feeding frenzy on the back of my neck as it got dark, and now I'm lying here tormented by the itching."

I chuckled sympathetically but switched to wincing when pain shot through my hip. "I gotta turn over, I'm sorry. I know we worked hard for the reverse–Fruit Roll-Up arrangement here, but my hip is killing me."

"No worries." He rattled the edge of the crinkly blanket. "I'm not sure how much this thing is doing anyway. It's fucking freezing out here."

I shivered as I rotated. And then again when I was situated. He returned to hugging me. It was starting to feel normal. "I'm not sure this is doing anything, either," he said, giving me a little squeeze to indicate that "this" referred to the horizontal hug.

"Eh, it's doing something in the keep-Gretchen-from-freaking-out-about-bears department."

He tightened his hold on me. "OK, good."

I wasn't lined up with his neck this time. We were face-to-face, and I could feel his breath on my skin when he spoke. "Why are we whispering?" I asked, trying to resist the absurd but intense compulsion to reach out and touch him. Like, I wanted to run my hands all over his face as if I were a blind person? Huh?

"I don't know," he whispered back. "Can bears hear?"

His breath hit my ear in such a way that it tickled. I snaked an arm up to scratch. And then...I don't know...His face was so close.. I still wanted to touch it. And my hand was *right there*.

He didn't react as my hand settled on his cheek. He had a serious five-o'clock shadow going. I could hear the raspy sound my fingers made as they slid over his whiskers.

I only had to move a couple inches to touch my mouth to his. His lips were as soft as his face was sharp. It was a chaste kiss, on the surface of things. Brief, gentle, no tongue. But my insides roared to life. I was suddenly remembering my ill-fated date with Scott. Not the date itself, but the idea behind it: one last hurrah. I never got that.

"What was that?" he asked after I pulled away—or as away as I could get, which was only a few inches. He spoke gently—he didn't seem upset. He had kissed me back, after all.

"I believe that was a kiss," I said.

"But you're retired from dating."

True. But also: "Is this a date?" I asked in such a way that there could only be one answer.

Which he gave me: "No. God, no. This is a brush with death that we will tell as an amazing story on Monday at sunrise circle."

"But we'll leave out the kissing part, right?"

"We'll leave out the kissing part," he agreed.

"Does that mean we're going to do it again?"

I still had my hand on his face, so I could *feel* him smile.

He got right to the point, opening his mouth on a groan and letting his tongue slide into mine. It wasn't subtle this time. It was *hot*. So hot I wondered how I had ever been cold. It had been so long since I'd been so well kissed. I felt like someone had come up to me and hit me with a baseball bat. In a good way.

I would have said I saw lights. That fireworks went off.

Except I did see lights. Flashlights hitting the trees. And I was pretty sure the fireworks were actually flares.

I heard it then. "Teddy! Gretchen!"

And I heard *him*. He probably thought I hadn't, because he mumbled it under his breath, but I heard him clear as anything, whispering, "*God damn it.*"

9
HORIZONTAL HUGGING

Teddy

What? The actual fuck? Was my life right now?

One minute I was lost in the woods, and somehow the next I was *kissing Sourplum*.

No, actually, let's go further back. One minute I was on tour with my band of seventeen years, and now I was bundled into a van wrapped in a blanket—an actual blanket, not a bullshit piece of tinfoil—after being interrupted *kissing Sourplum*. And I was annoyed by it? Because I'd rather have stayed lost in the woods? What?

Although, to be fair, *she* kissed *me*. She started it, anyway. And maybe the interruption wasn't an interruption so much as a blessing. Because yeah, even though, as she said, we sure as hell weren't dating, what the fuck was I doing? What was *she* doing?

I didn't get to talk to her alone because the low-level frenzy of our rescue involved park rangers and paperwork and Gatorade and medical exams.

Then Lena and Marion were in the van with us on the way back to camp. This was another situation I wasn't sure was a hindrance or a blessing.

But actually, it didn't matter. It was neither. Because what did I think? Gretchen and I were going to move the party into my cabin or hers?

As the van came to a halt in front of the camp office, I hopped out and reflexively reached a hand back to help Gretchen out. So maybe I *did* think we were going to move the party to my cabin or hers? Or my hand did, even if my rational brain didn't?

She didn't take my hand, just shot me a look I couldn't decode. But the not taking my hand was a very decided sort of not taking my hand.

Message received: party definitely over.

Which was fine—good, even. I did not need to be getting entangled with this complicated woman.

We were swarmed by the other artists exclaiming how glad they were we'd been found, or, from the ones who'd been on the hike, how sorry they were they'd lost track of us. Gretchen was her usually sunny self, accepting hugs, dispensing absolution, and telling them they hadn't needed to stay up to greet us. I found I wasn't annoyed by her Pollyanna shtick, because it allowed me to not have to talk. Maybe we made a good team that way: she talked, I brooded.

We rode golf carts back to Mr. Rogers' Neighborhood and said our good nights as people peeled off one by one at their cabins. Even if I'd harbored any hope of getting Gretchen alone at that point—which I didn't—it would have been impossible because Marion was apparently walking us all the way home.

"I'm really sorry, Marion," Gretchen said as we arrived at her door. I didn't think an apology was warranted. Had we gotten a little distracted? Yes. But had they left us in the fucking woods for hours? Also yes.

"*I'm* sorry," Marion said. "This is going to inspire us to

rethink our safety procedures. We're so concerned about not losing any kids, but clearly we need to think more broadly."

I mumbled good night, intending to leave them there, but to my annoyance, Marion jogged to catch up with me and followed me around my cabin to my porch.

I half expected her to ream me out for getting lost, or for never coming to sunrise circle, or for...something. I felt generically guilty. But she only said, "How have the first two weeks here been for you, Teddy?"

"Fine." I realized, though, that I should probably be more forthcoming and/or gracious. Not only had the woman mounted a middle-of-the-night rescue, she was putting me up for free all summer and not asking a lot in return. "It's been quite...mind expanding in a general sense"—I thought of Anna and the "girl" songs—"but to be totally honest, I've been frustrated with myself because I can't seem to get any writing done."

"Writer's block," she said, and I wasn't sure if it was a question.

"I guess, though I've never had it before." Finishing a song could be easier or harder, and that song could end up being better or worse, relatively speaking, but the initial noodling-around part had always been second nature. I'd always had more ideas, or bits of inspiration, than I'd had the time, or the discipline, to deal with.

"Perhaps you need a break," Marion said. "Art isn't like factory widgets."

"That's what my sister said."

"If you ever want to run anything by me, I'm happy to help. I know you probably think I'm a rich woman with too much time on her hands."

I started to protest that no, I didn't think that—I mean,

I kind of did think that, but it occurred to me that I had no actual evidence to support this conclusion. Even if it was true, it wasn't every rich woman with too much time on her hands who chose to spend two months a year living side by side with a bunch of kids and no air-conditioning.

"And maybe that's true," she went on. "But I love art—music, visual art, all of it. I've been lucky enough to make it a big part of my life. I'm not blessed with a lot of artistic talent myself, which I used to feel bad about. But then I realized that being a good audience member is a skill. I listen well and see well." She grinned. "And I *am* rich, so that doesn't hurt."

Hmm. "I don't want to assume anything about how old you are, but do you have any familiarity with folk music of the 1960s? Protest music in particular?"

"Sure do."

It was three thirty by the time I was finally alone. Ah, the great indoors. I collapsed on my bed, but although I was exhausted, I was jumpy. The adrenaline hadn't yet dissipated. After giving some thought to whether it was too late even for us and deciding that, nope, it wasn't, I FaceTimed Auden.

"I just got home from being lost in a state park for eight hours," I said before she could speak.

"What!" She'd been reading in bed, and she sat up, alarmed. "Are you OK?"

"I'm fine. It was wild, and I'm covered in mosquito bites, but I'm fine." I recounted the whole adventure. Well, I recounted the whole adventure minus the kissing.

She shuddered. "Oh my God; that is my worst nightmare."

I moved the phone closer and studied her. Her tone had been odd—not sympathetic, as I might have expected, but sounding as if she was truly terrified.

"It all turned out OK. I really am fine."

"I know, I know." She relaxed against her headboard, looking more like herself. "So what are you going to do now?"

"I have no idea. I should sleep, but I don't think I can. I'm too wired."

"What does that actually mean, 'wired'? You hear people say that, but what actually *is* it? What does it feel like?"

I considered the strange question. "It feels like I have too many fragments of thoughts and emotions clanging around in my head for there to be room for sleep. They have to burn off if I want to sleep."

"Write a song."

"What?"

"I'm not an expert, but it seems like writing a song might do exactly that—burn off the fragments."

"What happened to not pushing it? Not being reactive?"

"This isn't reactive. At least not in the tit-for-tat way we were talking about before. If you wrote a song now, it wouldn't be a revenge song. It wouldn't have anything to do with Scott, or Concrete Temple. It would be about a major thing that happened to you. Wouldn't it be weird *not* to write about it?"

Huh. She might have a point, but I didn't want to talk about it anymore. "How are you?"

"Oh, I'm fine. I'm always fine."

The way she said that seemed a bit off to me, but at the moment I was too self-absorbed to press her. The fragments swirling around in my head were...starting to coalesce a little? Maybe?

We said good night, and fuck me if I didn't haul my ass out of bed and over to the keyboard. I could count on one hand the number of times I'd written a viable song on a piano. Most of them had been when I was younger, before the band really hit, before I spent so much of my life on the road. Some of those eventually made their way onto Concrete Temple albums, but later it was easier, sitting around with Scott in studios and hotel rooms, to write on our guitars. I got used to doing it that way.

But Scott wasn't here anymore.

And I had this phrase in my head. It was only six notes, but I heard them, clear as day, and I heard them on the piano.

So I turned on the keyboard and got to it.

A couple hours later, as the sun was coming up, I had a song.

———

I was startled sometime the next day by a knock at my door—I'd been playing the new song—the new song!—over and over in almost a fugue state. I looked around for my watch to no avail. I wasn't the kind of person who could judge what time it was by the quality or direction of the light, so it could have been seven or it could have been noon. Or maybe I'd completely lost track of Sunday and it was Gretchen, come to rouse me for Monday's sunrise circle.

I stumbled to the door, and it *was* Gretchen, but I was pretty sure she wasn't here to rouse me for sunrise circle, because she looked like she had been cast in a comedy in which she was playing the role of Extremely Ineffectual Spy. She was wearing a hoodie with the hood up and drawn tightly over her head so only the center of her face was visible, and her eyes darted back and forth as if she expected someone to jump out at her.

"Hey," I said, smiling despite myself. I must have been feeling a sort of residual camaraderie from our time in the woods, because how else to explain the rush of affection I felt at seeing her in her silly getup and the accompanying bloom of pleasure that she was seeking me out?

"I need to ask you a question," she whispered urgently.

"Shoot."

"Can I come in?"

Yes. "Sure."

"I heard you playing. Am I interrupting?"

"No."

"I kind of am, though, right? You were playing, and now you're not."

I didn't want her to talk herself out of coming inside, so I changed the subject. "It's Sunday, right?"

"Yes."

"You want some bourbon?" Although maybe it wasn't bourbon time. "Is it noon yet?"

"It's eleven—close enough."

I stepped back to let her in. "We should probably eat something." I hadn't eaten anything since last night, when Lena and Marion had run us through a McDonald's drive-through on the way back to camp. I went to the kitchenette and got another bag of camp-store almonds, which was all I had. "You hungry?"

She didn't answer, and I was halfway through pouring the first bourbon when she burst out with, "I'm here to ask you if you want to do some horizontal hugging."

I would have liked to say that my startlement—I tipped over the glass—was due to the fact that she had basically shouted her question at me, but nope. It was the violence with which the answer roared through my body. The answer was *yes*. And not only because of the instant boner that sprang up, but because something in my stomach...I don't know, sort of thunked.

Thunked in a good way. As if my guts were settling after a period of unease.

This whole bizarre bodily response reminded me of my hand reaching back into that van last night to help Gretchen out even as my brain was confused as to what was happening. It was as if something inside me, something not of my intellect, or even of my conscious emotional self, had answers at the ready, answers to both articulated and unarticulated questions.

Maybe that was what had happened with that song last night.

But of course it wasn't that simple. Even if the answer to Gretchen's question *was* yes, it couldn't *be* yes.

So I got my shit together, wiped up the spill, and took my time pouring the drinks.

I turned and leaned against the counter, holding out one of the glasses to her. "Wow. I'm flattered, really flattered, but—"

"I have to say, I didn't have 'Dude tries to get out of horizontal hugging' on my bingo card. *That* never happened on Tinder."

Oh, shit. She was hurt. She was trying to be breezy, but she was overcompensating. She had a tell, I realized: she was her usual sarcastic self, but without the twinkle in her eye that tended to accompany sarcasm when she had the upper hand. This was defensive sarcasm.

She was backing away. Getting ready to leave. I didn't want her to do that. Even if I couldn't sleep with her.

It was confusing.

"I'm not trying to get out of it," I said, but I could tell she didn't believe me. I wasn't sure this was the right move, but I glanced down at the visible evidence of my excitement—my thin sweatpants weren't hiding anything. I didn't want to be creepy, but I wanted her to know I wasn't saying no because I wasn't attracted to her.

"I held my breath as her eyes widened. "Ohhh. Wow."

"Yeah. I'm trying to think with my brain here."

"Didn't you just give a speech last night about getting out of your head, about relying on muscle memory?"

"That was about playing music, and also, we don't have any muscle memory when it comes to this."

"We do, too. We have Fruit Roll-Ups in the forest. We know how to do horizontal hugging, we just need to...take it up a notch. Or several."

That cracked me up. *She* cracked me up. Once you got to know her, Sourplum was *funny*. Speaking of muscle memory, my gut apparently didn't have any memories of what it was like to laugh. It was sore from our laughing fit yesterday.

"You're right, though," she said. "This is a bad idea." She didn't seem hurt anymore, and she came to fetch her drink.

I had successfully delivered what I'd been aiming for—a rejection that wasn't being taken personally—so I had no idea why my next move was to open my mouth and say, "If this were to happen, what would we do for protection?"

She raised an eyebrow in a way that seemed to telegraph skepticism, or amusement—or both. "I have an IUD. A relic from my pre-crone days."

"Tell me more about this crone thing." This was the second time she'd mentioned it. "You mean like a wicked witch in a fairy tale?"

"Yes. I'm trying to become one."

Gretchen and her big blue eyes and cotton candy hair and impeccable posture were about as far from a crone as it was possible to get. I thought about asking her to sit down. I wanted her to stay regardless of whether there was going to be any horizontal hugging, but I feared that calling attention to the fact that we were still standing in the kitchenette might puncture this détente and she might bolt. So I stayed put and asked, "Why?"

"So I can be powerful and self-actualized and a little bit scary and totally self-sufficient except for my friends whom I periodically invite over for drinks I make in my cauldron."

I barked a laugh. This woman wasn't just funny, she was an honest-to-God comedian. But at the same time, I understood that she meant what she was saying even if she was saying it in a jokey way. "This is that reset you were talking about."

"Yes. The reset is that I become a crone."

"How does one become a crone?" And why was I so interested? Why was I taking us off the infinitely more urgent topic of potential horizontal hugging?

"I don't really know. That's the problem. I'm not sure you can just declare yourself a crone. You probably need a certain amount of life experience to become one."

"Maybe you need to lure some children to your house and eat them? Meet a quota of death and destruction before they give you your crone card?"

She laughed and took another sip of her bourbon.

I liked making her laugh, trying to match her wit, so I made another attempt. "I have another question: Don't crones generally live in the forest? Because, no offense, I'm not sure the forest is your most natural setting. Crones shouldn't be afraid of bears. They should enchant them and turn them into a bear army to do their bidding."

I got the laugh I'd been going for. "That was the idea of coming here this summer. It was meant to be a bookend of sorts—the end of one phase of life and the start of another. Go to the woods and become a crone. But realistically, I can't live in the forest forever. I'm going to be a city crone. A suburban crone. This summer was just meant to jump-start things."

As I was trying to think how to get us from crones back to the prospect of horizontal hugging—though I did realize it was my fault we'd gotten on this topic to begin with—she raised her eyebrows and asked, "So do you want to do some horizontal hugging or not?" The twinkle was back in her eye.

I told myself this was a terrible idea. I believed her when she said she wasn't looking for a boyfriend, or to date, but I also believed her when she said she was on her way to becoming a crone. I believed she had the power to fuck me up. So while I was glad we'd made peace, become friends, even, it was best to chalk up our ill-advised interlude as a visceral response to fear. Leave the kissing in the woods. In the fairy tales.

Which was why it made no sense that I opened my mouth and said, "Yes."

Her eyes lit up, which was hugely flattering, and I rushed to add a disclaimer. "As long as it doesn't..." I was struggling to articulate my reservations even to myself. "Mess anything up." I gestured to her and said, "The reset, the crone project." I gestured at myself. "The...whatever." Whatever the hell it was I was trying to do.

"Oh, for sure," she said. "Look, here's my logic. I know I just said we should set aside logic, but let's have one little session of overthinking this. Here we are in the woods. Not lost-in-the-woods woods like yesterday, but in this place that seems out of time. Contextless, like you said. I had planned to have one last hurrah before I gave up dating, and it...didn't work out. I would like that last hurrah. If you don't mind."

"I don't mind." Which was putting it mildly.

"And really, what do you have to lose?" she went on, though I was persuaded. "I mean, think about what you have to *gain*. Maybe I'll blow your mind so much that I'll become your muse and you'll suddenly be able to write all those songs you haven't been writing." She made an exaggerated silly face, and I snickered. "Are you laughing at me? You're not supposed to laugh at your muse!"

"Are you a crone or a muse? I think you have to pick one or the other. Also, you don't need to convince me. I'm in for one last hurrah. For you, I mean. I personally hope to live many more years filled with many more hurrahs." It was hard to imagine that now, as the hurrah at hand was taking up all the available space in my brain. "We just need to sort out the logistics. I don't think we should rely on the IUD. I'm clean— God, I hope I'm clean—but my ex was cheating on me, and though I had one round of testing, they told me to come back in six months, and I haven't had time yet, so..." Ugh. "Sorry, this isn't very sexy."

"It's OK. This is logic time, still. And actually, it *is* sexy."

"It is?" She was an odd one.

"Yeah. Like, being concerned about my health. It's very considerate."

"Well, I wouldn't want your last hurrah to end with antibiotic-resistant gonorrhea."

She snorted, and I gave myself a mental high five even as I asked myself why I was suddenly so fixated on getting her to laugh.

"Do you have any condoms?" she asked.

"I do not. Alas."

"What kind of rock star doesn't travel with condoms?"

"I do, usually." In the post-Karlie period, anyway. I hadn't used them a ton, but it was good to be prepared. Which I very regrettably was not at this moment. "I swapped my big travel bag, which I took on tour, with a small duffel since I didn't need as much stuff for this trip. I threw in toothpaste and deodorant, and I guess I didn't think about condoms—or bug spray or footwear, for that matter. So basically I came here woefully underprepared, and now I have generic orange Crocs and no condoms. Do you have any?"

"No." She paused. "I have the IUD, but I don't even usually tell guys about that, because I don't have casual sex without condoms."

She had an edge to her tone, as if she were challenging me, but I found her policy unremarkable, and I certainly wasn't going to push the issue. "What kind of crone doesn't travel with condoms?" I teased, and I could see her relax. I, however, was not relaxed. Was I going to have to run to the camp store on the highly unlikely hope that it would stock condoms at this camp for teenagers?

"Well, I guess you'll just have to deliver this last hurrah by going down on me."

That worked, too. She was kidding, but suddenly I wasn't. "Mission accepted."

"What?"

"That plan works for me."

Actually, it *really* worked, judging by the bolt of lust that struck at the notion of having my head between those legs I had been admiring for so long. But I played it cool. I took her bourbon from her and set it on the counter. Her eyes had gone wide—had she not expected me to call her bluff? "Get your clothes off and get over here." I detoured around her to the bed, taking off my T-shirt as I went.

When I turned, she was still standing by the counter with her mouth open. "At least take off your pants," I said. "I think that's the minimally acceptable degree of nudity required for what you're asking for."

When she still didn't move, I started to worry that maybe she'd gotten cold feet. So I sat on the bed, trying to make myself less, I don't know...looming. "Hey. You OK, Miller?" At some point, I wasn't sure when or who'd started it, we'd taken to addressing each other by our last names.

That broke her trance. "Yeah, yeah. It's just that you're being so...clinical."

"Did you want me to romance you?" I wasn't sure if I was teasing or asking earnestly. And if she did want me to romance her, I wasn't sure I should do that. Or if I even knew how. As much as I didn't want it to be, maybe my initial instinct had been right: this was a bad idea.

"No, no!" she said, and started pushing her pants down. She was wearing tight, cropped yoga pants, and she either hadn't been wearing underwear or she snagged them along with the pants, because when she stood...there she was. Her thighs were muscular and meaty and gorgeous. I couldn't stop looking at them. I'd seen her in a leotard before, and two different swimsuits, so I wasn't sure why I was so dumbstruck at the sight of some well-defined quads. I let my gaze rise slightly. Maybe it was her thighs in combination with the points of her hips and the thatch of pale hair between her legs. I smiled, realizing I'd half expected it to be pink-tipped like the hair on her head. By the time I was done with my fond ogling, she'd shed her shirt.

There was the pink—in the form of a bra. It was darker than
the pink in her hair, and it was a no-frills number that looked
like it was made out of cotton. She wouldn't want me to say
it, but with the pink hair and the pink bra, she did not look
like a crone. She looked like the girl lost in the woods who
would be lured in by the crone. She looked cute enough to eat.
Which, happily, was exactly what I planned on doing. I shed my
sweatpants—unlike her, I didn't need to be pantsless for what
was about to go down, but suddenly the idea of Sourplum's
bare skin on mine was all I could think about. I shot her a
wicked smile.

I thought maybe she'd get shy. Women sometimes did that,
and who was I to judge? The patriarchy, man; that was some
weird shit.

But not Sourplum; she strode toward me, turned, and said,
"Can you undo my bra?" Apparently she'd decided to embrace
the "clinical" nature of our encounter—though I intended to
disabuse her of that notion. Without "romancing" her. It was a
fine line, but there had to be a sweet spot between "romantic"
and "clinical," and I was determined to locate it.

Her back was as leanly muscled as you'd expect given the
state of her legs. I launched Operation Not-Clinical-But-Not-
Romantic-Either by standing and brushing my hands down
from the corners of her shoulders diagonally toward the center
of the bra's band. She hissed a breath in—good. As I worked
the clasp open, I allowed myself to check out her butt. It was,
like her thighs, thick and muscular.

None of this should've been surprising given her line of
work, and given what I'd already seen of her clothed, but *damn*.

I decided I didn't care if I came off as clinical. I needed my
face in there, stat. So I slid the bra off her shoulders, turned her

around, and gently pushed her to sitting on the edge of the bed. "Scooch back," I said. I was surprised when she did so without any sass, propping her upper body against my pillows; I was downright shocked when she let her legs fall open.

With her pink-tipped hair fanned out against the white pillowcases and her muscular body that I was apparently growing increasingly obsessed with casually splayed on my bed, she looked like a painting. A beautiful, obscene painting. I had the idea that crones were supposed to be wrinkly and ugly, but at that moment, she sure as hell looked like she had the power of the universe at her fingertips.

I checked myself. This wasn't the first time I'd compared her to a painting, and I needed to cut that shit out. Waxing poetic about paintings, even just in my head, was sliding a little too close to the romantic end of the spectrum here, so without further ado, I stretched out on my stomach and lowered my mouth. I started with her inner thighs, pressing open-mouthed kisses against the smooth skin there. I tuned into the noises she was making: little sighs and, when I experimentally let one hand float up and tweak a nipple, a shriek that was almost a scream. Once again: *damn.*

Gradually I made my way to her center, and she let loose a long, low moan when I first parted her and made contact with the hot, delicate flesh there. I had to reach a hand down and press down on my dick to get it to calm down a bit. I worked her with my tongue, but I had this odd sense of missing the thighs I'd just been kissing. And then I had a genius idea: I looped my arms under her legs and closed her thighs around my head like I was closing a book. Like I was closing my head, my entire being, inside the greatest book ever written.

Shit.

I needed a pause. And I liked the idea of drawing this out for her as much as possible, which I suppose is a nicer way of saying I liked the idea of torturing her. If this was her last hurrah, she should go out with a bang. A big one.

I pulled back gently. She made a squeaky noise that sounded like a cross between the word "What?" and a generic sound of protest. I shushed her as I moved up to kiss her stomach. Mm. I had thought I was so into her legs, but she had a great stomach, too, sleek muscles visible under soft skin.

"Ahh!" She was frustrated, which was where I wanted her. It would pay off later. I lazily played with a breast while I willed my body to chill out. She had small, perfect pink-tipped nipples—pink again; was pink my favorite color now? When she tried to reach for me, I batted her hand away. "We'll do me later."

"That's exactly what you said in the woods."

I hadn't realized that, but my logic was the same. I didn't want her to stop, to lose her footing on the track she was on.

"If we're 'doing me,'" she said, "can we get on with it?"

"Hey. I'm just trying to stretch things out a bit. If this is your last hurrah, it's gotta be good, right?"

"Fuck off, Teddy."

I chuckled and continued lightly massaging her breasts, and she seemed to surrender to my plan, to the frustration I was deliberately cultivating. With a groan that was half pleasure, half dismay, she let her head loll back.

"There you go," I murmured, and after a few minutes, I let my other hand drift south, finding her slick and hot. Jesus.

"Teddy," she whined, chasing the pressure of my hand with her hips, and oh how I wanted her to do that same thing to my mouth. Oh how I wanted to get back inside my book made of thighs.

"Yeah?" I teased, lifting both hands off her entirely.

"Come *on*."

"All right, all right." I returned to my happy place and went to town, kissing and licking, and when she inhaled sharply and held her breath and her legs stiffened, I gave a final little suck and she screamed.

Good Lord. I wasn't sure I'd ever been so turned on in my life. The men of Tinder were fucking idiots.

"Now we do you," she said. I wanted to tell her to stop and take a breath, recover a bit, but then I thought, *I bet dancers have really good cardiovascular health*, and I let her flip us around, so I was lying on my back and she was hovering over me. We made eye contact, and she grinned and said, "Thanks."

"No problem," I said, like I was talking about lending her a guitar pick.

We looked at each other for a beat longer, and her grin grew knowing. Then she did some dancer ninja move and before I could blink, her mouth was around my dick.

"Oh my God," I bit out. Who would have thought it? Sourplum, the woman who had annoyed me beyond all reason that first day: two weeks later, here she was, blowing me in my cabin. It was almost too much to process. Which was fine because I wasn't going to last very long, and I wanted to pay attention. I wanted to remember this. I let my hand settle on her head—not to push her or direct her, but because I wanted to touch the pink-tipped strands. She tipped her head back, even as she kept working me with her mouth. Her eyes sought out mine, and they were so bright, but so pale at the same time. They were like tiny bleached swimming pools. She smiled at me around my dick, and *fuck*. Maybe she *was* my muse.

The pressure was becoming too much. I laid a hand on her

cheek to guide her off me. She went, but she made a very gratifying mew of protest, and it was the final nail in the coffin. I
came, bucking my hips and cursing as pleasure spiked through
me. I had to close my eyes against the onslaught of sensation—
it had been a long time, longer, I guess, than I'd realized—and
when I opened them, she was stretched out next to me, close
but not touching. I didn't know what to say, so I echoed her
previous word back to her. "Thanks."

"No problem," she said, echoing mine.

What now? While I was trying to think of what to say, she
spoke. "Normally I'm insecure about my small breasts."

Huh? My gaze automatically went to the breasts in question,
two perfect little mounds. They were marked by diagonal tan
lines—from all the swimming, I supposed—that converged in
her cleavage. "But you're not insecure about them now? And for
the record, size doesn't matter." Except it kind of did. I loved
her big butt. But I also loved her small breasts. They were like
little bonuses.

"Not today," she confirmed. "I think it's the context, you
know, like we talked about?"

"What is the context here?" I was getting confused. This
was a lot of talking, and my brain wasn't fully back online yet.

"The context is *not dating*. I don't have any expectations or
hopes. No secret wishes. We don't have a future together. So
I don't feel like I have to watch what I say, or care what I
look like, because I don't care what *you* think I look like." She
barked a single delighted "Ha!" as if she found the notion lib-
erating. "I mean, I don't have any makeup on, things are not
particularly groomed"—she gestured toward the hair between
her legs—"and I showed up in a hoodie I spilled coffee on this
morning."

I had not noticed items one and three in her list of perceived shortcomings. I had noticed item two, but I hadn't seen it as a shortcoming. I was agnostic in matters of hair removal.

"You were just using me for sex," I joked.

"Well..." Her nose and forehead scrunched. "We were using each other. Right?" A hint of unease had crept into her tone.

"Right," I assured her. "I hope your last hurrah met with your expectations."

She smiled and stretched and looked for a moment like a self-satisfied cat. "It sure did. Can I lay here for a bit before I go? I'm so cozy."

"Sure." I wondered if playing with her hair was offside. Probably.

"But to be fair," she went on, rolling onto her back and contemplating the ceiling, "I also trust you. I even like you, to my ongoing surprise. I think that's important for context, too. I don't have to worry that you're going to call me a slut or whatever."

"That's true," I said through an enormous yawn, as I considered the fact that I liked her back—weird. When was the last time I'd made a friend in the real world, outside the Concrete Temple bubble? "I trust you, too. You never called the tabloids."

"I still might," she joked, running her hand down the bed. "Why are your sheets so soft? Why do you have nicer sheets than I do?"

"I bought them at Target. You know how you have your thing where you don't like to share food?" She nodded. "This is my version of that."

"Ah," she said, like she got it. She *did* get it.

Which made me want to say more. "When I was a kid, I

slept on a lumpy futon mattress on the floor. The sheets in our house felt like sandpaper. When I started spending nights at Scott's, I learned about thread count." I made a silly face. "And now I'm a diva when it comes to bedsheets." I was going for humor, but another yawn tanked it.

"You're sleepy," she said.

"That's because I haven't slept yet."

"What do you mean? You didn't sleep last night?"

"Nope."

"And you didn't get a nap in the woods, either," she said with real dismay in her tone. Gretchen's worrying about me was endearing. It had been a long time since anyone besides Auden had done that. Look at me: not only had I apparently made a friend, I'd made a friend who worried about me.

I'd made a friend who worried about me and also gave astonishingly good head.

It was confusing.

"I wrote a song last night." I didn't know why I was telling her, except it sort of felt like I was trying to impress her? Which was ridiculous. Was I twelve?

"Good for you. You did it." She sounded genuinely thrilled.

My inner twelve-year-old preened.

"What's it called?"

That gave me pause. If anything, I would have expected her to exhort me to play it. People did that. Or ask me what it was about—they did that, too. But no, she only wanted to know the title.

"It's called…" I hesitated, but I wasn't sure why. The song had been inspired by my secret nickname for her, but she didn't know about that. " 'Sweet and Sour.' "

"Like the sauce?" She laughed.

"Yeah, but it's just a placeholder." I did that: stuck too-literal titles on songs and later decided to be a little less Captain Obvious and changed them.

Anyway, the song wasn't about Gretchen, per se. I'd been thinking about "Lemon Tree." The idea of a lemon flower smelling sweet but the fruit being sour. And about how first impressions are often incorrect. Sure, Gretchen had been the example I'd been thinking about when it came to first impressions, but that just meant she'd been the vehicle for getting my head out of my ass and notes on paper.

Which, come to think of it, sounded an awful lot like saying she was my muse. She'd joked that our sleeping together might turn her into my muse, but apparently I didn't need to sleep with her for that.

All right, I needed to calm down. Slow my roll. It was one song.

And this was one hurrah. A last one, to use her terminology.

"Hey," I said by way of changing the subject, "I never asked you, how is Tristan working out?"

"He's…"

"If he sucks, you can tell me." I felt bad now, for sticking her with him. I hadn't been thinking about how he would actually do in the performance she was creating. I'd only been thinking of making him do something he wouldn't like. Which was actually kind of a dick move. Why had I done that?

It was confusing—why was everything to do with Gretchen so confusing?—and I was so tired. I yawned again.

"I should go," she said suddenly, and I wanted to know what had happened to lying here for a while. What had happened to cozy? But what could I say? I had signed up for a last hurrah, not a cuddle session.

"I'll see you tomorrow?" she asked as she shimmied into her yoga pants.

I shamelessly ogled her butt while she did so and felt a pang when it was tucked away under a layer of spandex. "Yeah."

"Were you serious about going to sunrise circle?"

"Yeah." I paused. "Pick me up?" Was that too much like a date?

She paused. "Sure."

"But we're not going to tell them about the kissing," I said. I wasn't sure if I was asking or telling. If I was asking, I wasn't sure what I wanted the answer to be.

"God, no. Or about..." She waved her hand between us. "The last hurrah."

"Noted."

As I drifted off, I experienced a small pang of regret over the fact that we hadn't kissed—like, on the mouth. Maybe I had erred too much in the direction of "clinical."

I fell asleep thinking about lemons.

———

I stayed asleep until I awoke to another round of knocking on my door. Three sets of knocks over the past two weeks. It sounded like a fairy tale—weren't things always happening in threes in those stories? The first time Gretchen had knocked, I'd rudely turned her away. The second, I'd slept with her. What would the third knock be met with? A proposal of marriage?

"I came early because I thought you might not be ready," she said, and God bless her, she was holding two coffees. "I saw that your light never went on last night, and I wondered if you fell asleep at some point while it was still light and then slept through." She paused. "I am aware this makes me sound like a creepy stalker, but, happily, due to the whole context thing, I don't have to care."

"Well, you got it exactly right, and I probably wouldn't have woken up, so thanks." Sleeping for unreasonably long stretches of time—that was another thing that happened in fairy tales. I nodded at a cardboard box she was carrying. "What's that?"

"I noticed you missed dinner last night—look at me, still a creepy stalker; still don't care—so I got you some food."

My stomach rose up and began singing the "Hallelujah" chorus. All I'd eaten since that McDonald's drive-through a lifetime ago was a few almonds. "You are an angel." I nodded at the glider on my porch. "Give me two minutes to tame my hair, and I'll meet you out here."

"Sorry no sushi or Caesar salad," she said, passing me a takeout box as I sat beside her. She had brought me eggs and pancakes from the dining hall, and never had cafeteria food smelled so good.

I started shoveling it in. I didn't care that I probably looked like a Neanderthal. When I felt like I was maybe not going to die of starvation after all, I slowed down and eyed her. "How're you doing there, Miller?"

She flashed me a somewhat sheepish smirk. "I'm great. I slept really well last night. Did you?"

"Sure did."

"Oh, you've got your off-brand Crocs on," she said, looking down at my sandal-clad feet. "Do you like them?"

They were ugly, but comfortable. "Sure do."

"Well, aren't you agreeable this morning?"

I didn't like the idea of being thought of as agreeable. Yeah, I'd survived a brush with death and had some mind-blowing sex, but I was still me. I grunted and shoveled in the last bite of pancakes.

When we got to sunrise circle, things felt...different. Marion gave me a wave, and Caleb asked how I was doing after the drama of getting lost. There were some whispers among some of the kids, but I guessed that was to be expected.

As the proceedings got underway, the artists sat back and observed as the kids and counselors did their things, which mostly amounted to a lot of peppy chanting and clapping. Not my scene, but I could, objectively, appreciate that it was probably fun if you were a kid. A normal kid.

And it was nice to be up in the cool morning air. It was nice to feel like I was part of something, as lame as that sounded. I wasn't sure if it was all the cheering and shit, or if it was the presence of a lot of artistically minded people, but there was a kind of charge to the air, a creative energy permeating the scene.

I used to feel that way in the studio when we were recording. I hadn't felt that on the last album. For the first time, I allowed myself what felt like a not unreasonable hope that I would feel it again someday.

Afterward, I found the music counselors. They were college kids. One played a ton of instruments, and the other was an opera singer in training. Because I had apparently taken leave of my senses, I said, "Hey, do we maybe want to get everyone to play something together for the final performance? Or is that too much like a high school band?"

"Something fun," the band guy said.

"Definitely something fun, light," the opera girl said. "It

could be the finale, after their individual pieces. They're all—mostly—working so hard on those."

I wondered if that "mostly" was about Tristan. " 'Bohemian Rhapsody'?" I suggested. "It's long, so we can rotate instrumental kids through solos. We can build to a sing-along with the audience—everyone loves that song." I turned to the opera girl. "Maybe you can take the falsetto bit and really do it up."

They were into it, and we made plans to start rehearsing. Later, though—I needed to take a step back before I stumbled my way into a participation trophy. I was still me, after all.

10
THE LEMON TREE

Gretchen

Teddy showed up at swimming on Monday afternoon. I would have said I was surprised, but somehow, the unexpected from him was starting to feel...expected.

I was holding on to the edge of a floating dock and chatting with Maiv, who had a kickboard, when I heard him talking to Caleb and Danny on the beach. As with the campfire the other day—which felt like a lifetime ago, maybe because it had happened before we got lost in the woods—he just appeared, as if it were normal for him to be here, inserting himself into the scene all low-key-like. I didn't say anything, merely noted his presence—and hoped I was doing so without blushing.

Maiv noticed him, too. "Looks like your boyfriend is here."

"What?" I sputtered. "He's not my boyfriend!"

"OK," she said mildly.

"Sheesh. Are you in junior high?" But inside I was panicking. Had she seen me skulking into—or out of—Teddy's cabin yesterday? I had taken pains to make sure the coast was clear before darting across the path. "Why are you saying that?"

"No reason."

"There is too a reason. You don't say something like that without a reason!"

"Who's in junior high again?"

I rolled my eyes.

"There really isn't a reason. I just get the sense that you two are suddenly kinda cozy. You showed up together at sunrise circle this morning."

"You weren't even there!"

"I heard."

"Oh my God!" The idea that people were talking about us was mortifying.

"And now he's here, when he hasn't shown any interest in swimming to date."

I was tempted to tell her that he had been swimming, once. I wondered why he hadn't been back after that one morning.

Did I *want* him to be back? Wasn't the whole point of my morning swim that it was a solo activity?

"Well," I said, returning to the defense I was mounting, "he's not here because of me, and in no way, shape, or form is he my boyfriend. You will recall that I'm here to get over boys. To transition into—"

"Yeah, yeah, you're here to become a crone."

"Which you said was cool! You said you were going to paint me!" Maiv and I had tromped out on one of the hiking paths, and she had taken a bunch of photos of me in all my croney glory because, she said, she was going to make a painting for the urban/wild series she was working on. I had been honored because most of her paintings didn't include people.

"Maybe becoming a crone is like becoming a nun," Maiv said. "You can change your mind, up to a certain point. Like, in *Sound of Music*, Maria's what? A postulant? And she decides not to renounce the material world after all."

"Oh for God's sake. There is nothing happening with me and Teddy. Being lost in the woods together inspired us to reach a kind of...détente." Détente with orgasms. Which still didn't make him my boyfriend.

"OK," she said again, with more of that maddening mildness.

I wasn't sure why I was being so secretive. Maiv and I had become close. We were camp friends. Of course, when Marion had introduced the concept, she'd been talking about the kids, but Maiv and I were on an accelerated track, friendshipwise.

I didn't have any experience with camp friends. Maybe you didn't tell your camp friends about your secret hookups.

Maybe Teddy was my camp boyfriend.

No. No. Teddy was my last hurrah. Past tense. One and done. Slam, bam, thank you, sir.

All right. I needed to get my shit together and stop thinking about Teddy. I had a video call later with my contractor. Justin couldn't start the job until after I took possession, obviously, but I had taken Rory's advice and set him up to do one of my walk-throughs on the property so we could start making a plan.

And speaking of Rory, she was joining Justin for the walk-through. I'd invited her because she knew me so well. I figured having her there was almost as good as being there myself. But her knowing me so well was going to cut both ways. I was half-afraid she was going to lay eyes on me and have some kind of ESP-fueled vision of what had gone on in Teddy's cabin last night.

"Well, that's it for me," Maiv said. "You staying in?"

We'd been in the water a long time—my fingers were prunes—but I wasn't ready to face Teddy in front of everyone.

If they were gossiping about us, I wasn't keen on fanning the flames. If this was even a fraction of what Teddy felt like when he was in the tabloids, did I ever sympathize with the guy. And honestly, I needed to get him out of my brain before I saw Rory.

"I'm going to stay out for a bit. But give me your kickboard if you don't mind."

I ducked under the floating rope that marked the boundary of the swimming area, paddled out a way, and pressed the board down under the surface so I could balance my butt on it. Sitting in the lake, watching the clouds go by. I loved this.

After a few minutes, I heard someone approaching but didn't turn.

Please don't let it be him.

Please let it be him.

Wow, I was all over the place.

"Hey, Miller."

"Hi!" I squeaked. So much for getting him out of my brain.

"How is it that you're managing to levitate in the water without any apparent effort? Is this part of your crone training? Witches don't drown, right?"

"Ha. No." I dismounted from my kickboard and showed him my trick.

"Ah." He had a board, too. He pressed it down and let it pop up dramatically. When I didn't react, he said, "Am I interrupting?"

"No, no." I gestured to the water next to me. "Have a seat." Once he got himself settled, I, apparently deciding to state the obvious, said, "You have a lot of tattoos."

I knew that, of course, having had three occasions now to see him shirtless. But the first had been dark—he'd been illuminated only by the light of his own phone as I spied on him.

The second had been that early-morning swim, and he hadn't been close enough to see. And of course there'd been yesterday. What can I say about yesterday? I guess I'd been too distracted for tattoo inspection.

And really, it wasn't that I hadn't *seen* them; it was that I wanted to know what they *meant*.

"Yeah," he said. "The ink got a bit addictive for a while there."

"What's this one?" I probably shouldn't touch him, given that our hurrah was over, but I reached a hand out and grazed a pair of letters—*AK*—near his collarbone.

"My sister's initials—Auden Knight."

That was sweet, but I suspected he wouldn't want to hear that. "She's named after a poet, too."

"Yep. Our mom was...a real piece of work."

I didn't know what to say. It wasn't a surprise given what he'd said about his childhood, but I wasn't sure if I should pry. So I moved my hand over his shoulder and down his upper arm, where there was another tattoo. He shivered. I wanted to flatter myself that it was my touch, but it was probably the cold of the deep lake. "This one is waves?"

"It's meant to represent this pool my sister and I spent a lot of time in when we were kids." He paused and tilted his face to the sky. "It was more than a pool. It was...a refuge. Also a place to shower."

"Ah." I understood, and when he said, "Yep," I knew that he knew I understood.

It was an interesting sensation, having this kind of short-hand with someone about our deprived childhoods—to be so easy about something that generally made me feel vulnerable and defensive.

He twisted and showed me, unprompted, a tattoo on his other arm.

"That looks like an intersection in New York?" I asked.

"It's the location of my bandmate Scott's parents' apartment. Ex-bandmate. They...they were good to me at a time in my life when I didn't have any adults I could rely on."

Well. The Scott plot thickened. "Are you still in touch with them?"

"That's a good question. I guess I'm not. My interactions with them were always via Scott, so..."

"They're your ex-in-laws, basically."

He huffed a bitter laugh. "I guess your divorce analogy wasn't so far off."

"And this?" I pointed to some music notes.

"A bar from the first song we wrote that got radio airplay. But also just music generally."

"Are these all..." The idea had just popped into my head, but I didn't know if I should verbalize it. I was probably reading too much into a bunch of tattoos. But hell, Teddy and I had told each other a lot of personal shit, to my ongoing surprise. "Are these the things that saved you?"

He didn't even hesitate. "Yeah."

I experienced a rush of pleasure at my crack forensic psycho-analytic skills, but doubt crept in. Why was I being so nosy?

Time to change the subject. "What did you do today?"

What did you do today? I regretted the question the moment it was out of my mouth. What did I think? I was his girlfriend? And more importantly, did I care what he'd done today?

He didn't say anything. Fair enough. It had been a stupid question, and he didn't owe anyone, including me, an accounting of his day. "Look at that cloud." I pointed. "It looks like a horse."

He eyed the cloud in question, but he said, "Today I tried to play this song called 'Lemon Tree' on the keyboard in my cabin."

Ooh. The "Lemon Tree" mystery. "Yeah?" I said, trying to pitch my tone as interested but not too interested. "I know that song." Of course, I left out that I only knew it because I'd eavesdropped on his conversation with his student a week and a bit ago and then gone on an investigative deep dive. "Peter, Paul and Mary, right?"

"There are several versions of it, but yeah. My mom was obsessed with that Peter, Paul and Mary recording. You know them, right? We sang a bunch of their songs at the campfire the other night."

"Right. You're having a 1960s protest-movement-music moment."

"Apparently I am. My mom grew a lemon tree in a pot. It was inspired by the song. I always thought it was ironic because the song warns against love and attachment, right? But she was obsessed with that tree. It was the center of our lives. It gave one lemon, once, when I was maybe ten or eleven. It never fruited again, though it never died. She bought all kinds of special plant food for it. She would decorate it for Christmas. In the summer, she'd make us carry it down five flights of stairs every day so it could get sun, and then back up every night. In the winter, when the heat got cut off, she'd put it in the prime spot next to this electric heater we ran off a generator. It used to...well, it used to enrage me." He was still looking at the horse cloud, and he seemed truly perplexed. "I don't even know why. It was just a tree."

The why of it seemed pretty clear to me. "She was buying plant food, but not human food. She prioritized a tree over you, her child."

He blew out a breath and nodded. "I don't know why it smarted so much, though, because she did that in all kinds of ways."

"Maybe because the tree was a physical object. A tangible manifestation of her screwed-up priorities. Possibly also because it was so absurd—a lemon tree in New York. It's already a lost cause."

"She was Don Quixote tilting at windmills," he said.

"Don Quixote tilting at windmills while her children raised themselves and fucking starved." My voice had gone all vehement there, and it must have startled him. He transferred his attention from the sky to me.

"It's shameful," I said, and I didn't care if I sounded overly invested. Teddy and I might have gotten off to a rocky start, but as with the Concrete Temple "divorce," I was firmly on Team Teddy now.

I really needed to tell him about my ill-fated date with Scott. It was starting to feel like I was keeping something from him, something he had a right to know.

"Still," he said, "I don't want to be the kind of person whose every move is secretly motivated by the fact that his mommy hurt his feelings."

"Well, I think that's unfair to trauma sufferers worldwide, and I think you're talking about a lot more than hurt feelings, but I understand." I hesitated over whether I should say more. Who did I think I was? A shrink? *His* shrink?

No, I was a wannabe crone, and crones didn't censor themselves. "I just think maybe the way to not be someone whose every move is secretly motivated by the fact that his mother hurt him is to stop resisting."

"What do you mean?"

"Let the feeling—your mom was shitty to you; she hurt you—be. Let yourself feel it. Lean into it, even. Then maybe you can discharge it and it will have less power. Resisting something can take a lot of energy, can make it more important than it is—or than you want it to be. But if you let yourself feel it, maybe you'll be able to let it go?"

"I don't think I can let myself feel it without talking to my sister."

"Then talk to your sister."

"What if *she's* not ready to feel it?"

"There's only one way to find out." I paused. "But also, what do I know? Don't listen to me."

"I think you know a lot."

I was stupidly pleased by that statement. "So you say you *tried* to play 'Lemon Tree'? What does that mean? You don't remember it?"

"Oh, I remember it."

"Where's your mom now?" I asked when he didn't elaborate about the song. "If you don't mind my asking. Have you ever, I don't know, tried to confront her?"

"I have no idea where she is. The last time I saw her, we had a huge fight over the tree. I'd forgotten to bring it upstairs, and she wanted me to go down and get it. I was in my pajamas and ready for bed, so I refused. Well, I refused until Auden got up to do it. So I did go down for it, but it was like something inside me had snapped. Like I could see the Matrix all of a sudden, you know? She was never going to give us any of the stuff a mother is supposed to give her kids. And I'm not just talking about food and shelter and all that."

"So you left after that?"

"No, she did. My reckoning was more internal. I wouldn't have left until Auden was done with high school, but at that moment, I understood that there was no point in trying to please my mom. Or trying to get her to be decent to us. Or…whatever it was I was doing; I'm not even sure. The point is, I gave up. Maybe she could sense it; maybe she somehow knew she didn't have any hold over me anymore. Regardless, she left that night—she said she was going out, but she never came back. Looking back, it was one of those *You can't fire me; I quit* scenarios."

"What! Did you try to find her?"

"Initially we assumed she'd turn up eventually. She sometimes disappeared, but usually only for a few days at a time, max. That time, though, a couple of weeks went by with no word from her, and one day we came home from school to find the tree gone. So we knew she'd been back to get it, and that she was really gone—for good."

"What?" This was all so egregious, I was having trouble wrapping my mind around it. "What did you do? How old were you?"

"We didn't do anything. We stayed in the apartment. She already wasn't paying rent. It was May, so the heat wasn't an issue. It was spring of my senior year, so I finished school and we stayed through the summer. Without my mom rallying everyone against the landlord—I guess she was good at something—the eviction notices eventually came with police. So Auden and I got a shitty studio apartment in Brownsville.

I was working full-time days to pay the rent and trying to make the band work at night. She was only a year behind me in school, so she kept going—and she got a part-time job, too. She was smarter than I was, so she got into NYU with a bunch of scholarships, and she figured out legally how to demonstrate that our mom had abandoned us, so that made her eligible for financial aid."

"And then the band took off, and she became an actuary, and now it's all fine."

"Maybe."

I wasn't sure what that meant. Perhaps that things were fine financially—which was the sense I'd meant—but not fine in other ways.

"I literally hadn't thought about that song for years. But then on my first night here I was standing in the dark in my cabin looking at that keyboard, and it just...rose up inside me. I think remembering it is what sparked the sixties-protest-music renaissance I seem to be experiencing. And I say 'seem to be experiencing' because it really does feel like something that's happening *to* me rather than something that I'm consciously doing. But even though I'm a regular Arlo Guthrie these days, I can't get through that particular song without...well, without feeling ill. I play the first few measures, and then I have to stop. So that's a very long answer to what I meant when I said I was 'trying' to play it."

"You're playing around it, or playing your way up to it."

"Maybe so." He shook his head and lifted an arm out of the water. "So yeah, that's the story of the ink." He was signaling that we were done with this conversation.

I took the cue and said, teasingly, "You and all your deep tattoos. And here I thought rock stars had tattoos of, like, badass dragons and shit. Or Chinese characters they think mean 'fierce' but actually mean 'rainbows.'"

He laughed, which was gratifying. And also my chance to take my leave. "I gotta get out." I held up my pruney fingers. "I have a FaceTime with my contractor tonight. He's doing a walk-through of my new building." I made a face. "So I have to turn my phone on."

He made a sympathetic face.

"Yeah, I'm about to spend a shockingly large sum of borrowed money on a risky new venture—I close on the purchase next month—and I haven't figured out a way to do that without a cell phone." I popped off my kickboard.

"Reality rears its ugly head."

Didn't I know it, Teddy Knight. Didn't I know it.

———

I thought about what Teddy had said as I showered and dressed. I thought about what he'd said as I grabbed dinner from the dining hall, and as I ate it in my cabin. I thought about it as I unearthed the planner that held my notes on the new building—skimming them made me feel like I was an archeologist discovering records of a past civilization.

Well, no, really I thought about *him*. Kid Teddy hauling that lemon tree up and down five stories. But also adult Teddy floating in the lake and just…opening himself. Telling me about his tattoos as if I were a person worthy of his confidences.

Not going to lie, I was also thinking about those tattoos in a purely aesthetic sense.

Also in the I-want-to-put-my-mouth-on-them sense.

But we'd had our last hurrah.

And it was good to remember that while we'd had fun, this was what was real. The studio. Studios, plural. This was my life.

I had to plug my very dead phone in and wait for it to come back to life. I was tempted to read the 207 emails and thirty-two texts I had notifications for, but I resisted. I had autoreplies on everything. This was only a quick dip back into reality.

"She lives!" Rory exclaimed when FaceTime connected. "Are you really not using your phone at all?"

"Not at all!" I confirmed. "It was completely dead, and I'm having to talk to you with it charging."

"Hey, Gretchen," Justin said. "Are you having a good summer?"

"I am, but I'm on pins and needles here. How does it look?"

"Everything looks good as far as I can see. There's just one thing we may have to worry about." He reversed his phone camera and pointed it at a spot where it appeared he'd removed some of the drop-tile ceiling and exposed the ductwork. "You see this tape?" He moved the phone and showed me a piece of yellow-brown tape.

"Yes?"

"That's asbestos tape."

"Ooh, that's bad, right?"

"It's fine as long as it's undisturbed, which it has been under the ceiling. But now that we're going to expose it, we have to get rid of it. And I don't do that."

"Who does?"

"Remediation specialists."

"Who are expensive, I'm assuming? Though how expensive can it be to take off some tape?"

"It's not the tape part so much, but they have to build a barrier and create a negative pressure situation, wear protective gear—it's a whole deal."

"Well, shit. Do I have asbestos tape in my dance studio? Why don't I remember this being a thing?"

"Your existing studio is in a building that's too new to have asbestos in it."

Justin had done the work on my studio when I'd first leased the space and needed to change it from a hair salon to a dance studio, cutting me a bit of a deal because I was so young and so clearly broke—and because he'd just been starting out himself. Look at us now, embarking on a giant-ass job complete with asbestos.

"Asbestos was more a thing mid–twentieth century," he went on. "Clearly someone did a reno on this place around that time—hence the ugly drop ceiling."

"So we have to deal with this."

"We do. I mean, I guess you could ask the seller to remediate it."

"I think that ship has sailed; that should have been part of the negotiation process. Why didn't the inspector tell me about this?"

"He should have flagged it." He shrugged. "But it's not the worst problem to have. It's probably going to be a few thousand bucks, and it's going to delay my start a bit, but it's not the end of the world."

"You know how you watch those reno shows on HGTV and there's always some catastrophic surprise, like black mold or something that's disastrously not to code?" He rolled his eyes to express what he thought of those shows. "You're saying this is not that."

"This is not that. With a place like this, you never know what people have been doing to it over the years until you pop the hood. This is what you get when you buy a building that's more than a hundred years old."

This was what you got when you bought a building that was more than a hundred years old in an attempt to cure a midlife crisis.

"It's got good bones, though." Justin started walking around, but his camera was still reversed. It was wild to see the space after so long away from it. From the idea of it, even. I guess the woods had really done their work.

Last time I'd been to the new building, on one of the visits I'd made when I was thinking about buying, the space had looked more like the out-of-business clothing store it had been. But now the racks and fixtures were gone, as was the huge cash desk that used to sit along one of the sidewalls. I guess the seller was getting a jump on getting rid of all that stuff.

What had once been the bones of an old store was now a blank box.

I owned this blank box. It was mine. Or at least it would be on August 31.

"I had a peek under the carpet," Justin said, pulling back a corner of the God-knew-how-old wall-to-wall gray carpet. "I'd been hoping for hardwood, but no dice."

"Yeah, but old hardwood is usually too wonky and uneven for dancing." Though maybe not for yoga. I wasn't sure about that.

Shit. Did I know enough about yoga to be opening a yoga studio?

"The underflooring seems like it's in good shape from what I can see," Justin said. "It will be easy enough to lay down wood, or laminate. We can talk about options, and costs.

"I do think you might consider swapping the dance and yoga areas," he went on. "At least based on the square footage estimates you gave me." He panned along the exposed-brick sidewall. "We can run a hallway down here." He walked toward the back of the building. "And then we can mount those Pilates machines to this wall." He gestured at the back wall, which was also brick.

"Yeah, but my thinking was that from the street, if people see a yoga or Pilates class going on, it will lead to walk-ins, whereas my dance clientele is going to follow me, and that side of the business is more word of mouth anyway." I relaxed a bit. I might not know anything about yoga, but I knew marketing.

"Ah. I get it. Well, we can make it work either way. And I know you want to leave the second floor as-is for now, but I was thinking those small rooms would only need some fresh paint and you could rent them out as massage rooms, or something like that."

He wasn't wrong. The second floor of my building contained a kitchen, a large room I was planning to use as an office, and two little rooms I'd vaguely thought I might someday combine into a small studio I could use for private lessons.

"Anyway, that would be an easy fix," Justin said. "You can keep it in mind. We still good to walk through together on August fifteenth?"

When I first hatched the idea to buy a new place and expand my offerings, I'd been filled with excitement. Just a month ago, when I was describing it to the loan officer at the bank, he'd remarked that my enthusiasm was palpable.

Now I was filled with…I wasn't even sure. Trepidation, in part. But to be fair, that was probably a logical response to asbestos.

Justin had turned the phone back around and was awaiting my response.

"Yes," I said. "The fifteenth."

"I'll bring some flooring samples now that I have a sense of the space," Justin said.

"With all the store junk gone, you can really imagine the new studio here," said Rory, who'd been with me and my Realtor on my initial viewing.

You really could. I could picture it perfectly: the new studio. My future.

I wanted to sign off. I wanted to go for another swim, though I'd only been out of the water for a couple hours. Or maybe I could round up some people for a campfire. I wanted to get out of this limbo, was the point, this spot where I was half in one world and half in another.

But Rory wouldn't let me. "Don't mothball your phone yet. I'm going to call you from my car. Stand by."

I sighed and waited for the incoming call. I tried to get back into my fun BFF groove. "Yes?" I said, making a silly face when I picked up the FaceTime.

"What's wrong with you?"

"What do you mean?"

She raised her eyebrows.

"Nothing's wrong with me!"

"You didn't seem very excited."

"I guess it's hard through a phone screen. You probably need to see it in context to really appreciate it."

There was that word again, Teddy's word: *context*.

"Well," Rory said, "it looks amazing. Now that it's empty, it's so much bigger than I realized." She shot me another weird look. "So you're liking it there? You must be if you've completely abandoned your phone. I have to say, I thought you were going to be calling me constantly, fretting over the new studio—and the existing one."

"I thought I would, too, but I don't know, I guess I really embraced the challenge of immersing myself here."

" 'Here' being camp? The woods? The dance stuff you're doing?"

Good question. "All of the above," I said, because I didn't want to talk about it. I wanted to get back to it. To "here," whatever it was.

It did occur to me that maybe the pull I was feeling wasn't *to* anything—to the woods, or to Wild Arts, or to *Little Women*, but *away*. From Miss Miller's of Minnetonka. From my new building. From my life.

But that wasn't a possibility.

"Anyway," I said, "I knew you'd call the camp if you ran into any trouble, so I've been assuming everything is fine."

"Yeah, yeah, everything's fine."

"And how's the chicken nugget?"

"Chicken nugget" is what we called her baby-to-be.

She groaned, and we talked about the unpleasantness of late pregnancy for a while.

"What do you keep looking at?"

"Sorry." I hadn't realized it, but I was looking out the window. "Just distracted by the trees—my cabin has a killer forest view," I said, realizing that I'd never told her about being lost in the woods. It was weird that I hadn't, and I wasn't opposed to doing so, but I wasn't going to do it now.

When we hung up, I turned off the phone, stashed it in my empty suitcase, and considered the concept of context. Teddy had remarked that we didn't know each other in context— meaning in the real world. That was why it had been so easy for me to have sex with him—to have sex with him in a way that allowed me to really get into it. Really let go. I hadn't cared

about how I was being perceived, either physically or emotionally. And why was that? Because this place had an end date. It
was outside of reality. There had been no stakes, was what it
boiled down to.

As a thought experiment, I considered whether sleeping with
Teddy once at Wild Arts and calling it my last hurrah would
be any different from sleeping with him for the duration of
my time at Wild Arts and calling it my last hurrah. What was
different about today versus yesterday in this place that was
already outside of time and reality?

Nothing.

I burst out of the door before I could talk myself out of it,
but came to a dead stop on my porch when I realized we still
had the condom problem.

The camp store had closed at five, and how likely was it that
a store at a camp for kids would have condoms to begin with?
I might be able to get one from one of the other artists, but
who? Maiv would be my obvious first choice, but she wasn't
getting it on with anyone here. At least as far as I knew—I did
entertain the idea that if I was having secret rendezvous, other
people could be, too. Still, I thought Maiv was a long shot when
it came to condom procurement, and I wasn't sure it was worth
outing myself for those odds.

Jack, I decided. He was exactly the kind of guy who would
pack condoms for his writing retreat. And he would be less
likely than anyone else to interrogate me about why I wanted
one.

He answered my knock with his eyebrows raised. I had
probably interrupted the writing of a Pulitzer-worthy sentence.

"Do you have a condom I could borrow?" I asked, deciding
to cut to the chase.

I'd expected a reaction of some sort, but he merely nodded and disappeared back into his cabin.

"I don't think 'borrow' is the correct word, though," he said when he returned with a little square packet. "I don't think I want it back."

There was the reaction. "Ha ha." I glanced down at it. "'Ribbed for her pleasure.' Wow, I wouldn't have thought you were the type to care about her pleasure."

"Maybe insulting the person who's lending—giving—you a condom isn't the best course of action here."

He was right. "Yeah, yeah. OK, thanks, Jack. I appreciate it."

I went back to my cabin after that, in case he was watching me. I needed to put on a hoodie, anyway. I made myself wait five minutes before heading out again.

"Hi," I said as Teddy swung open his door and looked me up and down. He was still wearing his swim trunks from before—they had dried—and he'd added his own hoodie on top. He was barefoot. I bit my lip. There was something about his feet, casually bare on the scuffed wood floor of the cabin, that seemed almost painfully intimate. Like I was getting a glimpse of Teddy Knight at rest, a rare thing most people never got to do. My stomach lurched with a mixture of lust and fear. "I know I said that there was only going to be one occurrence of horizontal hugging, but—eep!"

If I'd been unsure how Teddy was going to react to being propositioned again, I needn't have been: he literally picked me up and hauled me over the threshold, kicking the door shut behind us. I emitted yet another unflattering squeak when it became clear that he wasn't going to set me down, that he was, in fact, transporting us directly to bed. A shiver of anticipation radiated through me as I hitched my legs around his waist.

"Do you have a condom?" he asked as he walked backward toward the bed.

"I do!"

"This is better than when you brought me breakfast." His voice was low and a little bit growly. And a lot sexy. I was excited for this solo album of his—Concrete Temple had been wasting all that vocal talent relegating it to the background.

At the bed, I thought he'd turn and set me down, but he backed himself up against it and fell back, taking me with him.

I stared at him. He stared back.

I couldn't read his expression until he suddenly started laughing.

"What?" I told myself there was no reason to be offended. The man had literally carried me to bed.

"This." He grabbed the tie of my hoodie. "This very alluring getup you have now worn twice in your wily attempts to seduce me. I'm beginning to think this is a covert operation."

"Of course it's a covert operation! I don't want people to get the wrong idea."

His expression grew quizzical. "Which is what?"

Was he an idiot? "That we're together! Romantically, I mean!"

"We're together sexually but not romantically?" He undid the tie of my hoodie. "I'm just clarifying."

"We're not *together* sexually. I mean, we're sleeping together, but out of expediency."

"Maybe some mutual attraction is involved, too?" He looked amused. "Just a smidge?"

"Of course it is. But you know what I mean. There's a difference between having sex and 'being together' sexually."

"I see." His smile grew wicked. He slid his fingers under the ruched edge of my hood. "May I de-hood you now?"

"You may de-everything me now."

He did, and holy shit, I was afraid that from this day forward, the sound of a zipper slowly being lowered was going to send me into a fit of lust. He kept eye contact the whole way as the metallic zipper teeth gradually clicked open, and I swear, that mofo slowed down even more just to torture me.

I wasn't wearing anything under the hoodie—hope had sprung eternal back at my cabin when I was waiting my five minutes—and when he finally deigned to finish with the zipper, he drew open the two sides of the hoodie.

"Fuck," he muttered, and he looked angry as he stared at my chest. Which was, somehow, flattering.

"That's the idea," I said with exaggerated cheeriness, purely because I knew the juxtaposition with his cranky intensity would annoy him.

There was a moment where we stared at each other, teetering. Then it started. I wasn't even sure how, or who fired the starting gun, but the rest of the disrobing was as fast as the unzipping had been slow. We were jointly tearing at clothing—our own, each other's. I was frantic with a lust that was almost menacing, feeling like if I didn't get his skin on my skin—if I didn't get him inside me—it was going to be bad news. He must have felt the same—he was shoving everything that was in our way to the floor.

"Hurry," I panted as he slid out from under me and off the bed so he could struggle with his swim trunks. "The condom is in the pocket of that hoodie you yeeted across the room."

He stumbled away, tripping over his trunks, which were still on one leg, cursing like a sailor. It would have been comical if I hadn't been so wound up.

Then he was back, trunksless and condom-ified, and his eyes

were smoldering. Like he was Fabio or something. I reclined, and he paused, hovering over me. He actually looked kind of distressed, but I glanced down at his erection and decided he couldn't be *that* distressed. So I grabbed him around the waist with my legs and pulled him toward me.

"We should kiss this time," he said through a groan. "On the mouth."

"We should kiss next time," I said, pulling harder, causing him to groan harder.

"But dude," he said, sounding rather strangled. "Foreplay."

"But dude," I echoed, shaking my head. "No thanks."

He slid in, and I swear to God, his eyes started to roll back into his head, which made me positively giddy with the sense of my own power—or it would have if I hadn't been so flattened by lust. It made my brain heavy, my thoughts slow.

There was something about Teddy—well, let's be honest, there was something about Teddy's dick—that was just right. It was the angle between us, maybe. Or it was the way that instead of hovering over me and doing the classic jackhammer, he lay on top of me and rocked with relatively shallow thrusts. Whatever it was, it created a continuous pressure on my clit that had me so agitated I almost—almost—wanted to get away. But there was no getting away; there was just more of that relentless heaviness. The only thing to do was surrender to it…and come.

Oh! And come again!

"Fuck."

He was back to swearing, but I couldn't concern myself with him, beyond making sure that he didn't stop, that he didn't change anything about the angle or the pressure or the magic or whatever the hell it was that he was doing. "Keep going!" I ordered. "Don't change anything."

"Uhn," he grunted—in a way that seemed to signal acknowledgment.

Oh holy God, I was having a third orgasm. "Three!" I exclaimed in disbelief as my hips shook. Except they didn't shake. They were still pinned by Teddy's hips, which I suspected was part of what was making this all happen. They were shaking and still at the same time. Like there was a shaking inside me that he was…in charge of, somehow.

When the shuddering stopped, I was able to be less ruthlessly inwardly focused. I eyed him.

I hadn't realized he was watching me like a hawk. I grinned, and though I was pretty sure it was a goofy grin and not a sexy one, it seemed to summon something inside him. He shouted, "God damn it, fuck." With a great big groan to end all groans, he froze, and his body quaked with…I wasn't sure what. An orgasm, obviously, but it seemed like more than that. The effort of holding himself up on his arms over me all this time. Or maybe of holding back while I came—three!—times. I actually had no idea how long that had taken. Time had ceased to be real for me while it was happening.

With a final, soft "Fuck," he heaved himself to his side, but he left one leg and one arm slung over me. He was sweating—we both were. We were breathing heavily, too.

"That was fast," he panted.

I guess it hadn't taken very long. Wait. I started to worry that my three—three!—orgasms had looked too good to be true. They'd *felt* that way. "What are you implying?"

"Nothing!"

"I don't fake orgasms."

"I didn't say you had!"

"I know I told you about that time I faked enthusiasm over miso soup on that terrible date, but I never faked orgasms."

"Nor should you have." He lifted the arm that was slung over me and showed me his palm, a gesture of peace. "I absolutely was not complaining. I was merely making an observation."

"All right. But also, that wasn't normal. On a number of fronts."

He laughed. "What do you mean? Tell me about these fronts."

"Well, first, the only other times I've had more than one orgasm have been by myself." And even then, it hadn't been a frequent occurrence. It had always seemed like a lot of work to chase subsequent ones. They didn't usually just *happen*. But I didn't need to tell him that. He had a big enough ego as it was.

Well, no, that wasn't right. That was my reflexive thought based on my initial impression of him. I needed to stop doing that. It wasn't that he had a big ego so much as he was…a bit prickly. Hmm. People said that about me, sometimes, too. I filed that away to think about later. "Second, normally, the answer to the foreplay question is going to be yes."

"Noted."

"I mean, if we're going to be doing this again," I said hurriedly. I didn't want to assume. I had, after all, given him my crone speech. More than once.

"Oh, we are going to be doing this again."

I feared my grin was as dopey as they came—way worse than the previous one. "Yeah?"

"Are you kidding me?" He grabbed one of my thighs and

slung it over his legs, reversing our positions so he was lying on his back and I was on my side draped over him.

From this angle, I noticed that one of his shoulders was covered in mosquito bites, a dozen or so of them. "Wow." I ran my hand over them.

"Oooh, ohh, do that again but with your nails."

I switched to scratching, and he made comically exaggerated noises of relief. "That batch is from swimming earlier."

"It wasn't dark yet."

"What can I say? I guess you were right: I'm too sweet to resist."

I snorted and stopped scratching. "Back to the concept of doing this again."

"Damn, woman, give me five minutes, maybe?" he teased.

"Not *now*. Just…theoretically. I feel like some clarification is in order."

"By all means, clarify."

"This is still my last hurrah. I'm just being a bit more expansive in how I'm defining that. A camp affair, if you will. I want to put that on record."

"You're saying you don't want me to follow you back to your regular life in Minneapolis and hold a boom box over my head outside your bedroom window?"

"That is exactly what I'm saying."

"No danger of that." He grinned. "But if we're putting things on the record here, allow me to register that I do believe in kissing."

"What?" I laughed. "I'm not sure kissing is something you can believe in or not. It's not like God. Or, I don't know, the COVID vaccine."

"Sure it is. And I believe in it. Therefore, I'm starting to be a

little too aware of the fact that we've had two episodes of horizontal hugging now and there hasn't been any kissing—mouth
kissing, I'm talking about—involved in either of them."

"OK, so there's a work order for next time."

"Yes," he said urgently. "I think next time you should keep
your pants on until there's been a certain amount of kissing."

"What?"

He patted my hip. "You have very...distracting thighs."

"And here I thought I had very large thighs."

"You say that like it's a bad thing."

"Nah. I used to hate them when I was younger. I thought
they were huge. Well, I got told—usually by men—that they
were huge. But I got over it. I'm pretty neutral on my thighs
these days." I guess one thing that being of midlife crisis age
was good for was body neutrality.

"But you didn't get over it with regard to your breasts."

"Huh?"

"You told me yesterday that normally you're insecure about
having small breasts."

That was true. I shrugged. "I contain multitudes." That was
my standard line for when I was contradicting myself.

He smiled. "You sure do."

"Well"—he ramped up his thigh-patting—"there's something insanely hot about muscles that exist for a purpose. And
when you layer on that the purpose of these muscles is dancing?" He blew out a breath.

"What do you mean?"

"Well, you could have muscular thighs if you were, say, a
powerlifter. They would still be hot. But dancing is so...delicate.
No. That's not right. Precise. Like, the thighs power these intri-
cate, specific moves."

"Weirdo."

"I do kind of sound like John Cusack with a boom box now, don't I?" I made a laughing noise of agreement, and he gently slapped my outer hip and added, "I can't help it. You have superhot thighs."

"Well, you have superhot hands." It was out before I could think better of it.

"Really?" He sounded mystified as he held his hands up.

I grabbed one and examined it. "Yeah, the nail polish remnants, the cool rings, and I think these calluses are like my thighs—sexy because they're in service of something delicate. Not that Concrete Temple is delicate. But you know, guitar playing also seems like an exercise in precision."

"Mm."

As before, I wanted to stay. But even with my relaxed rules, staying was a no-go. There wasn't any amount of mental gymnastics that would make sleeping in Teddy Knight's bed, draped over his body, a good idea. I started to heave myself out of bed to go back to my place, but he grabbed me and pulled me back. "What are you doing?" I shrieked. I was laughing, and trying to get away from him, but not very hard. He grunted and maneuvered us so we were arranged in reverse order from when we'd first landed on the bed. I was on my back and he was on top. "I have to go!" I mock protested.

"I know. I know. I'm just getting a jump on the work order for next time."

"What?"

Oh. The light, bantery air around us evaporated, and I knew he was going to kiss me. He tilted his head as if he were contemplating the right way to go about it. He floated a hand down and brushed a strand of hair off my cheek, which, to my embarrassment, made goose bumps rise. He lowered his head slowly—this was the opposite of our mad, frantic coming together earlier—and when his mouth met mine, it was such a strange, profound relief that I sighed into it. His lips were gentle, and chapped. It was a relatively chaste kiss, given what had just gone down, but it felt…important.

Important? What was I on about? I shook my head, breaking the contact between us. But I flashed him a small smile to show that the kiss hadn't been unwelcome. He rolled off me, and I got out of bed.

He didn't speak, just watched me lazily as I got dressed, his long hair fanned out over the pillow. When I had my hand on the doorknob, he said, " 'Lemon Tree' is kind of delicate."

I understood that he was talking about the sorts of songs that would give him calluses, but also about something bigger. Something he was reckoning with. I was measured in my response. "On the one hand, yes, 'Lemon Tree' is delicate." I paused, thinking of the lyrics. "But it's also kind of savage."

―――――

I'm not going to lie, I pretty much walked around camp the rest of the week on cloud nine. I used my apparently superhot thighs during the day to dance, working on recital stuff for my studio and working with the girls on *Little Women*.

At night I wrapped my apparently superhot thighs around Teddy, who had procured a box of condoms from Target. I was in a sex haze. As last hurrahs went, it was pretty great. And happily, my sex haze did not seem to be interfering with my actual work. The dance girls continued to be a source of inspiration and creative energy. Everything felt like it was feeding everything else.

Out of all this creative cross-pollination, something was happening. I didn't know how to put it into words. Maybe words were not the point, because it—whatever "it" was—was coming to me in images. Fragments that would rise up through my mind when I was swimming, or sitting on the porch, or lying next to Teddy in the aforementioned sex haze. Eventually they started assembling themselves into . . . not a story, but little vignettes.

I didn't know what these vignettes meant. I didn't know what to do with them except to let them keep coming, to keep assembling them from the fragments that were floating through my consciousness. They felt like something. I didn't know what, but something.

11
LEAN IN

Teddy

Gretchen and I spent the rest of the week having sex, which was a twist I had not seen coming.

No, correction: Gretchen and I spent the rest of the week having sex when we weren't doing our jobs.

To my surprise, I was increasingly digging my job. The music kids were of wildly varying abilities—none of the others had anywhere near Anna's level of talent—but most of them, if you talked to them for a while, turned out to be cool. It took a certain amount of dedication, of seriousness of purpose, to spend a month in the woods working on your craft.

Don't get me wrong, I was still my usual grumpy self. Anna aside, I was still letting the counselors do the heavy lifting. But I was hanging around at the end of the day when the whole crew worked on "Bohemian Rhapsody." They'd even talked me into playing bass for it.

It was, to my ongoing surprise, fun.

And shit, when was the last time making music had been *fun*?

Anna and I were getting together pretty much every other

day. By the end of week three, I thought it was time to introduce the idea of making a demo I could send to Brady. I hadn't
brought it up after my phone call with him because I'd wanted
to sit with the idea, make sure it felt right—for me and for
Anna. But yeah, this girl was going places, and selfishly, I
wanted to be along for the ride.

She was astounded. "You were serious when you were talking
about me making an album?"

"Yeah, but you can't just 'make an album.' I mean, you can,
but no one will hear it without some kind of deal. I talked to
my manager after we spoke, and he said he'd listen to a demo."

"So I guess you do have a manager," she said wryly.

I smirked. "Turns out I do."

"But...how would this work?"

"We book some studio time, hire some session musicians.
Or maybe not even. Between the two of us, I think we could
play everything. We aim to record maybe half a dozen songs.
'Take It Easy,' but, like you said, mostly originals. If you're OK
with it, I'll start involving myself more in the writing. I've been
holding back a bit, conscious that here, I'm meant to be your
teacher and not your collaborator. They'll still be *your* songs.
But I think I can help—I have some ideas. We'll share songwriting credit with your name first."

I paused, trying to get a sense of how she was taking this.
She looked shocked but not displeased.

"If we don't feel like we have enough songs by the end of
camp," I went on, "which we almost certainly won't, we keep
in touch, send them back and forth. Do some Zoom rehearsals.
Then, when we're ready, we record."

"Where? Where do we do this?"

Good question. I knew studios in New York I could book.

But I could hardly invite a high school girl to crash with me in New York. "Minneapolis. I'll fly in when you're ready. And of course your mom can be there." I sometimes forgot that camp wasn't reality. Which was a bummer—on more than one front. "We'll run this all by her."

"I don't want my mom there."

"Well, someone should be there."

She was looking at me like I had two heads, which I guessed meant she felt safe with me.

"You mean in case you suddenly have a personality transplant and decide to offer me drugs and/or take advantage of me?"

I laughed, but I was stupidly pleased that she thought it would take a personality transplant for me to do something shitty. I was starting to get the feeling that this was going to work. Not just musically, but that Anna and I were going to mesh as collaborators in the real world, outside the creative soup of Wild Arts. "You know I'm not going to offer you drugs, and I know I'm not going to offer you drugs, but the world doesn't know I'm not going to offer you drugs. But we can work out the logistics later."

"What's in this for you?"

Ha. She was skeptical. Good for her. "I get to say I discovered Anna Sommer."

"Maybe *you* should be my manager."

"Oh God, no. You don't want that. *I* don't want that. But if you do get to make an album, I'd love to produce it, if you'll have me. And assuming we like working together on the demo."

She blinked rapidly, like she was having trouble assimilating what I was saying.

"You should know I have no experience as a producer. I

mean, I was there for all the Concrete Temple records, obviously, and I had opinions. But I was never *the* producer."

The blinking continued.

"Look, Anna, you're crazy talented. I truly believe you can make a career of this if you want to. I would be thrilled to help however I can. I admit I'm not exactly riding high on my own career right now." Hell, maybe I should join *her* band. "I know people, though. I can get your demo in front of them, and your songs will do the rest. Maybe it's too soon. Maybe you want to finish high school first. You *should* finish high school, whatever happens." Maybe I should have led with that. "But I don't see why you can't do both. It's not like a record deal is going to drop in your lap tomorrow."

"Honestly, I'm a little overwhelmed," she said. "I'm excited, but I never thought about my life going like this. I've been thinking of music as a hobby."

I thought about Tristan and his boundless sense of self-worth. I thought of Gretchen and her dancers and their theory about "girl" songs.

Had I stumbled into becoming a music-industry feminist? Was I the next Jack Antonoff? I chuckled. I could think of worse things.

"Let's focus on what's in front of us, why don't we?" I suggested. "We don't have to make any big decisions right now. Let's just work on the new song. We'd be doing that anyway." She had a song on the go about being the only person in a concert audience not filming the show, and it was awesome. It was a breezy, observational song on the surface, but underneath that, she was saying something about how we choose to experience—or not experience—the world. Like I said, she was a huge talent.

"Yeah, OK." She started strumming but suddenly stopped. "Teddy?"

"Yeah?"

"Thank you."

"No problem," I said, though I was pumped that she was open to the idea of working toward a demo. Like, disproportionately excited. Damn. Camp had made me soft.

————

I was conditioned to pop a semi every time there was a knock on my door, which was awkward because although most of the time the visitor was Sourplum, occasionally it was Jack.

So when a knock came around three in the afternoon on the Saturday of the third week of camp, I untucked my T-shirt and arranged it so it covered the front of my shorts, just in case.

It was Gretchen, but she wasn't wearing her usual spy getup. Which meant either she had dropped her devotion to the covert nature of our liaisons, or she wasn't here for that. I was voting for option A, so I wordlessly stepped back to let her in.

"I can't stay."

Well, that was disappointing.

"But I got you something." She handed me a plastic thing I couldn't identify. It was a small white cylinder with a pump-like mechanism.

"Is this a bicycle pump for a Barbie doll? Or, no, a sex toy for Ken? I mean, he doesn't have genitals, right? So maybe he needs some help?"

She threw her head back and cackled. It was a full-on witchy cackle. She was doing well on her crone-ification mission.

"It's supposed to extract the venom out of mosquito bites." She shrugged. "I went to town with Maiv this morning, and it was in a display near the counter at the drugstore, so I impulse-purchased it."

"That's…" Really nice. I was tickled she had thought of me. It felt like a long time since someone besides Auden had. "Thanks." I had to clear my throat. Damn, I *was* going soft: getting emotional over a mosquito venom pump.

But I was also going hard.

Life with Sourplum was confusing.

I decided to lean into the hard side of things. I was more comfortable there. I waggled my eyebrows. "You sure you can't come in?"

She had "come in" every night this past week, late. I hadn't been sure how weekends were going to work, but I was open to an afternoon delight.

Hell, I would do it anytime, anywhere with Gretchen. I wasn't sure if it was this whole last hurrah/no romance thing making it feel like the stakes were low, or if we just had chemistry, but damn. The woman made me come so hard I sometimes feared I was going to damage myself. And the awesome part was, it seemed to go both ways. She was multiorgasmic, but not, like, in a performative, porny way. It was really something.

"I can't. I'm meeting the dance girls for an extra rehearsal."

"How's it going?"

"Great, except for Tristan. I'm going to fire him today, actually."

I winced. "I'm sorry." I'd given her Tristan because he was a little shit, and had thought of the role as a punishment for him. That wasn't something I was proud of from this vantage point. *Little Women*, but with dancing, from what I'd picked up now that I was more present in the goings-on at camp, was sounding like it was going to be amazing. But even if it wasn't, what kind of person was I that my "help" was less than no help? Why would I give a fellow artist "help" that would hinder her? One interpretation was that I *wanted* to hinder her—or at least that I didn't care about hindering her. That I didn't respect what she was doing.

None of that was true, but that was a reasonable conclusion, given the facts. And the real truth wasn't any more palatable: I'd been so wrapped up in my own angst when I got here that I couldn't see beyond myself. I'd thought of most human interactions as battles. Me versus them. I would have liked to be able to blame that on Scott, but it takes two to tango.

"It's OK," she said in response to my apology.

"It's really not," I said. "I promised you a Laurie, and I got you a shit one."

"I appreciate that. All he has to do is count and spin in this scene—we've made it so he doesn't even have to dance—but he can't do it. *Won't* do it. Worse, he's doing these little 'subtle' sneers at my girls. I'd been trying to cut him some slack, thinking, *Well, he's a teenage boy, and he's been voluntold to be in this very girly production.* But you cut someone too much slack, suddenly you don't have a functional rope anymore. You don't have a show. So he's out."

She was such a badass. It was hot.

"Though I admit I'm not sure how firing him is going to go. I've ejected plenty of kids—or their parents—from my studio over the years."

See? Badass.

"But in that case, it's *my* studio. I can't kick Tristan out of camp, so I have to think about how I'm going to handle it."

"Let me fire him for you." It was the least I could do.

She squinted at me. "You would do that for me?"

"Well, I don't know if it would be 'for you' so much as it would be cleaning up my own mess, but yes."

"It's OK. I'll figure it out. But thanks. I appreciate the offer."

"You want me to get you a new kid? A good one?" I paused. I felt *really* bad about this. Which was weird, but it was what it was. "Or I can play the role myself if you like?"

That cracked her up.

"What?"

"While I would very much like to see you playing the part of Laurie, we are good."

"You sure?" I told myself to stop pushing. Did I *want* to be Laurie in *Little Women*, but with dancing? No, I did not.

"Laurie being played by our resident adult rock star would lend a distinctly creepy note to the proceedings, don't you think?"

"Yeah, I guess."

"How old are you, anyway?"

"Thirty-five."

"Ooh," she said laughingly. "A younger man."

"How old are you?"

"Forty at the end of the summer."

Wow. She didn't look forty.

"Hence the man cleanse, I guess," she added, shrugging. "Maybe once you turn forty they fast-track you for cronedom."

She was kidding. I thought.

"Anyway, I appreciate the offer, but I have a plan that requires no boys whatsoever."

"Kind of like your plan for life generally."

"Kind of," she agreed with a cheeriness that was hard to parse. It made me vaguely uncomfortable. It wasn't that I was going to be all torn up when Sourplum and I had to part ways,

but I *was* going to miss the spectacular sex. She, apparently, was
not. It was disconcerting to see how easily she was going to be
able to walk away.

She started to go—I could recognize that she was cueing up
a leap or a jump to dismount my porch—but I grabbed her arm
and said, "Come in for thirty seconds."

She made a mild noise of protest, but she came. I pushed her
gently against the inside of the door and planted one on her. I
was addicted to kissing her, now that we'd broken that barrier.

She had that heart shape in her lips, which I'd learned—
while tracing it with my finger and expressing admiration for it,
mortifyingly—was called a Cupid's bow. I just wanted to... eat
it. All the time.

It was strange, though, to be kissing her knowing it wouldn't
be leading to more. If we were having a last hurrah—meaning,
as she'd said, sex and not romance—what was I doing luring
her inside for the purpose of kissing her? Why was I getting
myself all riled up to no end?

I broke the kiss. She looked a little dazed but rolled her eyes
when I said, "Thanks for the mini sex toy."

I followed her outside. She leaped off my porch, as I'd
known she would, and something kind of... stuck in my chest.
I watched her jog off, but when she was a few yards away, she
turned back. There was something about the angle of the afternoon sun, the way it hit her hair, which was piled on her head
in a messy bun in such a way that the pink was extra visible.
The catch in my chest deepened. I told myself it was regret over
how profoundly I had misjudged her initially.

"Hey, Knight," she said, like she was trying to get my attention, though she had never lost it.

"Yeah?"

"Campfire tonight. You coming?"

"I am now."

She beamed at me and skipped off.

———

Damned if, a couple of hours later, I didn't have the bones of a new song. But I didn't know if it was any good, and I was exhausted. Even though the songs were finally coming— this was the third now—writing was slower than it used to be. Harder, too. Instead of songwriting feeling like solving a puzzle, the way it used to, it felt like solving a puzzle while wrestling a bear.

Maybe I worked better with collaborators. But I was increasingly feeling like whatever happened in the long term, the next album needed to be mine. Mine alone. Not because I needed to prove myself to Scott, but because I needed to...I didn't even know. Prove myself to myself? That didn't feel quite right. I knew that with Brady on board, and given the Concrete Temple pedigree, I'd be able to get a record made. It was more that the record that was beginning to take shape in my mind was a different kind of record. A solo record not just in the sense that it was me without the band, but a solo record in the most elemental sense of the word: a record made by a man alone in the woods. I guess because this album was about this place— Wild Arts, but also "this place" psychologically. This limbo I was in, which, once I stopped fighting it, was an interesting, if sometimes uncomfortable, place to be.

The record was going to be different stylistically, too, which was a bit wild. Three songs in, I had to accept the fact that I was writing a folk-rock album. I was playing the songs on the keyboard or acoustic guitar, so they maybe sounded extra folky at this stage. I *was* imagining giving them some edge in the studio. But there was no way around the fact that these songs had more in common with Peter, Paul and Mary than with Concrete Temple.

It remained to be seen whether this marked the beginning of a new era for me or was just something I needed to get out of my system—a one-and-done before I went back to the harder stuff. Or maybe I'd move into producing for people beyond Anna.

Regardless, I'd broken the logjam. I really was working on a solo album now, even if not as quickly as I might have hoped at the outset of the summer.

I grabbed my phone to call Auden since I had some time to kill before dinner. I'd ignored a FaceTime from her the other night because I'd been getting it on with Gretchen.

"Are you OK?" Auden asked when she picked up.

"I'm fine."

She cracked a smile. "I think we're the only family who gets alarmed when a call comes in during daylight."

"Ha. Yeah, I don't know, there's something about this clean air or some shit that continues to have me out like a light well before midnight." Of course, it could be the mind-blowing orgasms. Either way, these days I wasn't conscious during our usual chat times. "What are you doing?" She was wearing her darkroom clothes—she had converted a closet in her apartment into a darkroom.

"I've been experimenting with this thing called light paint-ing." She reversed her phone camera. "I don't know if you can see this." It was a dark scene—it looked like a forest, or maybe a garden?—with big circles of yellow light that almost appeared to be moving. "You use a superlong exposure on a moving light source—in this case, me in Bryant Park with a glow stick. You can also move the camera around a static light source. I haven't tried that yet. This is just practice."

As per usual, Auden's "just practice" looked amazing. "That looks like something you'd see in a gallery." Also as per usual, she waved me off. "I wish it was darker, though. Maybe I should go into the depths of Central Park."

"You should come here," I said, reviving my earlier invitation. "It's *dark* here. And there's a painter here, Maiv Khang. Look her up. You'd love her, and I think she'd be interested in this light painting thing. She's doing a series on the overlap of city and nature. And—" I felt like a huge dork saying the rest. "You could see my music kids do their final performance."

"Your music kids? Aww!"

"We're working on this big cheesy finale—'Bohemian Rhapsody.'" Which I suddenly very much wanted Auden to see.

If she came, maybe I could also talk to her about Mom. I hadn't forgotten what Gretchen said, about leaning into the pain Mom had caused as a way of trying to discharge it. I wondered if that was what I was doing with my album, with all this folk-rock.

I also hadn't forgotten what I'd said to Gretchen in return, that I didn't think I could do that—lean into the Mom junk—without Auden being willing to do the same, or at least willing to witness me doing it. "Please come," I said, letting the urgency of my desire infuse my tone. "It would mean a lot to me."

She paused long enough that I thought I might have won her over, but then she said, "I can't."

I sighed. Yeah, not everyone had jobs they could take off from at a moment's notice. "I know."

"No, I mean, I *can't*."

"What?"

"Teddy, I've never left New York City."

"That's not true." *Was it?* "You went to that retreat in the Hamptons last summer. We were just talking about that the other day."

"I went to that retreat for one day, had a full-blown panic attack while wading in the water, faked food poisoning, and left early."

What? My mind was having trouble grabbing on to the notion that my sister had never been farther from the city than the Hamptons. Auden was wealthy. She went to spas and Broadway shows and lived in a large—by New York standards—apartment filled with art. Some of it was by friends, but some of it was top-shelf stuff she bought at galleries. She had a guest room she wasn't letting me occupy this summer and a spare walk-in closet she used as a darkroom.

Surely she was overstating things, forgetting a business trip at the very least. Her firm had a secondary headquarters in Los Angeles. But...I thought of all the times I'd suggested she take the train up to Boston to see a show. She'd always declined. "I went to like three hundred Concrete Temple shows when I was a teenager," she would say, referring to our early gigs in dives around New York. "These days, I can see you once a year at Madison Square Garden and call it good."

"That promotion you turned down last year...," I wondered aloud.

"Would have required me to spend a ton of time at the LA office."

"Auden, I don't know what to say."

"You don't have to say anything. But now you know why I can't come to see your camp show. I would love to, but I can't."

"And that's it?" *You're just going to be like this for the rest of your life?* I didn't want to say it quite so bluntly, though. I was still reeling from this bomb she'd dropped, and I didn't want to overreact. The Hilton Garden Inn episode had represented my lifetime allotment of overreaction.

She sighed. "Sometimes I think maybe I should try another big city, one that doesn't feel that different on the ground from New York. Chicago, maybe? Toronto? Now that you're not touring so much, maybe we could...try to go somewhere together?"

"Of course, anytime. But maybe you need a therapist. Maybe you need—"

"Massive pharmaceutical intervention?"

She was trying to be funny, but I wasn't feeling it. "Possibly. But mostly a therapist. I feel like you can drug yourself, sure, and maybe that's part of the fix, but is it really going to get better—really, actually better—if you don't understand the root cause?"

"I'm pretty sure the root cause is Mom."

I huffed a bitter laugh. "Yeah." Of course it was. "But then you need to talk about the root cause." All that shit Gretchen had said—she'd been right. "You have to talk about it before you can get it to loosen its hold on you."

"I guess."

She didn't sound enthused. "Do you want to talk about it with me?" I was no therapist, but maybe I could get her comfortable with the idea of talking. Hell, *I* wanted to talk. Wasn't that half the reason I'd invited her to Wild Arts?

That gave me pause. Auden and I had talked a lot this summer, but it was always about me. What I was doing. What I was—or wasn't—writing. I wanted her to come visit because *I* wanted to see her. I wanted to feel the things I would feel if she came here.

"You know," she said quietly, "this is why I didn't want you staying with me this summer. I didn't want you to figure it out."

"I feel terrible that I never realized this."

"I worked hard to hide it from you."

"But you're not hiding anymore."

She shrugged, but the gesture was too casual. "I guess it's getting too exhausting to keep hiding it. From you, anyway."

"Is it agoraphobia?" My mind was searching for a diagnosis. A word.

"I feel like it's the opposite. Fear of empty places. In New York, there are always people around. You're always close to anything you could need—food, friends, hospitals. You can get anywhere on foot."

"What happens if you try to…push yourself? You said you had a panic attack in the Hamptons."

"Yeah. I get itchy. My skin literally itches. I get black spots in my vision, and I feel like I'm going to pass out." She paused. "And Teddy, it's getting worse." She squeezed her eyes closed for a moment, and when she opened them, she leaned closer to the phone and looked intently at me. "After you left, I regretted not letting you stay here. I realized that if you're not doing your usual touring stuff, where you have your army of handlers and a prescribed schedule, anything could happen. I think that's why I'm telling you about this now. Because it feels like…it's spreading to you. Not like it's contagious, but like I'm going to start having the same panicky feeling about you now. What if you got lost in a forest in Minnesota and I had to fly out there and, I don't know, find you?"

This was why she'd been so freaked out when we'd spoken that night. This was big. But it wasn't something we could solve right now, so I decided to try to lighten the mood. "They have park rangers for that."

"What if I had to fly out there and identify your body?"

"They have FaceTime for that." But maybe she wanted me to push her, not protect her, which was always my instinct. "I would, however, love to see you. But coming here sounds like it would be too much too soon. Why don't we plan to work up to taking a trip together? Somewhere less dramatic than northern Minnesota. But you need to talk to someone. Besides me. In addition to me. I can help you find the right person." I had no idea how people went about finding therapists, but I'd figure it out. "I'll go with you if you want. Hell, I'll find my own therapist. I'll get someone lined up for the fall, when I'm back in town."

Weirdly, this situation with Auden was making me feel better about the demise of the band. This was something that needed my attention. A way to be useful. Which I realized was just more of me making Auden's shit about me, but hey, baby steps.

She smiled weakly. "You'd do that for me?"

"Of course." I hesitated over saying more. But maybe it would help her to hear it. "Honestly, I've been doing my own reckoning up here, with regard to the Mom stuff. Realizing it has more of a hold on me than it should, or than I'd like it to. I'd like to . . . get out from under it."

She looked somewhat cheered. "So maybe we can...try to do that together? Or in parallel?"

"It's a deal."

"Tell me something about you before we hang up, so I feel like less of a freak."

I knew she was wanting to end the conversation on a lighter note, and while I normally never would have told her about Gretchen, I felt like she'd told me something big, and I wanted to do the same. Not that this was big. It was, as Gretchen said, about her getting her last hurrah. Though of course I was enjoying myself, too. So not big, but the kind of gossipy news that would make Auden squeal.

"I have spent every night for the past week sleeping with a woman here. That's why I haven't been answering your calls."

"What!" Her shriek was gleeful, which was what I'd been aiming for. "Is this the woman you got lost in the woods with?"

"Yep."

"Tell me about her."

"It's casual—a camp fling. There's nothing to tell."

"I'm not saying kiss and tell. Tell me some stuff about *her*. What's she like? Is she a musician? Come on. Throw me a bone."

"She's a dancer, the ends of her hair are dyed pink, and..." The next thing that came to mind was her thighs, but I couldn't say that. "She kind of pushed me into this reckoning I was talking about."

"Whoa, whoa, whoa. This does not sound casual."

"It is casual. Casual just means we're taking advantage of our circumstances. It doesn't mean she can't have an impact on me. She's smart that way. She grew up poor, like us. She knows shit."

"You sound smitten."

"I'm not *smitten*. I'm just telling you the facts. If you want to add wild interpretations to them, that's your business." I was getting annoyed now.

"Is Karlie still in your apartment?"

"I...don't know." I hadn't thought about Karlie for weeks. I also didn't know why it mattered. Except...it sort of felt like it did.

12

STUMBLE THROUGH

Gretchen

"I think I made a mistake assuming we needed a boy for Laurie."

I looked out at a sea of surprised faces and tried not to fidget. I'd called a special weekend meeting of the dance group, and I was here to apologize.

I'd never had to do that before, and it was making me twitchy. At my studio, I ruled with a (cheerful) iron fist. I enforced Miss Miller's Morals. I choreographed recitals and taught the kids their parts. I was the boss.

I wasn't the boss here. I was the artist in residence, though I still didn't really know what that meant. I was aware that the campers looked up to me, or at least to my position—the other artists in residence were bigger deals in their respective fields than I was in mine. I wasn't in charge, was the point. We were putting on this show together. Which, of course, was part of why I was so excited about it. It was a collaboration. The campers were the ones who'd inspired the idea for the theme of the show to be "girl" songs. We were still doing *Little Women*—kind of—but after all our chat about the book's themes, we'd decided to pick a few scenes and set them to iconic songs by women that referenced womanhood or girlhood in powerful ways. But we were also inspired by the title of the book in its regular adjective-noun format: little women. What is it like being a girl today? How does a girl assert her power in a world that doesn't naturally tend to give her any?

It was going to be amazing.

After I got rid of the dead weight.

"Last week wasn't the greatest, right? Not because of you all, but because of Tristan." A murmur went through the group. They were surprised I was speaking so openly. "I'm not sure what his problem is, but clearly he has one. But I've been thinking, I'm not sure we need to let his problems be our problems, you know?"

"Are you going to kick him out of the show?" Addison asked.

"I think I should." I had pretty much made up my mind but thought I ought to talk to the girls first. We were in this together, and I was the one who'd told the other artists to treat the kids like peers. "Do you all agree?"

"But what are we going to do without him? What about the ballroom scene?" asked Hong, who, in the role of Jo, was his partner for a large part of that scene.

"I have some thoughts about that, but first I really do want to apologize." I'd meant to open with that, but we'd gotten sidetracked. "From the start, Laurie should have been one of you. There was no reason to bring a nondancer in, even one who was going to be decent about it. And beyond that, the show is supposed to be about girl power, right? So why have we been so stuck on this boy? Remember when we first decided to do the ballroom scene? We talked about how Laurie would be the eye of the hurricane, the center of the scene?" There were nods of agreement. "That was wrong from the get-go, Tristan aside. And as we evolved the theme of the show to be more overtly about girlhood and the power of girls, it became even more wrong. I should have seen that sooner. I'm sorry I didn't."

"I don't think there's any need to be sorry," Addison said. "I think this is what choreography is like sometimes—it's probably what all art is like, or at least art you make with other people. It's a process. Sometimes you have to stumble your way through to the right thing."

Wow. I'd been correct in my early assessment of Addison as the smart one. And that *was* what was different about what I was doing here. At the studio, I unilaterally imposed recital choreography. I might consult Rory, but there was no "stumbling through" with the dancers themselves. There was no creating something together. Partly because most of them were so young. But partly because that just wasn't how a dance studio like mine operated.

"So let's stumble our way through this," I said. "We have one week till the show. What do we do about Laurie?"

Some discussion followed, and it was decided that a girl named Harper should play Laurie, because she had the smallest role in this particular number, so pulling her out of it would cause the least amount of disruption.

"But will she fit into his costume?" asked one of the girls. "Or can we get it altered?"

"We can get it altered," I said. "Or Jo could dance with a girl. Lori spelled L-O-R-I?" They laughed at that. "Remember that's what Tristan first thought it was when he heard the name? Then the costume is irrelevant. We could just dispense with boys altogether."

Hong raised her hand. "I actually like girls in real life. In, you know, *that* way. Not boys." She was blushing, and I kept my face open and neutral. I had no idea if she was out generally, if everyone else knew this about her. At the very least she was coming out to me with that statement.

"That's great." I was trying to be positive but to play it low-key. "And since this is acting as well as dancing, it will probably read as more authentic." I swung around to Harper. "Are you up for it?"

"I don't want you to feel weird," Hong rushed to say. "Or uncomfortable. It *would* just be acting."

It was Harper's turn to blush. "I won't feel weird or uncomfortable."

Then we ran the scene and damn, I was pretty sure both Harper and Hong did "feel weird," but in a good way. A way that was creating chemistry and making the number crackle with energy. Hong had *not* had this with Tristan. We should have made this change a long time ago. But, I told myself, it was OK: we were stumbling through together. And now it was going so well that no one would be able to tell we'd only had "Lori" for a week.

After we got the number nailed down, I sought out Tristan and fired him. Hilariously, he did a version of what the Mediocre Men of Tinder so often did when faced with rejection. He told me my show sucked, that he'd never wanted to be part of it anyway, that dancing was lame in general, that ballroom dancing was especially lame. The funny part was that he was talking quietly, so quietly I had to strain to hear him. But then I thought, *Why? Why am I doing this? Dude can't even speak up with his toxic bullshit?*

I laughed, and I didn't even feel bad about it. Maybe I should have, on account of his being a kid and my being an adult and authority figure, but I didn't.

That should have been it, but he followed me out of the studio, repeating his mumbled insults, except this time with less mumbling.

I was suddenly finding this encounter less hilarious and more of an affront.

I'd been headed to the dining hall, but I stopped and faced him. "You didn't even want to be in the dance show anyway. As you *just* said. And as you made abundantly clear every time you 'practiced' with us, so I don't know why you're so up in your feelings about this."

Never tell a boy—of any age—that he's getting emotional.

His insults turned personal. "Bitch."

Perhaps I shouldn't have been shocked, but I was. I guess I assumed a kid at Wild Arts, no matter what he was thinking, would be smart enough not to vocalize something like that. So I was set back on my heels for a moment, blinking, unable to quite absorb the fact that yes, this was happening now.

"Fucking dance bitches. You think anyone will ever—"

"You will stop talking now."

Teddy. Suddenly there.

He was clearly beyond angry at Tristan, but he wasn't expressing it with yelling or any kind of theatrics. "You are an embarrassment." His tone was cold—icy—and utterly controlled. Somehow that was scarier than a more overt display of rage would have been. "You are fired from the music group, and if I have anything to say about it, this is it for you at camp." They stood facing each other, Tristan blinking, eyes wide, and Teddy staring, eyes narrow. "Come with me," he finally said, and he turned, apparently trusting that Tristan would follow.

He did.

I did my best to shake off the encounter and went to dinner. I often got my food to go after a long day, but I was still feeling off. Unsettled. So I collected my taco salad and banana pudding—oddly, I was going to miss camp food—and sat by Jack, the only other artist present.

We nodded at each other and ate in silence for a minute.

"How's the book coming?" I finally asked, just for something to say.

He didn't answer. Why had I ever expected Jack Branksome to be chatty?

But then he said, "It's not. I haven't done shit since I got here, and to be honest, I hate myself for it."

I almost choked on a piece of taco shell.

Wow. I didn't particularly like Jack, but I didn't wish him ill, and the idea of him hating himself, much less copping to it, was making me reevaluate him. "Maybe that's OK. Part of the point of being here is resting and recharging. Creativity isn't a widget you can produce on demand." Lest he think I was being too presumptuous, I added, "I mean, maybe. I don't know. I'm not a writer."

He shrugged like I wasn't automatically and/or totally wrong. I decided to press my luck. "Do you have a hard deadline?"

"January first."

A little less than six months from now. I didn't know if that was a lot of time or not a lot of time when it came to book writing. "Maybe you can really crank on it starting next week when you're in between camp sessions."

"You'd think I could," he said in a way that was self-deprecating enough to make me continue reevaluating his whole persona. I wasn't sure how to respond, but I didn't have to, because I heard a low "Hey" from behind me.

Teddy, carrying a dinner tray, and sliding onto the bench next to me.

"Hi." I raised my eyebrows, not sure what to say in this context. *Thanks for rescuing me?* I didn't like to think of myself as the kind of person who needed rescuing. Especially from a teenager. But I could not deny it had been nice to have the Tristan problem handled. And more than that, it had been good to have someone have my back. Well, not someone. Teddy.

That was an alarming thought I should probably analyze later. Or not. I didn't have that much longer at Wild Arts, so why bother?

"I hope you don't think I overstepped with Tristan," Teddy said. I smiled. It was like he could hear my thoughts. "I happened to overhear what he was saying to you, and I felt responsible. He was a music kid, and I was the one who stuck you with him. But you were handling it. I should have let it be."

"No, I was happy to have him be your problem." I sent him a jokey smile, both to show there were no hard feelings and to cover my own unease at how much I had enjoyed being rescued by Teddy.

He squirted some hot sauce on his taco salad. "Well, he's Marion's problem now. She's kicked him out and called his parents, and she's driving him to Duluth to meet them."

Jack made a noise that was half astonishment, half inquiry, so I turned to him and said, "Shitty kid had a meltdown and called me some unflattering things, and Teddy went on the warpath."

"Mm." Jack looked back and forth between us. "I see how it is." He shot me a smile-smirk hybrid, but not an unkind one. I knew he was thinking of the condom he'd given me, but apparently he was going to keep that thought to himself and not be a jerk about it. Could have knocked me over with a feather.

"We were just talking about Jack's book, which is due January first and isn't coming along," I said to Teddy.

Jack rolled his eyes and said, "It isn't even starting along."

"Yikes," Teddy said.

"I'm about to email my agent and ask how long I can push it until they make me give the advance back."

"Maybe you shouldn't have been so quick to turn your nose up at Blair Kellermoon," Teddy said jokingly.

"Maybe so."

I waited for the sneer, but it didn't come. Had Wild Arts mellowed Jack? If so, forget crones in the woods, this really was a magical place. "We're having a campfire tonight. You should come."

Jack shrugged noncommittally.

"Seriously. Singing, s'mores, goodwill, camaraderie. It's right up your alley." I cracked up.

"Maybe." Jack pushed back from the table, looked between Teddy and me, and said, "I'll leave you two alone now."

I was about to protest that there was no reason to leave us alone, but I thought better of it. Protesting would only make me seem guilty.

Guilty of what? Of wanting to be alone with Teddy?

I *was* guilty of that.

It was a good thing I was out of here at the end of next week.

———

I was late for the campfire because I'd gone to the dance cabins to report to the counselors on Tristan's firing, and we'd gotten to talking. The kids were in bed, if not asleep, so the three of us went and sat on the porch of one of the cabins.

"I wish you were staying for the next session," Grace said.

"Me, too," Brianna said. "You handled the Tristan situation like a pro."

I was chuffed by their praise. "Honestly, I thought I was fumbling it."

"I wouldn't have had the guts to confront him like that," Grace said.

"Me either," Brianna said. "Or I would have gotten Marion involved. Regardless, I would have lost a ton of sleep over it. You just *handled* it."

"I did lose some sleep over it," I said. "But I've been thinking lately about how we—women, I mean—sometimes go to extreme lengths not to offend men. Or boys. Do you agree?"

"Yes!" they said in unison.

"I've been trying to stop doing that."

"Though to be fair," Brianna said, "I think there are situations where you *need* to not offend men, you know? Situations in which you might actually be in danger."

"Oh for sure," I said, alarmed. I didn't want to radicalize my counselors such that they got themselves hurt. "You have to read the situation. And I'm not saying any of this to tell you what to do. I'm a lot older than you. This attitude, which does not come naturally, by the way, has been a lifetime in the making."

"I wonder," Grace said thoughtfully, "if part of the problem is that sometimes, in the moment, it can be hard to distinguish between situations that might become violent and situations that probably won't. Maybe our bodies, our fight-or-flight responses, don't always know the difference."

"Yes," I agreed. Silence fell, and, sensing we were done with this heavy topic, I asked, "Will either of you come back next summer?"

Grace was going to, but Brianna wasn't sure, as she was going into her last year of college. "It depends what I can scare up jobwise after graduation."

I asked some questions about Brianna's upcoming year—she'd mentioned previously that she would be taking a choreography course. Hearing about it all was fascinating. I was a little jealous, actually, but I quashed it. There was no point in getting lost in the what-ifs. I'd done what I needed to do to survive, and that hadn't included an expensive four-year degree.

"Will you two keep in touch after this summer?" I asked.

"Oh for sure," Brianna said, and Grace agreed.

"So you're actual friends rather than just camp friends."

"Yeah," Brianna said. "Though I never went to camp as a kid, so I don't really know about the whole camp friend thing firsthand."

"Oh, I did," Grace said. "Every summer. Not arts camp like this, just regular camp." She smiled at Brianna. "But we're real friends, you and I."

"So you're an expert on the camp friend phenomenon," I said to Grace. "Tell me about it. Why can't camp friends port into the real world?"

"It's not that they *can't*. They just usually don't. You go back to your regular lives, you go to different schools that might not even be in the same city. If you want to keep in touch, you're reliant on your parents for logistics and transportation." She shrugged. "So you see your camp friends at camp, basically. You have this intense but time-limited friendship."

"What if your camp friend doesn't come back the next year?"

"It's sad. But you get over it."

"And do you think about them?"

"Maybe. I guess you think you were lucky to have had that summer with them."

You were lucky to have had that summer with them.

As I approached the campfire, Grace's words were reverberating in my head. I was going to keep in touch with Maiv. I vowed I would make it happen. She didn't live far from me, and we both had flexible jobs and were single with no kids. It was doable.

But the rest of them? Camp friends, probably. A bittersweet category of human relationship I hadn't even known existed before I came here. As I approached the fire and saw everyone gathered around it, the flames making their faces glow, I was struck with a longing, a kind of homesickness in reverse, for them, for this place.

Teddy was holding his guitar but not playing, and there was a spot open next to him. It would have been logical for me to sit there. It was right in front of me. But I was afraid we had the chemistry my Lori and Jo did. If people had been gossiping about us earlier in the week, I hated to think what they were saying now.

Also, I was starting to get spooked over how much I liked him. Actually *liked* him. Beyond the sex. Which I also liked.

Distance seemed prudent for a variety of reasons.

So I stepped over the log, skirted the fire, and sat in the other empty spot, next to Danny, noticing as I did so that the conversation had come to a halt.

"Wow, do I know how to bring down a party or what?" I joked, thinking that if my aim had been to deflect attention from my and Teddy's...thing, going out of my way to avoid him was probably not the way to do it.

Or I was overthinking this all.

Let's go with that.

"Jack was telling us about his book," Maiv said, and I was shocked. By the fact that Jack was talking about his book, but also by the fact that he was here to begin with. I hadn't noticed him initially, in my angst over where to sit.

"By all means, continue," I said.

"Eh, I think that's about it. I'm stuck. Not much more to say."

"I don't know anything about writing novels," Caleb said, "but when I get stuck on a play, I sometimes think about if I can tell that part of the story—or the whole story—through the point of view of a different character."

I expected Jack to say something snarky, but he just made a vague murmur of acknowledgment. Wow, was this nature-and-artistic-collaboration stuff finally working on Jack Branksome?

For a while, the only sounds were the lapping of the waves and the crackling of the fire, but then my second shock of the evening was delivered in the form of Teddy's saying, "Anyone want to hear a song I wrote?"

The group's answers ranged from "Yes" to "Hell yes." I said nothing because I wanted to hear his song so badly, the wanting opened a pit inside me.

The song wasn't a ballad per se. It was peppy, but it was acoustic. Well, of course it was acoustic; he only had a guitar with him. But it sounded like it was *meant* to be acoustic.

It was about...well, I wasn't sure. On the surface of things, it was about a lake, a lake that the narrator originally saw during a storm and found menacing. But then it turned out that the lake had moods, a kind of sweetness beneath the choppy waves. I wondered if this was the song he'd told me about called "Sweet and Sour." There was a line about lying back in bed at night and still feeling the waves that, for reasons I couldn't articulate, choked me up.

There was a moment of silence when he finished, then everyone started clapping and hooting. I kept looking at my feet, trying to stave off tears. The homesick feeling was deepening. I was going to miss these fires. Hearing people's music. Watching Maiv take a blank canvas and turn it into something breathtaking.

Everything everyone was making here was so beautiful and terrible. It was like watching baby birds hatch and leave the nest. I'd done that once, when a robin had made a nest in a planter on my porch. The things that came out of those eggs hadn't looked like birds at all; they'd looked like tiny alien reptiles. They were ugly, but I hadn't been able to stop looking at them, standing there on my tiptoes in my entryway, spying on them through the little window at the top of my front door. Over the next week, they grew feathers and doubled in size and seemed less like creepy miniature aliens and more like proper animals of the sort that belonged on Earth.

And then they were gone. Out in the world somewhere with flimsy new feathers that made actual flight seem like a long shot.

I was on my feet before I even realized it. I had to leave. Something was happening to me. Something was breaking inside me, or about to break.

"I didn't realize how tired I am," I managed to say. I heard myself speaking as if listening to a recording of someone impersonating me. "I have to be up early tomorrow," my impersonator said. "I have some work to do on a piece for the end-of-camp show."

Everyone said good night, and I was almost free when Teddy

said, "I'm going, too." He smirked. "Sorry to run off, but I kind of can't believe I played that song to you guys, and now I'm going to flee."

He didn't even try to be subtle about the way he followed me, bypassing his own front door. If anyone was watching us, it would be obvious. I was too freaked out to care. And tired. I hadn't been lying back there; I'd suddenly become overwhelmed with exhaustion, my limbs made of cement.

"Hey, hey, Miller."

I stopped, though I didn't want to. Or maybe I did. Maybe I just didn't want to want to.

"You OK?" The porch light from my place shone on his face. He looked genuinely concerned.

"Yeah, sorry. I'm really beat. I don't think I'm up for anything tonight."

He waved a hand dismissively. "Yeah, fine, but are you OK?"

Was I OK? I didn't know. I probably would be tomorrow. "Your song was phenomenal," I said, which I realized didn't answer his question, but it was the truth.

———

The next morning, I overslept so severely that I had to vault out of bed and run to the dining hall so as to not miss breakfast. I'd been so weirdly overwrought when I got back to my cabin last night that I'd forgotten to set my old-school alarm clock, so I'd missed my morning swim.

I'd freaked out last night, and I wasn't entirely sure why. The homesick-in-advance feeling had stuck around, kept me tossing and turning until the wee hours. I felt better this morning, but jumpy. I told myself I would chill as I worked on the new Lori dance, which was my plan for the day. I would, of course, be workshopping it with the counselors and the kids, but we were tight enough on time that I was going to get moving on some ideas.

I ate a big bowl of oatmeal with fruit and headed out. I took the extreme step of locking myself in the dance studio. Generally we kept the doors open. Because of the heat, but also because of the overall vibe of Wild Arts. There was something about being surrounded by people making art that upped your own game. I thought of the times I'd listened in on Teddy and Anna.

But not today. I could only hope that as was generally the case on weekends, the kids and counselors would be off doing regular camp things—there was a two-hour canoe trip this morning that at least some of the dance girls had opted into.

The Lori dance wasn't that hard. I knew Hong and Harper. Not just as dancers, but as people. I knew how the dance was meant to slot into the overall performance, in terms of both pacing and style. It was like adding a missing paragraph to an essay or finding a missing puzzle piece under your sofa.

As I ran through it one final time, doing Harper's new part, I found myself adding a calypso leap on the end. It didn't belong there. It made no sense within the grammar of the dance. But my body wanted to do it. To add it on like an exclamation mark at the end of a sentence. Except that wasn't right, because this leap wasn't a punctuation mark that signified an ending. It was more of a transition. A beginning, even.

I'd been doing this particular leap off Teddy's porch a lot. I didn't even know why, except that it just…came out. Maybe his porch was a good height.

Which made no sense, because the whole point of a leap was that you started on the ground and ended on the ground.

Starting from a higher vantage point, like a porch, gave you a head start. It was cheating, basically.

So why couldn't I stop doing it?

Why did I run over to the potting studio and liberate an unused bench they sometimes used to display pieces and drag it back to the dance studio and leap off it approximately a million times?

What did it all mean?

I wasn't sure, but suddenly there was a flash of lightning in my brain and I started thinking about the opposite concept: how would I execute a calypso leap—or any leap—if I wanted to start on the ground and land on the bench?

I asked myself again why I would want to. What it would mean.

What did it mean when I leaped *off* porches or *off* that bench? Why was I doing that?

I thought the answer was that it was an expression of joy. The head start made the leap extra big, made my body feel extra buoyant. I tried to put some specificity to that feeling. Like, what would be an example?

The first thing that came to mind was Teddy. Well, not Teddy per se, but that feeling I'd had when we were negotiating the last hurrah. *I don't feel like I have to watch what I say, or care what I look like, because I don't care what you think I look like,* I'd said, and I'd literally laughed out loud from the thrill of it.

So . . . I was leaping because I was liberated. That wasn't very deep.

I closed my eyes and summoned one of the vignettes that had been accumulating in my mind. It was a woman dancing up a hill. Not dancing in a happy way, but working hard against gravity, exhausting herself.

So if leaping with a head start—off a porch, or a bench—was liberation, was the opposite also true? If I tried to leap but started from "below" somehow, from downhill, my body having to fight against gravity to make it happen, would the resulting leap signify heaviness, strife?

My legs got jumpy.

I had no way to try out this scenario. I did consider actually trying to leap onto the bench, but it was narrow and rickety and I didn't want to hurt myself and leave the dance group leaderless. Instead, I...pretended. Imagined a giant slope that I never managed to crest. Did it over and over again, thinking about the woman in the vignette in my head until I became her.

The piece was about the shitty men of Tinder, it turned out. About what it felt like to be the recipient of their unsolicited opinions, even as one was doing one's best to live up to their expectations.

I suspected it was also about men generally. About *life* generally. What an uphill climb it was sometimes to exist as a woman in the world, in both the personal and professional realms. But when I thought about it like that, I got spooked. That was too big a theme. So I just danced.

At seven, when I emerged, I felt...new. Scraped clean, somehow. I decided to knock on Caleb's door, to tell him about my day. I'd followed my body through the negative-start leaping it had seemed to want to do, and, after doing it enough times, I'd started to get what it meant. The meaning was coming through the steps. I'd never done things in that direction. For recital pieces at my studio, I had selected music, often according to a theme, and then put steps to the music.

I stopped on my way to Caleb's. Would he get it, though?

Maybe I should find Maiv. She would give me some box wine and be thrilled to hear about my day.

I knocked on Teddy's door.

I mean, of course I did.

He answered with his eyebrows raised. "She lives."

"Yeah, sorry, long day."

"You didn't swim this morning."

"Did *you* swim this morning?" He hadn't been back since that one morning he'd joined me.

He paused. "No. I just...sometimes notice when you are." Another pause. "I mean that in the least stalkerish way possible."

I grinned. "You got anything to eat? I missed dinner. And lunch."

"In fact, I do. Jack and Maiv and I went into town, and I got some groceries. I heard you like Cheetos."

"Oh my God, I love them. Though I should probably try to go beg something more substantial from the kitchen staff, assuming they're still there. I haven't eaten since breakfast, and I burned a lot of energy today."

"I also picked up some of the famous Kuhn family cheese spread."

"Did you love it?"

"Eh."

"Oh come on. You loved it."

"I did, but I'm not keen on being the kind of person who loves a product labeled 'cold pack cheese food.' What does that even mean?"

"Cold Pack Cheese Food should be the name of your next band."

He smirked. "The problem is I ate all the crackers. Wait. I'm having a flash of inspiration." He made jazz hands. "I have some bread—and this hot plate." He plugged in the single-burner stove and bent down and rummaged through a cupboard and emerged with a beat-up frying pan. "Cold pack cheese food grilled cheese sandwich? With a side of Cheetos?"

I cracked up. "Sounds perfect. How come you have a loaf of bread? Seems random."

"I've been oversleeping breakfast—when I'm not noticing you swim in the least stalkerish way possible—so I usually just make toast." He made a face. "I may be doing better on the participation front, but I'm still not a morning person." He moved to the minifridge. "You want classic cheddar, port wine, or herb and garlic?"

"Wow, you really went all in on the cheese spread. I don't know what to pick!"

"I'm getting another brain wave. We'll make finger sandwiches. Little fancy sandwiches. Then we don't have to choose."

"Brilliant." I made my way over to him. "You want to cut the bread first or make the sandwiches whole and then cut them?"

He hip-checked me. "Shoo. I'll do this."

"I can help."

"Nah, you sit. I got this. You want some bourbon?"

"Sure."

He herded me to the little table and gave me a drink. "You probably aren't going to believe this, but I am an expert at grilled cheese."

"I believe it. Grilled cheese is classic poor-people food. Filling and cheap."

"Exactly. A brick of Velveeta, a loaf of Wonder bread, a tub of margarine, and you've got a week's worth of dinners." He was spreading cheese on bread as he spoke. "Though today you get your sandwiches fried in real butter, because that's what I put on my toast these days."

"Fancy." I sipped my bourbon and watched him work. He was shirtless, wearing only shorts and the orange rubber clogs. He had an unselfconscious ease in his body that was compelling. It interested my inner choreographer.

Oh, who was I kidding? It interested my inner horndog.

"I thought maybe you were done with me," he said over his shoulder. "When you turned in early last night and then I didn't see you all day." In another context the statement would have been loaded, but he didn't seem bothered.

Did I... *want* him to be bothered by the idea that I was done with him? Which I most decidedly wasn't.

I was overthinking again. "Not done with you," I said. "I've just been preoccupied."

I waited for him to ask with what, but he only said, "Mm," as he flipped sandwiches.

"I'm afraid when I go back to my regular life that it's not going to be enough for me anymore," I blurted, and whoa, I hadn't known I felt that way until I said it. *Yelled* it—I'd gotten rather vehement there.

He turned around and leaned back against the counter. "Well, shit."

"Exactly."

"You want to elaborate?"

"I spent the day choreographing. For the kids, but also... for me."

"That's... great?"

"Is it?"

"I don't know?"

"I made the beginning of this...I don't even know what to call it. Dance. Story. Story-dance. But I have no idea what to do with it. How to finish it. Whether to finish it. I barely even know what it's *about*."

"Making new things, new *kinds* of things, is scary as hell."

"Right. But here's the part that's new for me: the idea of *not* making them is, suddenly, also scary as hell. Or not scary, really, but, I don't know...soul destroying?" I laughed at myself. "That's too melodramatic. I'm just in a weird headspace."

He was looking at me really intently, gearing up to give me advice, I was pretty sure. I somehow knew it was going to be a speech on how I couldn't let go of this new creative side of me, how I had to make room for it in my life. Easy for him to say. He wasn't the one who had his entire professional and financial future on the line, tied up in a very expensive new building.

"I think your fancy poor-people sandwiches are starting to burn," I said, sniffing the air.

"Shit!" He danced around the kitchen for a minute. "I think I've saved them."

He plated them—he had made three sandwiches and cut each into quarters, so we each had six little squares. He poured some Cheetos on my plate and set it in front of me with a flourish. "Milady."

"Thanks," I croaked, suddenly emotional. I couldn't remember the last time someone had cooked for me. Someone besides Rory and her husband.

"Oh my God," I said through my first mouthful. "Why are these so *good*?"

"Mm," he agreed. "I wonder if you can get cheese spread in New York."

"Ha. I've converted you."

"Maybe so," he said thoughtfully, and after a minute of silent munching, he added, "You know what I do when I'm all up in my head over a song?"

"What?" A moment ago I hadn't wanted his advice, but when it came like this, with a window into his creative process, into *him*, I found myself desperate to know.

"I do the next thing. I write the next line, or I let a chorus I've been humming and ignoring come out. I try not to over-think it. I just do one thing." He paused. "Now, I'm not saying I always do this. But when I can make myself do the next thing without worrying about how it's all going to fit together—*if* it's all going to fit together—it usually works out."

"Hmm."

"I'm aware that I'm saying this like it's simple, and I'm aware that it is in fact not simple, but ask yourself, What's the next small thing?"

"I need to dig a hole," my mouth said.

"Literally?"

"Literally." Because I knew, suddenly, in a way that went beyond language, that it wasn't a hill my dancer-self protago-nist was trying to dance up, it was a hole she was trying to dance out of.

And so I found myself, post–cold pack cheese food sand-wiches, stealing a shovel from a shed where Lena kept her lawn mower and tools.

And we really were stealing it: Teddy was picking the lock.

"How'd you learn to pick locks?" I asked as the door clicked open.

"I can only do these crappy locks where the lock is inside the doorknob." Yeah, there was no deadbolt or high security here. "I used to have these phases where I'd go to school before it was open. The front doors would be unlocked, I guess because the custodians would be there, but none of the classrooms were. I used to break into the band room. But just to sit there. Maybe noodle around a bit—they had an electric guitar and amp there with headphones so no one could hear me."

"This is my first episode of breaking and entering," I said as I let my eyes adjust to the shed's dim interior.

Teddy grabbed a big shovel. "We're not breaking and entering. We're entering and borrowing. Come on, let's go."

I caught sight of a crate full of hand tools—spades and such—and grabbed a small hand shovel. When Teddy shot me a questioning look, I said, "Detail work."

We both burst out laughing.

After we tiptoed out, he said, "Where is this hole going? May I suggest somewhere off the beaten path so a camper doesn't fall in?"

"Yes. Also so no one sees me."

We settled on a spot behind the off-the-map shower building, and Teddy got to work digging. I kept expecting him to ask me what the hell I needed a hole for, but he just dug with cheerful diligence, refusing my offers to take a shift.

"You want to come in and measure?" he asked, after having established that I was going for knee height. We switched places, him jumping out and me jumping in.

"This is good," I said like I knew—like I had any idea what I was doing. "A good depth, but I think I need it to be a little wider." I needed to be able to get momentum.

Teddy started widening the hole, and when he was done, I could no longer stand how noninquisitive he was being.

"Why are you being so cool about this?"

"What do you mean?"

"I said I wanted to dig a hole, and you were like, 'OK, let's dig a hole.' Aren't you curious? What if I need to hide a body? What if you're an unwitting accessory to a crime? Don't you think this is at least a little bit weird?"

He shrugged. "I guess art is weird sometimes." He excavated a few more shovelfuls, paused, and shot me a wicked grin. "Anyway, I would help you hide a body any day, Miller."

13
CAMP BOYFRIEND

Teddy

I spent a lot of the next week using my phone to do research—so much for my big speech on how phones should only be phones or books or maps.

I looked up all kinds of stuff related to phobias—agoraphobia, but I also learned about kenophobia, which was fear of open spaces. It wasn't that I thought I could or should diagnose Auden, but I couldn't do nothing. Regardless of what label would ultimately be applied, it seemed like a pretty severe case of anxiety must be at the root of what was going on.

I also looked up therapists—read reviews, cruised websites, combed the listings in *Psychology Today*. I stopped short of sending them to her, but I did book a plane ticket home for the break between camp sessions. I needed to see Auden. Lay eyes on her. Even if it wouldn't solve anything.

I also needed to get my own house in order—literally. But also metaphorically. I needed to get my life ready for me to reinhabit it in the fall.

It wasn't all kenophobia and plane tickets, though. I worked with the kids, individually and as a group. "Bohemian

Rhapsody" was in good shape. It was a bit ragtag, but in some ways that was in the spirit of the song.

Anna continued to blossom. As much as I hated that word as a metaphor, it was apt. Every time I saw her, she had new stuff for me. It wasn't all album material, but a few of her songs were fucking phenomenal, and now that I was officially cowriting, I could roll up my sleeves and get in there. We had a couple songs that I was prouder of than anything I'd done with Scott. They made my limbs buzz with an energy that I hadn't realized I'd been missing. They made me want to get up and dance.

Dancing, of course, was not something I did. But one afternoon when I was getting the dancing feeling, I went over to the dance studio to spy on Gretchen's *Little Women* rehearsal like I was James fucking Bond.

Until I, in a very non-Bondlike twist, got caught.

"Can I give you a piece of friendly advice?"

That from Jack, who'd sidled up next to me.

"Can I stop you?" I asked.

"*I* know why you're here. *You* know why you're here." He paused. "Well, maybe you don't. Anyway, I know you're not skulking around looking at teenage girls in leotards, but you might want to think about the optics of this."

"I..." Could not argue with that. I wasn't spying on the kids—gross. But I *was* spying on Gretchen. The question was why. Jack said I knew, but apparently I wasn't as smart as he thought I was.

It made no sense for me to be here. I had Gretchen in my bed every night—the one night she'd seemed out of sorts and stayed away had turned out to be, as she'd said, just about her being tired. I'd thought she was ending our last hurrah prematurely. But no, she'd only been having an artistic crisis of confidence, apparently followed by an artistic blossoming—there was that stupid word again—to do with a hole in the ground. I got that. I mean, I didn't get the hole-in-the-ground part, but I wasn't supposed to. I respected both artistic crises of confidence and artistic blossomings.

And every night, after Gretchen danced in or around her hole or whatever, we went at it like it was our last week on earth. Which I guess, for our purposes, it was.

The point was, I had Gretchen's thighs in my bed. Wrapped around my waist. Or my neck. I didn't need to be ogling them as I slow-walked by the dance studio like I was a fucking teenager.

I hadn't been like this when I *was* a fucking teenager.

I went back to my cabin and wrote another song. Like it was no big deal. Like I was Anna, with a direct line to the songwriting mojo of the universe.

It was so easy it was almost scary.

When I was done, it was cocktail hour. But I put on my swim trunks before I walked over and knocked on Jack's door.

"Hey." He stepped out, bottle in hand.

"Let's go swimming."

"I'll pass, thanks."

"Come on. You came to the campfire last weekend."

"That was an aberration."

It was true that he hadn't shown his face much this week. I'd dragged myself to sunrise circle this morning—it being Friday, it had been the last one for this session. The other artists seemed to have had the same idea, but not Jack. I hadn't seen him anywhere except for our customary cocktail hour, and I wouldn't have thought it possible, but he'd been more sullen than usual this past week.

"Suit yourself."

When I got to the beach, Gretchen wasn't there. She was probably in her hole.

Which was fine because it wasn't like I'd gone to the beach to see her. I'd gone to the beach to swim. I would see her later. Tonight.

———

Where the hell was Gretchen? It was nearly midnight and she wasn't here.

I checked myself. Maybe I shouldn't assume we were going to have sex every night. Just because that was how it had been going didn't mean that was how it was always going to go. There *had* been that one night she'd been too tired.

We could take a night off.

Well, there was no *we* when it came to taking a night off. *She* could take a night off. *I* didn't want a night off. We only had two nights left, and if it was up to me, we'd make the most of them.

I got up and looked out the living room window, which faced her cabin. Her light was on. What was she doing over there?

I did some pacing.

I made a cup of coffee to keep myself awake, because I was apparently now the kind of person who couldn't stay up past midnight without the assistance of a stimulant.

I looked out the window again. No change.

I couldn't text her. I didn't even know her number. She didn't have her phone on anyway.

Well, hell, I was just going to go over there. We always got together at my place, but that was a habit, not a rule.

We didn't have rules. That was the whole point. We weren't in a relationship where we made demands on each other.

Therefore, it was perfectly reasonable for me to go over there and see what was up.

Which did not explain why I had butterflies in my stomach as I did so. I crept around my cabin, trying to be casual. I didn't care if anyone knew we were hooking up, but Gretchen did. I glanced around furtively. While this amateur spy shit was cute on Gretchen, I was aware that I probably looked like a fucking idiot.

The butterflies went into a frenzy as I knocked softly.

No answer. Maybe she wasn't in there despite the light. I knocked again, and I was about to give up when she swung open the door.

"Teddy?" She was all disheveled and blinking—and adorable. She was wearing a leotard and shorts, and she had creases in the side of her face. "Oh my God, I fell asleep. What time is it?"

"I'm sorry I woke you. I'll go." Disappointment sliced through my gut, displacing the butterflies.

"No!" She pulled me inside. I was probably more flattered than I should have been.

She sniffed her armpit. "I gotta shower. We had a big day—the final rehearsal. Then I spent longer than anticipated on the project I'm working on. I intended to lie down for a few minutes, but I guess I conked out."

"If you're tired, we don't have to...you know," I said, offering her an out I hoped she wouldn't take.

"Hell yes, we do."

I—and my dick—swelled with pride.

"It's our last chance, so we gotta make the most of it."

Wait. "What?" I tried to be casual. "We have two more nights before session one is over, right?"

"Yes, but my friend Rory is coming to the show tomorrow—

she's the pregnant one. She doesn't want to sleep in a cabin. So she's got a hotel room in Duluth that she's driving back to after the show, and then she's going back to the Cities the next day. It made sense for me to go with her. Plus, I've missed her."

"So this is it," I said, realizing how much I'd been counting on us having two more nights. Finding out that it was in fact just one... well, it stung.

"This is it," she echoed. Was I imagining that wistfulness in her tone? She was all business as she said, "I'll run and take a shower. You want to wait here, or should I come to your place?" So yeah, I guess any wistfulness in this exchange had been imaginary.

"Let's swim," I said, letting the impulse rise in my brain and flow directly out of my mouth.

"What?"

"Come on. It's your last night." It was *our* last night, but I wasn't going to say that.

She stared at me for a beat, and I could not read her expression. She looked more like herself when she finally said, "OK."

We made arrangements to meet on my porch, and as I waited for her, I thought about how if I'd known tonight was her last night, I would have suggested a campfire. A proper send-off. But it seemed like everyone was preoccupied with tomorrow's show.

Anyway, did I really want to spend my last night with Gretchen in the company of everyone else? I could give her a very proper send-off all by myself. Heh.

She appeared a few minutes later, the beam of the flashlight she was carrying slicing through the darkness—though it wasn't dark-dark. It was clear, and the nearly full moon pinned over the lake had poured a glaze over the night.

She lowered herself onto the glider next to me. She was wearing the Target swimsuit and carrying a shower caddy.

"Going for the full bathing experience, are we?"

"I really do not smell good, so I either gotta wash in the lake or take this to the shower afterward and you'll have to wait for me."

You'll have to wait for me.

A strange feeling came over me, like I would wait for her in any setting, for any amount of time. I quashed it. "Let's do the lake bath. I could stand to get clean, too. I'd suggest a joint shower later—I'm wagging my eyebrows lecherously, but it's too dark for you to see them—but although I'm always up for adventure, I'm not sure you want to risk discovery."

"Yeah, I'm not sure Marion would take kindly to her artists getting it on in the shower."

I chuckled as I rose, giving some thought to whether I should offer her my hand. Would it come off as too solicitous, too much like a date, which she was always insisting she didn't want?

It occurred to me that I was spending a lot of mental energy trying to make this last bit of time we had together exactly the way she would want it. Which felt an awful lot like I *was* approaching this as a date. Could it be a date and a not-date at the same time?

"You OK there, Knight?"

"Yeah." I was, of course, standing there like an idiot, paralyzed while I fretted over whether to take her hand or not. Fuck it. It was dark, we were going to have sex later. And more to the point, I felt like offering her my hand. She could ignore it if she wanted to. So I stuck my hand right into her beam of light, just to make sure this gesture that was almost certainly an overstep would not be ambiguous, and said, "Shall we?"

She took my hand.

Not only that, she handed me her shower caddy to free up her hand—she had her flashlight in the other—so she could take mine.

Something happened in my chest—there was...a bubbling up. Which was ridiculous, because all she was doing was holding my hand as we crossed the beach.

I needed to get out of my head.

She leaned down to set the flashlight on the dock, but she kept hold of me, so I did the same with the shower caddy. When we were both upright, she swung my hand forward to indicate we should jump in together. "Ready?"

"Yes." I was not ready for a lot of things, maybe—to make an album, to figure out how to help my sister, to face life after the last session of Wild Arts—but jump in a lake with Sourplum? Yes. A thousand times yes.

We had to separate as we hit the water, and when we surfaced, I could *feel* her grin. Her giddiness to be here, in the dark, quiet lake.

Or maybe that was my own giddiness.

She swam off, and when I caught up, she rolled over into a lazy sidestroke. "How come you never came back to swim in the mornings after that one time?"

"You said it was your time to get ready for the day, to get your head screwed on. I thought I shouldn't intrude." And after we'd talked that morning, she'd swum off and ignored me.

"Oh."

"Should I have intruded?"

"I...don't know."

Well. That was a big fucking missed opportunity.

We swam out farther until, as if by silent agreement, we

reached a spot where we stopped and trod water. Last time we floated in a lake together, at the official swimming area, I'd vomited out my sob story about my mother and the lemon tree.

I still felt sheepish about that, but what Gretchen said had really made a difference. It had changed how I thought about it and had led to that conversation with Auden.

I wanted her to know that. And this was—apparently—my last chance to tell her. "I was thinking about what you said about how I'm reacting to the lemon tree thing."

"What did I say?"

"You said to lean into the shitty way it made me feel. That holding on to things gives them power over you. I mean, not that I'm suddenly magically over my mother and all her bullshit, but you were right. And *that* made me think about how my sister said something similar about the album I was thinking I'd write while I was here—she said it was reactive, and she was right. I was doing it to get back at Scott. I was even thinking of it as 'the revenge album.'"

"Hmm."

I'd expected her to say more, to dispense more of her hard-to-hear but correct advice, but she only rotated in place while she trod water.

I assumed she was still listening, so I continued. "I've been thinking maybe I should reach out to Scott. Apologize. See if I can salvage something."

She stopped rotating, but she wasn't facing me. I could see her face in silhouette thanks to the moonlight. "You mean like a friendship or a professional partnership?"

"I don't know, either? Both?" Did I want that, though? I was clearly writing different kinds of songs, at least for now. And as for friendship, how would that even work? We'd never been friends outside the context of the band.

Gretchen hadn't said anything, so I asked, "You don't think it's a good idea?"

"Oh, no, I have no opinion."

"Say it like you mean it."

"You should do what you think is right."

You should do what you think is right? Something was off here. She was spouting generalities, and she was sounding uncharacteristically uncertain. "I'm just feeling like most of the way we left things is on me. Scott is not a bad guy. You'd like him."

"Does your sister like him?"

What an odd question. "Not so much." Auden had never come out and said it, but I hadn't gotten the sense that she was the president of the Scott Collier fan club. "But she doesn't really like anyone. She tolerates him, though." Or maybe I should say "tolerated," past tense. Because unless I did reach out, I probably wasn't going to see Scott again. That was a sobering thought. How could someone who'd been such a big part of my life just be…gone forever?

"I think I have to tell you something," Gretchen said, sounding more like her usual, decisive self.

"OK." My stomach dropped. But why? It wasn't as if I were getting dumped, which was what her tone brought to mind. You couldn't get dumped if you weren't in a relationship to begin with.

"I should have told you this a long time ago."

Now I was getting freaked.

"I don't even know why I'm telling you this."

Which is it? I wanted to ask. *You should have told me a long time ago, or you don't know why you're telling me?*

JENNY HOLIDAY

"It's not like it has any impact on what you do or don't do with respect to Scott."

Huh?

"It's not a big deal, is the point. I'm building it up like it's a big deal, but—"

"Will you just tell me!"

"I went on a date with Scott."

My blood turned to ice water. "*What?*"

"We matched on Tinder. He was my last hurrah that I mentioned."

"*What?*"

I couldn't think of anything else to say. *What?* was the only thought in my head right then. It was taking up all the available space, pushing up against the edges of my head—of my whole body.

"I didn't know it was him," she said quickly. "And even once I knew it was him, I didn't know him. I couldn't have named any of the members of Concrete Temple at that point, and I couldn't have picked Scott—or any of you—out of a police lineup. I only recognized you at the Minneapolis airport because I'd googled you after Marion wrote to us about joining the staff at Wild Arts."

I didn't like this feeling of having one giant, unsettling thought in my head. An angry thought. This was how I ended up smashing TVs in Hilton Garden Inns. Not that I was going to lash out violently here. I was more confused than anything.

But more than that, I needed to not be the kind of person who lashed out violently in general. Ever. So I forced myself to replay what she'd said and to react to it in a normal way.

"I'm sorry I was such a dick that day at the airport. I was...I was a mess. I was coming off more media attention than I'd ever had in my life, and it was all focused on behavior I wasn't proud of. The most attention I've ever got coincided with the worst day of my life. Not that I wanted *any* attention."

"You know," she said quizzically, "you always hear famous people saying they don't want to be famous, but it always seems at least partially disingenuous. But with you it seems real."

"It is. I accept that a certain amount of fame comes with the privilege of getting to make music for my job. If you want to make money playing music, you can't do it without an audience. But usually people recognize me only in specific settings, and that's how I like it. But…" I was trying to find a balance here, of not going all Hulk-smash but also getting my needs met. I needed to talk about this date. So I took the remarkable yet unremarkable step of opening my mouth and asking, "Can we talk about Scott, though? Can you tell me about this date?"

She proceeded to spin the most astonishing tale. Everything she said made sense. We had been in Minneapolis that night. Scott had been in the hotel room next door to me, for fuck's sake.

The way she described Scott was both familiar and not. As difficult as it was, I let her speak without interruption. The pit that had opened in my stomach when she first said she'd gone on a date with him slowly started to fill with…something. Dread, I suppose, though I felt it physically, like tar. I felt responsible for this having happened to her, though I understood with my intellect that Scott was not me and I was not Scott.

Maybe that was what I'd been needing to understand, to articulate, all along.

Scott was not me and I was not Scott.

We'd made a lot of music together, but it didn't necessarily follow that that was the only way we could do music.

Well, shit.

I told myself to shelve this revelation to examine later. Right now my job was to listen to Gretchen.

"He wasn't violent or anything," she assured me.

He wasn't violent. That was a low bar.

She cleared her throat. "But he was actually the one who inspired me to give up dating." Her tone was, on the surface of things, light. Almost glib. I could see beneath the surface, though. "Well, that's not fair. I'd already decided. I guess he was the nail in the coffin."

"So what you are saying is Scott turned you into a crone," I said. It sounded wrong, though. I'd been trying not to over-react, but I feared I'd come off like I was making light of what had happened to her.

"Well, remember I'm only an aspiring crone. But yeah. But also, not just Scott. He and all who came before him."

"For the record," I said, "maybe your encounter wasn't physically violent, but it sure as hell sounded...psychically violent."

"Yeah," she said quietly. "That's a good way of putting it."

"I kind of want to get out of this water, hunt him down, and break his face." It was the truth, but in my ongoing attempt to not overreact, I kept my tone calm, even.

"I assume you know that's a bad idea." She chuckled. "Though I do appreciate the impulse."

"I do know it's a bad idea." I paused. "I don't know if you read the tabloid stuff about me smashing a TV." I didn't wait for her to confirm whether she had. "I know probably every rock loser who's trashed a hotel room has said this, but I don't know what came over me. I'm embarrassed by it. I'd like to say that wasn't really me. I've been thinking about it all summer, and I guess I have to face the fact that it *was* me. It wasn't like that TV smashed itself. Anyway, my point is that while I say I'd like to break Scott's face, it really is, in this case, a figure of speech."

"Maybe it's Scott. He's the common denominator in these crappy encounters."

I wasn't sure if she was making a joke, but I took the proposition seriously. "He wasn't always like that." I paused. "Or maybe he was. That's the upsetting part. Did I just have bad judgment? *Years* of bad judgment? But anyway, I don't want to turn this around and make it about me. I'm sorry that happened to you. I'm sorry it happened to you at the hands of someone I used to call a friend."

"Used to call a friend" because this settled it. I'd answered my previous question about whether I should reach out, try to mend fences. Scott and I were done. Hopefully I'd get to the point where I'd remember the good stuff—the crowded van in those early days when we were so full of hope and ambition, the shared awe of our first stadium show, the addictive *eureka* feeling of nailing a song during a writing session.

"No need to apologize," Gretchen said. "You're not responsible for him."

"I know that, but to some extent we're judged by the company we keep, you know?"

"I actually did judge you, initially, by the company you kept."

"I don't blame you."

"I tried not to, mind you, but then you *were* kind of a jerk at the airport."

I couldn't deny it. I told myself not to try to explain away my behavior again. She'd heard me the first time.

"But then I realized you and Scott are totally different."

That was interesting. At the risk of continuing to make this all about me, I asked, "How so?"

"You're not smooth and charming like he was. You're a lot grouchier. Less appealing."

I barked a laugh. "Thank you very much."

"Initially," she clarified. "But really, you guys are inverses of each other. He's all smooth and charming, but he's rotten inside. You're all…"

"Go on."

"You're prickly on the outside, and you can be an asshole, but inside you're actually very upstanding. Honorable. Kind, even."

Damn. The water was cool, but I could feel myself flushing. "I think you're giving me too much credit."

"I'm not. Look at the way you booted Tristan out of here. The way you're helping Anna."

"Arguably, that is called doing my job." For some reason her characterization made me uncomfortable. I *wanted* to be those things: honorable, upstanding, kind. I just wasn't sure I *was*.

"Well, then you're doing your job well."

"Well, maybe, but I'm also lazy—I went to a grand total of two sunrise circles while the kids were here. And I *am* kind of a dick—I basically ignored a couple of the music kids because they were talentless wannabes."

She splashed me, signaling that she was done enumerating my good qualities, which was honestly a relief. "Anyway," she said, "I'm still not sure I should have told you about my date with Scott. It's been stressing me out not telling you, and when you brought him up, it felt like lying to keep silent. But maybe it was selfish, dumping this all on you. It's not as if you can do anything about it, and I've probably messed with your mental image of one of your best friends."

"We were never *best* friends, but we were tight. We worked really well together. And his family was...really good to me."

"Where did you meet?"

"We met at band camp, basically, if you can believe it. The band teacher at my school was pals with some other teachers in the city, and they organized an informal battle of the bands one summer—a round-robin tournament. I was in a shitty band at that point with some guys from my school. Scott went to a fancy arts high school, and his band was much better than mine. But we ended up vying for the title, and I don't know, I guess we had a lot of respect for each other. We started jamming. His parents were wealthy—they had that big apartment on the Upper East Side that I told you about—and I spent all my free time there until we graduated. Then they basically bankrolled the band through the lean years. And when I'd eat dinner there, which was often, they always sent me home with leftovers, which I'd give to my sister. They were good folks."

Which was why it was so hard to hear what a shithead their kid became.

But also, hearing the story of what a shithead Scott had been to Gretchen made me feel less bad about how *I* was feeling about him.

"Well, you show different sides of yourself to different people. Just because he was one way to me doesn't mean—"

"If you're about to say what he did to you doesn't make him a bad person, you're incorrect."

"I don't want you to feel like you have—"

"I don't feel like I have to do anything. I'm glad you told me. It makes it easier to just stay out of touch, actually."

"Are you sure?"

I had never been more sure of anything in my life. Her story was the last piece of a puzzle clicking into place. I was done with Concrete Temple. I was done with Scott. I was in another phase. My protest music era, or whatever. I didn't even know yet. But somehow, it was easier to be in a new phase knowing the old one was really, truly behind me.

"I've been wondering about his wife," Gretchen said.

"Meaning should you tell her he's on the prowl?"

"Yeah. I mean, I don't know how I'd do that. Send her a DM on Instagram, I guess."

"They've been separated more than a year now, if it makes you feel better."

"It does, actually."

"Well, good. Honestly, I don't know the ins and outs of their separation, but I think we can both feel OK about letting go of the Scott fallout in our lives."

She heaved a big, relieved sigh. "I feel so much lighter now that I've told you."

I felt so much lighter now that she'd told me. And I had gotten to explain the TV smashing incident. "I guess this is why people go to confession. Come on. Shampoo time."

We swam back to the dock, and I shimmied up far enough to grab her shower caddy and to angle the flashlight so it was illuminating us. I squirted some shampoo into my hand. "Hold on to that post."

"You're going to wash my hair?" she exclaimed in disbelief.

"This is a full-service confession, ma'am." I paused. "Unless you don't want me to."

"Oh, by all means, knock yourself out. And remember I paid for the shampoo with extra scalp massage."

I chuckled and got to work.

"Oh my God," she said after a few seconds. "That feels amazing."

I had never washed anyone's hair before, and I didn't know what had possessed me. I mean, partly it was that I was ready to move on to the indoor portion of our evening. But mostly I just…wanted to take care of her. Not to make up for what Scott did to her, but to show her that…I don't know, that she was worth caring about. Even if she was happily on her way to cronedom.

Sourplum: she was confusing. But I was used to it now. I could exist inside the confusion.

Eventually she submerged herself to rinse, and when she came up she asked, "Are you doing the conditioner, too?"

"Sure." I got started on that and said, "I've never really understood the point of conditioner."

"You don't use it?"

"Nope."

"How is your hair so shiny and pretty, then?" I chuckled, and she added, "I assume your masculinity isn't so fragile that you object to having your hair called pretty?"

"Nope. Remember I'm the guy who gets his nails done at strip malls in Cincinnati. So I'm fine having pretty hair. And as for why it is that way, I don't know. Conditioner wasn't something we had lying around as a kid. These days, they definitely put it on me when I get my hair cut, and sometimes I buy a bottle, but then it seems like an extra step that's just a time suck, and I fall off the wagon."

"Isn't your hair hard to comb through when it's wet, though?"

"Sure is."

"Well, this will help." She swatted my shoulder, seeming to want me to turn around. I did, and damned if *she* didn't start shampooing *my* hair. "Uhn," I said. It wasn't like I didn't know, objectively, that having someone massage your scalp felt good, but there was something extra about Gretchen doing it in a lake under the moonlight. Something that felt very close to what I'd been trying to make her feel: cared for.

She didn't linger, though. "Rinse," she ordered, and after I did, she combed conditioner through my hair with her fingers. "You're supposed to let it sit for a while, but I'm impatient."

"You are, are you?" I teased. "Why?"

"Because you're making sex moans as I'm washing your hair."

"You started it."

She swatted my shoulder. "Rinse."

"Yes, ma'am."

We both ducked—she still had her conditioner in. It took me longer to rinse—I guess my hair was thicker and longer—and when I came back up, she was soaping her armpits. Why was that so hot?

"You want this?" She held up the soap. "It's biodegradable and approved for lake use—so was the shampoo and conditioner—in case you were wondering."

I had not been wondering. It had never occurred to me that products used to clean would somehow be bad for nature, but as was well established, I was not a natural—pun intended—when it came to nature. "I'm good, thanks."

"All right," she said, plunking the soap in her caddy. "Let's get this show on the road."

She suggested we go to her cabin, where she said she had

some spray detangler that she wanted to use on me, so we crept across the road.

"You're missing your oh-so-effective hoodie disguise," I teased.

"Eh," she said. "I'm pretty sure everyone's onto us. Maiv and Jack, anyway."

Maiv I wasn't surprised by. Even if Gretchen hadn't told her, Maiv was perceptive. I suppose it was her painter's eye. "Jack knows?"

"Yeah. That time I came over to your place with a condom, I'd gotten it from him."

"Well, damn."

"He's never said anything, though." She wrapped her towel around her hair as we walked. "You know, I'm starting to wonder if I've misjudged him."

"I read his book," I said.

"Really?"

"Yeah. I downloaded it on my phone after my first few drinks with him." I shrugged. "I don't know, I was curious. And I've been thinking about how I used to read a lot when I was younger. I wasn't a great student, but my library card got a lot of use. I fell out of the habit somewhere along the way." If the next phase of my life was going to be less relentless, with its hippie folk music and its lack of punishing world tours, I intended to acquire the habit again.

"How was it?"

"It was great, actually. It really made me think, and it was just a good story—a page-turner."

"I was afraid of that."

"What? Why?"

She looked around as we mounted her porch and gestured me inside before saying, "Because he's such a jerkface."

I chuckled. "I think he's just insecure."

"I think you might be right. I feel bad I misjudged him."

"Well, he does come off as a jerk, and you can't be everyone's psychologist. Just mine." I winked. "But if Jack knows we're sleeping together and hasn't said anything yet, I think our secret is probably safe."

"Anyway, it doesn't matter who knows. I'm gone tomorrow."

"Right."

Right.

As I watched her disappear into her bathroom, I started to...I didn't even know. What was this strange fluttery feeling in my stomach?

I was nervous. I'd felt like this in the early years of Concrete Temple, when we'd started leveling up from dive bars to small concert venues, and then again in a bigger way when we graduated to arenas. Stage fright.

I told myself that was ridiculous. It was just Gretchen. We were old hands at this by now. We knew each other's bodies. There was no performance anxiety. She was, frankly, easy to get off. And she really did it for me, too.

It was going to be strange not to have her around.

"You know that song 'Moon River'?" she asked as she emerged from the bathroom holding a hairbrush. She made a game show hostess gesture to a cascade of moonlight angling in through her window.

"Look at that, we've got our own moon river."

She shimmied out of her swimsuit, and she stood and wrapped her towel around herself, securing it under one armpit. I did the same, tying my towel around my waist—and then I shocked the hell out of myself by holding my hands out and saying, "Dance with me."

I'd shocked the hell out of her, too, judging by the face she shot me.

I moved into the moonbeam. "Come on." I started humming "Moon River."

"You are such a weirdo."

She came into my arms, though, and rested her head on my chest. I switched from humming to singing as I got to the line "Wherever you're going, I'm going your way." Ironic, given that this was our last night.

"What do you think a 'huckleberry friend' is?" she asked after I was done.

"I don't know, but it sounds good." I ran through the lyrics in my head. "Maybe a friend you go on an adventure with? A friend you can roam free with?"

"Like a camp friend. Remember Marion talking about that?"

"Yeah." Though *camp friend* felt like not a strong enough designation for us—if in fact she was implying we were camp friends.

We kept swaying even though the song was done. That was the nice thing about dancing in the moonlight to imaginary music—you could do it as long as you wanted to.

"You know," she said, her voice muffled against my chest, "at some point I started thinking of you as my camp boyfriend."

"What?"

"I know I'm the one who's been hyper over saying nothing we've done was a date and we aren't together—and nothing was and we aren't. But I don't know..."

"Dancing in towels in the moonlight is a pretty romantic thing to do."

I expected her to scoff, or to deflect, but she just said, "Yes."

"But also illegal, according to the Gretchen Miller view of the world."

She laughed. "Also yes. But maybe there's a loophole if you're only my camp boyfriend, you know?"

"Is a camp boyfriend one step up from an imaginary boyfriend?"

"Exactly. Low effort. Superlow in this case, as you didn't even know you were my camp boyfriend until the eve of our breakup."

She was saying all this laughingly, with a hint of self-deprecation. I couldn't get with the vibe. I couldn't stop glitching on this idea that she'd been thinking of me this way and I hadn't known. "Except," I said, "I think if you're using the camp friend analogy, the idea is that camp friends see each other every summer, right?"

What was I saying? That I wanted to see her next summer? I wasn't going to be back next summer.

Was I?

Would I even be invited if I wanted to come back?

"Sure, sometimes," Gretchen said, "but I was talking to the dance counselors recently about this very topic, and they said sometimes a camp friend doesn't come back."

"And what happens then?"

"Nothing. They're sad for a while, but there's enough else happening that they get over it."

I for one was never going to forget Gretchen. I wasn't sure if what I'd undergone this summer was attributable to the place or to her or to some alchemical combination of the two, but I was a different person from when I'd arrived. A better person.

I didn't know how to say any of that, though, so I let the hand that had been wrapped around her float up and rest on her cheek so I could tip her head up and kiss her.

She sighed into my mouth, and something like a sigh

happened to me, too, to my whole body. I wasn't sure if I'd ever been so relaxed, so rooted. We kissed for a long time. Maybe we were making up for those early, kissless encounters. Or maybe we were banking kisses for the future. Things eventually heated up, but not in the usual way. Normally when we had sex, things were frantic. We'd be tearing our clothes off and going at it like teenagers—that was why we'd skipped the kissing initially. This time, though, it was slow. I would have said lazy, but that wasn't the right word. We were exacting in our ministrations, careful as we let hands glide over skin, as we let towels fall to the floor. *"I went to the woods because I wanted to live deliberately."* The line snaked through my consciousness as we touched each other with such focused intent.

Eventually she led me to her bed, and we lay on our sides facing each other. She stroked my face, like she had that night in the forest. It felt like she was trying to memorize me. I wanted to do the same. Not that I was in any danger of forgetting her—that was impossible—but I wanted the sense memory. I wanted to caress her face and tangle my fingers in her hair. I wanted my hands to remember what she felt like. So I did all those things. I wondered if she'd been struck with a similar impulse, because she brushed her hands over my tattoos—the ones she could reach, anyway. She would find one, rub her fingers over it in a little circle, and look at me with an expression I couldn't decode. Something that contained fondness, but also sadness.

When she was done with her tour of my ink, which felt like she was done with her tour of my life, she heaved a big, shaky breath and turned away to get a condom. She tipped me to my back and climbed on top. I grabbed her hands, and she rode me, staring at me and holding my hands like she never wanted to let go. I knew I didn't. She was upright, and the moon river hit her, painting her shoulders and breasts in its white light.

"Gretchen, I—"

"Shh." She shook her head, and I swallowed the rest of the sentence. Once it was gone, I wasn't even sure what it had been.

Slowly we carried on, staring at each other and holding hands as she ground herself on me. When she came, it was with an almost surprised-sounding cry. And it was a cry. A wail, almost.

I knew this feeling. It was building in me, too. It was pleasure, but pain. Sorrow. It was goodbye.

When we'd finished, she slumped forward and buried her head in my neck. We lay there a long time. It reminded me of when she'd slept in my arms in the woods. Except this time, when we got up, it would be the end.

I wasn't used to being in Gretchen's cabin. The nice thing about mine—aside from not having to do the James Bond walk of shame to get home—was that I didn't have to make the decision about when we were done. She could leave whenever she wanted. Which, historically, had been not long after our encounters. She'd usually loll around a bit. We'd even had one or two serious post-sex conversations—about teaching, about our childhoods. But she never fell asleep. She always left.

So I should probably do the same.

But now, with us wrapped up in each other after the most intense sexual experience I'd ever had, I didn't know how to leave.

We'd been lying silently for a good ten minutes when she shifted against me. "Is it OK if I stay a bit?" I whispered into her hair.

"Assuming you don't mind slumming it in my low-thread-count sheets, sure," she said, turning onto her side to face away from me. She flashed me a smile over her shoulder that felt like it was scooping out my insides.

Would it have been that easy all along? If I'd asked her to stay over at my place any of the nights we'd gotten it on, would she have?

It seemed that skipping morning swims wasn't the only opportunity I'd missed this past month.

I lay there in my big spoon position thinking about how we'd never done her leave-in conditioner, or even combed our hair. We'd gone straight to dancing in the moonlight. I was going to have a mess of tangles in the morning, but I didn't care. I wondered what Gretchen's hair would be like when she woke up.

"Mm," she sighed.

I hadn't realized I'd started playing with her hair. She liked it—she was angling her head into my touch like a cat chasing scratches.

So I lay there stroking Gretchen's hair as she fell asleep. Until long after she fell asleep, actually. I was content, partly. But underneath that contentment was a hole, and as Gretchen's breaths expanded, so did the hole. I had the oddest sense that like Gretchen's literal hole, I'd dug it myself.

14
REALITY IS FOR LOSERS

Gretchen

I woke up to the sound of a piano. I was confused at first, thinking I'd fallen asleep in Teddy's cabin. But then last night came rushing in. The swimming, the shampoo, the dancing. "Moon River." My huckleberry friend.

My camp boyfriend.

It was still dark. And dawn came early here, so I could be fairly confident it was still night.

I let my eyes adjust. There he was, sitting at the keyboard in my cabin. He was playing—

Oh my God, he was playing "Lemon Tree."

I sat up, but then I froze. I wasn't sure if he wanted an audience. But I also didn't want him to stop.

This was a big deal. This song that had been haunting him all month, this song he said he could never seem to make himself play. But here it was, now, the music at least. It felt like he was doing some kind of ritual. An exorcism, maybe.

He turned and made eye contact with me. I expected him to stop playing, or to look away at least, but he didn't do either.

He had to break with my gaze occasionally to look down at the keys, but he always found it again.

As the song neared its end, instead of winding down, he segued into starting over, and this time he sang. "When I was just a lad of ten…" He made a face like, *Can you believe this?*

I nodded vigorously. I hoped he understood what that nod meant. *Yes. I believe it. I believe in you.*

It was a funny song to be serenaded with, because it was very much not a love song. It was, as I'd thought the first time I'd heard it, the opposite of a love song.

Of course, he wasn't serenading me. I just happened to be here. He was doing his ritual. And I was a crone in training, right? Rituals should be right up my alley. Before I could over-think it, I joined in on the next chorus.

The smile he gave me was a blow to the chest. I was no singer—I didn't know how to harmonize, and I had to trail off on the verses because I didn't know the words, but it didn't matter. We were singing together.

The second time the song ended, he stopped. Left his hands on the keyboard and just looked at me.

I didn't know what to do. Usually this was the point at which I'd get up and leave—I had been careful all summer about not overstaying my welcome with Teddy or doing any-thing that could be considered too coupley—but we were in my cabin.

He stood. He was dressed. I wanted to tell him not to go yet. I wanted him to stay until morning.

But those were not things I could have. And really, they weren't things I *wanted*. They were like craving another drink when you'd already had one too many.

I reminded myself that I'd gotten exactly what I wanted from Teddy. I'd gotten my last hurrah—boy, had I ever.

I was trying to think what to say when he shot me a crooked, fond smile and said, "See you, Miller."

The minimalist approach. I liked it. I did have to swallow a lump in my throat, though, in order to say, "See you, Knight."

———

I wouldn't have thought it possible to fall asleep after Teddy left, but a couple hours later, I awakened to the beeping of my alarm. I lay there staring at the pine ceiling, "Moon River" and "Lemon Tree" zipping around inside me.

I was seized with more of that nostalgia in advance. I felt it in my chest, a physical ache. I was missing camp while I was still here. I was missing my camp boyfriend.

I couldn't have Teddy, not for real. I didn't *want* him, not for real. But that didn't mean I wasn't going to miss him.

Eventually I got up and, in preparation for reentering the real world, turned on my phone. Rory was going to text when she was close.

It felt strange in my hand. Alien. As it found a signal, notifications started rolling in. I felt ill.

It was good to see Rory, though, when she arrived that afternoon. It hit me how much I'd missed her. She wasn't my camp friend; she was my real friend. We'd been through some shit together. I hugged her, and she was solid. Real.

And so very pregnant. "You look amazing!"

"I look huge is what you mean."

"You look amazing," I reiterated. "Feeling OK?"

"Pretty much. A bit of swelling at the end of the day, and

it's getting hard to find a comfortable position to sleep in, but I'm hanging in there."

"Let me give you a tour. Unless you want to just go chill in my cabin until the show?"

"How about a minitour followed by chilling? I brought you a treat that I may need to eat ninety percent of myself." She produced a bag of Cheetos from her purse.

Which made me think of the last time I'd had Cheetos—as a side dish with cold pack cheese food grilled cheese. Made by Teddy last week, or a lifetime ago, one or the other.

———

The show was a hit.

Everyone did great. There was a gallery of visual art that everyone perused at the start of the evening, the kids standing by to answer questions about their paintings and sculptures and pots while Maiv and Danny hovered like proud parents.

The performance part of the show started with readings from Jack's writer kids. As with the paintings and pots, a couple stood out from the crowd—a poem from a small, quiet boy who never looked up while he read, and a viciously funny short story from a goth girl.

The drama kids went next, performing a one-act play set in a British air-raid shelter during World War II. I only caught the first ten minutes or so because we were up next, but they did a great job.

The girls gathered backstage in their costumes. They seemed to be looking to me for words of wisdom. "I guess I'm supposed to give a pep talk here?" I was unprepared. "I don't know what to say except I know this is going to be great. We've immersed ourselves in these stories, these themes. There's no way it can go wrong."

When I got a few skeptical looks, I fell back on Miss Miller's Morals. "And even if it does go wrong, it's just dancing. Dancing is supposed to be fun."

Some of the artists had opened their sections of the show with introductory remarks. I skipped that. I felt the work should speak for itself. And it did: my girls stormed out for the ball scene set to Beyoncé, and it was *great*. I'd run around and was watching from the back of the audience, which erupted into cheers when Meg and Jo broke out of the formal quadrille and started a modern duet. And I hadn't been wrong about the Jo/Lori chemistry. The audience was feeling it, too—everyone grew quiet and attentive, and I could feel the crackling tension in the air.

Obviously the audience was biased, but when at the end they leaped to their feet and hooted and hollered as my girls, beaming, took their bows, I had to wipe away a tear. On paper this wasn't that different from the recitals I ran twice a year at my studio, yet it was. I knew what had gone into this. Well, I knew what went into my recitals, too. I guess the difference was that *more* had gone into this. The recitals were fun. I taught the steps, the dancers danced them, and the parents clapped and cheered. But there was no story, no overarching narrative. There was no meaning.

As the applause went on, I saw a few girls wipe away tears through their smiles as they bowed. I was so proud, I about melted into a pile of goo. When they called me onstage and group-hugged me, I think my soul left my body momentarily.

It was the greatest moment of my professional life, as overwrought as that sounds.

The music kids closed out the show. As with the other

groups, some kids were better than others. Until Teddy's music prodigy kid, who went last, blew us away. She played an original on banjo that had the breezy but brutal wordplay of Taylor Swift, the twang of the Chicks, and a delicate, high soprano that reminded me of Billie Eilish. It was really something. I sneaked a look at Teddy, who was standing off to the side, his hands folded under his chin in a really intense way. When she was done, his face lit up like a Christmas tree, and when she looked over at him, he punched the air. Then he got onstage and joined the music kids and counselors for a rousing version of "Bohemian Rhapsody." By the end, we were all singing along. It was transcendent.

Rory turned to me after the final curtain call. "Wow. Just... wow."

"Pretty great, isn't it?"

I was so glad she'd made me come here, and I started to say as much but was interrupted, pulled away by girls wanting me to meet their parents, and later by Brianna and Grace, who had duties yet this evening—they had to supervise the moving-out process—which was for the best because it made our goodbyes less emotional than they otherwise might have been. "I've learned so much from you both," I said into our group hug.

"Are you kidding?" Grace said. "*I've* learned so much from *you*. And not just about dance, but about, I don't know, leadership." Brianna echoed Grace's sentiment, and I was on the verge of tears again.

Eventually the kids and parents were herded outside by the counselors, who were leading everyone back to the cabins to get their stuff, which left Rory and me with the artists and Marion. I introduced her to everyone, congratulating myself when my voice came out normally during the Teddy Knight intro.

"Usually I make this speech at the end of the second session, but since Gretchen is leaving us, you'll get it early," Marion said as we stood in a loose circle at the back of the auditorium. "I've stayed out of your way, but now you're going to get some unsolicited advice—from someone who's never made a painting or written a song in her life."

Everyone smiled. Marion was a good egg.

"It's been easy here. Not literally, perhaps. In one sense, you've been roughing it without air-conditioning or the comforts of home. And some of you got literally lost in the woods." She winked at me. "But you've had very few demands on you. That's a gift. I'm not trying to pat myself on the back; it's just a fact. I think most of you have used this time either to nurture a burst of creativity or to rest and recharge. Both are valid, and important.

"But neither is going to be easy to do when you go back to your lives, where you may have day jobs, teaching commitments, shows, exhibitions, and so on. Not to mention families and friends."

I didn't have those things. Well, of course I had my mom and sister, but we didn't see each other that often. My personal life was pretty much limited to hanging with Rory and her family, and they were getting ready to turn inward when the new baby arrived. Which left work. The hustle. The thing that was going to ramp up big-time when I got home. The thing that had always felt so central to my identity.

"My hope for you," Marion went on, "is that you hang on to some of what being here gave you, whether it's a sense of creative expansion or merely permission to rest. I hope you can find a way to get some of that in your real life."

Rest. I should prioritize that when I got home. Have phone-less days.

Maybe I should plant a garden. Put up a hammock. Yes. Both those ideas appealed.

I felt better having made that plan.

Marion approached. "I have to go oversee the tangle that is the parking lot." She gave me a firm hug. "Between you and me, I wish you were staying. I'm sure Irina Petrov"—Marion had gotten a dancer from the Joffrey Ballet for session two—"will be great, but you really had a way with the kids. You're a natural teacher."

I was chuffed by the praise. "Thanks. I've had such a wonderful month, but it's time for me to get back to that—teaching."

Why wasn't I more excited?

I was excited about the hammock, I reminded myself, and about my future garden.

"Well," I said to the assembled artists. "I guess it's back to reality for me."

"Reality is overrated," Caleb said jokingly, and at that moment I couldn't say I disagreed.

"Yeah," Danny said, "Reality is for losers. Stay!"

"I can't. My reality involves closing on a new building next month, and I have a ton to do."

"Yeah, I know," Danny said, "you're our resident entrepreneur."

Resident entrepreneur.

I guess that was right. Despite my late-in-the-game burst of choreographic creativity, I was going back to my small business. My soon-to-be-larger small business. There would be no leaping out of holes for me. I mean, I had thought about it, but where would I even do it?

I had thought about *that*, too, and for a moment I thought, *Hey, I just decided I should start gardening. What is gardening but digging holes in the ground?*

But I gave myself a reality check. Sure, I could work on the piece, but to what end? It wasn't ever going to get mounted anywhere, even if I didn't have a full-time job—a more-than-full-time job—sucking up all my time and energy.

It didn't even seem real, all those hours I'd spent mucking around behind the shower building. From this vantage point, it was starting to feel like a dream I'd woken from and could only remember in fragmented flashes.

Maiv kicked off the rest of the goodbyes by throwing her arms around me. She didn't say anything, but she was teary, which made me teary, too. We *were* going to stay in touch, we had already decided, so it wasn't really goodbye. Caleb reiterated his invitation for us to work on something together, and I deflected. I could see Rory gearing up to ask questions, so I moved on to Danny, who gave me a beautiful vase. Its dark-blue glaze was the same color as the lake at afternoon swim time.

Next up was Jack, who shook my hand and said, "Be good."

I smiled at him—genuinely. "Good luck with the book. Or are you not supposed to say that? Is it like with plays, where you're supposed to say, 'Break a leg'?"

"I'll take it. I need all the luck I can get."

"Nah, you don't need luck. You've got what it takes." Look at me, complimenting Jack Branksome. Maybe I'd even follow in Teddy's footsteps and read his book when I got home.

And then there was only Teddy left.

"Am I allowed to say that I'm going to miss you?" he asked.

"Of course. I'm going to miss you, too."

We hugged, but it was awkward—we both moved to the same side and ended up doing a little dance, but not the swaying-in-the-moonlight kind. How was it we'd had the ease of longtime lovers last night, but here we couldn't make our limbs cooperate?

It was akin to the way my phone had felt strange in my hand that morning—a relic I wasn't familiar with. Suddenly Teddy was the human version of that.

Which was good, in a way. It would make my departure easier.

"We're not going to stay in touch, are we?" he whispered in my ear, his breath making me shiver.

"I don't think it's a good idea," I said as I pulled away. Just like the hole dance didn't fit into my real life, neither did my rock star camp boyfriend.

"What's not a good idea?" Rory asked.

"Right," Teddy said. "You'll be busy with your empire. And your crone duties."

"Your *what* duties?" Rory said.

"Bye, Miller," Teddy said, stepping back from me and lifting a palm.

"Bye, Knight."

And that was it.

How could something that felt so monumental end with so little fuss?

It hadn't been monumental, though, I reminded myself. That had been the whole point. It had been convenient, and now it wasn't anymore.

Last hurrah: I could check that off my list.

———

To my surprise, Rory didn't get on my case as we pulled away from camp. We talked about the show, and she filled me in on the happenings at the studio: someone's check for the fall session had bounced, Keira—a little shit I was this close to ejecting from the studio—had written on the wall under Miss Miller's Morals, the phone bill was due tomorrow and Rory hadn't known how to pay it.

I was being bombarded by the minutiae of my empire. Of my life.

I didn't care about any of it at the moment, but I was happy to let it wash over me, because it meant Rory was keeping her mouth shut on all matters camp.

Until we hit Hinckley, where we stopped at Tobies for their iconic caramel rolls. I had let my guard down, because when she said, "You have something going on with that Teddy guy, don't you?" I spilled my coffee.

I bought time by grabbing some napkins and cleaning up the mess. I considered lying, but what would be the point? I wasn't going to see Teddy again. He had served his purpose in my life, as had I, I hoped, in his. We'd had some spectacular sex, and as a bonus, I felt like he'd worked out some of his mental junk. Not that I took credit for that exactly, but I liked to think I'd helped.

Not bad, as far as last hurrahs went.

It was weird that I hadn't told Rory about Teddy. She and I told each other everything. I could blame the fact that I hadn't on having ditched my phone. Now, though, I was back in the real world, and in the real world, I didn't keep secrets from Rory.

More importantly, there was no *reason* to keep Teddy a secret. Yes, I'd skulked around camp trying to be incognito, but that had to do with not wanting to be the subject of gossip, with not wanting people all up in my business.

"I *did* have something going on with him, past tense." I

waggled my eyebrows. "We had a camp-friends-with-benefits thing going."

She slapped the table. "I knew it! Tell me everything!"

"There's not much to tell. We got lost in the woods together, and one thing led to another."

"I can't believe you didn't tell me!"

"I wasn't using my phone."

"Yeah, but you were getting it on with a famous rock star! You didn't think that merited telling me?"

"I'm telling you now."

"I didn't tell you about Mike to begin with."

That was true. She'd kept her dealings with her now husband on the down-low for a long time. But I didn't see what that had to do with anything. "So?"

"I didn't tell you because I was afraid of how real it felt. I thought if I told you, you'd make me face up to it."

"Calm down. That's not what's happening here."

"It's not?"

"There's nothing to face up to! We had some fun." I did the eyebrow waggling thing again, but it felt like I was performing.

15
THE STANDARD ADVICE

Teddy

On break between sessions, I flew home to take care of a few things. Namely making sure Karlie was actually going to be out of my apartment before I returned for good at the end of the summer, and accompanying my sister to her first therapy appointment.

The Karlie part was anticlimactic. I'd texted her a couple days before I was set to arrive, saying I'd be in town and wanted to chat. When I got to my apartment, I found it empty. There was a bottle of bourbon on the kitchen island with a note in her familiar loopy handwriting that said, "Thanks for letting me (over) stay."

Well, that had been easy. Unnervingly easy.

I didn't have an Instagram account, but I went to a browser and checked out hers. She hadn't posted for a week, which was unlike her.

Now I was officially worried. I FaceTimed her.

"I thought you were staying till the end of August," I said when she picked up. I'd just wanted to make sure we were on track for that. I'd been planning to offer to hire movers if need be. "You didn't have to vacate immediately."

"I kind of did, though." She smiled fondly. "That's the problem with you; you're too nice."

"You're the only person in the world who has ever said or thought that."

"Yeah, well, you don't let people know you, not really. Not anyone but your sister, anyway. And maybe Scott." She quirked an eyebrow. She and I had not spoken about the band's demise, but presumably she'd read about it.

"Yeah, I thought I might try to make up with Scott, but I think I'm gonna leave it."

"That sounded like a question. Are you looking for my opinion?"

Why not? "Sure."

"You outgrew him. You outgrew the band. Maybe he did, too. It sucks, but it happens."

"You got all this wisdom since I last saw you. What are you up to? You have a place to stay?"

"I have a new project." She set the phone down, stepped back, and pulled the shirt she was wearing—an oversize men's button-down—tight over her...pregnant belly.

"Holy shit!"

She came back to the phone, laughing. "I can see you doing panic math there, but dude, I'm only five months along, and you and I haven't had sex in almost a year."

"I know, I know. I'm just surprised."

"You and me both."

"Not that it's any of my business, but is everything good with the father?"

"Yeah, yeah. He's great. But it's been...interesting. This wasn't planned, but we decided to go for it, both in terms of the kid and the relationship. He's excited about the baby—he's really cute about it, actually—but he doesn't want any of it on social media. Like, *any* of it. Not the pregnancy, and not the kid once it's here."

"Sounds like a smart guy."

"He is. It's caused me to have to seriously think about why I do what I do—or maybe did what I did. Was influencing about the money? Or was it something else? Attention?"

"And what did you conclude?"

"I don't know yet. But it was easy enough to take a step back, at least initially, because I had bad morning sickness."

"So this guy is treating you well."

"Yeah, yeah. I'm happy." She paused. "I know it seems fast."

"It doesn't seem fast."

It did seem fast. But maybe that was how it happened sometimes, when it was right. "I guess I was never Mr. Right."

"It's not that. Well, maybe you weren't Mr. Right for me. It's more that I always thought relationships were supposed to be hard," she went on. "You hear that, you know? Like, marriage takes work, or whatever. But maybe that's not actually true. Maybe when it's right, it's not that hard." She snorted. "Though I *am* rethinking my entire career path and identity, so maybe relationships *are* hard."

"Maybe that's not hard so much as it is an overdue reckoning."

" 'Overdue reckoning,' " she said thoughtfully. "That's a good phrase. That should be the name of your next band."

I chuckled. "I actually think I'm going to put out a solo record." But wait. What was this "I actually think" equivocation? I tried again. "I *am* going to put out a solo record."

"Good for you. You must be having a good summer, then."

"I'm having...a really interesting summer." And it was only half-over. I was surprisingly excited to go back for the second half, though at the same time, the prospect was daunting. I wasn't sure I could take another month of such intense creative and personal upheaval. "I made a lot of progress, chilled out a bit," I finished, keeping things purposefully vague.

She smiled. "I'm glad. You've been running yourself ragged for literal years."

I had been. I could see that now. I thought about what Marion had said to us about the importance of rest.

"So anyway," Karlie said, "thanks for letting me overstay. I haven't really been in the apartment in any meaningful way for a couple months. I was more just holding on because I do like having my own space—but of course it was never really my place."

"Yes it was. It was yours and mine." I paused, not sure what else I wanted from her but not quite ready to hang up. "We good, Karlie?"

"Yes, of course. I'm sorry I was a shit a lot of the time."

"Well, it took two to tango."

"We had some fun, though."

"We did."

"Anyway, I gotta go. I'm getting more into the furniture stuff, and I have a potential buyer coming to look at a piece."

"Bye, Karlie. Take care of yourself."

"See you around, Teddy."

Well. Knock me over with a feather. Apparently item one on my list had taken care of itself.

Which left Auden. I was due to see her tonight. What was I going to do with myself in the meantime?

I was going to rest.

I headed for the bedroom. I really did have some fancy-ass sheets.

———

"How was it?" I asked Auden the next day in the elevator on the way down from her first appointment with a psychologist. I'd offered to accompany her, and she'd wanted me to but asked me to wait in the lobby, which I'd been happy to do.

Well, not happy. More like nervous, worried, consumed with guilt that I hadn't seen all this shit my sister had been carrying around for so long.

She didn't answer right away, which was fine. I wasn't going to push it. I mean, did I desperately want to know everything that had been said? Yes. But I also understood that wasn't my right, or my role.

She spoke to the taxi driver and exchanged pleasantries with her doorman, but she didn't speak to me.

We rode the elevator up in silence, and I started to fret that she was mad at me. I wouldn't blame her. I'd always thought we were close, but I'd missed a hell of a lot.

As soon as I closed her apartment door behind us, she burst into tears.

Auden didn't cry, generally. She got mad. Maybe sometimes she got a little teary watching a sad movie. But even when we'd been kids and things had been *bad*, she hadn't been a crier.

I was having some kind of adrenaline-fueled fight-or-flight response. I felt like we were kids again, at that low point, when we realized Mom was well and truly gone. The worst period of my life. The panic over how to make sure Auden graduated high school. Where we would live. How we'd get money for food.

I took a breath and told myself that we were safe. We had food. We had homes—nice ones with Egyptian cotton sheets and shit. There was nothing to fight, except maybe Auden's fears, and I didn't know how to do that. But I could learn. I could rely on her to guide me.

So I opened my arms, and she stepped into them. I didn't know what to say—I didn't want to offer false platitudes—so I said, "Remember the lemon tree? The actual tree but also the song?"

"How could I forget?"

"I don't know. I sometimes don't know if what I remember is the way it actually went down, or if I'm giving things more importance in retrospect than they actually had."

"We hated that fucking tree."

"We did, right?"

She pulled away, wiped her face, and studied mine.

I beckoned her farther inside. We stopped in the kitchen, where I filled two water glasses from the tap and led her to the living room.

"There was a keyboard in my cabin at camp," I said, "and the first night I got there, 'Lemon Tree' came into my mind, and it...got its claws in me. I couldn't stop thinking about it. But I also couldn't play it. I think I played every other fucking song we sang with Mom back in the day, but I couldn't play that one."

I wasn't sure why I was telling her this. Maybe it was just that I was trying to do what Gretchen said—lean into the bullshit as a way of trying to discharge it. Maybe doing that would help Auden. Show her that it was possible.

"But then the second-to-last day," I said, "I suddenly played it."

"And?"

"I don't know." Well, that was dumb. I had been there. It was hard to explain, though. But wasn't that part of the point of the lean-in exercise? Putting to words things that felt ineffable? "It was anticlimactic, but in a good way. It felt like...just a song. I mean, I guess it will never be just a song. But the feelings I used to associate with it felt further away."

"Why does she still have so much power over us?"

That was the big question. "I don't know."

"Over me, anyway," Auden said. "It sounds like you're making progress."

"If I am, it's accidental. Well, no." That wasn't giving credit where credit was due. "It's more that..."

"What?"

"A friend from camp told me something that resonated with me. She said that when you're in a situation like we are, where a person, or a memory, or whatever, has a hold on you, you should lean into it."

"What does that mean?"

"In my case, I thought about those old days. Sang those old songs. The idea is that trying to avoid this stuff only makes it retain its power. But if you face it, you can discharge it." I shrugged. What did I know? "Maybe?"

"I think that's basically what the psychologist told me today, though not in exactly those words. And I gather that in my case, the 'facing it' part is meant to be slow and controlled and supervised."

"But you got a good feeling from her? Because if not, you know you can try someone else."

"I think she's good. Good enough to get started, anyway. And she recommended a psychiatrist who can prescribe meds, which she thinks is a good idea."

The relief I felt was massive, but I didn't want to freak her out, so I just said, "Good."

"I told her about my past in broad strokes. It was only a quick overview today. But do you think you could..."

Yes. I didn't even have to know what she was going to ask to know that the answer was yes. But of course I had to let her speak.

"Do you think you could come with me to some of the sessions where I tell her about..."

"...the lemon tree?" I supplied when she trailed off, knowing it stood for all this junk we were talking about.

"Yes. The lemon tree."

"Name the time, and I'll be there." I'd fly in from anywhere. Except Wild Arts. "After August, though. I can't leave Wild Arts in the lurch." Apparently, even though I'd started off phoning in my artist-in-residence duties, I was now committed.

She raised an eyebrow. "You can't leave Wild Arts, or you can't leave your 'friend' you're hooking up with there? The dancer with the pink hair, right?"

I made a face at her. "I can't leave Wild Arts. Gretchen isn't even there for the second session."

"Gretchen," Auden said quizzically. "And can I assume *Gretchen* is also the one who gave you all this sage advice about Mother Dearest?"

"She is," I said warily. "Was." I kept having to remind myself that Gretchen was in my past. She'd specifically said we weren't going to keep in touch, but I still hadn't absorbed the fact that I would literally never see her again.

"You like her!" Auden said in a singsong voice, teasing me in a juvenile way she never had when we were actual juveniles.

I took that as a kind of progress—for both of us. Life had been dead serious, for the most part, when we were kids.

"I do like Gretchen. Did." I was doing it again. "But not in that way. She was…fun." That was understating it entirely.

"Fun and wise. Maybe you shouldn't have let her go."

"Maybe it wasn't up to me." That was as close as I would come to admitting that if more had been on offer, I might have been down with it. Auden was still looking at me with that damned raised eyebrow. "Anyway, I can't get into something now. Isn't the standard advice after a breakup—and I've essentially had two, if you count Scott, which I kind of think I have to—to take some time for yourself? Be alone for a while?"

"Oh, screw the standard advice."

"Well, I don't have Gretchen's phone number. I don't know how to get ahold of her," I said, like this was my only, or main, obstacle.

"OK," Auden said, backing off in a way I found both uncharacteristic and destabilizing. "I see how it is."

I suddenly thought about how Karlie had said my next band should be named Overdue Reckoning.

I thought about it on the flight back to camp, too. I was having my overdue emotional reckoning, right? I'd played "Lemon Tree." Not only alone in my cabin, but in front of Gretchen. We'd sung it together. And I'd grappled with what it meant for my life, what it stood for in terms of acknowledging how much damage my mother had done. I'd decided to let Scott go. I'd written some new songs. Auden had confided in me about her troubles, and we were making a plan to tackle them. I'd made peace with Karlie. When I came back to New York in a month, my apartment would be waiting for me.

That was a hell of a lot of reckoning for a month. I should be happy. Or if not happy, exactly, satisfied. Content with a job well done.

Then why the hell was I so sad?

Sad was a new one for me.

I wondered if that was because sad was subtle. Maybe sad could hide beneath other, bulkier emotions like fear and anger. Emotions that could make a person smash a TV in a Hilton Garden Inn. Maybe I'd finally excavated the sadness that had been under the surface all along?

That didn't feel quite right, but what the hell did I know? I was a beginner at this emotional shit.

16
REARVIEW MIRROR

Gretchen

The thing about coming back to reality was there was a lot of reality to deal with.

When you abandon your life for a month, especially when the main item on your life to-do list is "Expand empire," a lot of stuff piles up. Admin for the existing studio. Getting ready for the fall sessions, which were more numerous and better attended than the summer sessions. Writing job descriptions because I was going to have to hire a receptionist/studio manager for the new place. Historically, I'd done that role myself with some help from some older students who covered the front desk when I was teaching my own classes in exchange for free lessons, but I wasn't going to be able to scale up that informal approach to things. I'd only ever hired teachers, who were independent contractors who invoiced me, so this was a whole new ball game involving payroll taxes and all kinds of stuff that hurt my head.

I had stuff to do on the home front, too, most urgently making nice with my cats, who were mad that I'd left them with my sister for a month—Ingrid had moved into my place while I was gone, so it wasn't like they'd been uprooted. But still. They were prickly. I understood.

I meant to go shopping for a hammock, but I never got around to it. It was still written on my physical to-do list, though. And the garden, I decided, would have to wait for next spring.

And of course, the new building. My baby. My enormous, time- and energy-sucking baby. I struck a deal with the sellers for them to do the asbestos remediation before closing.

I was entitled to one more walk-through, and Justin and I did it together. He drew up plans, I signed off on them, and we started purchasing materials and booking subtrades so he'd be ready to hit the ground running after closing, which was fast approaching. I found myself uncharacteristically indecisive when choosing finishes, though. From flooring to wall color to the countertops in the kitchen on the second floor.

"You want me to hook you up with a designer?" Justin said one morning while we were looking at toilets at Home Depot. "I have one I use on some projects. Mostly residential, but she's good."

"Oh my God, what is the matter with me that I can't even pick a toilet? I couldn't even tell you what the toilet at the current studio looks like."

"Doing a space from scratch is a lot different from moving into a rented space," Justin said diplomatically, when what he should have said was, *Choose a damn toilet, lady.*

One morning at the studio, I was waiting for a rep from a software company to come by and demo some software I was thinking of buying—unlike the dance side of things, yoga and Pilates were going to be drop-in, and I wanted to automate payment, waivers, and attendance taking. Take the pressure off the receptionist. Who I still had to hire.

And what was I going to do when the receptionist got sick? Or took a vacation? Did I need a backup?

I was the backup. Which probably meant I should, at least initially, cut back on how many dance classes I taught.

Which would mean I'd need to hire more dance teachers.

The door opened, and it wasn't my software dude; it was Rory, carrying two coffees.

"What are you doing here?" She was in her final month, and she wasn't teaching the last summer term.

"I'm bored."

"Aren't you supposed to be resting and making Mike rub your feet and wait on you?"

"Boring."

I grinned. I was glad to see her. "You know what else is boring? The presentation I'm about to hear on software."

Rory kept doing that—showing up at random times with coffee, claiming to be bored. Over the next few weeks I kept telling her to go home and put her feet up, but she wouldn't listen. She came with me to pick out flooring and bathroom fixtures—I finally settled on a freaking toilet—and a front desk setup for the new space.

"Are you OK?" she asked one morning.

"I'm fine." She didn't say anything, so I added, "Do I not seem fine?"

When she still didn't speak, I said, "What?"

"I don't know. You seem subdued. Or just kind of...off."

I *was* off.

The terrible truth was that I missed camp. I missed the stupid hole dance that had no place in my real life. I missed Teddy, who also had no place in my real life.

Earlier this summer, before camp, I'd decided that my

Midlife Crisis: Averted project had two pillars. Pillar One was the new building. The new empire. Become too busy expanding my empire to be in crisis. Pillar Two was giving up on dating, on men. Going to camp was supposed to jump-start Pillar Two. Go to the woods and become a crone.

So why was I back from the woods missing my camp boyfriend and unable to choose a toilet for my new empire?

This wasn't me. I didn't dither over toilets and moon over dudes. I shook my head. "I'm just stressed about everything I have to do."

"How can I help?"

"You are helping." I held up the coffee she'd brought me. "Also, without you I'd probably have a completely subpar toilet."

"You remember when I was in my old apartment after Ian moved out? You used to come over, and we'd dance in the empty living room."

"Yeah." I smiled. Those were good memories. I had a whole dance studio to myself after hours, but somehow Rory's empty living room—her ex had taken all the furniture—had inspired bursts of creativity. We'd organized an entire Go-Go's-themed recital in that apartment.

"Maybe after I have this baby and you get going in the new space, we can work on the holiday recital."

"For sure. And that sounds great."

I thought about telling her about the hole dance. But it would sound so stupid. What would I even say? *I made up a dance that was maybe about the patriarchy and there was a lot of leaping out of holes?* The piece was fading from memory. It wasn't that I couldn't remember the steps, more that the urgency I'd felt about doing that choreography had faded.

Rory and I had talked lately about her nervousness about

labor and delivery, about how women always say you forget the pain of childbirth. "How can you forget the pain of pushing a human out of your vagina?" Rory had exclaimed incredulously.

I thought I understood. The experience of life after childbirth—of keeping a baby alive, of dealing with the rest of your life, whether that meant other kids or jobs or relationships—made the "bigness" of the birth experience shrink.

Time stripped emotion from an experience, and without emotion, you just had plot. Things that happened: *I gave birth. I made a dance.*

I made a dance once. Not that long ago, even. But from this vantage point, I couldn't remember why.

17
OVERDUE RECKONING

Teddy

The second session of camp went fast. I missed the hell out of Gretchen, and I wrote a fucking album.

I wondered if the two things were related. I kind of thought they were, if only logistically. I had been spending so much time with Gretchen the last session, and toward the end of that session I'd broken my writing logjam. This session, with the writing flowing and Gretchen gone, what the hell else was I going to do?

I did try to do a more respectable job this time around with the teaching and mentoring and shit. And getting up at the ass crack of dawn for sunrise circle. Still, that wasn't enough to fill the days.

Or nights.

So I wrote. Way more songs than I'd need for an album.

The other weird thing? I became friends with Marion.

"I was thinking of playing lead guitar myself," I said one morning over tea in her office after sunrise circle.

The Marion thing had started when I'd taken her up on her previous offer to help, asking her if she'd listen to a song. She'd liked it, and her feedback had struck the right balance of enthusiastic and constructive. She'd been right: she was a good audience member. That had led to her asking me to tea, and now I was a semiregular at post–sunrise circle teatime.

"Actually," I added over a sip of Earl Grey, which I'd surprised myself by liking, "I'm thinking of playing all the instruments myself on this record." Not in a power tripping kind of way, not because I didn't trust anyone else. More because I wanted to feel my way through the songs as I recorded them.

"It doesn't seem all that remarkable to me that you'd want to control the process pretty tightly for a record that is going to be your first without your former band—and one that makes a break stylistically from your old work. What's the downside?"

"I guess if I ever want to tour. But I just came off a year of touring, and honestly I have no desire to do it again anytime soon."

"You can cross that bridge when you come to it."

Marion wasn't telling me anything revolutionary, but she was smart and accomplished, and having her stamp of approval meant something.

When I called Anna—we'd been staying in touch—to see what she thought about my plan to do everything myself on my new album, she was similarly unfazed. She said, "It's your *Speak Now* album."

"It's my what album?"

"Taylor Swift. *Speak Now.*"

"Right…" I was as much of a fan of Taylor Swift as anyone—the woman could *write*—but I wasn't getting it.

"Her third album. Every song was written solely by her. No collaborators, no cowriters. She'd taken some heat about being a hack. You remember the whole Kanye West thing where he cut off her speech? And when she did that duet with Stevie Nicks and everyone criticized her singing?"

"Kind of?"

"*Speak Now* was her eff-you to the public. But also it's very introspective, reflective."

Hmm. I guess I needed to go listen to *Speak Now*.

It was not lost on me that Anna was mentoring me as much as I was mentoring her.

Also that it was the summer of the girl: girl power songs, Anna the girl prodigy, Marion the patron of the arts.

Gretchen.

I thought about what Gretchen had told me about her dating travails. I thought about her experience with Scott. I thought about how she weathered it all, how she absorbed criticism and...well, abuse and just kept going.

I sometimes wondered, if all of that stuff hadn't happened to her, would she have given me her phone number? Did I meet her too late?

Too late for what, though? I asked myself when my brain went in this direction. It wasn't as if I were in the market for a relationship, even if Gretchen had been.

"I've been thinking about *my* album, too," Anna said. I could almost hear her grin through the phone. "I still can't believe I can say the words 'my album' and have it be, like, a legitimate concept."

"Honestly, I think self-belief is half the battle." For some reason I'd never had any problem in that department, at least artistically. Thanks to my education this summer in sexism and double standards, I wondered how much of that was because I was a dude.

"I go to a pretty rigorous school," Anna said. "I had to fight my mom to let me go there because it's not my local school. Getting there is a pain. She won't drive me, even though she doesn't work. I have to take two city buses, and my days are long. What if we worked on the demo, but, like, slowly? Maybe we could do some studio time over school breaks, if those times work for you. I know that's probably the opposite of the way it should work. You're probably supposed to do it all in a big intense burst of creativity."

"Screw how it 'should' work. There are no rules. And I think this is a great plan. Finishing high school is important. Probably college is important, too." I hadn't gone, but I wasn't as smart as Anna. "So yeah, let's squeeze it in when we can. And honestly, if it's a success, your life is gonna change. So I think it's good to have as much of your education done as possible by that time."

"And if it's not a success, I still have an education."

I agreed with her, but only because I didn't want to sound too crazy-intense by assuring her I knew she'd make it. But I did. I knew she'd make a successful album more than I knew *I'd* make a successful album. Oddly, I was OK with that. I just wanted to record my songs. We'd see what happened after that.

"I'll look into booking a studio in the Twin Cities," I said. "Marion will probably have some leads. You want to send me the dates of your winter break? We can book some time, noodle around, and see what comes of it."

———

The end-of-camp finale the second session was "Hey Jude." It went fine, and the music kids did a respectable job collectively and individually. But the music counselors and I agreed after the fact that we should have repeated "Bohemian Rhapsody," which had been a smash instead of merely fine.

Fine basically summed up that entire second session, aside from my songwriting, which had gone more than fine. But the public-facing, camp part of things had been unremarkable. Gretchen's replacement had been a Russian ballerina named Irina who mostly kept to herself. Without Gretchen as the ringleader, evening artists' swims fell by the wayside. Maiv got lost in a flurry of work. I barely saw her, and when I did, she was covered in paint and mumbling to herself. I still had drinks with Jack, but we'd never talked much to begin with. I hadn't had any prodigies this session, which was for the best, as I could probably only handle one prodigy at a time.

Marion knocked on my door the morning after the final show and handed me a printout of an email. "This is an engineer-producer I made contact with through a mutual friend. He said he's happy to help with your project. In general, but he also apparently has a cancellation next week if you want to jump right into it. He's got four days of time free."

"Tempting, but I should go home."

Right? Auden would need me.

"I was just thinking Anna probably doesn't start school until after Labor Day," Marion said.

Hmm.

"You'd have momentum, camp still being fresh in everyone's minds," she said. "You could try out this engineer, then get serious about booking more time later, whether it's with him or someone else."

"Let me talk to Anna."

"Did you meet her mom and dad at the end of last session?"

Mom and *stepdad*, I wanted to correct, but I held my tongue. "I met her mom." Her stepfather had not come, which, given what I knew about him based on Anna's delightfully vicious song, had not been a surprise.

"Did you float the idea of doing some recording with Anna?"

"Yes, and she was fine with it. Too fine, actually."

"What do you mean?"

"I'm not going to insert myself into Anna's family dynamics, but I feel like her mom has the potential to turn into a big-time stage mother. She said she would clear her schedule to be at any and all recording sessions." Yet she wouldn't drive Anna to school. "Anna won't want that." Which I knew on account of Anna's making a dramatic choking motion from behind her mom when her mom said that. I didn't want it, either. How were we supposed to lay down tracks about her shitty stepdad with her mom in attendance? "I'm afraid her mom will ruin the vibe, you know? I don't think Anna can be her usual creative self with her mother hovering."

"Ah. Sometimes the parents of our campers can be... challenging."

"But I do feel like we need a chaperone for the studio sessions. I mean, we *don't*, but we do, you know?"

"I would offer to do it, but I need to be here next week, doing some wrap-up. How about asking Gretchen Miller?"

The idea was jarring, but also... galvanizing? Like a bee sting.

Or a mosquito bite.

"You think?"

"Yes, she knows Anna; Anna knows her. It's perfect."

It was perfect. Except for the part where Gretchen didn't want to have any more involvement with me. But maybe she would see this less as involvement with me and more as involvement in Anna's artistic and career development.

That was what I told myself, anyway.

———

Given that I wasn't going home to New York, I hitched a ride to the Twin Cities with Jack.

"You want to come back next summer?" Marion asked as she hugged me goodbye.

I started to demur—if things went to plan, I would be busy next summer on the new album—but she said, "Don't answer now. Just think about it."

"All right," I said. Not declining outright was the least I could do. Marion's invitation to come to Wild Arts, even though I'd had no idea what I'd been saying yes to, had changed my life.

"You're not going to invite *me* back?" Jack said, drawing our attention. I'd thought he was serious—Jack was always serious—but he shot Marion a wink. Could have knocked me over with a feather.

"There are two kinds of artists," Marion said. "Those who thrive when you take away external distractions, and those who don't."

"And I don't?" Jack said.

"Am I wrong?"

He chuckled. Wow. Maybe Jack had been having tea with the artistic fairy godmother, too.

"In fact, I think what you need," Marion said, eyeing Jack, "is a part-time job. A brainless one, but one that sucks up twenty hours a week. Starbucks or something."

I expected Jack to object—God's gift to the literary world was going to sling Frappuccinos?—but he said, "Maybe."

"What was that about?" I asked as we pulled away.

"Marion's been giving me some advice."

"And you've been taking it?"

He smirked. "I've been not rejecting it outright." I whistled, and he added, "What can I say? My inability to write this book has humbled me."

Jack and I settled into the companionable silence we seemed to have mastered. When we got to the outskirts of the Twin Cities, he asked, "Where am I dropping you?"

I'd made a hotel reservation, but instead of asking him to drop me there, I said, "I don't suppose you have Gretchen Miller's phone number?"

"Why do you need Gretchen's number?"

"I'm going to ask her if she can help with a recording session I have scheduled with one of the music kids from the first session." I was, right? I hadn't exactly decided what to do. I should have just asked Marion for Gretchen's number. Or I should have had Marion ask her on my behalf. I had myself all tied in knots, wanting to respect Gretchen's desire not to hear from me, but also just…wanting her to chaperone me. Us. Anna. Whatever.

"The kid who played the banjo?" Jack asked.

"Yeah."

"She was phenomenal."

"I know. We're going to make a demo for her. But she's only fifteen. And I'm a volatile asshole rock star."

He glanced at me, then back at the road. "Are you, though?"

"Does it matter? It's gonna be a middle-aged dude sound engineer and me. I can't have a teenage girl in there without a chaperone."

"So you're going to ask Gretchen to do it."

"Yeah." Right?

Yes. I was going to do it.

"Are you also going to tell her you're in love with her?"

"*What?*" The seat belt lock mechanism engaged as I twitched, pinning me against the seat.

"Are you going to tell Gretchen you're in love with her in addition to asking her to chaperone your recording sessions?" Jack said with an astonishing degree of sanguinity considering what was coming out of his mouth.

"I'm not in love with her!" When he didn't say anything, I added, "I'm not the kind of person who falls in love."

"Never?"

"Well, certainly not in the span of one month."

"But according to you, you're also not the kind of person who writes folk songs."

"They're not *folk* songs." I liked Jack better when he was grumpy and silent.

"What are they, then?"

"They're folk-informed rock songs."

Jack's snort told me what he thought of that distinction.

"What is your point?" I asked shortly. Were we close enough to the city for him to let me out so I could get an Uber?

"My point is that people change."

"Do *you* change? Are you going to get a job at Starbucks where you'll have to mingle with the subliterate masses?"

"No, but I'm not as evolved as you."

"Oh for fuck's sake."

"I was being serious."

"Fine." I didn't want to talk about this anymore.

"I'm just saying, everyone could see that you and Gretchen were into each other."

OK, maybe I did want to talk about this some more. A tiny

bit more. Because I needed some clarification on that. "You mean 'everyone,' like a generic anyone-could-see sense?" Which probably just meant Jack. Gretchen had gone to him for that condom.

"No, I mean literally everyone," he said, his tone almost gleeful. "We all talked about you behind your backs. Well, they talked. I'm not much of a talker. I listened."

He sure was doing a lot of talking now.

"Great. So glad everyone has the wrong idea about Gretchen and me."

"Anyway, do what you want; no skin off my nose. I was just thinking you might have an ulterior motive in all this. There must be a million ways you could solve your chaperone problem without asking the woman in the middle of opening a new business."

Ah, shit. I'd forgotten that part. Well, not forgotten it, but I hadn't really thought through that she wasn't going to have time to sit around doing nothing in a recording studio.

"Marion suggested it," I said, like that mattered.

"Did she now?"

"What does *that* mean?" I *really* preferred Jack when he was silent. And if he wasn't going to be silent, could he at least speak plainly?

"Nothing," he said in a way that seemed to mean the opposite of nothing.

"Well," I said firmly, "if Gretchen can't do it, she'll probably know someone who can."

And if she didn't?

Then it really would be goodbye.

"So where am I dropping you?"

"You don't have Gretchen's number?"

"I don't have Gretchen's number," Jack confirmed. "I can't imagine why you'd think I would. I also can't imagine why *you* don't."

"We, ah, agreed not to keep in touch."

He cracked up, which...was fair.

"Doesn't she have a dance studio? Miss Miller's or something? Why don't you look it up and I'll drop you there?"

"Or I could just ask Marion for her number."

"Yeah, but I think a declaration of love is better done in person."

"I'm *not* declaring my love for her. I'm asking her to chaperone a recording session."

"Right. Still, it would be nice to see her."

I...could not argue with that. And if I had Jack with me, it would, hopefully, seem a little less weird that I was showing up unannounced.

"Fine." I looked up the address and directed him to a highway that would take us to the western suburbs. Soon we were pulling into the parking lot of a strip mall in a place called Minnetonka.

Well, shit. This was one of those fancy strip malls where all the businesses had the same type of understated sign, and there she was, nestled between a dentist and an ice-cream parlor. The sign that read "Miss Miller's" didn't look any different from its neighbors, but there was something about seeing it, about being poised to enter Gretchen's real life, that threw me for a loop. There was no temporary "context" here; this was just her life.

Would I fit into it?

Whoa. All I was doing was asking if she would hang around in the studio with Anna and me.

Jack was out of the car and on his way to the door while I was still all up in my feelings about contexts. I had to hurry to catch up.

Gretchen's friend Rory was behind the front desk. There didn't appear to be anyone else around.

"Hi!" Rory exclaimed.

"Yeah, uh, hi. I'm looking for Gretchen."

"Hi, Teddy. I'm Rory. We met at camp."

"I remember."

She looked me up and down. "Gretchen isn't here. I'm about to lock up. There's a party at the new building tonight. Gretchen closed on it this morning, and it's her birthday, and she's having a party to celebrate both occasions."

Shit. Gretchen had referenced turning forty "at the end of the summer," and of course, I'd known she was taking possession of the new building—she'd done that virtual walk-through with her contractor—but she had never said the exact date of either.

"Can we crash the party?" Jack asked, then added, "Jack Branksome. We also met at Wild Arts."

"I know. You're the guy who turned down Blair Kellermoon."

"I am indeed," Jack said with an odd cheeriness.

"And you want to come to the party," Rory said, her tone quizzical.

"Wouldn't miss it." He smirked at me before turning back to Rory. "Also, I'm procrastinating my book."

"All right. It starts at six." She reached for a business card and scribbled on it. "Here's the address."

"Can we bring anything?" I heard myself say. What? Like I was Martha fucking Stewart all of a sudden and I was going to go whip up some canapés? I was utterly befuddled by this invasion of Gretchen's reality.

"Nope. And it's a demolition party, so if you get any ideas about spiffing yourself up, don't bother."

I looked down at my ratty cutoffs and Metallica T-shirt. "Noted."

"But maybe change your shoes. The contractor says no sandals. Not sure if those count, but…"

Yeah. I was wearing the orange rubber monstrosities.

"Don't tell Gretchen we're coming," Jack said. "It can be a surprise."

"Hopefully a good one," Rory said, narrowing her eyes at me.

18
TRUTHS

Teddy

Was I...friends with Jack Branksome now? Like, in reality?

In some ways, that felt like the biggest change I'd undergone in the past two months, though I recognized that objectively, there was no way that was true.

It was wild, though. He took me to his condo, ordered some food, and reverted to his usual silent self.

I crossed to a wall of windows and looked out. Jack lived exactly where you'd think he would—high in a condo building overlooking the Mississippi River. "Killer view."

"Yeah, I bought this place with the advance on my first book. Hopefully it's appreciated enough that I won't be in the red when I have to sell it because I have to give back the advance for my second book."

I turned. "You want to talk about this?"

I guess we really were friends now.

"Not really."

Or not.

"You're the one who keeps bringing it up," I said.

He shrugged. "I guess I'm trying to get used to the idea that I might have been a one-hit wonder. Saying it out loud helps."

I thought about giving him a pep talk, but then I thought, baby steps on this whole friends thing. We watched a movie and ate Thai food until it was time to go.

The setting for Gretchen's new studio was totally different from the strip mall. It was a cute little main street, in what was probably once its own stand-alone small town, as the buildings looked historic.

"I've never been here," Jack said as he parked. "This is some twee shit." We got out and started walking. "There it is." He pointed at a redbrick building on the other side of the street.

There was a taco place a few doors down from it with a sign that said "Cold Beer," and I started to suggest we duck in for a drink, but Jack took my shoulder and physically steered me toward Gretchen's building. The front door stood open, and I swear to God, I had a rush of stage fright worse than any I'd ever experienced.

What was *wrong* with me?

We'd stepped into a big empty space with maybe a dozen people milling around. At the back, a couple people were swinging sledgehammers at some built-in cabinetry. I could hear music thumping from the floor above us.

I saw her before she saw me. She was wearing a hard hat and her back was to me, so I'm not even sure how I recognized her, except that I *knew* her. In any context.

And that made the damnedest thing happen: it made all my fear evaporate.

And I suddenly understood why I was here. It had nothing to do with Anna's recording session. Jack had been right.

I was in love with Sourplum.

Of course I was. She had floated with me in the lake, in her ruffly marshmallow swimsuit, and told me—gently—what was wrong with me. She told me how to fix it. And I let her do that because she understood me. Because in a lot of ways, we were the same. She was ambitious and brave and a fighter. She was also a bunch of things I wasn't: wise and cheerful and beautiful.

We'd talked so much about contexts. About what was and wasn't allowed. We could sleep together because we weren't dating. It was "allowed" because we were at camp, which was somehow a different category from reality. She'd set it up as if we were exploiting a loophole.

I didn't want a loophole. I wanted reality, a reality that included camp. But also this. I wanted all the contexts.

"I'm going to do it," I whispered to Jack.

"Holy shit. Really?"

Yes. I was going to shoot my shot. I had never been more sure of anything in my life.

Overdue reckoning was about to come due.

My surety took a hit when I realized that Gretchen was low-level freaking out. I motioned to Jack to join me in hanging back to the side of the entryway, and to my surprise he did so without comment.

Gretchen was talking to a tall man also wearing a hard hat. "What do you mean?" she asked, her voice high and thin.

"It's not the end of the world. It will add some time and money, but not a catastrophic amount of either. And there's no mold, so it must be recent. Maybe triggered by when the seller uninstalled the dishwasher before the move."

"This *is* like one of those shows where the contractor brings the bad news," Gretchen said, her tone verging on hysterical.

It was strange: I hadn't known hysterical was a mode Gretchen did.

Rory, who had been huddling with Gretchen and the tall man, saw us and made her way over.

"Is everything OK?" I asked, still eyeing Gretchen.

"It will be. The contractor discovered a leak in the kitchen upstairs. Gretchen is taking it uncharacteristically hard." She tilted her head and watched Gretchen take her hard hat off and run her fingers through her hair. "She usually rolls with the punches better than this."

Yeah. Like her voice, Gretchen's overall energy was very not Sourplum. She was stiff and she started pacing. I was no expert on body language, but to my mind she didn't look like a person celebrating a milestone birthday and a business triumph. She looked like someone who would rather be anywhere but here.

"Do you think this is a good idea?" I asked Rory carefully. "The new studio, I mean."

She whipped her gaze to me. "Do *you* think it's a good idea?"

"You know her better than I do."

"Do I?"

She seemed to want me to talk, so I did. "I don't know. Just that at Wild Arts, Gretchen started doing some choreographing. Not for the studio, but some kind of personal project. I don't know that much about it, except that she was on fire with creativity and...well, it was something to see her like that. And then it all went away when she was getting ready to leave."

Rory nodded as if she'd expected this answer, but when I asked, "She told you about it?" she switched to shaking her head no.

"But I can tell something's been going on with her since she got back." We all watched Gretchen pace as Rory added, "She wanted to do something else. Something more. She thought this"—she gestured around—"was it."

"Maybe it is." Who was I to say otherwise?

She turned and did the narrowed-eyed thing at me again. "Why are you here, Teddy?"

Aww shit. Well, here went nothing. "I have...certain things I need to say to Gretchen."

That seemed to be the right answer. "Gretchen!" Rory called. "Look who's here!"

I was a deer in headlights as Gretchen turned. I couldn't move anything below the neck, but I could feel my eyes widen and my mouth fall open like I was a fucking idiot.

It was OK, though. She would smile at me—or smirk, or roll her eyes—and say something snippy but fond, and I would be OK.

I caught sight of Maiv, making her way toward us. Normally, I would have greeted her, but she must have sensed the tension in the air because when she got within about six feet of us, she listed to one side and made like she'd merely been walking in a big circle near us. Jack guffawed.

"Jack," Rory said, looking between Gretchen and me, "can I interest you in taking a giant pronged hammer thing and using it to destroy stuff?"

"You can indeed."

Which left me and Gretchen. Sugarplum. Sourplum.

"What are you doing here, Teddy?"

There had been no smile or smirk or eye roll accompanying the question, just an unnervingly blank expression. I started to panic.

I thought about leading with the chaperone question, but I had enough functioning brain cells left to realize that wasn't a good idea. Clearly Gretchen didn't have the time to be lazing around in a studio for a week helping me with my shit.

"I think you *are* my muse," I blurted.

"What?"

"I think you're my muse," I said again, as if the only problem here was that she hadn't heard me the first time. "Remember when you told me I should sleep with you because maybe I'd get over my inability to write songs?"

"I was kidding about that."

"I know, but I'm not."

"So I'm your muse," she said with what seemed like a strange lack of inflection.

"Yes."

"Well, no thanks."

I blinked. "I'm not sure it's something you can accept or reject. It just is. 'Sweet and Sour' is about you, you know. I mean, it's about a lake, but it's also about you."

"No."

I didn't know what to do with that. I hadn't asked a question.

"Have you listened to anything I've been saying?" she said, her voice rising. "I'm done dating."

"I know, but—"

"You can't be here," she said slowly, like she was talking to a child. "I didn't agree to this. This is the opposite of what I agreed to."

I could not argue with that. I was supposed to be her last hurrah. Maybe I'd been promoted to camp boyfriend there at the end, but I should know that camp boyfriends weren't reality boyfriends. Look at me, I'd somehow gotten Jack as a real friend and Gretchen had to remain a camp friend.

Well, fuck.

I guess sometimes you shoot your shot, and you get shot down.

I could feel a kind of hysteria taking root in my brain. I pushed it away. If Gretchen never wanted to see me again, I was going to tell her some shit she probably didn't want to hear. Because that was what you did when you loved someone—which I still did, even though it wasn't mutual. "Can I say one more thing? Something unrelated?"

"Can I stop you?" she said, her voice resigned in a way that made me sad.

Here went nothing. Maybe I was wrong. But I didn't think so. And if I was right, it needed saying. "You're using the studio as a shield. You're using this whole businesswoman/entrepreneur identity as a shield. A distraction."

"What the *hell* are you talking about?"

"I don't think you want to be doing this." I gestured around the room.

She didn't say anything, just looked at me with a degree of affront that made me feel shaky. But I pressed on. "You don't want me. Fine. But I think you want to be a choreographer."

"Fuck you, Teddy," she said, and I recoiled as if she'd struck me. "Go back and listen to 'Lemon Tree.' I'm the fruit. I'm sour. By choice. Don't be telling yourself I'm sweet. Listen to the lyrics."

I kept going. She had already rejected me, so I was determined to say what she needed to hear. "What happened to the hole?" I still didn't know exactly what had been up with that, but I didn't have to. I'd seen how it energized her. "You were on fire for a few days there."

"What happened is that in normal life, you can't fuck around digging holes. In normal life, you have to do your job."

"I'm making a solo album," I said. "I'm going to play all the instruments. I've got more songs than I can use. I wrote a ton over second session when you weren't there."

"So you were inspired by my *absence*," she shot back. "Sort of seems like I'm the opposite of a muse."

Normally, a comeback like that would have been delivered in a bantery way. It would have delighted me, and I'd have dished something back. But there was no bantering here. She meant what she said.

So I kept pushing forward. It was all I knew to do. "These songs are completely different from Concrete Temple. They're folk-rock."

She didn't say anything, just continued to gaze at me with a blank expression that freaked me out.

"I'm doing something new," I said, in case she wasn't getting the point. "I'm as scared as you are, but I'm doing my scary thing."

There was a pause that felt like it lasted a year, but it was probably only five seconds, before she said, "I'm not scared. I'm busy."

The way she was looking at me as she lied to my face: wow. She knew I knew she was lying, but she did it anyway. That was what hurt the most, more than her not wanting to be with me. To me, it said that all our frank conversations in the woods, in the lake, in bed, hadn't meant anything. I understood the concept of camp friends, or a camp boyfriend, or whatever, but wasn't half the point of those camp relationships that they cut out the bullshit? That without the distractions of technology, of cars and cities and jobs and family, you skipped straight to the truth? Confronted your own bullshit? Had your overdue reckoning?

I certainly had. I wasn't the same person I'd been ten weeks ago. Some of that was down to the setting, to Wild Arts itself. But a lot of it was down to Gretchen. She floated next to me in the lake and listened. She lay in my arms—in the reverse Fruit Roll-Up and, later, in my bed—and told me her secrets. I'd thought. A prickling sensation started behind my eyeballs.

Fuck. I had to get out of here before I started crying.

So that was what I did. Turned and hightailed it out of the building in which Gretchen was preparing to imprison herself.

Jack followed. "Hey, let's get that beer now."

"No thanks."

I crossed midblock, aiming for his car. When he didn't follow, I got out my phone. "I'll get an Uber."

"OK, OK." He jogged across the street. "Get in."

I got in because it was the path of least resistance—the path that would get me out of there the fastest—but I would have preferred an Uber. My mind was reeling and my skin was hot all over. Shame, I was pretty sure. This was what shame felt like.

"Was that supposed to be your declaration of love?" Jack asked as he pulled away.

"Uh, yeah?" Jesus. Had he heard anything I'd said?

"I heard that song you wrote, that night at the fire at Wild Arts. How can you be so, to use a phrase I abhor, emotionally intelligent but also so utterly dumb?"

"Huh?"

"How can you write a song like that about the nuances of human relationships but approach your own like a caveman with a cudgel?"

I didn't know what a cudgel was, but I suspected the idea of me having and/or using one was not a flattering portrayal.

"Look. I know I was hard on her, but I thought I owed her

some straight talk. She's making a mistake walking away from choreographing. I truly believe that, regardless of my feelings about her."

"Right. And what are those feelings?"

"I would have thought that was apparent. You're the one who's been telling me I'm in love with her."

"I told you, sure, but *you* didn't tell *her*."

"Yes I did. I—"

Wait.

"You made a cryptic, awkward speech about how she was your muse."

"Yes, but…"

"My dude. You never told her how you felt about her. Only what she did for your music."

"Well, *shit*." I hadn't intended it to sound like that. I'd only meant that she was so fucking amazing that she'd knocked me out of the pity party I'd been having and made it so I could write again. "What do I do now?"

"Maybe you should think about telling her how you feel independent of all this artistic bullshit."

"How do I do that?"

"Hell if I know. I'm sorry you've ended up with me as your advice-giving sidekick, but I have reached my limit for the day—for the year—of navigating other people's interpersonal problems. In fact, this is all so cringy that the idea of going home and working on my book seems less painful."

"Glad I could help."

———

The thing was, Jack wasn't wrong. When I rewound the tape of the evening, I could clearly see the moment I was struck with how much I loved Gretchen. She'd been standing there in her hard hat at the center of her party, and I'd been overcome in a way you are when you finally see the truth. Overcome and energized. But then I'd seen the *other* truth, the mistake she was making. And I loved her too much to let her make it, or at least to watch her make it without saying anything. The worry had overtaken me, and the expression of that worry had crowded out the expression of what was in my heart. And since she had—seemingly—so soundly rejected me, I'd become fixated on knocking her off this wrong path. A parting gift, if you will.

I got my truths out of order.

Maybe she was making a mistake with the new studio. But who was I to say that? Who was I to *lead* with that?

God, I was such a fucking idiot.

I called my sister. Who would tell me I was a fucking idiot, but hopefully also tell me what to do in a more concrete way than Jack had managed.

I explained everything, and she said, "You need a big gesture."

"What?"

"You know, a grand gesture. Like in a rom-com."

"Like Lloyd Dobler holding the boom box over his head?" I asked, thinking back to my joking reference to exactly that at camp—I'd known that Gretchen would find such a thing distasteful and creepy.

"Exactly."

A wisp of an idea floated through my brain.

"You know what I actually need?" I said. "A gesture that is both grand and funny." Assuming I was going to try again.

Was I? I closed my eyes and tried to will the wisp into something more substantial. Something actionable.

Did I dare?

Well, shit, of course I did. I could hardly make things worse.

"A gesture that's grand *and* funny," Auden echoed. "How are you going to pull that off?"

I didn't know if I *was* going to pull it off. But I was sure as hell going to try.

19
CONTEXT

Gretchen

The nice thing about having a confrontation during a demolition party taking place over two stories is that bystanders don't notice it. In an attempt to keep drywall dust separate from eating and drinking, we'd designated the second floor for partying and the first for demo. Most people had been upstairs while Teddy was here, because that was where the DJ, bar, and food were. Only Rory, Jack, and Maiv had witnessed the train wreck. Jack had left with Teddy, and Maiv had disappeared somewhere.

Which left Rory. I braced myself for either a freak-out or an over-the-top display of empathy. I certainly didn't want a freak-out, but I also didn't want empathy. I didn't want to *talk* about it anymore. I just wanted to get on with my life. Which right now meant tearing some shit down, which ideally would have the side effect of calming my brain, which was on fire.

Rory only said, "What's all this stuff about a lemon tree?"

"It's a song. It's about a kid whose dad tells him not to trust love. It was an important song for Teddy when he was a kid, and he's returned to it lately."

"Important how?"

For some reason I found myself telling her about Teddy's mom and the actual lemon tree. God damn it, had she tricked me into talking?

She got out her phone, and soon the song was playing.

"I've heard it," I said—peevishly, but I couldn't help it.

"I haven't."

"OK, well, I have demo to do."

I was shaking, but what could I do but keep on going? That was what I did. I made a plan, and I executed it. That's what had gotten me this far. I looked around. Everyone was here. Well, most people were upstairs, though I did have hard hats and sledgehammers on hand down here for folks who wanted to channel their inner Hulks. But upstairs were all my people. Rory's husband, Mike, and his daughter, Olivia. Friends from college. Suz and some folks from the strip mall. Current and former families from Miss Miller's. My mom and Ingrid. I could see them up there in my mind's eye, chatting and smiling and dancing.

I was lucky. I had a great life. I had built a community around my studio. It was normal to have cold feet when you were on the verge of a big expansion like I was, but I had to remember what I was doing, and why.

"You OK?"

Maiv. Even Maiv was here. I'd been glad she'd accepted my invitation, but now I kind of wished she hadn't. I didn't need someone else on my case.

But she didn't get on my case. She was holding two sledgehammers, and she said, "I've been eyeing that weird diagonal wall near the back door. Your contractor says it's not structural. There are some weeds growing through the asphalt in the parking area in back, and I was thinking if we took out that wall, we might be able to see the parking area through the door. Then if you don't mind, I thought I'd prop open the door and take a photo showing both the inside and outside and maybe paint from it later."

Weeds in asphalt: exactly Maiv's thing. And, handily, right now beating the shit out of a wall was exactly my thing. We put on respirators and got to work.

"So Teddy and Jack showed up?" she asked after we'd gotten a few swings in.

I grunted vaguely, the same way Teddy had when I first met him.

Fucking Teddy. How *dare* he come in here and threaten not only Pillar Two of Midlife Crisis: Averted, but Pillar One? I was his muse *and* he thought the building I'd already bought and was renovating literally as we spoke was a mistake?

Maybe I'd been too hard on him, but one thing I do not appreciate is being backed into a corner by men who think they know what's best for me.

I took a big swing, and to my shock, tears started leaking out of the corners of my eyes. My body was confused. I'd been powering through my confrontation with Teddy on adrenaline, and then I'd crashed. But now I was literally tearing down a wall, which required...more adrenaline? Strength? I don't know, but it required something I didn't have right then.

I kept trying, though, lifting the hammer and bringing it down on the drywall as my eyes leaked.

Maiv, being an excellent sort of human, didn't say anything, though I could feel her watching me.

Rory, though she was also an excellent sort of human, did not do likewise. I guess she was an excellent sort of human who knew me too well, because she marched right up and said, "I've listened to the song a bunch of times."

I sighed and swung, morbidly satisfied when a chunk of the wall came down. But then I put down my sledgehammer. Even though Rory was on my last nerve, I didn't want to asphyxiate her with drywall dust. And ultimately, I knew I wasn't getting out of this without having a conversation. Or at least listening to a monologue. At least my eyes had stopped leaking.

"I think it's you who's taken the message of the song literally," Rory said when I took off my respirator and aimed a resigned sigh in her direction. "You're the one who's afraid of love."

"I'm not afraid of love. I'm retired from trying to find it. It's not the same thing."

"But what if love finds you? Have you thought about that? Because it seems like it has."

"Ooh." That had come from Maiv. I glared at her, but it had no effect. She just looked at me like, *What?* Damn it. I should have left her as a camp friend.

I turned back to Rory. "This is all fine for you to say, from the vantage point of your one-in-a-million happily ever after, but the song *isn't* wrong. That's why it's so lovely. It's devastatingly true. The lemon flower is sweet, but the fruit *is* sour. I mean, it's a perfect metaphor for love."

"Maybe the issue isn't the lemon, or the flower," Rory said. "Maybe it's just that lemon trees aren't meant to live in pots in New York."

"Huh?"

"It's about context."

There was that word. It kept coming up this summer. "What do you mean?"

"Lemon trees don't thrive in some conditions, but they might in others."

What was she on about? "Are you saying I'm taking the wrong metaphor here?"

"Well, if you're taking the song to mean love is hopeless, that any relationship is doomed, I'm gonna go with yes."

This was all so confusing. "So what do I do with my meta-phorical lemon tree, then?"

"Plant it somewhere properly?"

"It's a *song*!"

"Do I need to remind you," Rory said, annoyingly undeterred, "that I, too, once had an imaginary boyfriend who became real?"

"Oh my God, this isn't *The Velveteen Rabbit*! It's OK to have standards for what you will and won't accept. It's OK to have boundaries. As I've told you a thousand times, I'm retired from men. From love. From all of it." Maybe I needed to explain the pillar thing, if we were dealing in metaphors here.

"Yes," Rory said, "but is it possible that the boundaries we put in place, often with the best of intentions, can end up get-ting stretched?"

"Only if we let them."

"That's my point. Sometimes we need to let them."

I was about done here. I wasn't mad or buzzing with demoli-tion energy anymore; I was tired. "Can you just speak English?"

"I think you're making a mistake sending Teddy away."

I glanced at Maiv, who had remained silent, but I'd felt her attention on us. She gave me a shrug that seemed to signal agreement with Rory.

"All right," I said looking between them. "Noted."

"I also think it's possible he might be right about this place," Rory said quietly.

Wow. Wow. I felt like she'd stabbed me in the back. It was one thing for Teddy to swan in here and tell me I was making a mistake, but Rory? The person who'd been by my side on the professional front for years? Who had come with me to showings and helped me pick out a damn toilet?

I took a breath. Rory *had* been by my side professionally. But also personally. For so many years.

Did I...need to consider the possibility that she was right? About all of it? Were my Midlife Crisis: Averted pillars about to come crumbling down? Or, worse, had they only been made of cardboard to begin with?

"I..." Didn't know what to say. My mind was reeling, and I feared that if I tried to talk, the eye leaking would start again.

"Happy birthday to you!"

A crowd of people approached, making their way down the stairs, led by my sister holding a cake with a little bonfire on top.

Right. It was my birthday. I was forty.

I felt like I was floating outside my body as I listened to the rest of the song. I looked at the blaze and missed camp with everything in me. I missed the hole behind the shower building. I missed Teddy. Even after what he had done, I missed him.

"Hello?" my sister said, making me realize that I was just standing there. "Make a wish and blow already. There are actually forty candles on here, and the ones I lit first are already nubs."

I drew in a breath, looked at those candles, and thought, *Is this all there is?*

———

I awakened to the strains of "Moon River." Great. Even my subconscious was on my case.

Somehow I'd made it through the rest of the party, mostly by returning to beating the crap out of my building. But as I'd swung that sledgehammer over and over, I'd started to think.

What did it mean that I was still asking myself Dad's old question? I'd thought I'd answered that question months ago. I'd retired from dating and I'd bought the new building. I had a mortgage to show for my trouble. Not my trouble. My *ambition*.

Unlike Dad, I'd responded to the question by *doing* something. By *changing* something.

But, as I'd let my tired arm fall, as I'd stopped beating on the walls of my building—the walls of my life, it felt like—I'd had to face the idea that maybe I hadn't answered the question *correctly*.

Well, I'd answered it correctly in a technical sense. *Is this all there is?* No. It hadn't been. So I'd changed my life.

But had I made the correct changes?

Had Rory been right? Had Teddy been right?

Teddy.

I could barely stand to think about him. I'd been so set back on my heels over the idea of being his muse. It should have been flattering. And in some ways it was. It was amazing to think I might have had anything to do with that song I'd heard.

But I didn't want to be a muse. I wanted to be a girlfriend. A partner.

Or I had. Before. I'd excised that wanting, though. Completed my crone-ification quest. Taken the weakness, the rot that was holding me back, and cut it out.

Right?

There was a little voice inside me that was hard to hear

underneath all the demolition noise. Demolishing a building is loud. Demolishing your life is louder.

But when I held my breath, closed my eyes, and really *listened*, I could hear the voice, clear as anything. It was saying, *Maybe we got it wrong.*

I was afraid, so afraid, that I'd lashed out at Teddy earlier not because I was offended by the idea of being his muse, but because I was in love with him.

Pillar Two came crumbling down.

And now I was dreaming "Moon River." I'd been dancing in the dream. On a stage. I'd had to squint, had been blinded by a light shining on me. I remembered the way the light glinted off the sweat on my forearms.

How would I have worked up that much of a sweat dancing to "Moon River"? All I could come up with was that "Moon River" was a reminder of camp, and camp was a reminder of what I wanted to do when I was allowed to follow the wanting in a pure sort of way.

Or maybe I *hadn't* been dancing to "Moon River." I was pretty sure, based on the lights and the sweat, that I'd been dancing to something else. That I'd been *performing*.

Perhaps my subconscious wasn't on my case so much as it was telling me that I'd gotten it wrong. That I had to go back and do a retake of the *Is this all there is?* test.

Pillar One came crumbling down, too.

A swell of violins had me bolting to seated. I was *actually* hearing "Moon River." It wasn't in my head, an echo from a dream. It was here—like, *here*. In reality for losers.

I went to the window, suddenly knowing what I would find. Dreading what I would find.

But inside the dread was a sliver of something else. It felt an awful lot like hope.

Which was funny because what had I been doing since I'd decided to retire from men but giving up hope?

But hope, it finds you, the sneaky motherfucker.

It wasn't exactly like the movie. I lived in a little bungalow with a small yard. It was only one story. So there was no looking down from a great height, Juliet style. There wasn't a lot of distance between us, either. He was *right there*, a foot from my window, jammed in between my house and a lilac hedge. In the movie, Lloyd was somehow illuminated even though it was night. Teddy was illuminated, but not in a romantic, cinematic way. He was blinking against the bright, motion-triggered floodlights I had mounted to my house outside my bedroom—hey, a woman alone needs to be careful.

In other ways, it was exactly like the movie.

He was holding a boom box over his head, Lloyd Dobler style, and it was playing "Moon River."

I laughed. Which was probably not what Teddy was going for. But it was all so absurd. But also...happy-making. When I examined my croneish heart, when I examined it honestly and not just defensively, I found I was *happy* Teddy was here. That was my first reaction. It was that God damn hope again.

I opened the window warily. I wasn't exactly sure why I was wary. I was nervous about what he was going to say, I guess. But I was also afraid of my own reaction, of this hope that was starting to flow through my body.

"This would work better if there was a moon," he said.

"How did you know which window was my bedroom?"

I did realize that asking logistical questions was perhaps not the point.

He didn't seem to mind. "I walked around your house like an unhinged creeper and looked in all of them—some of them had a crack in the curtains big enough to figure out what room it was—and made my best guess."

"What are you doing here?"

"Following you back to your regular life in Minneapolis and holding a boom box over my head outside your bedroom window," he said, quoting the joking line he'd given me about what he was never going to do.

I was so glad he was here.

"I'm sorry," we both said simultaneously.

"You should put that down," I said when, after our in-stereo apologies, he didn't move. "I'm not sure that movie has aged well. Standing silently outside the bedroom of someone who has rejected you is actually kind of creepy if you think about it." I winked to show I was kidding.

I winked to cover my fear.

"The other thing the movie doesn't get right," he said, wincing as he set the boom box on the lawn, "is how much it hurts your arms to hold a boom box over your head for so long. You took forever to wake up. This song has looped like twelve times." He pulled his phone out of his pocket and stopped the song.

"The music wasn't coming from the boom box?" I exclaimed. "What a rip-off!"

"Hey, man, you try getting a boom box in the middle of the night, forget a *cassette* of 'Moon River.'"

"Where did you even get a boom box?" And why was I still asking logistical questions?

"Marion hooked me up with an ancient friend of hers who uses it to teach aqua aerobics for seniors."

I smiled at him. I couldn't help it. It was very un-crone-like. Bordering on goofy, I feared. "What are you sorry for?" I knew what *I* was sorry for, but since he was the one standing on my lawn with a boom box, I thought I'd let him go first.

"So," he said, "here's the thing: I love you. I'm in love with you."

The light went out, and for a moment I thought I had died. That my heart had stopped and I'd literally died. But then I realized no, it was only the lights timing out.

"Wave your arms around," I said, and he did. This hadn't happened to Lloyd, either.

"So," I said, "you love me, and you're sorry about it." Ouch.

"No. I'm sorry I crashed your party and didn't lead with that fact. That truth. Which, just so we're crystal clear, is that I love you."

"But you're not sorry for anything you actually said." I paused. "You're not sorry you told me I was making a mistake with the new studio."

"For the way I said it, maybe. But for what I said?" He paused. "No."

He wasn't sorry, because he wasn't wrong. I was going to have to face up to that fact and decide what, if anything, to do about it.

The lights went out again, and he waved his arms like he was flagging down a passing car.

"Why'd you play 'Moon River'?" I asked when he was re-illuminated. "Why not that song about the lake that you said I inspired?"

"Two reasons. One, I see now how that whole muse speech came out wrong. You *did* inspire that song, but it doesn't mean you're responsible for it. Two, dancing to 'Moon River' that night was the most romantic thing I've ever done. Ever *wanted* to do. And I would very much like to do it again someday."

"Yeah." I paused. "So would I."

So this was it. This—standing in front of a man and telling him you loved him—was scarier than taking on a ginormous mortgage and renovating a building full of asbestos and leaky pipes. But it helped that my "So would I" triggered the biggest, goofiest grin from him.

The lights went out.

"God damn it!" he exclaimed, and he was starting to sound annoyed. When the lights came back on, he said, "I know you're scared. *I'm* scared. But I think this"—he waved his hand back and forth between us—"is a thing. I think it's real in any context, not just in the woods. I don't know if there's a fairy tale where the crone and the asshole in the cabin across the street live happily ever after, but there should be." He blew out a breath. "I'm bad at speeches. I'm better at songs. But yeah, I love you."

The stupid eye leaking was starting again. I didn't want him to see me cry.

But wait. That was part of my problem, right? If someone was going to be your person, they were going to see you cry every now and then. The prospect made me feel sick. But also hopeful.

He cleared his throat.

I loved him back. I loved him so much.

He dug in his pocket, looked down at his hand, and said, "Ten dollars for your thoughts."

"Well," I said, "you better come inside, then, because I have a lot of them."

EPILOGUE
AND THEY LIVED

Gretchen

And they all lived happily ever after. Just kidding. Well, kind of. It's after, and we're happy. We're not living together, but that's how I wanted it. Baby steps, you know?

Hi, it's me. Gretchen the badass. Studio owner, dance teacher.

And now it's April, and I've added a couple other titles to my résumé:

Dance company artistic director. We'll get back to that.

And, wait for it...real estate investor.

I decided to flip the studio building.

Yeah. I didn't really want to expand into yoga and Pilates. I'd thought I did. I'd had my midlife crisis and asked Dad's question. *Is this all there is?*

The answer had been no, so I'd started reaching for more. Expanding my empire.

Turned out, I'd been expanding in the wrong direction.

I say that without any implied criticism of my existing studio. I love teaching. I believe in what I do, and in how I do it. Miss Miller's Morals has created a dance studio I'm proud of.

But Wild Arts showed me that I didn't want to grow my existing empire; I wanted to do something else entirely.

Who am I kidding? *Teddy* showed me. Remember when we were lost in the woods and I was delivering my midlife crisis monologue and he said something along the lines of *Can your studio be great but also not enough for you at your current stage of life?*

Yeah, I didn't remember that, either. At least not initially. I wasn't ready to hear it when he said it, I guess, which is funny because Rory went through this whole phase where she was always talking about holding two contradictory truths in your mind simultaneously. Sounded fine when she said it. Sounded fine when Teddy said it. But it didn't sound like something *I* could actually do, so my brain let it slide away.

But Teddy was right. I loved the studio, and I needed more. The *and* in that sentence was key.

I'd been thinking about it as a *but*. I loved my studio, *but* I wanted more.

When really it was: I loved my studio, *and* I needed more.

A simple switching out of the conjunction in that sentence made all the difference. So I decided to keep Miss Miller's of Minnetonka going in the strip mall by day and to start a modern dance company by night.

As for the building, Justin and I worked out a rehab budget and a plan that would give prospective buyers an inkling of what the building could be but that didn't go over the top with high-end finishes. Turned out that with that brief in mind, I was *great* at picking out floors and fixtures. And toilets.

I netted seventy grand on the sale, and Justin invited me to go in on another reno with him. So we bought a run-down duplex. It's mostly his money and all his labor, so I'm only getting 25 percent of whatever we end up selling it for, but as passive side hustles go, yeah: real estate investing. Who knew?

My other side hustle was not passive. It was exhausting. And, in some ways, ludicrous. A dance company? Who starts dance companies?

But when you think about it, someone does. Every successful dance company out there was started by some person at some point. So why not me?

So I was back in my strip mall studio by day. And also by night. Because the handy thing about having a dance studio targeted at kids was that it wasn't occupied late at night.

I wasn't getting a ton of sleep, but I was loving working on the hole dance. Which had become a trench dance. It was about fighting the patriarchy using a metaphor of a literal World War I–style trench. Was that too heavy-handed? We'd find out. I'd rented a theater for a run of shows in May. It felt like a vanity project, like putting on my own recital, but really, wasn't that what any performance-based artistic endeavor felt like at the beginning? That's what I told myself, anyway.

And I was lucky in that I had an army of helpers. Maiv made our website—turns out she used to do web development before painting started paying the bills. Caleb got me a deal on the theater we're renting. And then there was Marion. She was my patron, I supposed, but I preferred to think of her as the general of my army. She activated her rich-person network to help me get grants—which was not something that had occurred to me to pursue. But she got me applying for a shit ton of them, some of which I got, and assured me she would get butts in seats in May, primarily by hosting an "opening-night gala." I didn't really know what that meant, but she told me not to worry about it, so I didn't. Much.

I wasn't paying my dancers—the grants were nowhere near enough for that—but we would be sharing the box office. So if the show went well, I supposed this new enterprise would be less a dance company and more a dance collective.

But the grants turned out to be handy for all kinds of stuff, including building a false stage at the theater so we could have trenches. We tried experimenting with trapdoors, but for my vision to really work, I needed dancers leaping out of trenches. So we were building a second stage to go over the first, like those bathtub liners you stick over your old 1970s seafoam-green tub. Except raised enough over the original height that we could fashion trenches.

Remember how I thought I might want to get into gardening? Turns out what I got into was digging an elaborate series of trenches in my backyard so I could practice. Well, more like directing Teddy doing the digging.

Oh, Teddy.

He was part of the army, too, composing music for the show. Composing! Weird instrumental stuff that went with my admittedly dark show. It was even further from Concrete Temple than the album he was working on. And he was really working on an album—he signed a deal with Columbia Records, which was not Concrete Temple's label. He had a deal *now*, I should say. Before that, he released his first single on his own—the one about the lake that still made me want to cry when I heard it.

It charted. I didn't know that much about the music business, but apparently it was rare for an independent single to do so well. He had to get into the economics of streaming, which

I gave him shit about because he was definitely using his phone for things that didn't exist before cell phones. But he broke some Spotify records as everyone lost their shit over the idea of an acoustic song from Teddy Knight. *Rolling Stone* called, and he told them about the composing for my show. Not in a braggy way, but to drum up interest in my company, or collective, or whatever the hell it was going to be. The result was a story called "A New Morning Dawns for Teddy Knight." He was embarrassed about it, but, I could tell, chuffed.

I sometimes felt guilty. If the show was a success, it would be largely thanks to the interventions of my rich patron and my famous boyfriend. But when I started to fret about it too much, I told myself to shut up. I'd made it all on my own the first time around, and the result of that was that I met all these amazing people who liked and/or believed in me enough to help with round two.

Speaking of Teddy, the bell on the studio door jingled. He was due in from New York, and I'd commanded him to come directly to the studio because I'd missed him so much. And also because I was going to ask him to move in with me and I was so nervous about it, I needed to get it over with. So yeah, I was graduating from baby steps to ginormous steps.

Mind you, he stayed at my place a lot. He was officially splitting his time between New York and Minneapolis. He was hanging out with his sister in New York and "resting," which was his new thing. When I suggested that maybe sleeping in his bazillion-thread-count sheets wasn't what Marion had meant by "resting," he just told me to try it sometime. In Minneapolis, he was working on his album, and Anna's, and when he was here he was, theoretically, staying with Jack Branksome. He didn't want to rush me or crowd me. He once told me that he was treating "courting" me—yes, he used that word; gag me—like approaching a spooked horse. I told him that comparing one's girlfriend to a horse was gross. But I got his point. I was a tough nut.

I was getting softer, though. Because Teddy was a fantastic boyfriend. When he was in town, he hung out at my house and wrote songs—I'd gotten a keyboard for him—and let me do my thing. One or two of the songs, I suspected, were about me, but he didn't make a big deal about it. He made me cheese-spread grilled cheese sandwiches. He told me about the therapy that he was doing in parallel with his sister. He hung out with my friends—and helped me babysit my now-seven-month-old goddaughter.

"Let's take five," I said to the dancers when I heard the bell, and I ran out to the front desk.

"Hi," he said, crossing the lobby in a few big strides and pushing me up against the front desk and kissing me.

"Hi," I said breathlessly when he pulled away.

"Holy shit," he said, looking me up and down. "You're a princess."

I was. Unfortunately. We were running the show this evening in costumes. Our characters were archetypes of women—nuns, princesses, mothers, career women—and we were fighting a literal war. Hence the trenches. You can probably guess that I didn't want to be the princess. But neither did any of my dancers, and did I mention I wasn't paying them?

So yeah, I was dressed in a puffy dance version of a princess dress, and I had a tiara pinned in my hair.

He cracked up.

"Thanks a lot."

He didn't stop laughing. Seemed like he couldn't stop.

"You want to move in with me?" I said, raising my voice so it was louder than his laughter.

That shut him up. "Really?"

"Really. I mean, when you're in town."

He stared at me with his jaw hanging open. I guess I'd shocked him. I'd anticipated this, so I'd come prepared. I reached into my bra and extracted the ten-dollar bill that we now passed back and forth when someone was dumbstruck, which happened more frequently than you might think.

"Yes," he said as he took the bill. "I don't have complicated, ten-dollar thoughts. Just yes."

"All right, then."

"Are you sure about this, though?" he asked. "I have studio time booked for Anna over her spring break. And I tacked on two weeks for me, so that's three solid weeks."

"I think I can handle it."

One of his rings got caught in my princess skirt as he tried to pick me up and twirl me around.

"God damn it," I said as we got more and more twisted up in the pink tulle.

Pink tulle. Because I was a fucking princess.

The part that's hardest to swallow in all this is that I don't get to be a crone. Yet.

I guess a girl can't have everything.

ACKNOWLEDGMENTS

As usual, this book was made possible by regular writing sessions with my friends Christine D'Abo and Sandra Owens. Sandy also read an early draft and provided immensely helpful feedback.

My thanks, as ever, to agent extraordinaire Courtney Miller-Callihan, who ran so much interference for me in 2024, aka the Bad Year.

Thank you to Leni Kauffman for the perfect cover illustration (Metallica!) and to Daniela Medina at Hachette for art directing.

And most of all, to the Forever folks: Junessa, Sabrina, Jordyn, Mari, S.B., Estelle. It is, as ever, a joy to work with you.

Marion Kuhn won a silent auction to have a character named after her. We were raising money in support of a local family struck by childhood cancer. If you are feeling charitable and looking for an outlet, may I recommend your local Ronald McDonald House chapter?

My Facebook reader group, Northern Heat, helped me come up with campfire songs. None of which made it into the book as I ended up going a different direction in that scene, but I love talking about books—mine and others—with y'all!

YOUR
BOOK
CLUB
RESOURCE

Visit **GCPClubCar.com** to sign up for the GCP Club Car newsletter, featuring exclusive promotions, info on other Club Car titles, and more.

Find us on social media: **@ReadForeverPub**

READING GROUP GUIDE

JENNY'S TWO-COURSE CAMPFIRE DINNER

You know how when you see recipes in the back of a book, they're always amazing? They're usually there because food is woven into the story you just read. These "recipes" are not that. Let's face it, most of the food in *Into the Woods* is of the processed and dyed-orange variety.

But I can provide instructions for a fun and satisfying dinner that will delight your inner child and also any actual children you might have running about.

You do need equipment, namely a thing that is variously called a campfire sandwich maker or a camp cooker. It's a long wooden thingy with two cast-iron plates at the end. Also, you need a source of heat, if not fire. I used to make these over literal campfires, but I am now retired from camping, so I make them over a backyard firepit or a charcoal grill.

1. Preheat your camp cooker. Insert it somewhere around the edge of the fire and get it hot. You'll have less sticking this way. Once hot, open the cooker over a rock or on a

surface that can handle blisteringly hot cast iron. Spray the insides of the plate with oil and lay a large tortilla on one side.

2. Plop sandwich fixings onto your tortilla. My personal fave is brie, prosciutto, and fig jam—'cause I'm fancy. But you can let your imagination run wild. Kids love pizza sandwiches—pepperoni, mozzarella, and pizza sauce. You do need some kind of cheese to melt everything together, but it needn't be actual cheese. I have made these for vegans with "cheese" with great success.

3. Once loaded, carefully fold your tortilla so it's closed and not larger than your plates. (*Why don't you use bread, Jenny? Doesn't the picture on the camp cooker packaging show bread?* I used to use bread, but a neighbor turned me on to the tortilla method. It creates a much better ratio of filling to casing.) Clamp the plates shut and return your camp cooker to the edge of the fire. As with making s'mores, slow and patient is your best approach. If you put the plates directly in the flames, you will end up with burnt tortillas and raw fillings.

4. The cookers and the sandwich inside will be wickedly hot, so unload and eat with caution.

5. Repeat the above steps, except this time you're making dessert. Load your tortilla-ed cookers with cream cheese and a canned pie filling of your choice. I am partial to cherry. I mean, you can also do the more traditional

Nutella and bananas or whatever, but try the cream cheese and fruit approach. I have converted many a neighbor.

That's it. But I'm telling you, there's something weirdly satisfying about cooking a two-course meal over a fire that isn't your usual hot dogs + s'mores. And about having each course encased in its own little pocket. Who doesn't want smoky dinner in a pocket?

QUESTIONS FOR READERS

1. The idea of "the woods" is central to many fairy tales. What role do the woods play in Teddy and Gretchen's story—their individual character arcs and their romance?

2. Also on the topic of fairy tales: Gretchen starts the book keen to embrace her inner crone. Crones or witches are usually the villains in fairy tales. Do you think this is justified?

3. Neither Teddy nor Gretchen makes a good first impression on the other person. Discuss the ways they might have gotten the wrong idea about each other. How important are first impressions in real life?

4. Gretchen and Teddy initially bond over the fact that they both grew up poor. How does having a similar background affect their burgeoning relationship?

5. At camp, Teddy finds himself drawn back to the music he grew up with even though it's not really "his" kind of music. What role did that music play in shaping him? Discuss what it feels like when you hear the music of your youth.

6. Some people might say that Gretchen is independent to a fault. Can a person be too independent?

7. Gretchen decides to stop using her phone at camp, and it takes her a few tries before she succeeds. How does unplugging affect her creatively and personally?

8. Gretchen spends a lot of time thinking about the concept of camp friendships—intense relationships that develop over relatively short time frames because of the isolation and camaraderie of camp. Did you ever have camp friends? Are there any circumstances in which adults might enter into these types of friendships?

ABOUT THE AUTHOR

Jenny Holiday is a *USA Today* bestselling author whose books have been featured by the *New York Times*, *Entertainment Weekly*, the *Washington Post*, and NPR. She grew up in Minnesota and started writing when her fourth-grade teacher gave her a notebook to fill with stories. When she's not working on her next book, she likes to hike, throw theme parties, and watch other people sing karaoke. Jenny lives in London, Ontario, Canada.

You can learn more at:
   JennyHoliday.com
   Facebook.com/groups/NorthernHeat
   Instagram @HolyMolyJennyHoli